“THE JOCK CONNECTION”

On the trail Of the Comic Billy Bagman.

Rob Little

Part 1:
Part 2:
Part 3:

In memory of Patricia, my loving wife of fifty years, and for Susan, Dawn and Louise, my cherished daughters, and for Christopher and Guy, my every bit as special grandsons.

Special thanks to Philip Ptolemey for creating the internal artwork.

I will send a donation from each book sale to the Nicola Murray Foundation, ovarian cancer charity.

Nicola Murray Foundation <info@nicola-murray-foundation.org.uk>

THE JOCK CONNECTION
CHAPTER 1
PART 1

Their place of duty that August morning thrilled Metropolitan Police Detective Constables Hamish MacNab and Harry MacSporran. They were on stakeout in one of their favourite places, a curry house, on their favourite quest: ready to arrest the suspects expected to arrive soon to blag the restaurant. It was much better than another day stuck in the office.

They were watching for traffic leaving London's busy Commercial Road, E1, and entering the backstreet one-way system. The restaurant side of the street was old London and looked ready for a facelift. Opposite was a building site with high scaffolding that ran for the length of the street in front of the new construction. Donkey jacketed figures wearing safety hats worked on every level. The transit van carrying back up didn't look out of place parked adjacent to the restaurant.

It was the Monday morning following the August bank holiday weekend. The capital baked, was getting back up to speed. Lorries delivering building supplies were the main users of the street, but it had gained few visitors of interest to them. From their vantage point, a window looking out of the Regency Indian restaurant, viewing was clear to the junction.

The restaurant clock was showing 11:20 when Hamish spotted a Ford Mondeo turning into the street. 'Here's a likely one,' he said. 'Its nearside indicator-light is lit but not winking. The car's korma-coloured now, but was probably canary yellow new.'

The Mondeo slowed as it neared. Both detectives stepped closer to the glass.

The driver and two passengers were black men. The six dark irises and white circles of their eyes rotated as the car came alongside, scanning the restaurant frontage, the two passenger's noses close to the glass. Then the eyes steadied, glancing briefly towards the window, having a stab at penetrating the gloom of the interior.

Hamish had leaked sweat in buckets that morning, fussing and looking busy around the restaurant tables positioned nearest the window overlooking the street. Cocooned in a burqa with no airflow wasn't helping. For half-an-hour, he and Harry had kept up the pretence, waiting the appearance of a suspicious vehicle. If the report they'd received was correct, a vehicle of interest had to appear. If their disguise worked, passersby would only see two shuffling Muslim women, preparing tables for opening time, only a few minutes away.

Hamish stepped back from the window, summed up what he saw. 'It could be them. They've that I'd pinch the elastic from my grannies' knickers look about them. That's if the old dears wear any.'

'Your Govan nose is working well this morning,' Harry said, then chuckled.

The restaurant had warmed as the morning progressed and was now steamy, smoky and aromatic. In the nearby kitchen, the chef was searing garlic, onions and red chillies in a pan. A simmering stockpot was adding vapour and spicy whiffs to the pungency.

Hamish's nose wrinkled. The smells were agreeable. Snaking a hand from a floppy sleeve, he extended a finger into the gap in the headgear and stroked away the sweat bubbles forming on his forehead. 'We've ten minutes before opening time,' he said, 'there's time for the Mondeo to pass again. If it's the company we're expecting bang on opening time, we'll get another take on them then.'

Robbery Squad stakeouts had put Hamish and Harry in many different situations and guises. This one had them in the sticky, airless apparel. Complete with masks, they thought it the perfect kit not to scare off any team out to blag an Indian restaurant of its weekend takings.

At 11:25, the Mondeo reappeared, slower driven this time.

'It's the same car. It has the same faulty indicator and bits hanging from the nearside-door mirror. There are identical bashes in the front wing,' Hamish confirmed as he watched the car approach. He shuffled closer to the glass and stood there polishing a spoon with a napkin. As the car passed, his eyes moved from one suspect's face to another.

'There couldnae be two like that,' Harry agreed.

'I'm sure they're all African. The driver has a narrow face, probably Somali. He has a Jimmy Hendrick's haircut. The front-seat passenger is black and dreadlocked, as is the backseat chummy. Both passengers are now clocking the front door. They're trying to hide their faces behind a hand, but are taking it all in through splayed fingers.

Harry was of the same opinion. 'That's what I see. I also think you're right about their grannies' loss.'

The deception seemed to be working. The Mondeo kept its slow speed until it disappeared from sight.

Hamish's mask was sweat sodden, but billowed as he said, 'It's a team alright. I can smell the thieving rats, even in this lovely reek.'

'Me, too,' Harry said, 'tasty looking bunch.'

'You're right, but we'll be ready for them.'

Since teaming up with Hamish, Harry had learned to trust his partner's instinct to spot potential collars; his ability had gained them a reputation as thief takers within the Met. Commendations for their skill, dedication to duty and bravery had come from magistrates, judges and the Commissioner. When results kept rolling in, their CID colleagues had tagged them "The Jock Connection".

Off duty the previous evening, they'd been on a crawl of several East End pubs. As their tenth pint of Guinness was going down, a peckish feeling had turned up. The Regency was a short stagger away.

The curry-house owner, Abdul Khan, had never charged a copper, on duty, or off, for a meal, cordially welcoming them with a smile at the restaurant back door, or front. And many coppers had mumped a meal there. The street running behind the restaurant had an alley leading from it to the back door. The street was a division between two beats. Two beat coppers could meet and mump at the same time. Occasionally, if one copper was a dog handler, he had three hungry mouths to feed

Abdul had looked worried when he joined them at their table, pulling up a chair before they'd given their order. They quickly guessed something was seriously amiss; his native-tongue jabber was incomprehensible, his eyes darted wildly and his hands he couldn't still. Customers were taking note so they moved to a quiet corner table.

Only when he calmed, spoke in his broken English, did they understand him better; he was looking for a return on his generosity to cops. A worrying phone call he'd just taken from a friend, told him of talk that an illegal-immigrant gang, wielding baseball bats, was going to rob him of his weekend takings, as his business opened the following morning.

The information was of interest to members of the Robbery Squad.

Abdul agreed with their advice: to take a taxi home when he closed for the night, not to travel alone, to deposit the takings in his bank's night safe. Before leaving the restaurant, they assured him of a police presence in his restaurant, before he opened for business the following morning.

A short walk took them to Leman Street nick. There, with Squad members working the night shift, they arranged the stakeout details.

The burqas disguised them well. 'Deep cover,' Hamish had described them. He was five foot ten inches tall, had wavy black hair, weighed sixteen stone and had a permanent grin, as if he found everything that life threw at him amusing. The burqa stretched around his shape. Harry was six-foot tall, a beanpole of a man, with crew-cut black hair, dark, bushy eyebrows and a long, gloomy face. His burqa hung around him like a collapsing tepee.

The mask's narrow slits weren't the best of viewing apertures. Through them, they'd seen enough to make a judgement. The blag was underway and it was imminent.

Although seasoned detectives, they were always tense during stakeouts. Two squad members, positioned in the kitchen, were acting as the close support they might need if things turned rough. The pair had reputations as curry hounds. The detail pleased them. Food preparation smells told of a curried brunch that they'd successfully mumped from the chef.

The transit van had aboard a sergeant and twelve squad members. The sergeant, in the front passenger seat, and the driver, would be monitoring the situation to the rear through the side mirrors. The back up in the van would be alert, wouldn't be happy cramped-up and sweaty in heavy clothing, but watching keenly for the situation to unfold, through the blackened, rear facing windows.

Discordant sitar music had played all morning through restaurant speakers, jangling nerves. Without warning, the recording ended. Too much cacophony for the waiter, it seemed. He was cowering nervously sat at a distant table, as far away from the front windows as he could get.

An adrenalin rush hit Harry. With a knife in each hand, he began circling a table, playing drum rolls on the side plates and the metal condiment set.

Hamish tried to lighten things up. 'Harry,' he asked, doing a little shimmy, 'is my bum big in this?'

'Yes!' Harry answered assertively, without looking.

'I feel like Cinders,' Hamish said, squeaking his words.

'How come?' Harry asked, then danced his feet around to face Hamish.

'Vindaloo… I'm getting fire down below!'

Harry gulped. The previous evening, he had put away the same fiery ration as Hamish. Mixed with Guinness, it had history: gut-rumbling volatility troubling them both. The twinge could soon arrive for him, warming that same tender spot. 'Watch you don't drop one and set the place ablaze,' he said, 'this carpet's saturated with oil and stuff.

'If I drop one wearing this outfit, it'll whistle straight past my nose on its way out this slit!'

'If you drop one in there, it's all yours.' Harry turned his back, sidled away, out of range.

It hadn't taken them much thought to work out why robbers would make their bid as the Regency opened for business at 11:30 that morning; then, it should be empty of customers and still have the long-weekend's takings on the premises. Weekday mornings, just after opening, was when Abdul, against all advice freely given by the many coppers recipient of his hospitality, usually left the restaurant to do the banking.

The clock ticked round to opening time. The Mondeo crept into view and drew-up outside.

The three men inside the car pulled black balaclavas over their heads. The driver positioned his head to the front of the accomplice sitting next to him, peering towards the front door.

Hamish shuffled slowly to one side of the porch, Harry the other. Both began fiddling with cords, adjusting the window blinds, alert for the robbers exiting the car.

Primed to do so, and acting naturally, as Hamish had indicated to him, the waiter passed through the inner batwing doors. He turned the key in the outer-door lock. Then he changed the closed sign hanging inside it to open. The unlocked door he left slightly ajar, as instructed.

The waiter moved back through the batwings. That was a signal to the robbers. The nearside car doors burst open. Two men got out.

They hadn't hidden the sawn-off shotguns they carried, just kept them close to their bodies, pointing downwards.

Hamish breathed in sharply and muttered, 'Fuck! They're tooled up. Harry, get hold of the rope, quick!'

They'd previously used the rope on a stakeout to stop robbers in their tracks – but they'd been unarmed. Now it lay on the floor, ready to use, far enough away from the batwings not to snag on it as they opened.

Its use this time, Met Police would give the tag: "the Indian rope trick that went with a bang".

The front door flew back to its stop with a crash, shouldered open by the leading robber. Side-by-side, they took a batwing each, the doors walloping back as they stepped inside the restaurant. Together they brought the guns up, swinging them from side-to-side, ignoring the burqa-clad figure to each side of the door.

The robbers were taking a pace forward when the rope jerked viciously, lifting them from their feet, to tumble awkwardly, the guns pointing towards the floor. A shot discharged from each. Cordite and curry smells mingled. Dust and carpet shredded by the blasts lifted into the air. Pellets ricocheted into the furniture, peppering the ceiling and the flock wallpaper. The noise was deafening, deadening the sound of the waiter screaming and shitting himself as he dived beneath a table.

Quicker still, Hamish and Harry, their cowls already ripped from their heads, their faces shiny and sweaty, leaped on top of the robbers and began wrestling the guns away, out of reach. The robbers were wiry, but only slightly built; they were no match for Hamish, when he spread his bulk over them, keeping them prostrate and gasping, their faces denting the pile of the oil-laced carpet.

Harry had the cuffs fitted before the backup waiting in the kitchen reached them, wiping curry sauce from their lips with tissue, as they raced to assist.

Outside, the Mondeo driver made to move off as the guns blasted. The van driver had the engine turning over. He was in gear, ready to move off on sighting the guns. As the robbers disappeared into the restaurant, he spun the van into the road to cut off the car's escape route. In the van, squad members were exchanging looks of consternation. This hadn't turned out as expected and they only had truncheons for protection; the car driver could also have a gun and they couldn't see what was happening inside the restaurant.

That a colleague might be down energised them. Quickly, they were out of the van back doors, some setting about hauling the driver from the car and pulling him to the ground. Others hunkered down, peering through the restaurant windows, assessing the situation inside. Truncheons drawn, they rushed in, ready to assist in the apprehension and arrest.

*****

Some pre-1990s plods will have you believe that the "Golden Age" of policing disappeared about the same time TV's Police Constable George Dixon retired from Dock Green nick. For Metropolitan Police Detective Constables Hamish MacNab and Harry MacSporran, continuing interest in policing "Goldenly" vanished within weeks of their most notable arrests, at their peaks as thief takers.

In the late 1990s, the Home Secretary of the government of the day appointed a new Metropolitan Police Commissioner. His mandate was to cultivate a culture of Political Correctness within the Force and to deepen its brain pool. Facilitating the rapid rise through the ranks of those university graduates encouraged into the force with a swift-promotion carrot had some success. Most senior police officers blindly adhered to this policy, fearing a mighty fall from the promotional ladder if they didn't.

Some senior CID officers saw gung-ho and cavalier detectives, more interested in results than being PC, as the culprits most likely to grease the rungs of their particular climbing device with something akin to STP engine-oil treatment (the slipperiest substance known to man). Such detectives became the first victims of the new guidelines, making way for those recruits deemed suitable for fast tracking.

Hamish and Harry had earned reputations as able and fearless detectives. However, their Divisional CID Commander, Dai Evans, saw the partnership as having that most slippery of substances ingrained into their characters and swiftly demoted them to uniform duties.

They were not alone in their return to uniform branch. Some detectives took their demotion calmly, citing wives pleased with their more-social hours for their lack of discontent. The seriously disgruntled committed acts of revenge and for months after, retribution raged. The disappearance of important case notes; the liberal pouring of sugar into the petrol tanks of private cars; the dumping of dung and ready-mix cement in home driveways, were some of the acts blighting the lives of those senior officers deemed guilty of instigating the demotions.

Hamish and Harry, more pissed off than any of their demoted colleagues, showed their discontent in their own way…………………

Chapter 2

It was a cool Wednesday morning in early October of the same year. Hamish had just completed ten wearying, mind-churning, foot-damaging nightshifts of a three-week stint at West End Central nick. Chugging his way eastwards, to his police apartment in Bow, astride his 49cc moped, loathing for his beat-policeman's lot was still eating him up.

Jenny, his wife, was still curled-up in bed and blissfully asleep in their police apartment home when he arrived there.

He made himself a cuppa and a slice of toast in the kitchen. He tried to settle his head, before he took to the stairs; it hadn't given him peace since he learned of his return to foot-beat duties.

About 7.a.m., he quietly entered the bedroom, undressing at the bedside, throwing his clothes casually onto a chair. Naked, he slid beneath the duvet. His chilled backside brushed against the same anatomical area of Jenny, lying with her nightie displaced. A similar event had happened on each successive morning since the nightshift tour began. Each time, Jenny had been sleeping soundly. Each time, it had been a shocking moment for her. Awakening now with a start, she swung her legs out of the bed. It had become a well-practiced movement.

He caught something she muttered as she strode away about him being a thoughtless fat bastard.

Unperturbed by her remark, Hamish wriggled his bulk across into the warm spot she had vacated and settled there. Closing his eyes, he awaited sleep to engulf him.

It didn't and hadn't after each of the nightshifts he had just completed. Each time his head hit the pillow it was spinning, the same agro unsettling him: the Job only wanted silly boys with degrees nowadays. Gov'nors would soon learn that a rookie possessing a degree was no substitute for an experienced detective. That Commander Dai Evans should cover his back. That he would look for his chance to avenge that bastard's decision… and take it!

Then there was the prank he had played on some of his uniformed colleagues: ones he thought smart-assed. He'd have to watch his back if they were vengeful types. The collection of pornographic photographs he had found, evidence for a past case, he had taken to the nick one day-shift, a harebrained idea in mind, a sort of mental relief. Unnoticed, he had slipped a naughty picture into each of those coppers' London A to Zs.

Later, that same shift, one copper, assisting to direct two lost nuns from the Vatican towards Westminster abbey, had the misfortune to see one fall to a pavement. The nuns had also got an eyeful; to all of the details, as it transpired. Murphy's Law dictating, the photo had landed saucy side up, showing a naked couple in a doggy-fashion entanglement.

The outcome of the incident had been a complaint against police. Hamish's body had shaken with laughter, wide-awake or trying to sleep, each time he pictured the nuns' distressed reactions to the photo's lewd contents. It had been the only moments of release he had experienced on many a morning. The tottering steps back, the rasping, perturbed gasps, the fingers hurriedly counting beads and the hands flying repeatedly upwards to make the sign of the cross over well-camouflaged breasts.

Sleep didn't come again and Hamish continued to toss and turn. About 10 a.m., he turned onto his back, opened his eyes and looked down the bed to his feet. Sticking out of the duvet, they looked rag-rolled in shades of red, white and blue, and roasting. He closed his eyes again and drifted into a restless slumber.

It was 11 a.m. when he shook himself and surfaced from a nightmare. In it, he had awakened, in the dark, in a cemetery, sleeping in full uniform on a green-mould-covered horizontal tombstone. He had rolled off and had fallen into a bottomless grave. He was somersaulting, grabbing for sides he couldn't reach. On his hair-raising descent, he thudded into Harry. He was also shouldering a uniform and tumbling alongside him. Both were screaming 'Fuck these foot-patrols, they're killers,' at the top of their voices.

Hamish slid from the bed and listened: had Jenny heard his panicky cries. Raucous, girlish laughter erupted from what he thought was a chat show on the TV downstairs.

Jenny didn't bawl up the staircase enquiring after his health so he put on his shirt, trousers and socks. To the boozer for a bellyful of Guinness with a fiery ruby to follow was the decision he again made; on the last eight mornings, sleeplessness had driven him to seek the same cure. Ten pints of Guinness, drank any time of the day, he knew to be a potent soporific – curry he just loved.

Jenny would be hard to placate. He was always in a merry state each afternoon he returned home from supping and feeding his face, Jenny rebuking him candidly on his many bad habits. Too frequently smelling like a curry mumping, beer swilling, reeking arsed ignoramus pig were but a few of her disparaging comments. Usually she insisted that he explain his conduct as he tumbled into bed. Oblivion usually came quickly, he found. Her attention exasperated him, but with the fix, sleep came quickly.

*

At 10:10 p.m., that Wednesday night, Hamish was still in the doldrums. He paraded for duty at West End Central. Before hitting his beat, he joined some other coppers for a warming beverage in the upstairs canteen. The air was abuzz with different conversations. Hamish caught various snippets of the chat as he carried a mug of tea towards an unoccupied table, where he pulled out a chair and sat down.

A group of fresh-faced rookies were quietly voicing criticism of a pushy sergeant. The sexual preferences of a new WPC on the relief were also receiving an airing. Grizzlier plods were grouching loudly of bills, morning court appearances whilst working night shifts, piles, the spiralling price of canteen food and other's sweaty feet. No change there, he thought.

Suddenly, the amiable buzz was shattered. Some wide-grinned coppers, with an agenda, were doing their tea quaffing in a chummy huddle. Their loud, inane remarks and silly sniggering were turning many heads. Hamish recognised the coppers as each being recipients of a naughty photograph. It quickly clicked with him: he was their target.

Sitting alone and within easy earshot, he began to hear, (discussed brutally when outbursts of laughter quietened), his size, shape, weight and his protestations of injustice regarding his recent change of duty.

'The haggis basher doesn't like walking beats,' was the first jibe to cock his ears.

'Roly-poly, fat Jock bastard,' he heard repeated, and the quick 'sure is' of agreement.

'Couldn't catch the cold,' was his perceived thief-taking abilities.

'Egg on legs,' one thought his shape, which had titters erupting from each copper sitting at the table.

'Humpty Dumpty cannae be deeeeed, then,' he heard said in a hammed-up attempt at a Scottish accent, which received the loudest guffaws that suddenly ceased. All the baiter's eyes were tear filled and tea, weak, sweet and milky, was jetting down nostrils, out of control, choking off their mirth.

Hamish had worked at West End Central nick as a probationer. Then, he was renowned as a master of the wind-up and was popular for his genial nature. Other coppers present, who knew his character, expected him to ignore the jibes, even laugh along with the ribbing.

Hamish's head was still alive with his own agro. His bugbears had correctly chosen the moment to probe his touchiness: to exact some payback for the childish prank he had played on them.

Hamish had swiftly sussed their drift. He gave nothing of his mood away, showed no telltale signs of irritation. Nursing his mug, he sat stony-faced.

A minute later, he was downing the last sip of tea and rising noisily from his chair. Faces turned in his direction.

Avoiding any eye contact, Hamish sauntered with languid grace to the servery and laid the empty mug in front of the counter girl. Hamish liked her. Shiny black curls cascaded over her forehead, giving her a mysterious appearance. She had rosy cheeks, responsive smile, come-to-bed eyes, a cuddly bum and a lilting, Hebridean voice he thought too beautiful ever to rise and bollock a man.

'Your mam has taught you well…'

'Er! What?' she asked, her eyes widening, before her face creased into a mischievous smirk.

'…the magic of conjuring six mugs of tea from a single teabag. What else did you think I might say?' Hamish said, smiling back cheesily.

'You never know how the ozone of the night's affecting you lot or what's coming next. Teabags leave behind no lees for a reading. You're correct, though, she did,' the girl replied, her voice squeaky, thoughts witty, 'She was a Jock four-by-two, just like you.'

The girl was smothering a titter as Hamish turned away and looked towards his banes. His face was grim; there would be no smile of any sort for them; their verbal assault needed replying to, sorting out. His intent set, he swung into stride. Bustling away from the counter, he narrowed his eyes, checking that his course was true.

The coppers sitting at the table were still drying eyes and didn't see him nearing. Then he was there. Swinging his backside into the gap between a sprawl of legs, he clipped the corner of the table. Hot brews sloshed onto all of their laps.

'Bastards all', he bawled towards them as he passed by.

Coppers hollered in pain and chairs squeaked noisily across the floor, drowning out his utterance. The table shot backwards, scattered with their toppled mugs. Hamish turned to face them, walked two paces backwards and gesticulated upwards, Churchill-like, with raised fingers.

Hamish didn't hang about; the result was good. Halfway down the staircase leading to the station yard, his luck changed. With his belly swinging, he skimmed over the steps, his pained, booted feet flying. Then he slipped and lost his balance.

'Fuuuuuuuuuck,' he erupted. His body rocked backwards, forcing his feet to rocket forwards; stinging consequences – juddering, inclined and an uncontrollable descent being the upshot. His boot heels connected with each step until an audible whoosh of air gusted from his lungs as he clipped the last one. His boot soles pointing downwards, he then prepared for the crash landing on a threadbare coir rug.

Hamish landed awkwardly, hunkered, blowing and winded. His heavy thighs crashed together, trapping his testicles between them, squeezing them line astern in the un-supple gap. Rocking and rolling aboard the unstable mat, his movements were unrepresentative of the sedate Victor Sylvester School of Ballroom Dancing. Extending his arms, his palms smacked onto the staircase walls. It stung. Preventing his sixteen stones frame from crashing headlong through the swing doors of the exit, needed a countering jerk of his hips, a grab for the banister rail, a firm grip and the uttered a cry of 'Sheeeiiiiiiiite!'

Usually I'd have to be as "pissed as a rat" to survive a slip like that, he mused. Still wobbling, his heart pounded. He repositioned his tunic, as wet dogs do their coats, with a quick shake. Gingerly, he extracted the Y-fronts rammed high in the cheeks of his backside, like a magician pulling on the silk handkerchief about to turn into a white dove. With an extra deep breath, he expressed his relief there was no splits in his pants.

Hamish straightened his helmet and pushed through the door. In the station yard, lights blazed from windows, upstairs and down, in the main block. No faces peered concernedly from them towards him. Thank fuck, he mused.

He viewed two young probationer coppers, their fresh faces beaming with success, pushing an unsteady drunk, walking on his heels, towards the charge room door. Under a spotlight, the wireless operator and the plain-clothed observer of a patrol car were easing a stroppy, handcuffed chummy out through its rear door.

He thanked fuck again. They, too, hadn't heard his tumble. The cooling night air had yet to calm the cause of his haste, though, and he felt he just had to broadcast his thoughts. 'Bloody failure, couldn't catch my breath, roly-poly fat bastard Jock, they said that of me. They think that of me, do they? One of the better detectives I was. One of the best criminal-catchers, thief-takers, of any rank the CID ever had…that lot upstairs in the canteen have no savvy! They ken nowt, by the way!'

The patrol car crew, to a man, stood startled.

'What's your problem, Jock?' asked the patrol-car driver, smiling evilly, his arm encircling a prisoner's neck and tightening around it.

'They bastards back there,' Hamish bawled. 'The sauce, the lip of them, talking loud enough behind their hands for me to hear, they were. Aggravating shite, it was. For fuck's sake, the porno pics were for a laugh, a bit of a joke, by the way, not to draw insults about my abilities,' Hamish said, incensed. 'There was no need for them rubbing it in, like the arseholes did.'

'A few of your relief were in a huddle yesterday, discussing getting you going for winding them up,' the wireless operator said. Grinning broadly, he slouched against the patrol car, his eyes moving from the cigarette he was rolling to watch his driver restraining the prisoner whilst steering him towards the charge room door.

Smirking again, ready to laugh, depending on Hamish's reaction, he said, 'Being peeved about returning to beat duties from CID, complaining victimisation, unwarranted university graduate selection, your knowing fuck all, thick as pig shit and all that, that's what gave them the idea. The porno bit was the incentive. They've wound you up tight, like a drum. You've bit and now you're bitter, big time at that.'

'Shower of bastards, by the way,' Hamish grizzled then strode towards the street.

His stride slowed on Savile Row. He still seethed. Settling his breathing rate wasn't coming easily, either. Vehicle-exhaust fumes tainting the air weren't helping his strained inhalations, which whistled hissingly through clenched teeth.

His pet hate got the rough edge of his tongue as he stood muttering on the doorstep of 13 New Burlington Street that had a sheltering porch when raining. 'Commander Dai Evans, the bastard! A lot to answer for, he has!' he blasted. The street was quiet. Taxis were dropping customers off outside The Queensberry Hotel that took up a great deal of one side of the street. He walked on until he reached Burlington gardens. Then he took the equally quiet Vigo Street, glancing into the display window of Suitsupply tailors as he passed, but nothing on display fitted him. By the time he turned onto Regent Street, he was convinced that some Force members had perpetrated every possible injustice against him. The mutterings were little consolation and his feet were developing an ache.

The three-week stint of nights was Hamish's first such duties for twelve years and he wasn't enjoying the experience. Losing his Detective Constable rank sat badly with him; up to the demotion, previous treatment and respect from his senior officers had all been good. His wife's caustic comments on his habits hadn't sat well. Nor had the canteen wind-up or the thought of any beat duties, on any manor, on any division, at any time, day or night, with attendant pain, until he retired. It all had gotten to him. As his ire overheated, so his crabbedness grew.

It was now 10:20 p.m. Regent Street was still busy, a riot of sound. Slow files of traffic, revving in low gears, horns honking like outraged geese. At times, the noise was tremendous.

Hamish let out a prolonged, unstifled yawn as he waited at a pedestrian crossing. Shuddering in its wake, his arms bounced into the air. His shoulders relocated to the attention position and he beat his chest with a fist, aiding the uplift of trapped wind. Then he belched boisterously. The resultant bellowing was a measure of his discontentment with his policeman's lot. He was expressing it gustily, while also demonstrating the burp-inducing capacity of hot, weak, police-canteen tea.

The milling crowd of late night revellers gathering to cross with him placed him at the centre of their interest. Some revellers cupped hands over their mouths. Some turned their faces to gawp. Others just reeled away. The outburst, the sizeable police officer's torso quaking, had shaken them all, stunning them. As had his ribcage, thrown so high, expelling the belch.

'Bad gas, officer, better try a "Seltzer",' drawled an American with a big breasted, honey blonde woman clinging to his arm.

Detecting the interest in him, Hamish didn't look to see who was waiting to cross with him, but slipped nonchalantly into detached mode. Staring straight ahead, he raised his hands quickly upwards to hook a thumb behind each his top tunic pocket buttons.

Lifting a foot, he rubbed the dull boot toecap on the backs of his trousers, rotating the ankle before replacing the boot on the pavement. While stork-like on one leg, he knocked the raised boot-heel against the kerb, seeking more space for his swelling toes. He repeated the exercise on the other foot.

A dribble of perspiration ran from beneath his helmet. Unhooking a thumb, he searched a trouser pocket for a handkerchief, which he dabbed at his forehead.

Interest in his presence subsided. Skylarkers in the crowd had begun jostling for position, pushing and shoving in inebriated frivolity, vying to cross first on the green-man signal.

'Has someone pressed the tit?' a sonorous voice asked.

A woman reveller, conceiving some humour in her reply said, whilst attempting to smother a high-pitched giggle, 'Don't dare, the constable might fall over.' Then she let a screech rip.

Most beat coppers tolerated harmless banter from the public. The tit thing tickled Hamish, easing his mood, renewing his interest in public contact. He reacted to this in a way he thought fitting. An affable smile sweeping across his rounded jowls, he parted his knees, waxing them in that well-known, music-hall-policeman routine.

Some in the crowd applauded. Perhaps they thought an utterance of 'Evening all,' Dixon of Dock Green style, would accompany the act. Could it be a prelude to a presentation by a member of the Metropolitan Police Leg Waxing Team, or "The MPLWT." for short? They were wrong. Hunkering low, he let go a loud, rasping fart then rapidly flapped a hand over the seat of his trousers.

Stiletto heels screeched jarringly. Other footwear scuffed. Some overbalancing occurred as revellers scrambled to withdraw. 'Fucking cracker, officer, I'll give it foive!' A Brummie-accented male roared.

The riposte had some of the female revellers laughing stridently as well as tottering. 'Bravo, officer, that's an early one for the sin bin tonight,' a quickly recovering reveller responded, before shouting, 'Encore, again if you dare!' and awarding, 'Five-point-nine for artistic ability, officer.'

'Terrorist bomb! Let's get t'fuck outuv here!' someone shouted in a phoney Irish accent.

'Houston, we have a problem. There's thunder over the boondocks tonight.' The drawling American had added his cent's worth.

'I'm not hanging about here,' a squeaky-voiced misfit bawled and egged on others to set out for the next crossing.

The green-man showed, the traffic stopped and the signal to cross sounded. Hamish was rocking gently, feeling less stressed now. Having contributed noisily to the party atmosphere, he made to move on. Leaning a little towards the street, he stepped down from the pavement and slowly ambled off. No one shared the crossing with him.

A voice he hadn't heard before said loudly, 'My respect for the British Bobby has just soared. Your action proves they're normal humans.'

The American voice, replied, 'You might find New York cops have some disgusting habits, but you wouldn't get that in Frisco where we're from.

Some others were laughing uproariously. Others appeared simply affronted and challenged others to cross over with Hamish.

In Beak Street, one pavement was crowded so he dawdled along the other. Suddenly, heavy footsteps were catching him up fast. It worried him for a moment. It was a turn of his head that reassured him: it was Andy, a young probationer copper on the same relief as him and newly out of Hendon. Being an ex-police cadet with A-levels, he was destined one day for the higher echelons of the Force. Changing his stride by skipping and missing a step in parade ground manner, he got into step with Hamish.

Hamish saw the flash of Andy's highly polished boots synchronise with his duller TUF variety. Synchronization in stride and spit and polished toecaps meant all to the probationer copper destined for the top. 'I didn't see you up in the canteen supping tea before you hit the streets, by the way,' Hamish greeted him. Coppers who didn't attend traditional night-shift brew-ups had always made him suspicious of their snivelling intentions.

That night shift duty, Hamish had set out to plod what some people thought were the seedier areas "up town": bits of the West End and streets towards Soho Square. Progress to his beat would be leisurely. His feet were now aching too much to force them past one another at anything like the advised walking pace.

The youthful enthusiasm shown by probationers advocating their suitability for early promotion, boasting of keeping their numbers up, he'd tolerate for a while, but Andy would have to plod along at his pace.

They talked as they walked. 'No, I've little time for the likes of that,' Andy said. Animated in the way Hamish expected, Andy began shining his torch into shop windows. Nothing suspicious showing in the thin beam of light, he gave passing traffic his attention. A drunk sang in a doorway. Andy told him to quieten down or he'd arrest him. Passers-by got the sniff test as he sought the aroma of smoked marijuana. 'While you've been wasting time drinking tea, I've been doing a major traffic process.'

In his present unbothered attitude towards the Job, any embracing of the "devotion to duty" ethic vexed Hamish… gov'nors wouldn't get it from him! Not now!

He saw Andy's over-keen face shaded by the regulation-placed rim of his helmet and retorted, 'A traffic process tonight, already. *You're kidding*?'

The wind funnelling between the tall buildings picked up Big Mac wrappers, other assorted waste paper and dust, swirling the lot around their boots. Hamish wasn't worried: the blackening could scuff; it was twelve years old and he now thought smartness of uniform was "a load of old bollocks", in any of its forms.

'I thought it quiet on my way in tonight until I saw a Jaguar XJ6 parked on double yellow lines outside a restaurant. That stirred me. I get a kick out of prosecuting monkey-bastard Jag owners,' Andy said, his lips twisting into a sardonic leer.

'Aye, some of them are all of that, by the way,' Hamish interrupted.

'I dashed from the nick straight after parade and went to the eatery, the "Prime Aberdeen Angus" steak house. Chummy was slicing his way through a T-bone grilled rare when I confronted him. His face reddened. A bit like the blood swimming on his plate it was. I hauled him out and "Stuck him on". Keeping numbers up is the name of the game.'

Hamish shook his head. The rookie had learned some police jargon, which made him think he was already an experienced plod.

'Tonight's station sergeant got my report quickly. My eagerness to bring in worthwhile process really pleased him,' Andy said. Rolling along, he smiled towards Hamish, but he was in the wrong company to expect praise.

Hamish halted and grabbed hold of a lamppost, 'Fucking boots,' he erupted while ramming each of his heels into the pavement in turn. 'Quiet is the way I like it, by the way. I'm sweating like hell. My feet have played me up every shift since coming back to beats. Nothing has changed tonight. I've only fifteen years in. I'll have to do the same again before blessed pensionable retirement.

'Putting the time in on beat duty isn't going to be easy. Gutted and pissed-off sums me up. It's all happened since my last gov'nor returned me to uniform duties, by the way. Retirement can't come my way quickly enough. My new gov'nors will get very few processes or collars out of me between now and then.'

They moved on. Andy looked Hamish up and down. 'You trundle too much weight about. That's your problem. Gov'nors won't put you behind the steering wheels of any police vehicle, unless the Met is supplied Saracen armoured cars.

'Nor will they put you behind a desk… you'll demolish the chairs. They'll never consider you for the Community Safety Unit either. You'd scare the shit out of the needful public. I'll give you this, though, you look outstanding in your winter baratheas cunningly tailored to lift, separate, support and, with any luck, disguise. The epitome of contour camouflage, some might say.'

Hamish squirmed and sucked at his teeth. Earlier, the piss taking had included his weight and his shape, severely irking him. Now, Andy had the audacity to attempt to wind him up over the size of his new uniform. Was he doing it knowingly? Did he have the nous to upset him? Were he and the canteen wind-up merchants working to the same agenda? Or was Andy just naïve and thinking himself helpful?

Hamish didn't know and he didn't want Andy's opinion, anyone's opinion. How his uniform camouflaged him was his business. 'So…you think my weight's a problem?' he asked anyway, a trifle truculently.

Andy smirked. 'Well, you've often had the relief laughing their socks off at meal breaks with your own comments about it. Your accounting of the number of fields of turnips farmers fed the sheep producing the wool to manufacture the material the police tailor cut and sewed up into your uniform had some coppers in serious stitches. A bit like the police tailor has had to use to contain you now, I suppose.'

'You think I should have included a few more acres of neeps and woolier sheep: merinos, cheviots or the likes?' Hamish asked, mockingly.

'Neeps?'

'You wouldn't know,' Hamish said, dismissively. 'It's turnips, to us Jocks.'

'Oh! What I was going to say was trundling your blubbery gut about must be exhausting. It's easy to see why you're slouching your way to your beat. Maybe you should use your overweight to your advantage. Approach a cartoonist for a modelling assignment or something. You'll easily find one eager to draw archetypal coppers your shape.'

Hamish forced a grin and lofted a hand to tilt Andy's helmet. 'You're a bit too cocksure and smart-arsed for my liking, by the way. So okay, my wife doesn't approve of my eating and drinking habits. Gov'nors might not be happy with my shape, my fitness level or me, but I'm happy with them...'

Feeling the draught, Andy ducked his head out of the way. 'Your weight,' He interrupted. 'Was it the haggis, the staple you jocks are supposed to exist on?'

'Don't knock it until you've tried it. It happens to be great with neeps and smash,' Hamish erupted quickly.

'What about greasy mutton pies, black puddings, porridge and…'

'Piss off!'

'…treacle bannocks?'

'You wouldn't know a treacle bannock from a heap of cow shite, by the way. You're a Sassenach. Been reading too many Sunday Posts, you have, trying to learn something about us Jocks. So okay, what if I was a butterball as a bairn and wee Govan gangsters dropped me from our tenement steps to see how high I bounced? I changed at puberty.

'All my puppy fat dropped off me. There wasn't a pick on me and I became a bit of an Adonis. All the lassies were after me. Birds flocked. They liked my arse when they saw me in tight jeans. I was muscular, cock o' the walk.

When I was sixteen, I went away to sea in the British Merchant Navy. I worked my way up from Scullion to Second Cook. I toiled in the galleys of many ships, under some of the finest chefs. I learned how to make a pot of broth, mince and tatties, to bake a loaf of bread and a passable ruby. I even passed my cooks ticket.

When I changed my career to policing in the Metropolis, I was the same weight I was when I joined the Merch. My weight now is entirely attributable to putting away too many pints of Guinness and Rubys during all those happy years I had in plain clothes. It was peer pressure, by the way…'

'Rubys?' Andy interrupted.

'Ruby Murray's. Do you know anything worthwhile? It's Cockney rhyming slang for curries. Get it? It took the police tailor a fortnight to sew up this uniform to fit my expanded waistline. My new gov'nors must have worried they'd ever get me walking beats again.'

Hamish's podgy hand wafted past Andy's ear again. It persuaded him to think better of winding Hamish up further. Unwittingly, Andy remained on dodgy ground. 'You were a bit reluctant to come back to uniform, then?' he asked.

Hamish scowled and snorted his disgust. 'Aye, too bloody right I was. A sad bloody day I can tell you. It was mentally painful then. Still is. My feet ache in these laced up boots. I cannot wear trainers and that's another irritant. I was mortified when I realised my days in plain-clothes were gone. My arrest record was excellent. Some were notable, made the press and TV. I was sure I'd get a permanent transfer to the Flying Squad.

'Oh, how I'd have loved life in the Sweeney Todd. Pitching my abilities against all those supposedly first-class detectives would have given me the greatest pleasure. I thought I was a cert for selection. That degree-loving, dream-destroying bastard, Commander Dai Evans, he kicked that wish into touch, didn't he?

'A vertically-challenged recruit replaced me. He'd be four-foot-four tall, if he's lucky, but he'd have a Desmond in fucking Zoology,' he ranted. 'How fucking tall is that,' he asked, spit flying from his lips.'

'About 1.3 metres,' Andy said, sounding smug.

'Litres, metres, saltfuckingpetre, I don't understand or give a fuck about,' Hamish erupted, venting his displeasure. 'The freak's knuckles will be trailing on the ground, that's what I think. The short-arsed bastard will be more use as a vet, spending his time shoving his gravel-damaged fingers up vertically-challenged Shetland ponies' arses on some stud farm…….. Dinosaurs are what some gov'nors now class experienced DCs, dinosaurs.'

Hamish was becoming animated by his ranting, rocking from side to side.

'It's silly boys with degrees that the Job wants nowadays. Big mistake,' he said, shaking his head so hard his helmet dislodged. 'Big mistake,' he repeated as he finished the repositioning. One-day, gov'nors will realise that a degree is no substitute for experience. I served on the front line. I investigated serious crimes. I got results. I served on the murder squad. I witnessed the horrors, all the gore of one particular murder scene. It was a domestic situation with children battered dead. I dealt with my demons and following my own gut instinct, when senior officers didn't, found and arrested the murderer. My gov'nors took the credit.

I did stakeouts. My last arrest was of tooled-up blaggers. I've had two Commissioner's commendations, my name in Police Orders five times, all that shite.

'I know the modus operandi of many criminals. When a member of the degree-holding fraternity arrives on the scene to arrest an unruly chummy, they'll find their fancy, educated words won't cool the ire of an obstreperous criminal. A clout to the back of the head, a biff in the guts, a boot in the bollocks, that's the only law some chummies appreciate.'

Andy had heard a few coppers whingeing since joining the nick and he considered that some of them must have had genuine grievances. Hamish obviously felt deeply about his gripe. 'Things change and it's just bad luck on…' he just about got out.

'It was a bad fucking deal all round,' Hamish snapped. Both my partner Harry and I got the shitty end of the stick thrust at us, we did. Made to grasp it, we were. Not bad luck, by the way.'

'This is an interesting patch. You can get involved here,' Andy enthused, trying to sound upbeat, 'It may be quiet now, but there'll be something going on somewhere tonight. I've had an arrest every night for the last six nightshifts. Drunks mainly… two pickpockets red-handed and a drug-pushing Rastafarian with twelve ounces of hash were the best. I won't want to take my days off when they come around. I can't get enough of beat duty.'

'It's *you* who will change. Just wait and see,' Hamish said.

'No. Don't say that. Your experience in the CID will be useful to you on the streets. Don't let it go. I won't let anyone knock the keenness out of me. I have to admit I did upset last night's station sergeant. He wasn't at all happy when I hauled a flea-infested vagrant back to the nick in the van. Piss, shit, spew, infestation, he had everything sticking to him. I later learned of two coppers, on the strength at Marylebone Lane, seen dragging the vagrant from their beat onto mine. Didn't want to do the dirty work, they didn't. For the rest of the shift I scrubbed out the van with disinfectant.'

Hamish read 'Sucker' on Andy's keen face. It sounded as if somebody had set him up with a doorway-dosser. Had his pal Harry MacSporran been up to his tricks? He worked that patch now. He would have seen the humour in transferring a vagrant between divisional doorways. If he were a culprit, he'd have hidden up in an adjacent shop doorway afterwards, watched for a copper working the beat to jump in, restrain the dosser and phone for a van, then have laughed his bollocks off.

As a probationer, Hamish had developed a theory: mumping was a harmless pastime, relieving tedium and bringing him close to the community he policed. All gov'nors, officially, frowned on the practice. Hamish reckoned they'd all have taken a cuppa in a back street café whilst on duty and that they couldn't admit to it on gaining sergeant's stripes.

Hamish had elicited some good information during such sorties off beat, enabling him to make arrests. Then, he had known the way to the backdoor of every curry house and Chinese restaurant on the manor: anywhere a cuppa or a nosh was available free to a plod.

Hamish thought Andy wasn't the type to mump anything. In ten years time, if the lad hadn't gained promotion, he might be mature enough to wander off his beat on the quest and in the process become a decent copper.

Guessing the reaction, Hamish thought he'd tease Andy with a mind-blowing prediction, by telling him of another experience from his probationer days. 'Aye, you'll change after a bit, mark my words. In a wee while you'll be hauling a brass up a dark alley for a free blowjob, rather than run her in.'

'Come off it… I never would… That…It'd make me *puke*… Don't tell me you did that…on duty…or off?' Andy stuttered, genuinely aghast at both suggestions.

Hamish nodded. 'I did, often and loved it. I couldn't get enough. There were plenty of good lookers on the game back then and my gov'nors loved a freebie. They were sneaky. I often followed and watched them. I thought it worthwhile to know information on them that I could later use if similarly caught. The gov'nors of today won't be much different; all coppers plodding beats on this division will have had similar perks.'

'They never would!'

Hamish nodded again. 'Just watch your back when you're up a dark alley, groaning in ecstasy, your eyes are closed and a brass is giving you lip service, siphoning out your prunes and you're halfway to a happy ending,' he warned with a grin. 'You'll shit yourself when the inspector taps you on the shoulder wanting two's up.'

Hamish looked up ahead. A gathering of immigrants dressed in ragged clothing, mothers with babies strapped to their backs, were hanging about begging. Worse still, drunks were taunting the immigrants. Several destitutes were humping cardboard boxes in his direction, looking for unoccupied doorways.

Leaving Andy to go his own way seemed sensible. With Andy's enthusiasm for the Job, he could jump into something serious, arrest a vanload of miscreants, require back up, and Hamish wasn't looking for hassle, or spending next morning in court.

An arcade entrance close to Bridle Lane seemed a good place to rest the "plates". The drunks and immigrants might disperse after a while. Hamish motioned Andy into the entrance. 'Have a break,' he said. 'You probationer coppers are always too impetuous for your own good.'

From the entrance, Andy looked out worriedly in both directions. 'At Hendon, we recruits were warned not to loiter in places like this,' he said.

Hamish gave another snort of disgust. 'Wee nooks and crannies the likes of this are the natural places of shelter for the beat copper. You should remember the snippet. It's amazing what you can see going on from a hidey-hole like this. If you're ever looking for me on a beat in the next fifteen years, try a deep, out-of-the-way shop doorway. The one you know has a settee or a comfy chair.'

'I wouldn't want tonight's sergeant to catch me here, he's pleased with me,' Andy said, concern edging his voice.

Hamish gathered his thoughts and gave Andy a swift butcher's. Most new recruits were green, falling for the "old chestnuts" spun by the Force's wind-up merchants. With his eagerness for knowledge, Andy fitted that profile. Hamish wasn't going anywhere fast and thought it worth a try. 'Mind you, Andy, you're not alone in dealing with a foul situation,' he began. 'I did some of my probation over in Chelsea. One enquiry took me to a nice little but and ben....

'What's a but and ben?' Andy interrupted.

'It's a wee Scottish hoose, if you ken what one of them is,' replied Hamish, knowing he was taking the piss. 'Anyway, as I was saying, the but and ben was in a posh street. I really got up a sergeant's nose on that one.'

'Oh, how did you manage that?' Andy asked, his eagerness making Hamish smile.

'It was a trivial complaint. Kids kicking a football about, something innocuous like that,' Hamish continued. 'I had to call to see the complainants. It was a white-painted house and a big, scrawny Alsatian dog lay across the doormat sunning itself. I ignored the beast and walked straight through the open gate.

'When I got to the door, I leant over the dog to rattle the knocker. The rattling aroused it, but it didn't look too bothered, just stood up, squinted around and shook itself. I wasn't too keen on it, especially when it began sniffing around my boots and knees.

'The door cracked open. Two identical faces, one slightly behind the other, stood there, looking out. "We're Mavis and Martha Fitzhugh, and this is my twin sister," the sisters said together. Wizened faces with sprouting hair, flesh nodules, alopecia and acne they had and looked seventyish, maybe more.

'Their asthmatic wheezing sounded like San Izal toilet paper ripping along the perforations. I remembered that sound from school. The dog squeezed past them and walked into the living room. It seemed at home all right and turned several times on the Chinese carpet. Then it sprawled in front of the gas fire. I thought to myself, you're at home here, boy, make yourself comfortable and warm your belly.'

'The dog sounds as if it was spoiled,' Andy observed.

'You're right, it was spoiled,' Hamish agreed. He had him hooked. 'I took my notes and gave the old biddies some good advice. Then they offered a cup of tea and a cream bun. I couldn't refuse.

'I'd supped my tea and was licking cream from my fingers when the dog lurched to its feet, spun around, gave a yelp of pain. As it turned, it tottered, its back legs shaking. Then it squatted. In fact, it quaked so much I thought it about to tumble into the fire. It had definite stomach problems. Worms, I thought, when shit squirted out of it in a yellowy stream, spraying the carpet.

'The old biddies screamed, pulled up their aprons and covered their faces. The flapping aprons and the heat from the fire spread the fumes more. Tearjerkers, I can tell you. So bad I nearly puked over the pair of them.'

'Phew, it sounds as if they were feeding it the wrong diet. We use Wuffitmix or something similar at home,' Andy said, seriously.

Hamish had difficulty keeping his face straight and talking without bursting out laughing. 'I found a hanky and dabbed my eyes. I don't think I'd ever risen to my feet quicker or approached an exit taking longer strides. The slightly less acrid atmosphere of Chelsea proved a pleasure. A few paces into the street, I looked back. The sisters were standing at the door, their concerned old eyes peering at me over the top of their aprons. Together they said, "Aren't you taking your dog with you, officer?"'

Suspecting a hook, but not seeing it yet, Andy narrowed his eyes. He looked at Hamish in the half-light and asked, 'Okay… then, how could you have got into bother when you didn't know it wasn't their dog?'

'Well, I went off duty soon after. The sisters complained, as you would imagine, still convinced it was my police dog. A sergeant attended. They locked the doors and kept him captive until he had helped clean up the stinking mess. I wasn't flavour of the month with him, I can tell you.'

Hamish peered out the doorway. Two men were arguing as they stood at the junction with Carnaby Street. Andy was on his shoulder, taking the situation in. He was about to step towards the pavement when Hamish grabbed his shoulder and drew him back, saying, 'I'll say goodbye to you here and walk on at my own pace.' Hamish moved off, looking everywhere but at the junction.

'Watch things don't go tits up for you,' Andy said, striding away, a spring in his heel, eager to feel collar.

Hamish chortled. Andy had bought the chestnut, uncracked.

Ponderously, his feet aching, he made towards the side streets filtering from Soho Square. He didn't feel much like stealth on the loose; his manufactured-sole boots were too tight.

Policing wasn't on Hamish's evening agenda; sauntering along the quieter streets, stopping frequently and resting up was. In Great Marlborough Street, he heard over the babble coming from a pub's open window the bar staff calling “Last orders”. Uninterested in checking on any rowdiness or drunkenness on the street at throwing-out time, he moved on.

Around the next corner, and further along the street, a burglar alarm clanged outside premises. Hamish thought taking a look a hassle-free task. A call on his mobile phone to the nick to report it would be sufficient. Gusting winds or passing heavy goods vehicles occasionally set off alarms, as well as shop-breakers. Anyhow, monitoring stations usually covered alarms in this part of the capital and already someone might be attending to it.

Outside the premises, Hamish’s keenness to deal with the situation rocketed. It was a sex shop’s burglar alarm clanging and he hoped there had been a break-in; looking through the goodies found in such premises appealed to him. Visible through the wire netting covering the windows were suggestive artefacts: kinky underwear and some soft-porn magazine front covers.

The Metropolitan Police Instruction Book contained important directives for officers investigating break-ins, the self-defence section dealing with the tackling of armed thieves found leaving premises. Hamish knew all this well and occasionally he had used his brawn as well as his brains to deal with a dangerous situation. Since returning to beat duties, he had sworn never to knowingly place himself in a position requiring any brawn. This instance didn’t count; the intrigue of viewing sex shop goodies wiped out any thoughts he had of a risky encounter with a dangerous chummy.

Hamish inspected the shop door for signs of forced entry. There were none and he prodded it with his truncheon. He let out an’ Ah ha,’ as the door pushed open. Keeping it ajar with a shoulder, he stepped inside into a small, square-shaped shop, brightened only by street lighting. No shadowy figure with a bundle of porno mags stuffed high in an armpit leaped at him out of the dark. Only the sickly whang of incense, rubber, leather and baby oil hit him.

There had been no break-in. It looked more as if a shop assistant, on leaving, just hadn’t locked the door behind them. Happy to be on safe ground, he let the door swing closed.

The flickering glow of a computer screen bathed the counter. Flicking on his torch, he allowed its beam to fall on glass cases crammed with kinky underwear and fearsome articles of sadomasochism. To study the shop contents better, he stepped forward. Some switches when operated lit the shop, but dimly. Rattling the handle of a cupboard door proved it locked. The absence of stairs up or down said there was no basement or any upstairs rooms attached to the shop.

Behind the counter, the till lay open with some small change on view in the drawer. He expected this; a forced open, locked and empty cash register was just as costly to repair as a full one. Using his mobile, he informed the station of the alarm and the unsecured premises.

The station responded quickly: the key-holder would arrive within fifteen minutes.

Behind the counter, Hamish faced shelves stacked with magazines, all with lurid covers. He chose an interesting bundle through which to thumb as he waited. Soft-porn shots, pictures of sex aids and advertisements for pornography to suit all tastes filled the pages. 'Rip-offs', he said loudly. They weren't the acme of porn magazines; not like what the "porn squad" had seized in raids on dodgy newsagents and pictorial bookshops on a manor where he once worked.

The amateurish posing of fat, ugly, tit-drooped women in the "readers' wives" section took his interest. A large blonde woman, with perkier tits than the others, ample love handles and a large bottom, interested him the most. 'I'd give her one. Big cuddly bum, whooooa, that's for me,' he said loudly. Then he quickly looked towards the door, thinking someone might have heard him.

The back pages of one magazine contained several columns of adverts under the "Adult Relaxation" banner. Hamish perked up. He immediately knew of a gov'nor who would find all of the sexual practices on offer in them nauseating: Dai Evans, the Commander who had reassigned him to beat duties, a man legendary as a gov'nor easily upset by matters relating to sex, unnatural or otherwise.

Titillations advertised would appeal to punters with preferences for "A" and "O", "Golden Rain", "SM", "Greek" and "Troilism". In another, Tattiana the mulatto transvestite offered any male reader exclusive, she/male services: a well-hung man with nice tits and arse. Contact was by telephone for home visits or… you… could… cum… to… his/her place.

Some wife-swapping contact columns he perused briefly before replacing the magazines. Taking his eye on the same shelf was a box of cigarette lighters with a price of £1 each, one of which he examined. The interest was a naked couple, in the classic 69-position, floating up and down inside the small fuel tank. It would be a topic of discussion among the practitioners frequenting the canteen at the meal break, if he had mellowed enough to talk to them. He took another, put both of them in his pocket, and placed two £1 coins in the open till.

Hamish paused in front of the computer screen. The screen saver was of a postman, strutting comically along a street, stuffing porn magazines into vertical letterboxes fixed between the cheeks of vast buttocks. It gave him an outrageous idea and he began blowing hard. If he had the balls for it, the notion afforded an opportunity to inflict revenge. Having those balls would mean retribution time had arrived: time to address the perceived injustices perpetrated against him by Commander Dai Evans.

Dry of mouth, he ditched the screensaver and studied the desktop screen. The computer had earlier churned off a mailing list for next day posting in plain brown envelopes. He could see they were the latest updates of available sexual aids and toys, transvestite adaptive clothing, pornographic videos, magazines, and other assorted kinky paraphernalia.

'Aye… aye, I see what I need to do and I have to do it now. It's too good an opportunity to miss. An occasion like this might never occur again. I must get my own back on that bastard,' Hamish muttered aloud.

Humming "Scottish Soldier", he moved the mouse on the pad and watched the pointer flick across the screen. Finding the mailing list, he scrolled it to the end, his future in the Job far from his thoughts. Opening the necessary window, he typed the name and home address of Commander Dai Evans, which, luckily, he knew.

Shaking a little with the humour he saw in his actions, he opened another window. There he placed an order on the Commander's behalf, payment on approval.

Clicking on urgent, next-day delivery, he chose a complete set of porno magazines and a full year's back numbers, an animal farm video, a set of sadomasochist's leathers with chain-link accessories and a set of handcuffs. As an afterthought, he considered the Commander would appreciate a postie delivering to him a blow-up doll, and a portable vibrating vagina, with the additional orifice at no extra charge.

On the counter were leaflets listing the monthly updates, which the Commander would definitely require. To ensure minimum delay in him receiving them, he put it in an envelope, printing on it his name and address. Spitting on the gummed edge, he sealed it, stuck the envelope in the franking machine and applied first class postage. Then he placed it halfway down the pile of mail ready for next-day posting.

The early part of the shift had gone well and by 1a.m., nothing more serious than reporting the alarm bell had occurred. Hamish's meal break, due at 1:30 a.m., meant starting a restrained amble now would get him back to the canteen in time to join a card school.

At the junction of Oxford Street with Great Portland Street, he saw his Scottish colleague and ex-partner, Harry MacSporran, walking with a younger copper down the other side of Oxford Street. He cheered up. A couple of weeks had passed since they last chatted. The bitterness they both felt about returning to uniform duties had dominated their conversation then; he doubted anything would have changed since.

Harry waved, signalling they should meet. At Oxford Circus, the traffic stationary at a red light, they met on the island in the centre of the street.

'How's the missus?' Harry asked as he approached.

'Giving me gyp. She's like these boots. How's the girl friend?'

'That W-plonk I was knocking off?'

'Aye.'

'Aw, I kicked her into touch last week. Got a bit snooty, she did. I could tell she didn't like the idea of getting her knickers off for an ordinary plod,' Harry said, bitterly. 'Talking of plodding, the old "plates" are giving you hell, are they?' he asked and playfully went to tap on Hamish's boot with his.

Hamish moved away and tapped his boots against a lamppost. Scowling, he said, 'My feet are killing me. Sod this beat duty for a lark.'

'Aye ah ken. I'm not hacking it very well either. Would have been attending a lock-in at a pub, had we still been in plain clothes.'

'Och don't mention it. This is a load of old bollocks, by the way. The perks we've lost, it fair gets up my nose so it does.'

'I fancy the CID,' said Harry's young colleague, his eyes shining.

Hamish grinned at him. 'I think I know how to interpret that loaded remark, son, but there's many that wouldn't. You mean you'd like for to *join* the CID, become a detective?'

Now Harry grinned. 'And *you* mean join as in enlist. Not as in back-scuttle?'

'I think I'd better head for the canteen and have my grub before I say something I regret,' Hamish said and turned to go. He would tell Harry the details of his deeds at the sex shop next time they met. He'd have loved to give him the account there and then; they'd have rocked together laughing. He'd say nothing with a jug-eared recruit listening. 'I can't hang about, grub beckons, but I'll be in touch to go for a pint next day-duty.'

'Stay out of mischief,' Harry said as if guessing Hamish's thoughts. Turning, Harry set off across the street back to his beat.

'And you,' Hamish answered. Happier than he had been for a while, he set out towards West End Central.

Chapter 3

Harry checked his tunic pocket as he walked off. Hamish had slipped something into it when his young companion wasn't looking. He found the cigarette lighter featuring the plastic models in a pornographic pose, gave it a quick glance and said beneath his breath, 'Trust you, Hamish.'

That night shift, Harry was pounding the streets of the capital in as bitter a mood as Hamish, having suffered identically. He had already taken his meal. Returning to his beat after the meeting with Hamish, the pissed-off feeling got the better of him.

'Life was great working in plain clothes,' Harry moaned. Jason, one of D division's eager new recruits, who had joined him as he left the canteen, turned his head to listen.

'In CID quite a while, were you?' Jason asked.

Harry nodded. 'Aye, Hamish, my mate you've just met, he and I worked together in plain clothes for many happy and very successful years. As well as being successful thief takers, we were also a bit of a comic duo. My tall, lanky appearance and my sad hangdog face hid my love of nonsense. Hamish laughed at everything, couldn't keep his belly still. We lived on free nosh. Among Hamish's many great gifts was his ability to cultivate Indian restaurant owners to be generous to coppers. He had them serving us curries at any time of the day or night.

'Many a wheeze we pulled while on stakeouts with the Robbery Squad. We were unique. Our methods brought us some noteworthy collars. One time, we were just wolfing a carryout whilst standing outside a chippy, observing a betting shop robbery in progress next door. The chummies never sussed out whom the clowns were throwing chips at each other until it was too late.'

'Did you pull in many?'

'Och aye, van-loads,' Harry said casually, as if it was an every-day occurrence. 'Our gov'nors knew we could just about pull anything off. Before political correctness reared its ugly head, they would use us in situations needing something bizarre to mask the obbo. I bought VIZ regularly and always had a copy sticking out of my back pocket. I used the "Funny Half Hour" until it disappeared from the newsstands. Most chummies never knew what had hit them when Hamish and I rounded them up.

We got no thanks for it in the end. It was a case of "Back you go into uniform, P.C. MacSporran, and you too, P.C. MacNab, we've two graduates to replace you pair of has-beens." It was hard to bear. We were the best. We got more than our fair share of collars.

'And we drank some gov'nors under the table nightly. In one respect, I was lucky. For all the piss and nosh I put away, I didn't gain a pound of weight. The uniform hanging in my Section House wardrobe for the past twelve years is the one I'm wearing now. Hamish's weight ballooned.'

'The Serious Crime Squad interests me long-term. The CID will do for me when I complete my probation,' Jason confessed.

'Well, I had experience in various squads. I was particularly keen to finish my time in the Diplomatic Protection Service, protecting royalty or a government minister. That bastard, Commander Dai Evans, thought differently.'

'Yes, I've heard the Force is trawling universities looking for graduates, whatever their degree,' Jason said, rather haughtily, 'guaranteeing appointments to CID and the DPS. That being why you were transferred back to uniform, then you must feel really disgruntled.'

'Aye, disgruntled is too light a word for it. My grievances with the Job are extreme. The thought of a decent pension when I've done my thirty is an attraction, I admit, but it won't make me start looking for chummies to nick. The Job's not the same. Nowadays, hardly anyone in uniform has a sense of humour. Doing things by the book fair pisses me off, it does. Street crime's out. You won't get me looking for drunks and druggies to keep my numbers up.'

'Surely, it can't be that bad!' Jason said, grimacing, confirming negative thinking appalled him.

Harry nodded. 'It is. Traditionally, on night duty, tired beat coppers from Marylebone Lane nick crossed over to the southern side of Oxford Street. Kipping in a sheltered shop doorway on C Division, out of sight of our beat sergeants, was a bit of a perk back then.'

'There's too much work on this patch for me to get bored. I won't be hiding myself away,' Jason said, 'I'm dedicated totally to policing in the MPD and will be throughout my entire service.'

Harry ignored him. 'Nothing's the same since that senior gov'nor from Manchester had his consumption of Chinese meals investigated by a Chief Constable. Now gov'nors go barmy if they suspect a copper drops off somewhere for a cuppa. Mooching across there for a kip has also become a no-no.'

'We were all warned at Hendon to refuse offers of unofficial refreshments,' Jason said, 'you won't catch me mumping.'

'In plain clothes, I wrote up all my reports in the Nags Head with a pint of Guinness and a pork pie at hand,' Harry said. 'Missing that part of the Job, nightclubbing, the odd invite to the home of a tasty-looking brass, free drink and nosh, hurts like hell.'

Harry noticed Jason's eyes roaming, looking for some poor cove to arrest, to keep his numbers up. It was time to calm Jason, get the lad to take the Job less seriously. 'Those were happy days and I long for them now,' Harry stressed with a sigh. 'Aye, those were days of fun galore in the Job. I remember a four-storied derelict building in Portland Street, close by the nick, with a Nurses Home opposite. One night shift, after parading at ten, we followed a well-rehearsed routine before hitting the streets. The whole relief, including some older, hoarier types, all of us desperate for titillation, would enter the derelict building. From the top floor, we could keep an eye on the nurses. Many a nude show from behind windows without the curtains drawn is what we saw.'

'You never did?' Jason let out, more interest in his voice now.

'Aye, we did. Had the place been back in my old stamping ground of Leith, I could have sold tickets for the show. We saw some very tasty nurses prancing about their rooms naked. I was sure some of them knew we were there. The saucier minxes amongst them trying to get us worked up by revealing their encyclopaedic knowledge of self-stimulation.'

'They never did! Fingering! You witnessed all that?'

'Aye, many a womanly habit we witnessed. Some were disgraceful. One in particular proved the suspicions lurking within the minds of most men.'

'What was that?'

'Some women *can* piss into a sink like a man.'

'You're having me on now!' Jason said disbelievingly.

'No, it's true. The lazy bitches wouldn't walk ten paces to the bog. The fascination lasted for many months. Then an adventurous young copper, a lot like you he was, eventually spoilt it for us.'

'Why was that?'

'He wanted more than the regulation eyeful and leaned too far out of a window. His silvery helmet badge reflected a streetlight, alerting a cod-faced old matron who guessed there might be voyeurs loitering opposite. She dialled 999. Information room alerted the desk sergeant and nightshift inspector, the only officers available at Marylebone Lane nick, and guess what?'

'What?'

'The desk sergeant stormed into the building, torch blazing, and found twenty-seven coppers loitering in questionable circumstances.'

'Did you all get away with it?'

'Och aye, the sergeant stayed and had a blimp himself. He even joined us for a couple of nights. Then he lost his nerve and warned us off.'

'Is the building still there?' Jason asked, eager for an affirmative answer.

'It was pulled down years ago.' Harry watched Jason's face turn bleak. 'Mind you, when I was a probationer finding fun in the Job was commonplace. Like up in Little Venice. We used to park a police van outside a brothel. The van roof gave us a good vantage point and four lads at a time had a safe, line-of-sight view into the working-bedroom of a brass. I found it interesting, educational and revealing, I can tell you. I've always been lithe, fit and, in those days, dead keen. I made sure of regular eyefuls from the roof.'

'Did that last long?' Jason asked.

'Like all good things it ended after a few weeks. An impatient probationer, as I recall,' Harry said, raising his voice and taking a meaningful glance at Jason, 'waiting his turn in the shadow of the van, threw a stone through the working-bedroom window while work was taking place… if you catch my drift. Two of the lads on the roof leapt down onto the pavement. All they suffered was some ankle pain. The other two panicked and jumped into the canal.'

'What happened to them?' Jason asked, once more absorbed.

'Two of the lads stripped off, dived in, and dragged them to the bank.'

'Did that end the viewing from the roof?'

'Yes, we gave it up thinking we'd been lucky to get away with what we did. Today, van roofs are not constructed the same. They're flimsy. They would break easily under the weight of one copper, never mind four of us.

'The fun has gone out of the Job. Ancient police scrolls I've read indicate it's an inevitable process. Between the wars, a copper paid a fine of three quid for passing wind on parade. The other three quid fine was for aggravating the offence. In stern terms, the charge stated that he shook his left leg to the amusement of the constables on parade. It seems the sergeant taking that parade was as humourless as some of those around now.'

Reaching the beginning of his beat, Jason said, 'I'm off here.'

'Proceeding to one's beat, are we?' Harry teased. 'Good luck,' he wished him.

'Watch things don't go tits up for you,' Jason replied.

'Knowing police jargon off pat will get you nowhere,' Harry shouted after Jason, quickly crossing the street to his beat.

Revellers and beggars were leaving the streets. Traffic had thinned to the occasional all-night bus or prowling taxi. At 3a.m., after an aimless patrol free from hassle, Harry developed a sudden, urgent desire to find a toilet. Rushing, clenched of nether cheeks, he headed towards an all-night Gents just off Wigmore Street. He knew that some "uptown" Gents were disreputable, but his need pressed and he cared little; any pervs likely to be frequenting them would quickly disappear on sighting a copper in uniform.

Harry rushed down the steps, into the gloom. He pushed open cubicle doors and checked for cleanliness, before choosing one that was central and lockable. Inside and secured, he placed his helmet on the cistern and hung his tunic on the door catch.

Preparing for a lengthy sit, he took the copy of VIZ from a tunic pocket. After the first plop sounded, his concentration on the job in hand produced some grunting and encouraging. On the "Billy the Fish" pages, he found the outrageous humour he craved, Billy's latest antics tickling him, generating giggles, interfering with his concentration.

Engrossed in the comic, Harry didn't notice the adjacent cubicle gaining an occupant. With the "Billy the Fish" story read, and about to turn over to see whom "The Fat Slags" were shagging in this latest edition, he sensed something was amiss. The light flickering across Shirl and Tracy and distracting his attention was coming through a large hole in the plywood wall separating the two cubicles.

The hole was directly above a short wooden support designed to hang the bog roll holder. For the first time, and with a drop of a lip, Harry noticed the bog roll was missing. 'Bollocks,' he muttered.

Seeking supplies elsewhere, his eyes roamed onto bits of graffiti scrawled onto the door back. Aimed at aiding the economic recovery of the country, one doodle suggested the use of both sides of the toilet paper. It didn't amuse him as much as the other piece: an anti-police Gents user suggested clients pull the flush twice, it being a long way to the nearest police station.

Harry screwed his eyes up in despair at the lack of tissue of any sort, anywhere. 'Damn,' he mumbled, realising the act of wiping would sacrifice a page of VIZ. Fizzing, he ripped a page out and softened it by rolling it into a ball.

He had torn the page into usable strips, smoothed them out and had lined them up on his thigh ready for use, when he saw the rampant black cock thrusting through the hole in the partitioning wall.

The cock's appearance might have had bog users expectant of its arrival salivating and in fits of excitement. Unwary users might have boggled at the sight of it, departing hastily, trousers around ankles, shouting "Police!" Harry decided to deal with it in his own way and muttered 'Thank you, Hamish.'

Now, he needed it to remain sticking through the orifice long enough for him to get the cigarette lighter from his tunic pocket, judge six inches from the protruding knob-end, which was now jerking feverishly, before flicking the lighter into life.

Moans, possibly of impatience, from the other cubicle were now accompanying the jiggling. Suddenly the movement ceased. Harry pointed the lighter and pressed down on the igniter. Yellow flame shot out, enveloping the cock. Harry smelled singed hair before he heard the howl of pain.

The cock withdrew.

Unsatisfactory wiping completed, Harry pulled up his pants, tightened his belt, put on his tunic and helmet. Outside the cubicle, he waited to greet his unknown neighbour, whilst smacking the base of his truncheon into the palm of one hand. He intended to arrest the person who had subjected him to such indecent behaviour, for the laugh of it.

Listening to the groans and mutterings in the strange tongue of the incumbent had him grinning broadly and lifting up on the balls of his feet. In a short time, the cubicle door opened inwards with a crash. A black man reeled out, bent almost double, shock and pain raddling his face. He wore an Armani suit, crocodile-skin shoes, and had a wet handkerchief bound loosely around his scorched cock. Harry stepped forward, placed a hand onto the man's shoulder and his truncheon across his throat, forcing him to stand upright.

At full height, the man reeled backwards, to lean against a doorframe. His eyes were rolling and his groans were increasing in volume and pitch. He had recognised the uniform.

'You're nicked,' Harry told him, and took a firm grip of his shoulder. 'You're not obliged to say anything,' he quoted briefly from Judges' Rules. 'But if you do, it will be a great laugh down at the nick,' he said beneath his breath. Harry was sure the circumstances surrounding the pervert's arrest would generate laughs in the canteen.

Certainly, there were a few chuckles when he frogmarched him into the nick with the hanky still in place.

Later, however, and unknown to Harry, the station sergeant was investigating the man's claims of diplomatic immunity.

Meanwhile, Harry was sitting with a cup of tea in the canteen, his mind unworried, relating his experience in the Gents to other coppers taking their meal breaks, whether they were interested in hearing them or not. Finishing his verbal report, he began some upsetting antics, which only disrupted the concentrations of coppers playing card games… a crime itself in police canteens.

'A low orgasmic moan reverberated through the plywood,' Harry said, and gave his impression of the mating cry of a seal. Laid on his back, on a canteen table, he clapped his hands and boots together like flippers. 'I heard great lips puckering with pain,' he said, rolling his lips back and plucking them with one index finger.

Some coppers encouraged Harry with cries of 'Show us your flipper.' Dissent was present, too. 'Oh come off it, Jock,' cried one copper holding a poor hand, more in annoyance at his bad luck than in disbelief.

'Bugger off and leave us alone to play cards, you crazy Jock fucker,' said another, irritably.

'There's more,' Harry pleaded. 'I'm sure I could identify withdrawal symptoms and supplications to a favourite witch doctor. Other noises sounded too, like those of an unfit contortionist, attempting impossible positions in a futile attempt…'

'Fuck off, Jock,' cried the copper with the bad hand, throwing small change across the table to the winner.

'… *listen*… at kissing himself better.'

A hush settled over the canteen. The entrance door had opened and the Station Sergeant's head poked in. 'MacSporran,' he called, and waved Harry out into the passage. 'You've only arrested the Cultural Attaché from an African embassy. His claim for diplomatic immunity is real,' the sergeant said and looked closely at Harry for a reaction. 'To make matters worse, he's made a complaint against you. He's also asking to see everyone from the Commissioner up to the Prime Minister to complain of the brutality *you* inflicted on *him*. In fact, he has accused *you* of assault. He says you aimed a flamethrower through the hole in the cubicle wall, while he sat innocently defecating. Talk yourself out of that, Jock.'

'Suffering fuck!' Harry said. 'It cannae be true. You're no going to believe somebody who'd stick his cock through a shithouse wall and wave it at me, against what I say, are you?'

Chapter 4

On the evening of the first Thursday in October, just before 7 p.m., silly altercations were taking place inside Paddleworth Towers, a tree-surrounded mansion, situated north of the Thames and on the easternmost fringes of the Metropolitan Police District. The Towers is the home of Algernon Rideout, Mayor of the Metropolitan Borough of Clegham, and his wife, Myrna. Friends and most citizens of the borough knew the mayor as Algie. His drunken antics were pissing-off Myrna.

Myrna was doing her damnedest to complete dressing Algie; he was reeling like a cartoon drunk, his eyes rolling in his head. Myrna was holding his hand tightly, her knuckles turning white, trying to tug it towards the sleeve of a dark-suit jacket. 'You'd never have gotten out of your poverty-ploughed rut in Plaistow, you bitch,' Algie lambasted, truculently. Bolshie when filled with booze, he was keeping his arm stiff, preventing Myrna from directing his hand into the sleeve.

Myrna dragged him closer, turned her head away from his foul, whisky-tainted breath and bawled, 'Rotten-mouthed bastard, relax.'

Wheezing, mouth agape, Algie swayed until a spittle-drenched 'ach' sounded his defeat and Myrna was finally able to insert a hand into an armhole. The hand appeared through the cuff. Grabbing it, fearful of him relapsing into defiance, she pulled the jacket over his shoulders and straightened the collar around his neck. Taking hold of his face in both hands, she steadied his head and straightened his tie. Algie threw his arms up, knocked hers away, mouthing, 'Bitch, bitch, bitch,' spittle flying in her direction from close range. Braving the spray, Myrna stepped in and brushed down his suit, checking his smartness for the Masonic Lodge meeting he was leaving to attend.

Myrna was taller than Algie, easily seeing over the top of his head. The extra inches were hardly menacing, but a tough Plaistow upbringing gave her the skills to hold her own in any discourse with him. She took a step back, placed her hands firmly on her hips, ready for him. 'Just because I was born in the East End, was a Dagenham Girl Piper and an assembly-line worker in Ford's, where I met you, remember, there's no need to insult me… arsehole.'

Since Algie's election to the Mayoral office, he had become bloated of girth and redder of already heavy jowls; the result of drinking daily whilst entertaining associates as a part of his civic duties. His drunken arguments were unwelcome; they got up Myrna's nose, as did his halitosis.

'My brothers are real East End boys. Know all about crooked council officials and their brotherly dealings, they do. Would put you away in a big hole, you little fart,' she said acidly. 'They'd never allow an arsehole the likes of you talk to their sister the way you do.' Turning, she picked up his regalia box from the sofa, held it tantalisingly out in front of her, inviting him to take hold of it, pissed as he was.

Algie moved towards her, crablike, a hand outstretched, his mouth slowly opening and closing. Clawing at the case handle, he missed it. 'You can't make your mind up whether I'm a fart or an arsehole,' he said, slurring his words. 'Your fancy friends won't like such improper talk.' Wobbling towards her, he grabbed at the handle, missing it again. The effort caused him stop, to hang onto the sofa-back and stand breathing heavily.

'Look at the state of you. You should lay off the piss. Get going to your silly Lodge, your Brothers and your daft handshakes,' Myrna countered. He reeled forward; she shoved the regalia box into his grasp.

'My little Saluki, I can see a sticky end coming your way, both to you and the girlies waiting outside for me to leave,' Algie replied, rocking bodily and spitting out his words. 'A fucking big comedown it will be too, something that'd never happen to any of us brethren.'

Myrna knew he'd say anything, even something silly, so long as he had the last word. 'I'm not your little Saluki,' she yelled at him. She raised a hand for her fingers to run through her shoulder-length blonde tresses. Shaking her head, she wondered what use, if he mistook her hair for dog's ears, would he be to fellow Masons, so pissed.

Algie's chauffeur-driven Mayoral car pulled up outside. Myrna caught his jacket sleeve and tugged him in the direction of the door. With one hand clutching at each side of him, she negotiated him through it without damaging him or the door. Taking the steps down alongside him, one at a time, she reached the waiting car without him stumbling.

The chauffeur was standing holding open the car back door. Smiling at Algie's drunken state, he watched Myrna send him headlong onto the rear seat. Myrna turned and scampered up the steps. From the top, she watched the car slow as it reached the gateway from the drive.

7 p.m. was striking on a hall clock. A jumbo was rumbling overhead; banking to leave the Ongar stack, it straightened up and settled on its glide path towards Heathrow airport. Myrna said aloud as she looked up towards the plane, 'Lucky bleeders have been on a proper holiday.' In the distance, an illuminated Tube train streaked from the tunnel in a ribbon of light. Unheard, like Myrna's words beneath the jet's rumble, it plunged on towards its terminus in rural Essex.

The car lurched into the storm drain gratings at the foot of the drive and its junction with the tree-lined avenue. Myrna saw the silhouette of Algie's head rocking back and forth in the back window. 'You're just an alcoholic dwarf,' she called after him.

Lodge nights were also girls' nights out; sometimes, they referred to the meetings as those of The Masonic Widows Society. For her and her three friends it had become a regular feature during their husbands' Masonic year.

Normally, it was a fortnightly get-together in each other's homes. All their husbands were members of the same lodge and attended fortnightly meetings.

Myrna was hosting this particular meeting. She expected the girl's arrival any minute, knowing they'd be waiting around the corner in their cars, watching for Algie to leave. Arriving before he left, which they'd only done once, meant running the Algie gauntlet. Preference was for not having their bottoms pinched, slobbering lips of greeting puckering on their cheeks, leaving unwanted dribbles or being nauseated by his bad breath.

Myrna turned and walked back through the tall, sandstone portals into her home. Bum-hugging Levis clung to her fetching figure, a low-cut blouse revealed the ampleness of her breasts and that she wasn't wearing a bra. She left the door slightly ajar for the girls and dallied in front of the hall mirror. It told her she had reddened slightly around her high cheekbones. 'Upsetting little wanker, so he is' she said to her image, before walking quickly into the lounge.

An arrangement of goodies supplied by "Annie Slobbers", a home-party company specialising in erotic wares and kinky lingerie, lay on the coffee table. In fact, the company dealt in eroticising artefacts of interest to any sexy woman wanting more from her bed sports. Myrna thought she had selected the right items to titillate her girlie friends. She had an important reason in mind.

Proceedings at past Masonic Widows' nights had exasperated Myrna. They had mainly yielded mutterings on dull family matters, opinions on neighbours and their husbands' promotion prospects. With the new Masonic year underway, things just had to change. In her opinion, topics for discussion needed a subject boost. Seeing, and handling if they dared, the sexy artefacts should inject real spice into the evening. It was her intention, if this entirely diverse approach stimulated any interest in subjects other than the norm, to raise the question of them spending a long-weekend away together in Blackpool. She was sure two of the girls would be agreeable, and that a drastic approach was required to move a certain sober-minded guest to consider the proposal.

All three of Myrna's expected guests were the wives of police officers. Each had telephoned during the day, confirming their presences that evening. They would arrive by rank; an unwritten protocol existed on arrival times. Something to do with not upstaging the boss's wife, she thought. Daphne Dewsnap, the wife of Metropolitan Police Commander Jack Dewsnap, the girls considered senior. She always arrived first.

In front of the chair Daphne Dewsnap preferred, Myrna had placed a box containing a large, black dildo. It had a fearsome head, a set of authentically hairy balls, which, when filled with a suitable viscous liquid and squeezed, faked an ejaculation. Myrna chuckled. She thought Daphne would like that. Daphne had often made coy reference to Jack's prowess in bed and the size of his cock. Gloria, wife of Superintendent Ivor Bunce, had thought that too much information. She had always butted in, putting a damper on such topics of conversation getting anywhere. She would be the attendee most likely to pooh-pooh her weekend in Blackpool idea.

Gloria preferred the recliner. Lining up her massive derriere between the chair's arms, she would launch herself backwards into it, her feet rising from the floor. Myrna had often listened to the sounds of straining springs and stressed metal hinges with some unease. Then, equally, she marvelled how Gloria extracted herself without help. Gloria sported a bun in her auburn hair; Myrna was sure it was unconsciously fashioned in the shape of a car's gear stick.

In front of the recliner, Myrna had placed a box of French ticklers. The various, horrendous-looking, bulbous knob-ends were pictured on the box top. Myrna wondered if the imagery might encourage Gloria into not being her usual overbearing, party-pooping self. Myrna expected Gloria would quiver at the thought of using one. Quite often, she had unashamedly boasted of the browbeating to which she subjected her husband Ivor, and in their apparent abstinence from all sexual activities.

Myrna also expected the arrival of young Maggie, the wife of the Scottish sergeant, Murdo Shrapnel. A recent transfer to the Met from the Lothian Force, he was well up in Masonry and had been "through the chair" in Scotland. From Algie's incoherent prattle, she had learned that both Jack and Ivor had earmarked him as a groveller, but set for rapid advancement in the Met.

In front of Maggie's chair, Myrna had placed the latest model "Stallion Pump" penis enlarger, newly imported from Holland. According to the accompanying literature, many happy wives reported the satisfying results achieved by their men, but Myrna wondered if the thing worked as well as the bumf implied. Maggie had once girlishly mentioned her husband's shortfall in the cock department and that she wasn't getting much satisfaction. Welcome to the club, had been Myrna's thought on that subject. 'This ought to get the silly little Scots lassie wetting her panties,' Myrna said quietly, shuddering herself at the size of the thing. Fussily she checked that the position of the box gave maximum affect.

Myrna placed some tall bottles of bath salts in the middle of the table. Covering the lot with a tablecloth, the result resembled a circus tent. It would keep the surprise intact until they'd all sat down. She hoped that once uncovered, the items on the table would shock the girls into discussions differing greatly from their old ones.

A car pulled up. Seconds later, Myrna heard a cheery 'Cooee.' Daphne pushed the front door open and walked in. Myrna was screwing an opener into the mandatory bottle of alcohol-free wine when Daphne walked silkily into the lounge, her hips rotating sexily, her face vivacious. Her titian locks and pale complexion put her well ahead of the other girls in the looks stakes. Her healthy, wrinkle-free bloom, after twenty years of marriage, she attributed to the lusty sexual relationship she maintained with Jack. 'You're looking wonderful, Myrna. I can see the holiday in Brighton did you good.'

'Spent most of the time on my own, Daphne, didn't I? Algie just hung around the hotel bars all day. He got rat-arsed most days, stocious he was sometimes.'

Two more cars pulled up. Gloria, with Maggie a pace behind, walked into the lounge.

Gloria's idea of dress sense, nurtured during her Salvation Army days, did nothing for her pear-shaped figure. 'My, you do suit lime green,' Myrna said kindly as Gloria slouched towards her wearing a trouser suit with turn-ups.

'It's good to get back into the old routine,' Gloria said, catching hold of Myrna by the shoulders, stooping and brushing her cheeks with hers. Turning towards Daphne, she grasped her by the arms and greeted her similarly. She ignored Maggie.

Daphne noticed Myrna's glance of exasperation at Gloria's rudeness. During the previous-year's meets, she had often snubbed Maggie, Myrna and Daphne thinking it because she was only a sergeant's wife.

'Hi,' Maggie said cheerily and smiled at them.

'Hi,' Myrna responded.

Daphne echoed the greeting.

'Have you lost some weight to fit into that tight skirt?' Myrna asked Maggie.

Maggie, her elfin face smiling shyly beneath her urchin cut, brushed her hands over her blouse and skirt. She directed a sniff towards Gloria, turned, and placed her bag on the chair-back. Gloria's overbearing greeting of the others embarrassed her too, but she said, 'Just a wee bit, I think, Myrna.'

'Did you enjoy the summer holiday with Jack?' Myrna asked Daphne, while busy pouring the wine and handing flutes around. Moving their usual chairs back, they all sat down at the table, Gloria with the usual protests from the recliner. 'You'll just have to wait to put the glasses down,' Myrna said quickly to them all, her eyes rolling suggestively, 'There are surprises beneath the cloth that should really take your interest.'

Before Daphne could reply to Myrna, Gloria butted in loudly. 'I didn't know you were away anywhere, Daphne. Ivor and I went nowhere as usual. I messed about in the garden all summer, cutting and trimming the lawn. Ivor moped in his shed, hoed his turnips and weeded his onions. Most of the time, he complained about a sore back, twitch and chickweed. Quite animated he got about his twitch.'

Daphne sipped at her wine whilst Gloria had the spotlight, then said, 'We went to Scotland and had a wonderful holiday touring the Trossachs and further north. We stayed in farmhouse B and Bs mostly. The midges were a nuisance and bit us unmercifully most days, especially when we were walking in the hills or by the sides of lochs.'

'Och aye, the fresh air would have done you the world of good, though,' reckoned Maggie, glad to have her Lothian-twang heard, 'especially around the Trossachs.'

Gloria looked hard at Maggie and pitched her voice higher. 'Trossachs, Trossachs, I say, it sounds like somewhere maggoty, somewhere to avoid to me. What horrors do you Scots keep hidden there, doon in the glen?'

'It's certainly not like that, Gloria,' Daphne said, turning to support Maggie, 'it's one of the nicest parts of Britain. Jack and I were quite envious of the Scots. The fresh, pine-tinged aromas of the forests made us a trifle heady. The wind howling through one glen nearly knocked us over. The walks along beaches on the Cromarty Firth I found most bracing. They certainly perked Jack up. He couldn't get enough of me, could he? Wrecked a few mattresses at the B and Bs we stayed at and flattened heather in some lonely spots.'

Myrna noticed Daphne wink when she finished her holiday report. She seemed to love emphasising Jack's bedtime prowess.

'You're all so lucky with your men,' Myrna said, tossing her head and sniffing. 'That Algie just can't get it up. He's always Jimmy Riddled. I haven't had a Harry Wragg for years, have I?'

Maggie had learned to remain silent at these times, embarrassed at having once revealed her misgivings about her husband's measurements.

Gloria humphed.

Gloria's humph suggested to the girls that Myrna's rhyming slang wasn't to her taste. At their meets, she had never admitted to having a sex life and the frank revelation which followed came as a surprise: 'Suddenly, soon after we married, Ivor became reluctant to engage in the sexual act. I must say I lost the keenness I had for it after I'd trapped him and I haven't missed it much since.

'Once, I recall, he had me shuddering with the heady delights an orgasm brings to a woman, had me shouting out in something that sounded Swahili, but that was on our honeymoon. If I really wanted to embark on a sexual interlude with Ivor now, limp as he is these days, then I think he would require perking up in the erection department. I suppose there must be some exotic chemical available, like Spanish fly. When I was young, people talked of it in awe, as if it was some magical potion.'

Gloria at least recognised something called sex existed, Myrna thought, which prompted her to reveal her surprises. She grabbed at the middle of the tablecloth and drifted it away, revealing the packages, '*Voila*!' she said for effect. 'Goodies!'

As Myrna had hoped, the artefacts generated both astonishment and mirth. She knew Daphne liked a bit of fun. As a trained nurse, she had worked in

A&E and had spoken of various nursing duties from her past. To giggles from her and Maggie, but to shushes from Gloria, she told of rescuing the strange artefacts humans stuck up orifices that nature had deemed “off limits” for such things.

Unperturbed by the surprises on view, Daphne clapped her hands together and said, ‘Bravo, Myrna, what a novel idea.’

It didn’t surprise Myrna that Daphne gave her support and treated the articles so lightly.

Daphne let out a chortle, lifted the box and broke the seal with her thumbnail. In a trice, she had removed the dildo from its wrapper. The sight of the cock-like thing resting in Daphne’s hand distracted Gloria from the box resting on the table in front of her. She let out a short squeal of disgust and exclaimed, ‘Whatever is that beastly thing? I’ve never ever laid my eyes on anything like it… it’s so huge… grotesque… and black!’ She looked from girl to girl, seeing only amusement in their eyes. ‘Are you trying to kid me that that is one of life’s pleasures?’ she asked, her eyes returning to Daphne’s hand.

Gloria’s fascination with the dildo as it lay across Daphne’s palm was plain. She opened her mouth wide and shook her head. Dragging her eyes away, they came to rest on the box with the revealing pictures. ‘My word, what do I have here?’ she shrilled, lifting the box closer. ‘I must say, at first glance all of the images look like the head of that Alien thingy; the thingy that popped out of the man’s chest in the film of the same name.

‘“French Ticklers”,’ she erupted, her eyes widening in disbelief, her top lip vibrating. ‘I’m aghast. Abhorred,’ she said loudly. ‘One look at them is enough. Of course I’ve heard of such things… read about them in women’s magazines… but I never thought I’d come face to face with any. Myrna, what is the meaning of this? In future, are we to degrade ourselves at each of the meets we have at your home? I say… I don’t like this at all!’ Satisfied she had made a point, she thumped the box down on the table. Throwing herself back, she crossed her arms and slumped into the chair, po-faced.

The box containing the lengthy glass tube and the words “Stallion Pump” mesmerised Maggie. Turning it end-over-end she found the instructions explaining its intended usage. Sitting, her legs crossed, she was trying hard to conceal a slight tremor. The small print promised increases in penis length and thickness for men of Murdo’s age group.

Maggie read the prophecies wide-eyed, her mouth open. Her cheeks had turned a little rosy and Myrna drew Daphne’s attention. Without looking at anyone, Maggie said, ‘I might have been able to find something similar in Edinburgh’s Grassmarket, but certainly not on Princes Street or on the Royal Mile.’

‘Not looking for the price are we?’ Myrna asked. ‘My agent will do you a good deal on one, a proper discount.’

Maggie shook her head. 'Och no, it's just that it's such an odd-looking contraption. It's just a squeezy rubber ball connected to a glass tube by a length of rubber pipe,' she said shyly, suddenly wary of her interest being noticed.

Myrna reacted gleefully to the controversy she had created and set about selling them her idea. 'You're viewing these erotic bits and pieces that I've selected to see if they'll blitz you out of your duff lifestyles,' she said. 'I want to get your minds working differently, to consider us going away on a long weekend together, for heaven's sake. To do something we've never done before.'

'Whatever would we be doing wherever we're going? Opening a dodgy shop or something?' Gloria asked. Tutting, she bent forward and took a gulp from her flute.

'No, no, you've got it all wrong,' Myrna responded quickly. She saw in Gloria's dissension a dissuasive influence, putting off Daphne and Maggie from showing any interest in her idea. 'Wouldn't it be lovely for us all to go on a long weekend away to Blackpool? We will see the marvellous light display. We can take in a show, that sort of thing. Algie's chauffeur has given him some front row tickets for a comedian, with the intriguing name of Billy Bagman. His show is in one of the famous pier theatres there. To see Billy and hear his silly gags will make the weekend so much more wonderful, memorable and we will have laughs. So, come on, who's up for it?' she asked, cheeriness in her voice.

The erotic wares were not now at the centre of interest. Maggie, though, was noticeably slow in dragging her eyes from the prophecies on the stallion pump box.

'Well, I don't know about that.' Gloria felt she had to voice her opinion quickly. Twirling her hair with her fingers, her eyes looking towards the ceiling, she said haughtily, 'Blackpool? Whatever will you think of next for us, Myrna?'

Without her moral support, Daphne saw that Gloria would snub Myrna's idea. She knew stuff about Gloria. Stuff the others didn't know: stories from Jack's repertoire of humorous happenings whilst he plodded the beat. Gloria's stiffish ways once had chinks in them.

******

Gloria had spotted Ivor plodding his beat around Sloane Square about noon one Sunday, twenty-seven years or so back. She had joined with other disciples from the local branch of the Salvation Army, to sing hymns and bang her tambourine. To the tune of "Onward Christian Soldiers", Ivor had caught her eyeing him up over the top of her hymn sheet. He had stopped a little further on to listen and watch.

He walked past again and Gloria approached him, positioning herself in front of him on the pavement. Quite blatantly, she waved a collecting pot beneath his nose. He had no change and, although renowned for his stinginess, he bashfully placed his only note, a tenner, in the tin. He fumed for a week over the donation. After numerous days, denying himself his normal intake of chips in the station canteen, he made up the deficit. When shifts suited, he walked that route on Sundays about noon, smitten by Gloria's interest, but always with a pocketful of small change.

Gloria worked as a teller in the Sloane Square branch of the Westminster bank. When Ivor discovered this, he transferred his account there. He proved a thrifty account holder, appearing once a week to make a meagre withdrawal. On each appearance, he looked shy and smiled nervously. Often, he missed his turn in the queue, hanging back so Gloria could serve him. Doing the opposite of queue jumping and being present on pavements while she belted out hymns, Gloria was convinced that he had more than a passing interest in her.

No man had made Gloria their Valentine and if Ivor escaped her clutches or fell for another, she saw a slot on "the shelf" looming forbiddingly. She fancied Ivor and snaring him could change that unwelcome scenario.

In a moment of surging passion, she made her mind up to seduce him, to give him what she understood every boy wanted and encourage him into her arms.

Initially, finding him in a suitable spot proved difficult; only his shifts during the hours of darkness suited her plan. She stalked him during a week of his late-turn shift. Each time she had caught up with him, he was either about to book off or in the company of another copper.

During his next spell of night shift duty, her luck changed. She found him walking alone around midnight and she stalked him until he took shelter in a shop doorway from a sudden downpour.

Gloria swished casually in beside him, lowered, shook and parked her brolly. Seeing no threat, Ivor just smiled sillily at her. His anxiety surged as she began to breathe heavily, her breasts lifting. Panic quickly followed as a hand disappeared beneath his cape to grasp and squeeze his inner thigh. His breathing rate increased when she turned her face up, close to his, and fluttered her eyelashes. Puckering her lips towards his, she was sure only his shyness prevented him from taking advantage of her offer. He was proving tardy, so she leapt onto him, threw her arms around his neck and pinned him to the door.

Her threshing arms dislodged his helmet, which he fought to keep on. She began to undress him, tearing at his clip-on tie and hurling it behind her. Her hands went inside his shirt, her fingers pinching his nipples, pulling his chest hairs, making him squeal. Her quivering and rouged lips were everywhere on his face, smothering his protests with wet, messy, lingering kisses.

Ivor's beat sergeant passed by during the assault. Fortunately, his eyes were scanning the other side of the street, towards where another copper sheltered, and he missed Ivor's wrestling match.

Ivor was forever grateful for the sergeant's eyes being elsewhere, but the copper lurking in a doorway opposite witnessed it all. Despite Ivor's protest, Gloria managed to open his fly. Unashamedly, her warm, fat, little fingers had played with him, in and out of his trousers.

Later that night shift, Ivor spent time in front of a mirror, cleaning his face before showing it again in the canteen. Today, he still seeks the perpetrator of the gory and greatly exaggerated details that subsequently circulated among the strengths of inner division police stations.

Colleagues believed Ivor's marriage to Gloria followed her threats of further episodes of on-the-beat molestation if he didn't promise himself to her. As far as anyone was aware, he had enjoyed a spiritual, happy, for a time Salvation Army-dedicated, childless life with Gloria. They'd always lived genteelly, their standard of living escalating as Ivor's promotions brought in increased salaries. Moves to larger and more commodious homes, in nicer areas, were another prestigious result of his promotions. Now they lived on the same prosperous, upper-class estate as Daphne and Jack did.

******

'You'll have been there before, Myrna,' Daphne said, before Gloria had the chance to put a damper on the idea. 'So tell us a bit about it. I've often hankered after a trip to Blackpool.'

'Daphne, you'll love it,' Myrna enthused. 'The pleasure beach is magnificent, the miles of beach with scrawny donkeys giving rides to children a comical sight. After dark, the lights depicting cartoon characters are a wondrous spectacle. They'll amaze you and brighten your life. The entertainment is marvellous too, on all three piers and reputable other theatres. Algie and I did Blackpool often when Labour held their party conferences there. Had the time of our lives, we did. Lillian Gished every night, we were. We met all the Labour hardliners, Prime ministers, everyone of note.'

'I think it's a wonderful idea, Myrna. Murdo and I spent our honeymoon there. Brill it was,' Maggie said.

Gloria's 'Ahem,' indicated she wanted a say in any decision-making. 'And when do you expect to get this expedition into these uncharted northern regions underway?'

'Well, the earlier the better, I would say,' Myrna said, 'we ought to go when the weather is still decent and we can still enjoy a stroll on the promenade. Before winter when the winds begin blowing and sand stripped from the beach blasts our eyes, I suggest. In fact, I was so sure you'd all agree to go that I went ahead and made a provisional booking for four, at the Royal Hotel on the South Promenade, for next week.'

'Count me in. I'm sure Murdo will be agreeable,' Maggie blurted, eager to agree to something.

Daphne winked. 'Count me in too. You'd never get me saying no to a few days of harmless fun away with the girls. I'll be able to screw the money out of Old Chiselled Features Jack, literally.'

Gloria finished her wine with a gulp. 'The Royal Hotel, you say. That sounds classy, my type of hotel. I see no reason why I shouldn't be in the headcount. Ivor can huff and puff, inflate his florid puss, but he just wouldn't dare say no to me. There's a nice Salvation Army citadel in Blackpool I could visit. Now isn't that a novel excuse for putting one over on hubby?'

'Nice one, Gloria,' Myrna said. 'It's settled then. I'll organise Algie's chauffeur to pick us up from here and take us to Euston station next Thursday, to catch the two-thirty train. Blackpool here we come!'

******

Gloria and Maggie had little difficulty wangling a decision from their spouses. Maggie promised Murdo a super-duper stallion pump. He became highly excited as she told him of the amazing claims she had read and agreed to her request. During the night, she woke him several times and screwed him, whispering in his ear each time, 'A fortnight after you start using the pump you'll be as well-hung as some of the Blackpool donkeys I'm going to see.'

Gloria simply told Ivor she was going to visit Blackpool's Sally Army citadel; and that was that.

Myrna couldn't find a sober ear in which to tell Algie where she was going so didn't bother.

To Daphne's vexation, Jack offered absolutely nothing.

******

Jack Dewsnap stood six-foot-two, was slim-built, handsome in a rugged way, a Yorkshireman to the core. He had spent his formative years on a tough Rotherham estate. He was the son of honest and conscientious parents, who championed dedication to one's calling and decency as the passport to a better life.

Jack soon found his social conscience alone wouldn't take him all the way to the top in the Met. During his first week of basic training at Hendon, instructors told him his Ee-by-gum, Ecky Thump, painful pronunciation of the Queen's English would hold him back.

After assignment to a division, he attended night school, taking O level English and worked on his Yorkshire accent until only slight traces remained.

During his initial training at Hendon, find a good woman and settle down, was a piece of well-intentioned advice mooted by instructors. Discussions also took place on the type of woman who might be attracted to a copper's "lot". Nurses got the nod; shift-work similarly affected their lives and they were used to the stresses of working unsocial hours.

When Jack met Daphne, she was nursing at St Mary's Hospital, Paddington. It was love at first sight. They couldn't get enough of each other from that first moment and became a devoted couple, encouraging each other to pass the examinations necessary for advancement in their professions. Working shifts had never produced any sort of tensions between them. When their shifts had coincided, Jack had strayed off his beat to meet Daphne for sexual romps.

While policing the streets of the capital in his early days, senior officers encouraged him to keep his number up and involve himself in all aspects of policing. Working on a central division, he arrested a wide variety of miscreants. Once, he arrested single-handedly a murdering mugger. Deemed a heroic act, the Commissioner awarded him his commendation. In court, he confidently delivered the evidence required to put chummy away. By the time he had completed his probationary period of two years, he had a noteworthy and exemplary record as a constable.

A Chief Inspector invited Jack to become a Freemason. His father was a member of the Royal Antediluvian Order of the Buffaloes so he saw no wrong in accepting the offer. That a gov'nor should show interest in his future, he found hard to ignore. He appreciated the encouragement, became a committed Freemason and attended his Lodge regularly, swapping shifts to attend when they didn't suite.

While studying hard for exams, he gave up being "one of the lads". The drift away from those aspects of police culture meant missing the refreshment available at the back doors of oriental restaurants and the like. Attending unofficial lock-ins in recognised police watering holes with colleagues, he did rarely, only succumbing when a senior officer requested his company.

Jack's police promotions went predictably. In the Masons, he had worked his way to Senior Warden of the Lodge.

That night, his responsibilities were ordering and overseeing the catering for the harmony following the Masonic meeting.

Jack hadn't forgotten that chefs, in the curry houses in which he had mumped a meal in his early days as a probationer, prepared staff curries differently to what they served-up out front. Like many of the brethren in attendance, he had tasted the difference and preferred it. For this special occasion, Jack had brought in an Asian chef from his favourite restaurant to provide the catering.

The brethren had initially appreciated the chicken and the excessively fiery Madras sauce, the Patna rice and the garlic naan bread. As the evening progressed, many of them were prophesying the onset of "Ghandi's revenge" the following morning. Others agreed, saying the chef was a "wicked bastard" for being a touch too liberal with the chillies.

The spicy curry might also have been solely to blame for Jack's ensuing demeanour.

Jack had gorged on the lip-burning succulence of the traditional cuisine, even tucking away an extra portion, washing it down with tots of Johnny Walker Black Label whisky over ice. After the harmony, looming biliousness had joined his feeling of being stuffed. A vile-tasting mixture had continually erupted into his throat and he had struggled to prevent the involuntary regurgitations. His wish was to sit quietly and allow his digestive system to process the mixture without him throwing up.

After the harmony, a black cab dropped off Ivor Bunce before setting Jack down outside his house. It was 12:15 a.m. The twisting journey and the frequent pulling up at traffic lights hadn't helped his unsettled stomach. He felt tired, drunk, and quite desperate for that quiet moment. After wrestling with his key, he staggered through the front door of his home, regalia case swinging from his hand.

Daphne rushed forward and welcomed him excitedly. He hadn't expected it. For the first time during their married life, he didn't relish it.

'I'm going to Blackpool for a weekend with Myrna, Gloria and Maggie. Don't you think that's wonderful, Jack?' Daphne said, then began to deluge his forehead with kisses. His large frame slumped back onto the door, which banged closed behind him under the weight of his assailed body. 'Mmm,' then 'schlop,' sounds he heard. Soft, rouged lips were skimming his lips then moving on to his nose, cheeks and ears in turn. Daphne's warm breath was sweet with the wine she had sipped waiting to announce the surprise.

'I will bring you home sticks of rock, mmm, schlop.' Daphne circled his face with her lips. She cupped his face in her hands, consumed with a passion for him, oblivious to the foulness of his breath. 'A funny policeman's helmet with "Kiss me quick" I'll bring you. I know you will love that. I can see you wearing it in bed when we fuck,' she squealed excitedly. 'Mmm, schlop,' sounded again. Then she blew hot breath into his ear.

Jack pushed out and broke free from Daphne's passionate handling. Throwing his case down, he swayed his way into the lounge, feeling light-headed and desperately trying to keep down his stomach contents. He collapsed into an armchair and removed his shoes. His feet ached from pacing the Lodge floor while taking part in that night's ritual.

Daphne could see he had drunk too much, but she was persistent and followed him closely. Fluttering around, she tried to help him by moving his shoes away. Then she kneeled and hung her arms around his neck like a petulant teenager trying to screw lucre from a flush parent.

Jack didn't need that. He didn't find it helpful at all. Already he had made up his mind: no way was Daphne going to Blackpool.

Jack took hold of her wrists, removed them from his neck and held them tightly out in front of him. 'You intend to go *where* with these women?' He didn't really want to ask the question or to listen to Daphne's reply; the Blackpool trip was out and he roughly pushed her arms away.

'We're going to Blackpool, that marvellous seaside resort up in the northwest. It has world-famous lights and sideshows and amusement arcades and three piers brimming with entertainment. Great comedians too, Myrna tells me. Myrna is going, Gloria and Maggie, too. We're all eager, looking forward to it.'

Jack had heard enough and exploded. 'I know where bloody Blackpool is at! Neither Myrna, nor Gloria could see a dodgy situation approaching on a clear day if it sat tall and swaying on the back of a seven-legged donkey getting a hammering with long sticks from Arabs wearing flowing robes, hauling beer guts and singing Waltzing Matilda with cathode ray tubes sticking out of each ear. In fact, I doubt they could see anything dodgy approaching them with the aid of binoculars…or radar.'

Jack settled back in the chair and took a deep breath. Daphne stood up and took a pace back, smarting. She had never seen Jack's face so enraged; had never heard such cutting sarcasm from him.

Jack wasn't finished. 'And their husbands should have more sense than to allow their women the opportunity to embarrass them.'

Jack looked at her, straight in the eyes, convinced his protocol was the correct one. His certainty was prodding him on to speak to her more earnestly; he would have his say and get it all off his chest, even though he could see how upset his cherished Daphne was becoming. The rage was there in her eyes, which were welling, close to spilling tears.

Fixed of mind and a picture of grimness, he stretched his hands out towards her. 'You must also realise and really I shouldn't have to say this. *You*, of all people, ought to know that it is inconsistent with the dignity of the wife of a police officer, and most certainly the wife of a Commander of Police, to cavort off on a weekend caper to the rude… crude… vulgar… and trashy northern capital of sleaze and tackiness. You… are… not… going!'

Jack tried to get up from the chair, to stand and face her, but gave up on the idea. His face glowed, his forehead pounded, the whisky and his soaring exasperation with Daphne responsible. Then another thought struck him and he berated the Blackpool weekend with even more fury. 'Furthermore, why should I have to endure the ignominy that might follow a misdemeanour reported in a trashy Sunday tabloid?'

'But *Jack… Jack…* man, you're creating situations, circumstances which are never likely to arise,' Daphne howled, tears now streaming down her own reddening cheeks.

'I've come across it all before. A group of unescorted senior police officers' wives, together with a drunken civic dignitary's even dafter woman, would make the front pages of the Sunday Sport. Only gutter-press-worthy news would be reported.'

'I see it now. You have something against Myrna. That's what it's all about,' Daphne raged. Stepping forward she thumped his shoulders with her closed fists as he sat.

Jack's temper was going through the ceiling. Daphne's defiance was getting to him. He caught her flailing arms by the wrists again, stilling them. His breath was reeking obnoxiously; he didn't care if her face was close. 'Silly Myrna has the potential to do something outrageous. She'll get you all noticed in dodgy, embarrassing situations. Moreover, haven't I just pipped Ivor Bunce to the latest Commander's promotion? Furthermore, forthcoming retirements predict, surely, my advancement to Assistant District Commissioner sooner than I had expected. *Does… that… mean… nothing… to… you*?'

Daphne ought to have known better; there was no point in arguing, but being a woman and stubborn her hackles were well risen. Jack's decision was shit. She would never show meekness in front of him, never; she had a mind of her own.

Fleetingly, the thought that Jack had spoiled her, given her everything she asked for during their married life, tugged at her conscience. The moment flew past as if it had never existed. Her eyes blazed. Nothing would persuade her to see his side. Nothing. Jack was just a spoilsport, clenched-arsed, tight-fisted and penny-pinching. Her eyes flashed him the salient points of the news…beware, major incident ahead!

Daphne wrenched her arms free, stood back and stamped her foot repeatedly. She fired herself up and generated enough spitting rage to make her denouncement. Jack would find out that she possessed the balls to fight her corner, enough determination to make him suffer. Yes, long and hard, in the manner he'd dislike the most.

'You, Commander Jack bloody Dewsnap, are nothing but a conceited, stingy inconsiderate, holier-than-thou bastard.' These words she spat out viperously, slowly, clearly, summing up his future. There would be no special place for him in the marital bed. '*You…will…pay…dearly…for…this…decision. Never… again… will… you… find… me… compliant… to… your… every… sexual… whim. So…go…fuck…yourself.*' Then she walked quickly from the room, slamming the door closed behind her.

Jack remained sitting in the chair, aghast, heard her stomping up the stairs. Daphne's tirade had told him straight, but never had she sworn at him before.

'Go fuck myself,' he bleated, 'a bastard.'

The house had quietened. All seemed normal when Jack rolled into bed and snuggled into Daphne's back. The first of the horrors struck home when she physically demonstrated the real seriousness of the situation to him, repelling him with an angry and telling jerk of her body. Jack groaned, but moved close again. Surely, there would be a show of remorse. No such luck: a well-directed, backward-thrusting elbow rammed into his ribs accompanied a snappy 'Fuck off Jack.' He tried foot contact and slid the ball of his foot along her instep. She back-heeled him on a shin and yelled snappily, 'Keep your fucking distance, you bastard,' and yanked the spare pillow from beneath his head. Spitefully, she shoved it behind her back, forcing it in between them. It kept a distance, an area of permafrost between them. Lying perilously on her edge of the bed, she stayed out of his reach.

Jack lay away from Daphne, feeling woozy still, but lucid enough to realise that his situation had become desperate. His sexy, loving Daphne seemed determined to persist with the charade, and with some intensity.

Chapter 5

On the Monday afternoon following his last night shift, Hamish had paraded at West End
Central for what he thought was a week of late-turn duty.

Instead of receiving the expected beat to pound, the station sergeant marched him directly to the Commander's office.

Standing to attention in front of the Commander's desk, restraining a snigger, he could tell from the scowl of contempt on his superior officer's face that he wasn't too pleased with him…and had guessed why.

'Constable MacNab, it has been proved to my satisfaction that you sent that utterly decent police officer, Commander Evans, some dreadful material. You sent him apoplectic, thirsting for your blood, eager to pursue his complaint against you until the Met rid itself of your presence, jettisoning you back into civvy street,' the Commander began his lambast. 'Until you perpetrated your most stupid act, you had an exemplary record of service. In my book, you have become disgusting, reprehensible, a disgrace to the Force. Had we a surplus of constables, you would be dismissed the Force, forthwith. However, your past record and our strength shortfall have saved you.

However, you will pay a heavy forfeit for your shocking, infantile behaviour. West End Central is no place for jokers the likes of you. Today, I have authorised your transfer. Your next police station will be out in the sticks. There, one might hope, you will learn to respect your superiors. Goodbye.'

Hamish saluted, turned and left the office.

*****

That same Monday afternoon, at Marylebone Lane nick, Harry received a similar berating to Hamish. 'Your behaviour in that toilet was quite revolting, MacSporran,' raged his equally unimpressed Commander. 'Luckily for you, the cultural attaché's burns healed quickly and he saw the downside of pursuing his complaint further. Ridicule would have tainted his life; the embassy returning him to his home country, had his peccadilloes become general knowledge. The Met strength is at an extraordinary low level. That fact, together with your previous excellent record, has saved you from being dismissed the Force. You are still, luckily, a constable.

'However, I have authorised your transfer. You will next have the opportunity to engage your dissolute mind on police work, whilst trudging a beat somewhere out in the sticks. Close the door on the way out.'

Harry saluted, turned and left the office.

*

The "out in the sticks" station Hamish and Harry's Commanders had referred to was West Clegham, a quiet patch on the eastern edge of the Metropolitan Police District Initially, the strength there showed interest in the new arrivals. Their tag, "The Jock Connection", had preceded them. Even the sleepy, backwater nicks of the Met knew of them and their thief-taking record.

Daft acts, revealing them as "good for a laugh", also quickly grabbed attentions: like when they lit farts in the station canteen. Witnessing blue flames in stereo gushing through the crotches of barathea trousers, elderly Constable Albert Tonks, his mouth stretched wide in incredulity, spilled his false teeth into his tea. The same day he applied for early retirement.

Chapter 6

The girls had returned from their weekend in Blackpool that same Monday. The following Thursday, at lunchtime, Daphne was sitting quietly in the kitchen of her home, sipping coffee and eagerly awaiting news from one of them, confirmation, even, that the meeting that night was still going ahead. None had phoned her, perhaps through not wanting to exacerbate the bust-up she'd had with Jack, she thought. She hadn't wanted to discuss the matter and had refrained from phoning any of them. It had delighted her, though, when Algie's chauffeur had delivered a stick of rock on Tuesday with the words "Present from Blackpool" running through it, wrapped in a poster of the comedian, Billy Bagman.

At 1p.m., the phone rang, dragging Daphne from her thoughts. It was Myrna. 'Just wait until you hear of the weekend's experiences,' she blurted quickly on hearing Daphne's voice. 'We had a wonderful time of it. I'm not spoiling it all by telling you over the dog and bone. Just wait until tonight's meeting. You're coming, aren't you?' Myrna's voice trailed off.

'I'll be there. I'm sure you have many tales to tell. The comedian has an unusual, newsworthy nose,' Daphne said.

'Our Billy, you mean? Wait until you hear some of his gags. You'll wet yourself.'

'I'll need something to cheer me up.'

'You and Jack still haven't sorted things out, then?'

'The Friday you left for Blackpool, I went along to the local undertakers and bought a burial shroud.'

'What in heaven's name for?'

'I wear it in bed to emphasise the message to the mean bastard. He will get nothing over my dead body, that's what for!'

'I didn't know the tiff was so serious, lovey.'

'Bloody right it is!' Daphne said bitterly. 'I sewed all the different pieces together to make a passion-killing robe of the ultimate significance. It's my intention to keep wearing it in bed until I hear him screaming for my body.'

'I've a passion killer called Algie, the drunken little sot. He never gets it up. Completely dead in the bollocks area, he is, and here's me gagging for a good Harry Wragging.'

Daphne picked up the poster from the worktop and looked at it closely. '"Chubby Brown Can't Wipe My Arse",' she read aloud from the caption. 'I'm in the mood to let Jack know that the poster amuses me greatly. At teatime, when he arrives home, he will find it stuck to the kitchen wall. He will hate it. It's this thing with Jack, he's so politically correct these days, but damn him.' Daphne dropped the poster, opened a drawer and rummaged for some Blu-tack. Finding it, she pulled pieces off the strip, forming it into small balls.

'It's Gloria's tonight, remember?' Myrna said.

'I remember,' Daphne said and sighed. 'I'll be there to hear your jokes.'

'There's a lot more. Wait until you see Gloria. You'll see the difference a weekend in Blackpool makes to the once staid and humourless. Don't miss it. See you then, 'bye.'

''Bye,' Daphne said. Feeling wrathful, she turned, looked along the wall, seeking a position for the poster…right in Jack's face. Somewhere where he couldn't miss it, somewhere where he'd see it every day. Somewhere where the message she wanted to get over to him would hit him hard: not being able to go to Blackpool with the girls mattered a fucking lot to her.

Chapter 7

Messing with Jack's brain was Daphne's sexual rebuffing and her continuing attitude towards him since he made his decision on Blackpool. He had become a stranger to her, felt discarded, ignored and surplus to requirements each night at home, his bed a loveless pit. Each day at the office, he looked forlorn.

He had never questioned his decision; he knew it to be the correct one and for all the reasons he had given Daphne at the time. He still hadn't been able to understand her keenness to visit Blackpool; especially in the company of three women he thought mismatched and by their actions, scatterbrained.

Jack's lift from the station to his home that Thursday dropped him off at 5:30 p.m. He walked around the house and entered through the back door. On Lodge nights, he only snacked at teatime because he ate with the other brethren at the harmony later.

Entering the kitchen, he found his meal: a chicken leg with mashed potatoes and baked beans, smoking and going black beneath the grill. 'Shit,' he mouthed. Tossing hot plates from hand to hand was for comic jugglers and he hated baked beans. Under normal circumstances, he'd never have allowed them into the house. Daphne knew this well and was probably showing how she could make life even more uncomfortable for him. At Lodge meetings, he didn't need bouts of flatulence as he walked the lodge-room floor. Annoyed, he just switched off the grill and left the plate beneath.

The comedian's poster stopped him in mid-stride. It was at a level on the wall where his eyes couldn't miss it. He looked at it twice. It wasn't to his taste and he pulled a face. He began to walk away, but then turned and stood rubbing his chin. The comedian's face was unusual, but there was something familiar about it that he couldn't quite place.

In the front lounge, the TV blared. There was no "Keep Out" sign on the door, but he knew Daphne would be in there, sexily dressed to attend her stupid girlie night, wearing a sullen face, the one she wore especially for him, these days. He drew his cheeks back, baring his teeth and breathed in through them. He had heard too many ill-tempered 'Humphs' and ungraciously flung 'Fuck offs' from her, to consider popping his head around the door to ask how she was. She would keep up the cold shoulder treatment he had come to expect.

Before the bust-up, Lodge nights had always been a bit of a dash. After a quick, appetising snack, which Daphne always prepared with thought, he had showered early with Daphne eager to assist. She loved sex in the shower, their bodies slippery covered with body gel, her fingernails clawing into his crevice, him pumping harder. Drained from her advances he'd cool off on top of the bed before dressing.

Tonight he had taken a cold shower and cooled-off alone, carefully. Nothing had drained from him since before the bust up, particularly his balls. A pernicious balls ache had set in soon after Daphne's rejection of his sexual advances and showed no signs of abating. 'Fucking lover's nuts all over again…and at my age,' he grumbled, while gently drying his testicles.

By 7 p.m., Jack was dressed in his charcoal-grey Lodge suit. Holding his regalia box, he watched through a front window for the black cab to pull into the cul-de-sac with Superintendent Ivor Bunce already a passenger. When it did, Jack opened the front door and left without saying goodbye to Daphne.

****

It was unusual for Jack to have any interesting conversations with Ivor on the fifteen-minute journeys to the Lodge, situated near Stratford Broadway. They never talked shop and tonight he wasn't interested in the profusion of weeds plaguing Ivor's garden. He just agreed with most of what Ivor said with, 'Ah-has.' At the Lodge, he wanted a moment alone to talk over his problem with Brother Rowley, whom he thought his soul mate. Rowley Beaverton, Assistant District Commissioner of Police for the Metropolis and Worshipful Grand Master of the Lodge, was Jack's immediate superior.

His ADC was a womaniser and reckless with it. His flings had sometimes perturbed Jack, but he had maintained a long and successful friendship with him. A strong bond existed, their Masonic membership just a part of it. Dining out together at Chigwell Police Sports Club, Rowley with his current girl friend, he with Daphne, had been a regular occurrence. Many off-duty hours they'd spent together playing golf. Frequently, a millionaire Brother invited them to watch The Hammers from a private box at Upton Park.

Rowley and he had occasionally flown out to take in an open golf tournament on the Costa del Sol. The first time they were there, Rowley had paid a woman to visit Jack in his hotel bedroom with instructions to seduce him. Quite merry after supping a jug of brandy-fuelled sangria, Jack had welcomed her into his bed. Her beauty, her voluptuous body, her exotic perfume and her range of expertise had driven him nuts. It had been the first of many such dalliances inside the doors of adultery on the Costas, Rowley being responsible on each occasion.

Unquestionably, Daphne trusted him. Returning from these jaunts, she had never enquired other than on the weather, the quality of his golf and if he'd improved his handicap. His present of a nice piece of Lladro, his dragging of her to the shower, his tender loving, his confessions of loneliness and of missing her terribly, he had always presented with all the sincerity he could muster. Thinking of those dalliances now brought Jack the first pangs of guilt.

He found Rowley in the Worshipful Grand Master's changing room, a fusty, austere and basic place. After greeting each other with a Masonic grip, Jack asked him, 'You'll have heard on the grapevine of the rough patch that

Daphne and I are going through, that I've been cast adrift alone on the cruel sea of life?'

Rowley completed the knot in the cord tying the Grand Master's apron around his waist and then looked towards Jack.

Rowley had many faces Jack was sure. Tonight the one he presented was pale, sombre, looking kindly towards him, his grey-blue eyes twinkling. Jack wondered was he laughing inwardly at his predicament.

Rowley walked forward, kneeled and tugged at Jack's apron. Pulling at it, he straightened it around his waist. He stood upright, messed with Jack's sash and sat it correctly on his shoulders. Rowley's face was now level with Jack's, smiling boyishly at him from beneath his crew-cut blonde hair. Jack thought his haircut was a short one, the number three he advised for all probationer constables.

When Rowley spoke, his voice sounded caring and reassuring. 'Jack, the lifeboat will already have been launched, floatation devices aboard, at the ready, heading full-speed in your direction. When you're hauled aboard, everything will be sorted,' he said. 'You'll see. With the correct equipment, rescues from the rough seas of life are much easier to perform.'

Rowley must use his measured, purring, honeyed voice to pull the ladies, Jack mused, but when he replied to Rowley, he sounded much bitterer. 'It's the lover's nuts too. They're killing me, pernicious pain. Cold showers are doing nothing for it.'

'An ice pack, Jack; use for maybe up to two hours each session. The treatment has worked for me in the past.'

'I've tried that too. This is worse than the sore balls I suffered as a teenager.'

'Try the five-knuckle shuffle. We've all done it,' Rowley said, moving his half-shut hand in the advised way.

'That's adolescent! The last hand relief I had was twenty-odd years ago while sitting with a girl in the back row of a cinema, chewing popcorn. I'm not going to start wanking again now,' Jack said, angrily at first, but his voice tapered off.

'I suppose you're right. I often shared a packet of popcorn and used a randy girl's hand to rid myself of rampant balls ache. Once I had to endure a girl's fiercely pumping hand thrice during a two and a half-hour programme. I recall I didn't have enough hankies and had to use the popcorn bag. Sticky mess,' Rowley said, breathing in deeply, remembering.

Rowley wasn't taking him seriously. How could anyone possibly be interested that a girl had tossed him off three times? With no one taking him in hand, Jack wondered how long he'd suffer, how soon things might change for the better for him.

Two weeks from that night, Past Worshipful Grand Master Masons would install Jack in the rank of Worshipful Grand Master Mason of the Lodge. He had waited for the day since his initiation as an Entered Apprentice. Now all he saw ahead was an enormous problem. 'The problem's huge,' he said to Rowley, 'my installation comes soon…as you know. Then there's the ladies' night dinner and dance held soon after. I've worked hard to get through to the chair, merited it.

'Tell me. How can I take my place at the dinner dance top table without Daphne? Appearing alone is out of the question. What would the brethren think? I'm sure that Daphne, in her present black and unresponsive demeanour, will refuse to accompany me. Nothing I do pleases her. She won't talk to me, just fucks with me. She certainly won't fuck me. I'd look a right prick on the night without her.'

Rowley read despair in Jack's wavering voice and saw it in his face. 'Jack, Daphne is a good woman. Surely, she'll have seen some sense by then.'

'Not by the way she's acting. She doesn't recognise my presence in the house. Definitely doesn't recognise it in bed. My back's been stone cold every night for weeks. I've wished my balls were back there between my shoulder blades sometimes.'

'The passion will return. You've been together too long for this to persist,' Rowley encouraged him.

'I wish I could see it your way.'

'You met her through the Job, didn't you?' Rowley asked, encouraging him to talk.

'Daphne was a nurse at St Mary's, Paddington. I was a copper. Our eyes met over a pile of bloody surgical gauze infused with the smell of shit from ruptured guts and hospital antiseptic. The mangled male corpse pronounced dead on arrival and laid out on the wheeled stretcher, we hardly noticed.'

'There you are then,' Rowley said, reassuringly. 'Nurses are compassionate as well as passionate creatures. You've rubbed her up the wrong way. Women don't see the world as we do. We can and we do rub them up, easily, without really trying sometimes. I'm sure you didn't expect it from Daphne. Women can be stubborn. The sensible ones get down off their high horse before they fall off. Daphne's intelligent. She will come to her senses soon. Common sense will prevail… you'll see.'

'Her passion, that's what I miss most. Her passion has consumed me since she first offered me coffee and cake that nightshift duty. Then she took me down to the hospital boiler-room. We stoked more than the boiler fires that night,' he said, head bowed.

The bang and the creaking sound was a body lurching against the door. Algie Rideout, the Lodge Tyler, threw the door open without knocking and almost fell in. Holding himself up between the doorframes, his eyes glazed, he slurred a call for brethren to assemble, interrupting the conversation.

Rowley placed his hands on Jack's shoulders, shook them a little and squeezed. He looked into Jack's eyes and saw the sorrow ravaging them from close up. Jack had sounded pathetic, as if he begged brotherly help. Rowley was up to providing fraternal succour if he could. He had done so in the past. He thought of the Spanish seductresses he had sent to Jack's bed. Jack had appreciated those acts of brotherliness. Something similar looked necessary now and urgently so.

'Before we go, Jack, there's a vacancy for Commander coming up at Hendon Training College. If you don't fancy it, let me know later if you think Ivor might be suitable, will you?'

'I'm a copper, Rowley, not a teacher, but I'll let you know about Ivor.'

Chapter 8

As per protocol, Daphne arrived before the other girls at Gloria's home that Thursday evening. She noticed immediately how airy and how much happier Gloria was when she greeted her, smiling radiantly as they leaned in and pressed cheek-to-cheek. Her new hairstyle suited her, too. The severe bun was gone, she had a kiss curl pressed to her forehead and a green ribbon tying her hair where the bun had been, matching the colour of her trouser suit.

'You look down in the dumps,' Gloria said to Daphne as she entered the lounge, noticing the worry bags beneath her eyes. Her remarks hurt again, when she said, 'It's such a pity Jack wouldn't let you come along to Blackpool. We all enjoyed ourselves enormously.'

By the time the others arrived, Daphne was looking even more forlorn.

Gloria ushered them into the kitchen where the usual non-alcoholic wine was waiting in flutes. After first sips, Gloria slid her backside off a stool. 'All back into the lounge,' she said, bursting with enthusiasm. Daphne followed, bemused.

At the hi-fi unit, Gloria bent over and slipped in a CD. She fiddled with some knobs and suddenly the lilting sounds of "Looking Back Over My Shoulder", a Mike and the Mechanics number, filled the room. Daphne had always liked the tune, but she never thought Gloria listened to rock music, even the lighter variety.

It was the cue for Gloria, Maggie and Myrna to form a line abreast. With a hand on each other's shoulders, they began singing along and swaying to the number in "line dance" formation. Words of the song called for them to look back over a shoulder, which they did.

Daphne watched, mystified.

'Come, join in, Daphne,' invited Myrna. 'Billy sang this at the end of his show. Everyone in the theatre was singing it. What a tingling sensation it was, and what a spectacle. We all linked arms with complete strangers and rocked to the music. It sent us.'

'And we sang it on the way back in the train, too, rocking good music, we had a packed carriage of day-trippers to London joining in,' Gloria reminded them.

Reluctantly, Daphne placed her flute alongside the others, joined the line and unsmilingly attempted to follow their hand and foot movements.

The performance ended with Myrna, Maggie and Gloria letting out a 'Hooray,' throwing their arms around each other and hugging together in a huddle. Gloria looked up, caught hold of Daphne around the waist and pulled her in, 'You must get with it, Daphne,' she advised, gaily.

The music died. Gloria dashed for the wine bottle and topped up their glasses. 'To get you all in a good mood for going home, we'll play the track again before you leave,' she said.

'My word, you lot have really cheered yourselves up. You seem different women to the ones I knew. Was it the sea breezes, the reinvigorating air blasting across the beach while you each took a donkey ride that changed you so much?' Daphne asked.

'Forget the sea breezes and those poor overworked animals. Come, sit down, we have so much to tell you,' Gloria said, ushering them all towards the three-piece Chesterfield.

'Okay, we all said we'd remember a joke to tell Daphne,' Myrna said, enthusiastically.

'I think I have one, too. It was in my head yesterday when I told Murdo. I hope it comes back tonight,' Maggie said, a hand to her forehead, faking forgetfulness.

She was too late. Gloria butted in with her one first. 'Oh, I'm sure it will,' she encouraged, 'I remember the one about making love in the kitchen. Billy said something like this:

"I came down the stairs this morning and my wife said to me:

Will you shaft me in the kitchen?

Why the kitchen? I asked.

Because I want to time an egg, you smart twat.

Do you want a hard one or a soft one?' I asked.

I want a hard one, she said.

So I gave her a runny one and left."'

Maggie shook with laughter, snatched up her handbag and ran towards the bathroom. Tears welled up into Myrna's eyes and trickled down her makeup. Gloria sat back, pleased with her performance, gasping a little, her face beaming, her shoulders lifting, excitement increasing her breathing rate. The girls had reacted favourably to her joke. Myrna was crying. Maggie had wet her panties.

'You *all* enjoyed seeing the *blue* comedian?' Daphne asked, though now nothing would surprise her having heard Gloria's performance.

Gloria stopped shaking before Myrna did and responded, 'Oh yes; on the Sunday night show as I recall. We had a few gins. Our faces were reddening when we slipped into the Central Pier Theatre. We were a bit tiddly, I think. We linked hands, following behind one another. I'd say we looked like a camel train, slow and rolling of hip, hugging our handbags and slouched down, eager that no one saw us. The rest of the audience looked merry enough. Mostly northern from their accents, working-class men and women hungering for humour, bawdy and blue, I'd say. What did you think, Myrna?'

'I never took any notice. It was such a laugh. Billy looked even funnier in real life, compared to the poster. His wonderful Irish accent gurgled through the sound system, yet I heard plainly every word he said. '

'Perhaps you could confirm Myrna's view of Billy's accent?' Gloria asked Maggie, sheepishly returning from the bathroom, 'I wouldn't know the difference between a "heilander's and an Irish accent,' she said, her voice rising as she attempted to give highlander's a Scottish inflection.

'Myrna knows her accents, Gloria, being from the East End. I think it was the hairs sticking out from that thing on his nose, the wart or something that got me' Maggie said, recovered from the dose of mirth and in dry panties. 'It was especially entertaining when he crossed his eyes and looked down his nose at them.'

'His jokes were the best I've ever heard,' Myrna said. 'The one about not making it to the theatre got me. He said, "Mind you, I very nearly didn't get here tonight. I fell down the stairs at my hotel and damaged my foot…I was lucky…I just managed to get my bollocks out of the way in time." And all the time he was tenderly rubbing his crotch.'

'I'd heard it was impossible to remember jokes from a comedian's show,' Daphne said, miffed, realising that none of the humorous exchanges had included her. Once they saw her as the senior girl at their meets; now she had the feeling of being a complete stranger in their company. She hadn't been privy to their experiences and nobody seemed to be paying her much attention.

'I'll tell you the one about his outfit,' Maggie said, still too risible to acknowledge Daphne's comment. 'Billy said, "What do you think of my outfit? I saw a man standing on the pavement outside Marks and Spencers…his foreskin caught up in his zipper. I thought he was bleeding to death, I did…so I went into the store… told them I needed something to dress a prick with…and they sent me out looking like this."'

'That was a cracker,' Myrna said. 'Control yourselves, Billy told this one about his Mammy like this. Aye, me Mammy was at it too. She said to me, you were the sexiest baby that was ever born in the whole of Ireland and the rest of God's earth. Taken aback I was when the Mammy said that. How the feck do you know that, Mammy? I said. She said. I caught yeh masturbating in my womb. Get the feck out of here with that malarkey… what made you think that? I asked. She said, well you never made a feckin' footballer, did you, you fat fucker.'

Daphne sat still, looking wide-eyed. Gloria and Maggie were falling about in fits of laughter. Daphne had never known Gloria act this way. She had always been so sober-minded, hated the kind of behaviour she was now openly encouraging. Daphne had suspected that, in the past, Gloria only tolerated Myrna's small lewdnesses because she was the Mayor's wife.

The laughter subsided and the girls looked around to see who was going to follow Myrna. Gloria, seizing the moment, said, 'He also reckoned naval intelligence was present at his birth. A scan of his Mammy's womb showed, apparently, a submarine with its periscope up. His Mammy said he was the only kid on Earth born with an erection. He said the feckin' midwife belted him around the bobby's helmet with a two-foot ruler before she got his first feckin' nappy on.'

'Did you do nothing else? I mean cultural, like visiting the Salvation Army Citadel?' Daphne asked as another bout of giggling subsided and the girls had stopped quaking.

'Oh, yeh, culture, I almost forgot,' responded Myrna. 'I thought I'd better take them on a dummy run, knowing their innocence. I didn't want to subject them to blue humour without any experience of it, so I took them along to Funny Girls on the Saturday night. It's a burlesque club advertising talented lady-girls, behind the bars and on stage.'

'I completely forgot about visiting the citadel, I'd enjoyed myself too much at Funny Girls, I think,' Gloria said, bouncing in her wide Chesterfield armchair as if she was about to rise and demonstrate some act. She gave up on the effort, sat back and said, 'There were dancers, all men, very funny, peculiar indeed. Peacock plumage adorned the backsides of their gyrating, corseted bodies. I was sure their feminine appendages were stiff and phoney. They did pirouette so sublimely on a stage set behind the bar servery. I was gobsmacked, but pleasantly merry. I'd changed my drink for the night to rum and coke. It was to blame. I certainly found some hilarity in those queer folk.'

'Gloria may not be used to strong liquor, but she learned to handle it quickly,' Myrna said, nodding her head towards Gloria, stoking her ego. 'We never guessed that as we traipsed around Blackpool. Her face glowed on the rum and cokes. I never thought it would take so many drinks to get her into fettle.'

'Aye, I thought Gloria was tiddly when the penny dropped and she suddenly focused her eyes on the torsos of the bar persons,' Maggie said, and then asked, 'Gloria, do you remember saying, "Do my eyes deceive me or are all these bar-people of a dubious gender?"'

Gloria was leaning back, her face beaming, lovingly revisiting her liberating experiences and her ability to hold drink.

'I remember now,' Myrna said. 'You said, "They may dress a bit like women, but they serve drinks with limp wrists, and don't they speak to the customers huskily with manly, yet alluring voices?" And… "They may look like the real McCoy, but their blotchy breasts, shaven or waxed and tucked into their low-cut swimsuits, don't fool me one little bit."'

'I'm sorry, Gloria, but you were a wee bitty out of control,' Maggie said.

Maggie's comment surprised Daphne and that Gloria hadn't erupted or at the very least scowled at such a statement from someone as lowly as a sergeant's wife. The pleasant exchanges finally proved to Daphne that the weekend away really had changed them, brought them much closer together, but not to her. For that, she resented Jack's decision not to allow her to go even more.

Gloria's giggles egged Myrna on. 'Remember I said to you, "I think you're right, Gloria,"' she said, '"I've looked closely at them in the past when I've been here with Algie." And do you remember what you said, Gloria?'

'Remind me, Myrna?'

'"I still can't work out where they've stuffed their bollocks." Then you said, trying to explain yourself, "such words, I normally cannot handle. Even Ivor would never use one in a raw moment," then you said, "Oh, I'm making a silly ass of myself. It's testicles, isn't that the word for bollocks," and then you said, "Oh, there I go again, I cannot seem to get my mind above the navel tonight."'

Gloria remained unperturbed. The revelations on how she reacted "in her cups" were getting her some attention, as were her observations on Funny Girls. 'I remember making some comment about the outfits being jolly painful,' she said. 'It did concern me where their dangly bits might have been stuffed. Then it occurred to me they were tied up and stuck up between the cheeks of their nether regions.'

'A painful receptacle for such tender parts, Gloria.'

'Indeed, Myrna. I'm sure my Ivor would object to such a placement of his with a painful hollering. I can hear the eruption now if his little pair were ever twisted savagely and forced up between the cheeks of his tight, pert bum.'

'I've felt a need for a strong man to do the business with for some time. Algie's a useless proposition, him and his drinking. He's so fucked up I call his cock "Droopy." Do you know what? The next time a handsome gent appears on my doorstep, I'll drag him by the Jacob's, up the apples and pears, into Algie's born and bred and shag his arse off,' Myrna boasted, her eyes rotating, the girls taking notice.

'It's so funny you should say that,' Gloria said, showing no shyness, 'but suddenly, so very suddenly, I've been getting urges, little twinges in the clitoral region, ones I'd hitherto thought extinct. In fact, I'm so enjoying them I've begun the process of building up Ivor to a sexual peak. He doesn't know quite what to make of it yet. Most unamused he was this morning to find a pile of vitamin and ginseng capsules on his bedside cabinet. He complained bitterly when I forced him to swallow a handful of them with a mug of ginseng tea.'

'Murdo thinks I'm on something since I got back. He suggested I'd picked up something or other in a Blackpool herbalists that send women crazy for sex. Now he says he's had enough. Shagged out, his cock gone numb, he says,' confided Maggie.

Daphne pouted. It convinced her more that the weekend away, remembering gags from the comic's show, together with endless laughter, had startlingly affected the girls. Each had returned to their spouses with renewed sexual vigour. Gloria, after twenty-odd years of marriage, had rediscovered urges she had forgotten existed. Myrna's lusting bordered on born-again nymphomania… and no man was safe, or her husband's bed. Maggie was demanding endless sex from a husband with a small, overworked cock who thought his nookie basket overstocked with goodies.

'I never thought to see such an amazing change in you all after a trip to Blackpool,' Daphne said gloomily, her jaw held firmly in one hand, the elbow on her thigh, her eyes looking towards the carpet.

'Oh you should've been there, Daphne, you'd have loved it, darling. We missed you so, didn't we, girls? ' Maggie said, not realising how deep she had dug the knife.

Daphne let out a shallow laugh. 'The poster you sent will remind me of the good time you had. Jack will get to know it well, too. The charisma bypass I have maintained will continue. Tomorrow morning, I'll return to the local undertakers to buy more shrouds. I think I'll buy some silvery ones for daytime wear. Jack won't like them, but he can go fuck himself.'

Suddenly Daphne's eyes welled with tears. Dabbing at them with a handkerchief and sobbing, she launched herself from the chair. Running from the lounge into the hallway without looking behind, she swung and banged her bag against walls and doors in temper as she went.

Myrna levered herself from her chair and followed. She caught up with Daphne as she fumbled in a pocket for her car keys. 'Don't take it too bad, darling. Things can only get better,' she squeaked, breathlessly.

'I don't think so,' Daphne muttered, exasperated that the car lock didn't open immediately. She stood pointing the key at the window, pressing the button in frustration.

'If Jack's making you that touchy, perhaps you need another man to do the business with,' Myrna tried, thinking the suggestion might help.

The car door opened and Daphne slipped in behind the wheel. She closed the door behind her and opened the window. 'If you can get me a decent man, I might just be bloody well interested,' she said. The car started and she drove off, wheels spinning on loose stones.

The tears and sobbing didn't subside as Daphne drove homewards. She still felt bitter over her exclusion from the weekend away in Blackpool, taking it all to heart. The girls had remarkably bonded, were surprisingly happy in each other's company, had had an amazing experience, but not with her along.

She made her mind up to punish Jack further and into the house she stormed, banging doors, her temper raging. Thumping her feet on the stairs, she entered their bedroom. Frumpishly, she moved back and forth across the bedroom floor, removing her clothes and other essentials from the bedroom wardrobe and dressing table. Her clothes, underwear, toiletries, perfume and jewellery, disappeared into their daughter's bedroom. There, she made herself a refuge. Jack would get nowhere near her until their daughter came home from Hull University for Christmas and maybe not even then!

Midnight had already struck when Jack returned home, another lengthy harmony detaining him. He should have eaten more, but had no appetite. He had tried to drink himself happy on Johnny Walker Black Label whisky, but had only a couple of tots. In the past, that much whisky was enough to send signals of romance hurtling to his head and had always ensured a lengthy erection. The result that night would be no different; he was sure. But he had no reason to believe Daphne had relented enough to welcome him or his erection into the bed.

Relaxing in an armchair, Jack removed his shoes and then picked up the local newspaper, intending to scan quickly through it before going upstairs, but his eyes lost focus quickly. He didn't think he'd drank that much. The idea of reading the court-reports page abandoned, he took to the stairs.

Jack used the bathroom and then entered the bedroom. He undressed, brushed down his Lodge suit and hung it up in the wardrobe. In the light from the bedside lamp, he noticed Daphne's clothes were missing. He saw the solitary sexy nightie hanging there: the one he loved to see her wearing before bedtime, before he ripped it off with gasps and giggles and they entwined beneath the duvet in the nude. He was sure it was there to remind him of what he was missing. Bitch! Could it be a subliminal message for him to digest? A "Come to me, Jack baby, all is forgiven" type of message or a ruse? He intended to find out.

The gentle breeze from the bedroom window flapped the light curtains and cooled his brow. He recalled the holiday in Scotland where they'd walked into the wind on a sandy beach, watching the spume race past them. They'd frolicked among heather and gorse where he had spiked his arse through his eagerness.

Tonight, Daphne lay silently in the bed, as far away from his side as she could get. She intended to show her position was one of continuing and burgeoning hostility towards him.

In the pillow against her back, effectively partitioning the bed, he saw an ominous message. He felt so despondent…so desperate to take the pillow's position.

Daphne had heard the purring of the black cab pulling up out front around 12:30 a.m. She guessed that Jack, filled with whisky, would chance his arm, try a little passion when he slid into bed and attempted to cuddle up.

Daphne had set out her stall; she had placed nothing exciting on it for him. He'd only find the ladleful of passionless umbrage, carefully prepared by her.

Jack had expected Daphne to be wearing her new nightwear… the passion-killing robe of the ultimate significance, the impenetrable carapace now shielding her. Could he remove it? Remove the maddening thing shrouding her beautiful, milky-white body he loved so much, from her slender, kissable neck, down to the gorgeous bum he had cuddled so often, down to the curve of her pert little heels. Would she be compliant? Was she asleep? She breathed softly and evenly. She faced away from him. He saw it as a part of her cold shoulder campaign. He sighed and breathed in slowly. Why did she persist in her attitude, freeze him out, showing only bitterness towards him?

It was because of his decision on the Blackpool weekend, he knew. She might not be ready to forgive him. He had to go out on a limb; he had nothing to lose. His imagination rampaged. Lover's nuts or not, he would use his rearing cock, present her with the usual surprise, the bed snake. She had loved the bed snake. The bed once whirred to her romancing the bed snake. They'd made static electricity together in the days of nylon sheets, scorching themselves on tender parts with friction burns.

Jack rolled naked beneath the duvet, his face intent, silently praying for acceptance, expectant and hardly breathing. The whisky-induced erection he sported sprang and waved, as proud as he ever remembered one. He shuffled across the mattress like a snake across desert sands and took hold of the partitioning pillow. Gently, he moved it from beneath the duvet and tossed it from the bed.

Eager to assume the lover's belly-to-back position, he slithered close up to her. With his "surprise", he prodded her buttocks gently. He began to lift the tail of the shroud up over them, his breathing shallow. For one tantalising moment, making him quietly gulp, he felt Daphne's warm, silky skin beneath. In the good old days of nookie on demand, it only took a feather-light stroke of his hand to bring on sighs of longing and instant, welcoming sexual arousal.

Daphne had felt Jack's prodding. While he was sidling up closer to her back, she recalled his skill as a lover and his stamina always to meet her demands. Apart from her, she thought only a Matron with three skilled-for-the-job hands could nurse and harness the energy in the swing of his erection.

Daphne reacted with disdain and contempt. His bid to arouse her and his manly request for re-entry into her world would get him nowhere. Her body arched away, recoiled from him, as if touched by the devil. Her head lifted from the pillow; he saw only the back of it, not the grimness twisting her face. She threw the duvet aside, pulled down the shroud to cover her legs and slid them over the side of the bed. Her feet hit the carpet, moving away in one movement. Turning at the door, she shouted loudly at him, vocal chords cracking with emotion, 'Not on your fucking Nelly, Jack! The girls had a wonderful time in Blackpool, saw a brilliant comedian and laughed a lot! Not until I see his show will you ever cuddle up to my arse!' Then she disappeared through the doorway, onto the landing and into the other bedroom, like a spectre vanishing through woodwork, before he had time for a second thrust.

Chapter 9

Superintendent Ivor Bunce had one opinion on his promotion prospects: he had missed the boat. He neared his fifty-ninth birthday; at sixty years of age, his retirement was mandatory.

His expectation that one day he might become a Chief Constable of a small county Force hadn't materialised either. The succession of hopeful interviews he had attended, when he thought himself the best candidate, came to nought: his dream remained unfulfilled. Consequently, his stagnation in the rank of Superintendent irredeemably irked him. Throwing himself into the Job, he ensured, using nastiness whenever possible, that all ranks beneath him upheld the first principles of an efficient police force. Carrying out his duties so pedantically, resulted in the coppers serving at West Clegham police station hating his guts.

******

At 07:30, on the last Wednesday in October, the last before Halloween, Ivor accepted wakefulness with a mournful sigh. Even before his eyes had properly opened, he had become swiftly aware of Gloria's hand gripping tightly his half-hard cock and attempting to masturbate him. It was painful. Through sticky eyelids, he saw the duvet pulled back, his pyjama cord already undone and the fly of his pyjama bottoms wide open. Gloria changed her grip on his cock as his head moved, adopting a more delicate stroke using finger and thumb. Ivor tried to turn away. Quickly Gloria returned to the full-handed, firmer grip and held on, preventing his escape.

The last remnants of Ivor's sleepiness were disappearing rapidly, but his senses were a tad behind. He ought to have predicted what might follow. Gloria, post-Blackpool, was a different entity, sexy talk befouling every conversation she had with him.

'We're almost there, darling,' she said. 'I can feel the too-long unemployed coming back to life.' Then she rolled over and threw a leg over him in one movement, pinning him to the mattress with the spread of her buttocks. Her hand groped between her legs to find his cock. Roughly, she jammed him into her and sat down over him.

Bending forward, their lips almost touching, she swayed, her pelvis thrusting into his, her breasts swinging into his face, muffling his shout of 'Do you have to, you bloody insane woman?' Resting her breasts on his chest for a moment, she leaned forward, poised her lips close by his, ready to leave behind a juicy kiss. Seeing what she planned, Ivor turned his head away and started to wriggle his torso, lift his legs to arch his back in an effort to slip from beneath her. He was unable to budge her weight. Giving up that strategy, he complied with her thrusting, his face contorted, thinking a quick finish the best method of escape.

Ivor wilted. With no moan of pleasure, he let his load jerk from him. Gloria ceased her grinding motion, shuddered and let rip long woweeee, rolled from him and slithered from the bed, her face split into a smile of contentment. Wobbling as she walked she left the bedroom and headed towards the stairs and the downstairs kitchen.

She returned shortly afterwards carrying two steaming mugs of tea, one ginseng. The other Earl Grey, Ivor's favourite brew. In one hand, she was holding the two mug handles; the other held a handful of capsules, his reward. The ginseng tea and the capsules she placed on Ivor's bedside table. On the bed edge, her back to him, she sat sipping the Earl Grey.

'That accursed weekend you spent in Blackpool has a lot to answer for,' Ivor raged as he viewed the unpalatable brew. 'The collection of vitamin and potion boxes sitting on my bedside cabinet increases daily. First, it was vitamins E, B, D and C, now there are Ginkgo Biloba, Saw Palmetto, Korean ginseng and Kava root amongst them. Vitamins are okay in my book, but I'd rather get them fresh from the vegetables I patiently tend each summer in my garden.'

'Vitamins and dietary supplements from any source, organic or otherwise, will have you feeling cocky again quite soon,' Gloria responded nonchalantly over a shoulder.

'Cocky again soon, cocky again soon, you say!' Ivor thundered. '*You* have me worried! The Saw Palmetto and Korean ginseng adverts in gardening magazines that my eyes skirt over, swiftly, have grinning, hulking, muscle-bound satyrs leering out of the page at me. If you think you will ever have me looking like that… then you can think again…bloody cocky…what do you think you are? If my colleagues knew about your sexual appetite; they would think I had married a woman with a raving sexual compulsion!'

'I'm just an ordinary woman with ordinary womanly needs. It just happens that I now require a man who can get it up and keep it up, regularly,' Gloria told him plainly. She finished her tea and smacked her lips, knowing the sound would annoy him.

'I liked things the way they were before. Why can't I have my usual Earl Grey tea in the morning, tell me that?'

'Only when your performances improve, you're enjoying sex with me, at least twice a week and it's not a one-way ravishing. You will know when you're close to achieving the goals I have set for you. I'll be screaming my head off in Swahili, while experiencing orgasmic fury and your bottom will be thrusting like the proverbial fiddler's elbow.'

'Twice this bloody week I've been late for work.' Ivor raged again, looking at his bedside clock. 'That's all your adolescent charade has achieved in my book.'

Chapter 10

Coppers at West Clegham nick, often sufferers of their Superintendent's rebukes for tardy timekeeping, had quickly noticed the departure from his morning routine, the laxity surprising them. They also wondered why this sluggishness should begin soon after his wife had returned from a long weekend spent in Blackpool. Until the first week of October, he had never failed to arrive in time for his 9 a.m. start.

An overheard conversation between Sergeant Shrapnel and another suspected member of the daft-handshake brigade encouraged speculation among the coppers that the trip to Blackpool had changed something.

Those coppers with wit rather than foresight came closest to the reason behind the lapses. Their suggestion that Mrs. Gloria Bunce prevented their superintendent from rising swiftly from his slumbers, by sleeping on the tail of his nightshirt, deserved the short odds on offer.

Increases in stinging ear bashings resulted in beat coppers using their skills to dispose quickly of any task keeping them at the nick.

Warnings and messages passed between coppers went along the lines of:

'Let's scarper, Bunce's late.'

'See you up the kaff then.'

'Which kaff? We've already drank tea in three this morning.'

'Okay, make it the Taj Mahal; we might get a ruby there as well as a cuppa.'

'Why are we all rushing off like headless chickens?'

'It's possible Mrs Bunce has given him a stiff shagging this morning, turning him into a nastier twat, that's why.'

'Fuck! Let's get out of here, quick.'

At 09:27 that Wednesday, Superintendent Bunce arrived in the station yard and drove his Ford Scorpio into his parking place. Dressed in his uniform, he stepped out of the car. Upon his head sat his flat hat, its scrambled-egg-decorated peak precisely one regulation thumb-knuckle length above the tip of his nose. His small, carefully trimmed and waxed moustache, twitched. When he was annoyed, constables thought it had a mind of its own.

Superintendent Bunce's morning routine never varied. "Doing the books" came first: the well-established Met police routine in which the station's senior officer went through the latest entries made in the ledgers. His particular fetish was the garage book in which the drivers of cars or vans at the station logged the time of the beginning and the end of each journey. As a Chief Inspector at a previous station, he had disciplined the drivers of a night duty van and an area car for racing their vehicles to Southend. On the return journey, the van crashed outside the MPD boundary. Entering the front office with little enthusiasm for the task, he saw Sergeant Shrapnel hovering.

Half an hour later, the Superintendent had satisfied himself that the nick had functioned without mishap overnight.

The sergeant approached him with two mugs of tea, the Earl Grey teabag labels hanging so the Superintendent might notice them, and suggested he sit awhile. 'I'd like to run something past you, sir. Constables MacNab and MacSporran, they joined us ten days ago from "uptown" stations. Already they're having a marked affect on the constables at this station. Apparently, it's the jokes and observations on policing they relate that have the relief laughing like drains and leaving the canteen bouncing into each other with manic laughter. That can't be good for discipline, sir. They call MacNab "Extreme Drollery in a Bannock" and MacSporran "Fun in a Bun". I've learned they also arrived here with the handle "The Jock Connection".'

The Superintendent's face twisted. 'A play on "The French Connection", I suppose. "Popeye Doyle" would turn in his grave. Whoever heard the likes? I thought their transfer from "uptown" highly unusual and unfortunate for me. Two Herberts of such similar dispositions, arriving at this station and both at the same time, I couldn't believe. I could tell they were intransigent, showing no interest in the Job when I interviewed them on their first day here. That was before I read their damning, accompanying reports. Banished to the sticks for indescribable behaviour, would you believe?

'MacNab mailed to his previous Commander, Dai Evans, pornographic literature, fiendish sex aids and things only perverts could enthuse over and too disgusting for me to name. MacSporran, apparently, attempted to set fire to an African Cultural Attaché in a West End convenience. By all accounts, he was lucky to get away without an official complaint from the embassy,' the Superintendent said, sneeringly, his voice rising stridently. 'It sounds as if both of them are proving bloody mischief makers at West Clegham, too.'

The sergeant nodded his agreement. 'A dodgy duo if I ever saw one, sir.'

The Superintendent cast his eyes past the sergeant and took in the office, checking it for eavesdroppers. 'You're quite correct, Murdo,' he said. 'Commander Dewsnap visited the station yesterday. We shook hands in the yard… the full Masonic Monty, of course. Those pair passed by en-route to the canteen and I heard one say to the other, "It looks like they're trying to remove some adherent, glutinous snot from each other's knuckles."

'I didn't pick up who had spoken… all you Jocks sound the same to me… but I cast an icy gaze over them. Rest assured… one day *I will* get the two piss-taking bastards. The downside, of course, is this. If *I* can't stick them on for some breach of police discipline and rid the force of their presence, *I'll* have them at this station until *I* retire. I must say, being put out to grass now seems a favourable option.'

'The constables are very fond of them, sir,' said Sergeant Shrapnel, 'I heard a comment about there being "humour in uniform" again at West Clegham. Apparently, it was an episode in the canteen, inspired by them, that prompted your favourite copper, Constable Tonks, to take a sicky and put in his retirement papers. I believe there's more afoot that's exciting the constables.' The sergeant rolled his eyes up as he said this. 'It's something to do with Tonks' retirement fund. All very hush-hush and MacNab and MacSporran are heavily involved. I haven't been able to put my finger on the nature of the affair or been made privy to the knowledge of where it will take place. I think it must be highly irregular if they're keeping the arrangements away from my ears.'

'The constables had better watch their ways, sergeant… *stick* to the rules of the Job… or *I'll* have them!' the Superintendent barked shrilly. There will be no leniency for any police officers attached to this station who associate themselves with base practices. *Am I clear*?'

'I'll keep an eye on MacNab and MacSporran, sir. I can tell you now that they've done no practical policing since their arrival. There never are many arrests on your well-policed manor, sir, but there are always plenty of moving and stationary vehicle offences to keep beat constables busy. There's no sign of any traffic-related process coming from them,' the sergeant said, stressing the point. 'They're on late-turn this week and posted together to patrol Tonks' old community beat. I thought if they were useless, they wouldn't do much damage there. I also told them they could collect a bob or two from the neighbourhood watch participants, towards Tonks' retirement gift.'

(Constable Tonks had opted for the quiet life towards the end of his career, and had set in place one of the most innovative neighbourhood watch schemes ever seen on the manor. Vigilance was his watchword, instilling it into the minds of the local populace, especially the senior citizens.)

'Good idea, Murdo, the ideal place for them. Report to me any of their shortcomings. If they don't conform to the Met disciplinary code, don't keep their numbers up, I want to know about it.'

******

'This weather's too bad for walking far tonight,' Harry said to Hamish. It was now the evening of the same Wednesday and rain was falling relentlessly. They had taken their meal break and were now leaving the yard of West Clegham police station for their beat.

'We could get a soaking, that's for sure,' Hamish replied.

'On an "uptown" beat we could dodge from doorway to doorway. Here, the distance we have to walk to get to our beat is painful.'

'Right on all counts,' Hamish said. 'If we're to stay dry, then I suggest we take a bus.'

'Just what I wanted to hear,' Harry said. 'Let's get into a shop doorway further up the High Street, close to the bus stop.'

Harry did up the button around the neck of his waterproof and ensured the collar stuck up beneath his helmet. Striding out, he said, 'I don't know about you, but I'm beginning to feel knackered. The Mayor's wife really shagged the life out of me this afternoon.'

Hamish put his head down, braving the rain. 'Aye, me too, feeling a bit wobbly, but it was great. My cock's raw, which is always a sign of a brilliant rumpy-pumpy session. Have you thought what might happen if the Mayor finds out we're responsible for wrecking his beds and he complains to Bunce? I saw his Masonic apron case. He and Bunce are daft-handshake brigaders.'

'We'll tell him we're not going there again collecting for old Tonks' retirement fund until the Mayor gets stronger beds,' Harry said, stifling a laugh. 'She was certainly desperate for a good shagging. Rolled about on top of you and shagged you until she was nearly seasick.

'Before she reached the first of her many orgasms, you were shooting your dust, breathing hard and braying like a donkey with sore bollocks. Unhappy with your efforts, she rolled off, crossed onto the other bed, and impaled herself onto me. My back was going like a string on a duelling banjo…'

Hamish interrupted. 'I heard something twanging, by the way. Vertebrae or the bedsprings I can't say. You certainly were moving your arse, Harry boy.'

'Then when she had drained me she crossed back to you. Three legs fell off the bed when it collapsed. I thought it was about to move across the room. A good job you weren't on top when it gave up the ghost or we might have been looking at a serious accusation here,' Harry said.

'I've watched overweight WWF wrestlers land without damaging themselves or their opponents. She'd have been okay,' Hamish said.

'When you picked her up you had a hard job keeping her from sliding down your sweaty body. Then you squeezed onto my bed where I was recuperating, pushing me onto the floor. You destroyed that bed too. She clung to your body better than Captain Ahab did to Moby Dick in that film, and never came up for air once. It's making me breathless just thinking about it. What a nympho. It still worries me how the Mayor will react when he sees the demolition job you've done on his beds,' Harry said.

'Having a fit comes to mind,' Hamish said. 'And what was it she gave us, a measly pound wasn't it?'

'Probably wasn't too impressed with your efforts,' Harry said, pressing a hand into the small of his back.

'Took a long time finding yours,' Hamish said, wiggling a pinkie finger.

'After four shags in an hour, what do you expect?' Harry asked, grumpily.

'It was a tender and succulent fillet steak she cooked for us though. My knife went through mine like butter. Well hung, I'd say. A bit like me, I suppose. I hope it wasn't the Mayor's dinner. I'd be quite peeved if a steak of mine was given away to someone who had just podgered my missis,' Hamish said.

The bus routed through the High Street, then circled the Municipal Park before entering Tonks' old beat. Off the bus, they sought shelter. Between squalls, they walked the beat's length. The fruits of Constable Tonks' labours they confirmed many times. White-faced, cadaverous, skull-like apparitions on neighbourhood watch, bobbed up and down behind steamed-up windows, turning left, then right and then down again, like targets in a ghostly fairground shooting gallery. Some friendlier types waved at them.

'Old Tonks certainly has the pensioners working as instructed,' observed Hamish, waving back.

'Aye, he was a good mentor. Saves us a job,' Harry replied and waved along with Hamish.

The weather conditions suddenly worsened and created the fearsome sight of two constables striding out, heads down, with chinstraps shackling helmets to chins. Sleet reinforced by hailstones slipstreamed from the rear of their waterproofs.

'Harry, there's only one thing for it tonight.'

'What's that?'

'That Indian restaurant we paid a visit last week. The Taj Mahal, remember? It has a roaring tandoori oven. The kitchen will be nice and warm and the aroma appetising.'

'Lead on, MacNab,' instructed Harry and made to follow behind Hamish's bulk, 'I can't wait to get my damp arse close to that oven.'

Water gushed from a broken guttering, deluging over the stone steps of the path leading to the back door of the Taj Mahal's kitchen. Sodden themselves, they viewed the back door and dislodging rain from their waterproofs. Gloom descended, anticlimax, no nosh, no warm-up in the kitchen, no licking over spice-burned lips, the shock on their faces was plain to see. A scribbled notice said Taj Mahal closed.

With heads bowed, in single file, Harry still slipstreaming, they took a short cut down a poorly lit back street. At the other end, they would find a bus stop and transportation to a mumping hole elsewhere.

An Asian businessman, one of the many with the name Abdul Rashid, owned a dressmaking factory on their route. Approaching the darkened building, they heard one of its doors banging wildly in the wind. Hamish flashed his torch in the direction of the noise. 'Let's investigate,' he said. 'It might feel like we're doing some police work.'

The gate across an access to the site opened easily and they walked in. In a few strides, they reached the door. It was banging against a wall with a mind of its own, sending out a devilish, tom-tom-like summons.

'It's a sweatshop,' Harry said. 'The one I was at earlier in the week on an inquiry. They only employ Asian female labour. The women sit about all day cutting cloth and sewing up dresses for the street market trade.'

The banging door normally secured women in a spotless toilet. The Yale lock provided to lock it up at night was hanging open on the eye.

'I know I'm risking accusation that I've a fetish for these places, but this is far too nice. I just couldn't leave it like this,' Harry said, scanning the walls.

'Well, I'll not tell anyone if you don't,' Hamish replied, the hygiene of the surroundings impressing him too. 'Keep your lighter under cover. You got into enough trouble using it in one of these places, remember?'

'If you'd never given me the thing, I might've still been "up town".'

'Och, come off it. You'd have only missed me and asked for a transfer.'

'Oh, aye, it's maybe to that.'

Harry took a black felt-tip pen from his tunic pocket and unscrewed the cap. Satisfied with the ink flow, he began illustrating the walls with male genitalia of two sizes. Beneath the larger version, he wrote, "White man's cock". Beneath the tiny, almost mini-gherkin reproduction he wrote, "Asian man's cock". When he had covered the three pristine-white walls and the back of the door, in an artistic, but grotesque way, he considered the task complete.

Harry stepped back to admire his work. 'It's a great design,' he said, 'seamless, and it has a matching pattern. The Asian women will be dead chuffed with it. I can just imagine the look on the face of the first one who rushes in for a plop in the morning.'

Hamish rocked with laughter and grinned at him cheesily from beneath a dripping helmet. 'Yes, somebody will certainly shit themselves in the morning, that's for sure.'

'It's going to confuse somebody when they open up,' Harry said, chuckling away merrily as he swung the hasp around and clicked the Yale locked.

'When the plop house opens, mischievous gremlins will be blamed for the Asian womens' consternation,' Hamish said.

'Artistic gremlins cause Asian women to reconsider their choice of men after viewing the plop house walls,' Harry corrected, proud of his handiwork.

'Aye, come on, Van Gogh, you'll be doing portraits of the lads in the canteen next,' Hamish said.

'Aye, there are a few pricks back there and this will make a great topic of conversation when we have a brew-up. The lads will never guess I was so artistic,' Harry replied, grinning just as cheesily as Hamish was.

Chapter 11

It was the morning of the Thursday before Halloween. At 7:30 a.m., Gloria was already contributing towards another bad day at the office for Ivor. Throughout the night, programmed by the unsettling sexual assaults occurring on most mornings now, he had slept on his side, facing away from her, his hands cupped over his crotch.

Yet he jerked awake with foreboding. The bedroom light blazed overhead, telling him: you're on your back, sucker, and not all is well. The duvet was nowhere in sight, but he saw his cock poking out of his pyjama bottoms. On recent mornings, he had awakened to find it there and, as he could feel, Gloria was again gently manipulating his semi-erect flesh between a finger and thumb. Her other hand was tugging on the pyjama cord, loosening it. Then, moving both hands quickly, she grabbed and slipped the bottoms down over his buttocks.

Ivor kicked out, tried to wrestle free. He was unsuccessful: the bottoms were trapping his legs. He suspected what might happen next and hollered, 'Not another morning like the last,' and hurriedly flipped onto his stomach. Gloria, undeterred, stooped low and sank her teeth into his bare bottom. As he rocked his body to affect an escape, she put her arms under him, turning him onto his back. Then she cocked her leg over and straddled him, turning and facing his feet.

'You'll just have to guess if I'm enjoying this,' she teased. Her fingers began working vigorously on his cock, 'Come on, Big Boy,' she coaxed, 'you're taking a little more time this morning.' In a few strokes, it stiffened to her satisfaction and she said, 'He's ready for the tunnel of love,' and lifted sufficiently for her to slip it in.

Ivor grunted, cleared his throat, lifted his head just as his juices were leaving him and bawled at Gloria, as she slid off him and over the bed end, 'I'm utterly fed up with your wickedness. Yet again, you've exhausted me before I begin my day at the office. It will have to stop or my strength at West Clegham police station will begin to notice my lack of energy.'

Gloria wobbled towards the wardrobe and grabbed at it. Her breathing had become laborious, but she reconfirmed to Ivor her interest in sex wasn't about to wane. 'We will soon be trying something different… a little bit more on your legs… not something less energetic. One of Billy's jokes inspires me to try this new position with you.'

'For God's sake, woman, when will this insanity cease?' Ivor wailed. Sliding his feet onto the floor, he bustled past Gloria. Without giving her a glance, he left the bedroom. Hunched, he lurched towards the shower.

'Ivor!' she shouted after him, 'we have many years of sexual inactivity to make up for. Just think about it!'

The ravishing troubled Superintendent Bunce constantly during the drive to the station. He arrived there in a fiery mood, lips drawn back, tightly. It troubled him while driving into the yard and parking up. The rain had reduced to a drizzle but black, rain-bearing clouds jostled ominously overhead and the wind blew strongly.

Unfortunately, the wind was without enough puff to shift the worrying thoughts that what had occurred earlier was male rape, but more than enough for him to see panes of glass flying from his greenhouse.

He stood scanning the yard, viewing the canteen door through watery eyes. Sticking a constable on a disciplinary charge for overstretching his meal break was his uppermost thought. Contorting his face in anger and leaping up the canteen stairs two at a time hadn't always guaranteed a constable worthy of a swift rebuke would fall beneath his gaze. The stairs looked much steeper now, which persuaded him not to bother. Instead, he twitched his moustache and slapped his leather gloves into the palm of his hand, then onto the roof of the car with vigour and irritation, splashing rainwater high into the air.

Still tetchy, the Superintendent strode into the station front office looking as purposeful as he could. The greeting of 'All correct, sir,' from Sergeant Shrapnel he accepted with a brusque 'Carry on, sergeant.' As was normal, inspection of the front office and the perusal of various ledgers came first. Those duties done, he stood up and dallied in front of the beats roster. Running a finger down the paper, he attempted to put faces to the names of beat constables.

With a bang, the front door opened and together with some of the storm blowing outside, an Asian man walked in, an ex-Army greatcoat covering his traditional clothes. The frizzy beard he sported partially covered, in a thin straggly line from one ear to the other and down over his chin, a troubled face.

The Superintendent recognised him as Mr Abdul Rashid, the owner of several small businesses on the manor. He hadn't dealt with him before and wasn't looking forward to the experience now. Especially since Abdul had banged his coat and sprayed the counter with rainwater.

'Good marning, Superintendent,' Abdul twined, 'winter is coming up fast behind us and I'm not bladdy looking forward to frost and ice. It is not a bladdy very nice day today to be bringing you this kind of bladdy trouble, either, but some of my lady workers are not very happy.'

Sticking a hand into a greatcoat pocket, he removed a Polaroid photograph and held it up with one hand, the back towards the Superintendent's eyebrow-clenched gaze.

The Superintendent winced. The photograph could contain nothing decent: Abdul had poked a finger towards the side he couldn't see.

'One of my women went to the khazi early this marning. They're always going to there and sitting for hours. It costs me lots of money while they powder their noses and that sort of woman's thing. I'm sure you know what I mean, Mr Superintendent, sir. The woman in question came screaming back into the factory, deeply upset. "Disgraceful, disgusting and terribly filthy drawings of white men's willies and other unmentionables on the khazi wall," she said. I could tell by the look on her face that it was madly exciting her. Now the other women are excited too and want to view them. It is bladdy awful. I cannot get them to do any work. Terribly excited by it all, they are. What am I bladdy going to do?'

The Superintendent thought the outburst was never going to end and was about to leave the sergeant to deal with the situation when the Polaroid photograph thumped onto the desk under his nose, developed side up. The content of the mystery decorations was plain to see.

'You did lock the womens' khazi overnight?' the sergeant asked, using the Asian vernacular and looking suitably puzzled.

'Yes, and it was still locked this bladdy marning when we opened the bladdy factory, but the bladdy filthy drawings were on the bladdy wall just the bladdy same.' Abdul's head swayed from side to side, his agitation stoked at the cops daring to doubt him.

The Superintendent and the sergeant looked at each other ruefully. They had both latched onto the questions remaining unanswered: locked up premises didn't suddenly acquire the odious decorations they had quickly glimpsed on the Polaroid, overnight.

'But are you sure it was locked last night?' the sergeant asked.

'If it was locked this bladdy marning then surely it was bladdy locked last bladdy night,' said Abdul, heatedly, using the same flawed logic.

'There is nothing I can do to pacify your excited women,' the sergeant tried to impress upon him. 'But I can send around our senior Crime Prevention Officer. He will advise you how to protect your premises. Perhaps he might aid the search for another key. Finding one might reassure you and your women that it won't happen again. I can promise you little else.'

'There's not another bladdy key and if you send around a bladdy constable I cannot, in light of my womens' excitement, guarantee his safety,' Abdul said earnestly, slavers flowing into his beard.

The Superintendent nodded, but his dander was rising. His habit of uttering a succession of tongue clicks, his "I've had enough of this palaver" signal, was only another spluttered bladdy away.

Beset with the problem, he was glad Sergeant Shrapnel had taken the Crime Prevention Officer line. 'We will send around two steadier, older constables to look out for each other's safety,' the Superintendent said. He thought that should reassure Mr. Rashid and remove the problem from the station. He had had enough. An irritated Asian waving almost pornographic photographs around the front office, bladdying this and bladdying that, wasn't good for public confidence in the police service or for his dander.

Turning and scanning the map of the manor, whilst Mr Rashid's was more demonstrative, the Superintendent noted that the sweatshop was on Tonks' old beat, the one recently assigned to constables MacNab and MacSporran, who had patrolled it the previous day while on late turn. Having learned of the reputations these constables were acquiring for themselves, he immediately suspected a connection, "The Jock Connection". He said nothing, just frowned, whilst deep in thought.

Chapter 12

Rowley Beaverton, Metropolitan Police Assistant District Commissioner, a lusting lover of beaver, was willing to beaver in pursuit of happiness for his soul mate, Jack Dewsnap. An opportunity he saw ahead in the forthcoming Sunday night's Halloween celebrations, to break the ruinous stalemate pulling apart Jack's marriage, he thought worthy of pursuing.

Rowley knew Myrna Rideout slightly, noting her as woman most unlikely to repel his advances, when she consented to accompany her drunken husband to the Masonic balls they both attended.

Rowley thought Myrna fortyish, but she certainly didn't look it. Her tidy, tasty, five-foot-six, neatly stacked, doll-like figure had always looked tempting in pretty, body-hugging dresses. He guessed little use had been made of it…and he'd like to alter that.

Judging from the drunken states in which he saw Mayor Algie, Rowley reckoned Myrna hadn't enjoyed any nookie with her husband for some time.

At the balls, Rowley hadn't set out his stall to tempt Myrna with his fine body. Out of courtesy, he had danced with her. On the dance floor, he made every effort not to kick her accidentally, and avoided placing the soles of his shoes onto the toes of her pointed, sling-back stilettos.

He had noticed, when they danced slowly, Myrna had skilfully arced her breast across his tense abdomen until she had located his belly button. There she had neatly inserted her hardened nipple, like a jet fighter refuelling from a mother ship. He guessed she left it there knowingly so, breathing jerkily, enticing him. Habitually he crooned along to the music when dancing, the resonations from his diaphragm transferring to Myrna through toned muscle. Shivers of delight he had sent to the soles of her feet, especially when he hung onto a bass note. Could *she* now help him in the quest he had in mind?

Myrna thought Rowley thirtyish, a gangly gent, handsome in a boyish way and very, very humpable. Indeed, she thought him a potential beast to bed. Pangs of jealousy had twisted her insides at each ball she had attended, and he had appeared with an attentive, well-proportioned, giggling young woman hanging onto his arm. Myrna had prayed he might choose her for a dance at the balls. Until he did, she had contented herself eyeing him from a distance. He could certainly tempt her, especially if all his appendages were as large as his feet: as well hung as rumour had also suggested.

The first time he chose to dance with her, a waltz, she made sure he enjoyed the experience. She had danced close to him, her feet between his. He had left his dinner jacket unbuttoned, intentionally, she was sure, and she gave him the tit to belly button experience, leaving it there to entice him. Each other time, he had always chosen a slow, smoochy waltz to dance. When she had thrust her pelvis against his, the bulge there told her it had.

Rowley guessed he was setting a perilous course, but he felt compelled to steer Jack out of his doldrums. Jack's health was suffering, he had developed a stoop, looked gaunt, pathos raddled his face and he had begun to sound pathetic. If there were any delay, the fair wind of promise Halloween bore for Jack and Daphne would blow itself out and cease to exist.

It was the morning of the Thursday before Halloween. That night, the Lodge met. It was also the girls' meeting night. Before the day was out, it was vital he confirmed the arrangements he had planned for Jack and Daphne. He saw no other opportunity for him to do so before Halloween on the Sunday.

At 10:00 on that dismal, October morning, Rowley parked his Saab outside the gates of Paddleworth Towers. He watched the happenings in the vicinity and the street ahead. Frequently, his eyes looked up the driveway to the Victorian, sandstone mansion, half-hidden amongst trees. His view to the top of the driveway was clear to the mansion steps, and he could see any comings and goings.

Rowley listened to the latest Boyzone CD played through the earphones of his Sony Discman, enjoying Ronan Keating's singing. He believed he and Ronan had similarities; both were tall, slim, blonde, and attractive to women. His thoughts returned to the present and he sat tapping out the rocky beat on the accelerator pedal with his foot.

He wore faded tracksuit bottoms and a long, woollen sweater hung floppily over his shoulders. On his feet, he wore mud-spattered trainers. The baseball cap advertising "Archer's Peach Schnapps" he pulled down over his eyes to a jaunty angle. Inhabitants spotting him might assume, without suspecting otherwise, he was just another jogging enthusiast contemplated a morning run through the streets of their suburb.

Rowley sought no publicity. The undertaking he had embarked upon was truly personal. Driving him were strong fraternal feelings, a naturally felt Freemasonry, away beyond the bounds of mere cordiality for Jack.

He was peering through the windscreen when the chauffeur-driven Ford Granada, flying the Mayoral flag of office, turned into the street. It slowed down, signalled right, and turned into the driveway of the mansion. Rowley noted the entrance pillars had fixed to them a once colourful, but now paint-flaked, mayoral coat of arms. Etched deeply into the ageing, weathered sandstone was the name of the mansion and the number of the street: 69.

His Worship the Mayor, Algernon Rideout, was about to leave for his office to attend a series of meetings and later, constituency parties. Rowley knew the parties would keep Algie occupied most of the day.

Rowley looked towards the top of the driveway and the small roundabout there, overgrown with decaying shrubbery. The chauffeur left the car to open a back passenger door. Algie stepped out through the mansion front door, his short legs working briskly. His receding hair was gelled and he looked dapper in his white shirt, red tie, suit and Ulster.

Staggering slightly, Algie skipped down the steps. Missing the bottom step, he tripped and stumbled towards the Granada. The chauffeur, taking his briefcase, steadied him and assisted him through the rear door. Some banter passed between them as they drove past Rowley, heading towards the council offices. Algie, his head thrown back, was laughing at an apparently funny remark.

Sitting quietly, Rowley waited. The Boyzone CD finished, he locked the Walkman in the glove compartment. His eyes caught the movement of heavy drape curtains parting on the lower-floor front windows of the mansion, as someone pulled them wide and tied them to the side. He was sure that Myrna was alone inside the building.

A light illuminated the window at the top of the stairs, a shadow briefly falling on it, before flitting past. Then the light went out again. Then the bathroom, easily identifiable by its frosted-glass window, had interior illumination.

Rowley saw the silhouette of Myrna taking a shower, a long shower and the longer it continued the more Rowley enjoyed the blurred picture. He rubbed his gloved hands together, excitedly. Closing his eyes helped him conjure up a clearer picture of Myrna's body: frothy and fragrant, lathered in body-gel, the hot shower spray pinking her nakedness, her long blonde hair wet and straggly, foaming water trickling down her back and running into her perfect buns. He shuddered; already he was aroused.

Rowley left the Saab and locked it with a flick of his key fob some minutes after seeing the bathroom vacated. He walked casually towards the drive, looked right, then to the left, seeing nothing to delay his approach.

He reached the drive where the stones were loose and crunchy. Loping over them with long strides, he took a firmer route along the indentations made by vehicle wheels. Two red squirrels, disturbed from their nut collecting, raced up into the boughs of a high pine tree. Some brown-with-age toadstools, coppers-helmet-shaped heads thrusting lopsidedly skywards, lay shrivelled and dying in the long grass beneath the trees.

The mansion's sandstone portals supported a high lintel. The mahogany door was huge and Rowley stood looking up at it, his hands deep in his tracksuit bottoms. Clenched beneath an arm he carried a small, squeezable parcel.

The envelope gripped firmly in a hand contained a card on which he had printed some instructions. Before leaving these portals that day, he must convince Myrna to pass on both articles to Daphne.

He bounded up the steps and found the bell push. Without delay or looking around, he pressed it twice.

Myrna was making up two single beds in the master bedroom and fussing over them. They'd arrived late the previous day, brand-new, just after a plasterer had refitted the chandelier. Although her first night's sleep on the new beds had been undisturbed, comfortable, she just had to test again the foamy, almost marshmallow topping, the orthopaedic firmness beneath and the springiness of the new mattresses. Bouncing her bottom up and down on them, she thought them more comfortable and sturdier than the ones they replaced. 'Definitely superior to the hard, horsehair-filled things that scratched my arse when I lived in Plaistow years ago,' she said to herself.

Hearing the doorbell ring, Myrna turned an ear towards the stairs and wondered who might be calling on her. 'Bloody hawkers at this time of the morning,' she supposed, loudly.

She was happy with the new purchases. The sheets and duvets were tidy and the headboards aligned with the wall. She scampered down the stairs to the door, a loose-fitting housecoat drawn casually over her shoulders and tied up around the middle with cord. Around her head, she had wrapped a towel showing Blackpool Tower and a portion of the promenade.

Myrna opened the door, her face set stern for an encounter with such persons as hawkers.

The day before, she had thought lucky and perhaps unrepeatable. Two cheeky coppers, seeking donations for a colleague's retirement fund, had called and she had invited them in. Before opening her purse, she had telephoned Algie at his office. He being a Mason and all that, he might have had special instructions about the size of donation she ought to give a retiring copper. Sure, Algie had slurred his instructions, but they were clear enough and, she thought, encouraged her to perform as she had. Albeit later, Algie tried to wriggle out of his suggestion.

Dragging them upstairs, she had shagged them both repeatedly, wiping out her years of sexual deprivation in the course of the afternoon. She hadn't really fancied Hamish, the fatter of the two, grunting, slobbering and whooping Scotch obscenities in her ear, as she wobbled perilously on top of him. Making love to walruses was for walruses she had concluded the several times she rolled off his rotund girth. Hamish had egged on his mate, Harry, to wind himself up and go for it. Harry was wiry, well muscled, slim-hipped, and shagged like a rattlesnake. Eventually, her frolic had reduced them to two heaps of pallid, shrivelled, boneless flesh.

Later, when she didn't see any one of them getting it up again, she had led them to the kitchen and fed them exceedingly well.

Seeing Rowley standing there nervously, shuffling his feet, she instantly changed her face to one of welcoming allure. How could she be so lucky two days running? One hand instantly moved towards her head and flipped away the towel. Fingers of the other threaded through her damp tresses, teasing them out.

When she was sure he was ogling her, she slid her legs slowly apart. Then brazenly, she pulled open her housecoat, exposing the rise of her breasts and the depths of her cleavage. With an imperceptible quiver, she recalled the close encounters and the breast dockings at the Masonic Balls, where she had proved he was well hung.

Rumours said he had womanising ways, now she was convinced. She hadn't expected him to call at her home quite so openly, though, but now he was here, he wasn't going to escape easily.

Rowley saw the seductive look drifting over Myrna's face and the way she was making herself more pleasing to the eye. His eyes dropped as she opened her legs suggestively only to rise again as she pulled back her robe to reveal the depths of her cleavage. Her bosom rising on each gasping breath attracted his gaze, it lingering there longer than perhaps it should.

He recalled the Masonic Balls, the thrill of her breast arcing across his tense, expectant abdomen and the docking into his waiting receptor. Back then, he thought it was a teasing, "I'm yours if you've the balls for it" message. That action then and the one now he translated as a blatant offer of sex. He wanted her, oh yes, ever since she had first aroused him. Since then, lather had lashed from him during bouts of daydreaming. In his nocturnal imaginings, some of the dampish variety, he had dreamt of her clinging to his body in some of the more erotic positions of the Kama Sutra.

Some loose talk making the rounds of the Masonic grapevine since the last Ball had grabbed Rowley's attention: Myrna had threatened to drag the next good-looking man who stood on her front doorstep, up the stairs, into bed, and shag him. That threat was the crux of his plan and provided its "modus operandi".

On Halloween night, his plan had to work flawlessly. Only with his and Myrna's help did he see Jack regaining his rightful place up close to Daphne in the marital bed. If he were going to be as lucky as he intended Jack to be, in a moment or two, he'd end up in bed with Myrna wrapping herself around him. Rowley crossed his fingers behind his back. Would the fulfilment of both his most recent dreams reach fruition together?

A consequence of her afternoon with the coppers, the one causing so much annoyance to Algie, was the destruction of the two single beds. The sight of them trashed and de-legged was far from her mind as she grabbed hold of Rowley's sweater sleeve. Her tugging was full of zest. He didn't resist it. Her slippered feet were a blur pulling him from the door to the stairs. Grasping the banister rail with her free hand, Myrna let out squeals of excitement on the way up, calling out, 'Come on… come… fackin' on.'

On the landing, she positioned herself behind him and pushed him through the bedroom door. With one hand firmly in the small of his back, she began shedding her dressing gown from her eagerly shoving shoulders and urged him, 'In fackin' here… be fackin' quick.'

Rowley considered the two new beds appealing. With the duvets and sheets turned neatly down and back with the corners turned in a quarter, they invited entry.

Myrna tore at his clothing. It hung loose; stripping him of it quickly she found easy, especially with his help. Naked, she grabbed him, pushed him onto a bed and straddled him. After a brief kiss on the lips and a tweak on her already hard nipples, Rowley turned her around. For fifteen luxurious minutes in the classic 69 position, his tongue masterful, he administered cunnilingus, inducing a succession of body-jerking quivers.

She found his thigh jerked inconveniently each time one of her sharp incisors scored a hit, but continued giving him head. With tantalising licks and nibbles, overflowing with portent, she rallied him. Rowley, grunting like a migrating wildebeest, reached a sub-critical point on a burgeoning vinegar stroke. Myrna turned, lifted onto him and plunged his cock deep inside her vagina. Lifting her body gently and rhythmically, she neared the promised multiple orgasm. Ever closer, it was only a few resolute, controlled, knee-stressing buttock lifts away.

Her damp, straggly, blonde hair veiled her face; her lips were tightly drawn and set in concentration, her teeth bared in a silent growl.

Rowley grabbed the headboard behind his head with both hands. He arched his back, which was as elastic as an archer's bow.

'Ooh, ooh, aah,' sounded Rowley, his head leaping from the pillow in rhythm with her thrusting.

His eyes drifted around the bedroom, taking in the mahogany Victorian commode on castors with the chamber pot atop. Behind his head, he saw where someone had scrubbed at a patch of wallpaper to remove some indentations. An attempt to remove the figures six and nine from its surface had left blurred, but still discernible outlines. He focused on the spot on the ceiling where the chandelier hung and where new plaster around it still dried. It crossed his mind that an "Only Fools and Horses" type incident had recently occurred there.

Mouse-like squeaks punctuated Myrna's throaty croaks as lift-off time neared. Her G-spot signalling its proximity, she rode him right through her multiple orgasms until he had come too.

Sliding slowly off his writhing, sweaty body, their moans of pleasure subsiding, she crossed her legs, turned her back to him and lay by his side in silence, quivering with pleasure. It was no mock-modesty, just a time to savour, relive, make last, the ecstasies of her multiple moments.

Only Myrna's ribcage moved as she rested, recovering from the frantic searching of each other's bodies. Getting her breath back until she was ready to go again wouldn't take long. To rouse him quickly she turned, grabbed his head and kissed him roughly on his lips, flicking her tongue in, then out of his mouth, touching gently, playing around the end of his searching tongue. She whispered and sighed to him, 'You're so fackin' good in bed, Rowley, so fackin' good.'

'How would you like to organise a friend for a secret blind date Halloween party sort of thing, on Sunday evening?' Rowley blurted, butting into her praises of him. Leaning on one elbow, he looked down at her, his boyish face flushed, damp, his short, blonde hair laid flat like a rain-deluged cornfield.

'A fackin' what?' she spluttered, struggling to sit up, not believing her ears, her eyes looking owl-like from her face bedraggled with dampish hair.

'Is it possible to organise you and Daphne Dewsnap for a blind date on Halloween night?' Rowley asked, looking at her seriously. It was shock tactics, he knew, but he thought he might as well grab the nettles early. His physical efforts so far had pleased her, but he wasn't sure she would be compliant to his request.

'Daphne Dewsnap, why Daphne Dewsnap?' Myrna asked, clawing her hair to one side. Then she sat up, showing early interest in the idea.

'I'm trying to organise for Jack and Daphne getting together again. Jack is going through a hard time. You know what I mean. He has neither nookie nor happiness at home, but all the pain that lovelessness entails.' He now sat up more erect.

Myrna listened intently and said, peevishly, 'My Algie can't perform. He's always on the booze. Galloping brewers' droop that's what he has. He's not been near me for years, the sot.'

'How can you stand that type of deprivation?' Rowley screwed his face up with the displeasure of the subject. 'I'm especially sure Jack loves Daphne,' he said quickly. He didn't want to know more than he already knew about Algie's drink problem and suspected Myrna was about to reveal more lurid detail. 'I have thought a lot about this. I'm sure, because I know Jack so well, that I'll have to arrange this thing secretly if I'm to have any chance of success. In fact, I think, because of the fraught state of their relationship, they'll have to remain unknown to one another. If I can achieve that, then I anticipate they'll go so far up the cul-de-sac of a resumption of their relationship they'll not be able to turn back. I'm relying on you, totally, to get Daphne interested in the idea,' he said imploringly, looking into Myrna's eyes. 'Will you help?'

'It's a shame, isn't it?' Myrna said sorrowfully, 'Take Gloria Bunce. She's had no nookie for years and now she's seriously Harry Wragging poor old Ivor, regularly, if you can believe her. That's all happened since she's been to Blackpool and seen Billy Bagman, the comedian.' Her voice took on a degree of excitement as her long fingernails began a tender but earnest exploration of Rowley's scrotum. Her eyes roamed elsewhere and landed on the wrinkly skin hanging from his elbow. 'Here,' she squeaked, removed her scrotum-fondling fingers and tweaked the skin hanging there, 'I know what your maker has done with the leftovers when he finished making that,' Rowley made a grab for her. Hand-to-hand they writhed, giggling, legs entwined, lips pressed hard together.

Rowley was still flaccid. Myrna felt him hanging limp and broke off from wrestling with him. Quite plainly, he wasn't quite ready to go again. She composed herself and said, 'I like your idea, sport, even though I think you just wanted to bed me while you're here. Daphne will be a piece of cake. I only said to her recently she ought to get herself another man to do the business with if she was so unhappy with Jack. Do you know what? She smiled back at me and said with a sly, and I could tell, interested look, "I'll leave you to find me one then, Myrna". I'll telephone her first. I'll get her to agree over the phone and then explain it all to her at the girls' night tonight. I think she'll really be up for such a romp. Just leave her to me,' Myrna said, confidently.

'It's so wonderful to hear you say that, Myrna,' Rowley said, and shuddered, excited now at the prospect of success and Myrna's finger exploration widening in remit. 'Give her the disguise I have brought with me in the parcel and the letter containing the instructions for where they must meet. I'm sure Jack will be eternally grateful to both of us for hurling them back into each other's arms.'

Myrna looked quizzically at him. Playfully she skirted the periphery of his scrotum with her fingernails, trying to get him to notice her. Then, clutching its contents roughly with her hand and bouncing them up and down as if weighing them, she asked, 'You said about organising me, too, remember? What do you suppose we might be doing while Jack's meeting with Daphne, eh?' Pouting worriedly, her bottom lip sticking out, she exerted a little more pressure to tenderer, crinkly-skinned parts.

'That will be organised, Myrna,' Rowley gasped, the back of his head sliding up the headboard. 'Ha-ha-ha-ha, have you heard of the Saracens Head Motel, on the A.1, just south of Watford? There's a fancy dress ball there on Sunday night… I'll book us into the honeymoon suite overnight… bring your best frillies with you.'

'Would you like to eat now or later, Rowley, dearest?' Myrna asked, both of her hands now full, her fingers tenderly manipulating.

Chapter 13

Daphne's four-week defection from the marital bed was an uncomfortable time for Jack. Excruciating testicular pain that he couldn't touch, over-the-counter painkillers hadn't reached and bouts of mind-numbing depression. He suffered all the afflictions equally and couldn't face going to his doctor to talk about any of them.

For companionship in his home, there had been little more than the poster of Billy Bagman and he had talked to that. Daphne refused to recognise his presence, never made eye contact and would glide past him, dressed in a silvery shroud, silent, untouchable, a spectre of things past. When she forced herself to reply to any of his many entreaties, 'Fuck offs,' bitterly spoken, left her twisting lips to fly over a shoulder rapidly moving away from him.

In the kitchen, beneath Billy's gaze, he ate his breakfast, his supper, and late at night drank whisky. There were times, half way down the bottle, his throat tight with anguish and he close to tears, he cried out aloud to the poster, 'You bastard, Billy. If Daphne's girlie friends had never laid their eyes on you, been stunned by your act, my life would be less bloody painful today.' Inconsolable, he'd then wring his hands until the knuckles turned white.

The poster had become hard to ignore. Sometimes he thought it repulsive, other times, infectious. The strangely put together face of the comedian continually drew his eyes. The bulbous nose, its appendage with its hairy peculiarities was the features intriguing him most.

The more he looked at the face on the poster, although only a caricature, the more confident he became that he had seen it in the past; soon, a name to the comic's face would leap from his memory bank, he was sure. Nightly, as he sat sipping whisky, he said aloud the letters of the alphabet, forward, then back. In bed, dreaming, he would awake and sit up, expecting a name to form on his lips.

By morning, only his recollection of awakening in the night remained, no name had leaped out of his subconscious.

Recalling became a game. Probing his memory, he attempted to place the face amongst police colleagues. He thought that a policeman wielding such a belly, on whatever police duties and failing to keep to a strict diet, the Met would immediately medically sever. Even amongst the names of his arrests he had kept as a personal record, nothing registered.

On Thursday lunchtime, he was mulling over his lot in his second floor office and viewing the station yard through a window. He had no appetite for the nibbled at sandwich or the hardly touched cup of coffee or for the weather, which he considered was as bleak as his feelings. Rain fell in torrents from the windblown, cloud-laden sky and bounced from the rooftops stretching as far as he could see. The wind scooped at the run-off down slates, forcing it over the eaves and guttering to the ground. His constables, reduced to wearing waterproofs and leggings for protection, scurried about in the yard, hands holding helmets onto heads.

Nibbling at the sandwich, he wondered if the rain would ever cease. So hard did it pound, the droplets were rebounding off the yard cement.

A pale blue Morris Minor nosing its way into the yard took his eye. In two skilled manoeuvres, that had him believing he was watching a class-one Hendon Police Driving School trained driver at the wheel, it reversed into a spare parking slot. The driver's door opened and a straggly-haired, helmetless copper stepped out. He clutched a bundle of traffic-offence process books to his body and sped, as fast as he could, his belly straining tight his uniform tunic, through the rain to the front-office back door.

The Commander's eyes left the spectacle of the copper's belly bouncing and homed in on his bulbous nose. Immediately memory prodding and interesting was the hairy, nasal appendage. It occupied the identical position on the nose of face on the poster. 'Do I now have you, you bleeder...? Is it possible…? Can there possibly be another who looks like you…?' the Commander spoke aloud. The copper's name had slipped from his memory. He couldn't understand why; he had taken pride in knowing all his constables serving at the divisional station by name.

He walked stiffly to his desk, breathing out sharply; the discovery of the look-alike had surprised him. He picked up the telephone and rang the front office. 'Tell me quietly, sergeant,' he said when the station sergeant answered, 'what is the name of the constable who just drove the pale blue Morris Minor into the yard?'

'That will be Constable Beckham, sir, the community beat constable for the "I.Q.". You know, the dodgy Irish Quarter home beat down by the river. He's paying one of his infrequent visits to the station.'

The Commander spun around from the desk. Still holding the phone, he faced the filing cabinet, a brightness shining in his eyes. Without replying, he replaced the receiver, walked towards the cabinet, opened the top drawer and removed the file containing photographs of all officers on the Divisional strength. He flicked through the pages to those surnames beginning with B and found the photograph of Constable William Beckham.

Yes, the outline of Constable Beckham's face, complete with its blemishes, was the same as the face on the poster. Both had the bulbous nose, and even through the rain, he was sure he saw the dark spot with its four hairs curiously positioned at ninety degrees to one another. 'Who else in this world could look this similar?' he asked aloud.

Constable Beckham's record of service showed his posting to the "I.Q." had lasted for twenty-five years. In that time, he hadn't arrested anyone. The Commander mused: he has kept himself well out of the headlines until now. If he were moonlighting as a comedian, anywhere, he'd have had plenty of time to perfect his act in the "I.Q." Blackpool, who'd have believed it? I suppose he'd have to get well away from "The Smoke" to perform in secret, away from rubber heelers. He stood shaking his head for a time, before sitting down with a sigh and saying aloud, 'One of my constables, too?'

From his own experiences of the "I.Q.", he knew that only a constable with a rare sense of humour could have policed this home beat for twenty-five years. Many an experienced detective had returned from an enquiry there, confounded by the locals. 'If I didn't now believe P.C. Beckham was such a huge piss-taker I'd put him up for a bloody medal for serving there for so long,' he said aloud.

That afternoon the Commander left the station early. Defying the unabating downpour, he put on a civvy waterproof, walked to East Clegham Underground Station and took the Tube home. The evening ahead only offered the Lodge meeting. Before that, he needed to think. Walking in the fresh air, he was sure, would revitalise his thought processes. He had an internal disciplinary issue: Constable Beckham, by his moonlighting, had breached Met Police discipline. A judgement on the matter was required, but one favouring him; he had a reason for not passing the problem to a higher authority like the Special Investigation Bureau, the dreaded S.I.B.

Old and smelly, the Tube train ferrying him to Cleghamside underground station lurched and rattled. The vibration and motion of the carriage subjected his balls to more cussed pain. Completely involuntarily, without recourse to sexual thought, he developed an immovable and painful erection to accompany them. As the train sped through tunnels, windows reflected the grimness and unhappiness indelibly permeating his face; like the phrase "A Present from Blackpool" threading through that stick of rock he never got. The twists in his face were new and perplexed him further; like his top lip curling back in a rictus of displeasure.

The scribbled lewd graffiti on adverts for Dyno-Rod he found so idiotic and off putting. When he stood up to give an elderly woman his seat and grasped the knob hanging from the ceiling for balance, he shuddered. The knob jerked with the train's motion and reminded him of his lower body pain, the throbbing, the "lover's nuts". He completed the journey with his hands in his raincoat pocket, balancing with difficulty.

He dropped his head in Cleghamside Tube Station, having no desire to skim his eyes over the photographs of scantily-dressed women advertising Scandinavian undies. Outside, he strode out resolutely towards his home, conscious of his pained balls and his erect cock rubbing the inside of his Y-fronts.

Daphne was out when he arrived home. He guessed she was having her hair done for the girlie night. He dropped his briefcase onto a kitchen chair, removed his raincoat and hung it to dry. His fingers felt wooden as he took out his wallet, removed Constable Beckham's photograph and compared it with the poster. 'It's you right enough…It can be no other…I'll put money on it,' he said aloud, convinced. Stung and angry now, he mouthed aloud, 'Billy, you bastard.'

Chapter 14

At 7:15 p.m., the black cab arrived to take Jack to the Lodge, having already collected Ivor Bunce. Slipping into the back seat alongside him, he saw that Ivor looked facially different. His jowly face, usually tanned from the many hours spent in his garden, looked drawn, hangdog and pasty. Beneath his eyes hung brown bags of skin with numerous wrinkles and he was marked on his chin where a razor had slipped. Jack thought he had a soul mate in Ivor; he looked so sad.

Ivor had never responded positively to humour and what he was about to ask wouldn't have him guffawing uncontrollably. He asked anyway, while buckling up, 'What's up, Ivor, cats been pissing, shitting and burying in your onion patch again?'

'It's the shitty life I'm having. Not cats, Gloria. Since she returned from that bloody weekend away in Blackpool, she's been acting out her sexual fantasies on me. Tells me that it's all to do with the comedian she saw there and his bloody god-awful jokes. I'm fifty-nine and past it. All I want from bed is sleep. She tells me she wants sex more than twice a week. That's just to start with...and she's demanded we try different positions. She's even mentioned the Kama Sutra. Good Lord, Jack, I last performed sexual Olympics during our honeymoon. I'm at my wits' end with the cock-crazy woman.' Ivor was a sad spectacle. Only the moustache and his top lip were animated.

Ivor's situation was clearly desperate, unusual for a man who had always appeared in control of his life, a stickler for discipline and moral standards within his sub-division.

'That is interesting,' Jack said. 'Daphne is acting quite the opposite. Once my life was total sexual Olympics, now it's a complete disaster. A pain in the bollocks that won't go away is what I have to show for saying *no* to her Blackpool jaunt. Sleeps on her own now and I don't know when it will end.'

Ivor's moustache twitched. 'I woke up this morning to a cup of ginseng tea to wash bloody ginseng capsules over my throat. It tastes bloody awful. Gloria berates me that it will revitalise parts that other teas cannot reach. Among the various vitamin pots littering my bedside cabinet, is a bottle of "Pro-Plus". The silly woman bought them under the misguidance that the pills ought to rejuvenate my prostrate. How bloody dippy can one be? I've never felt so irritable.'

Jack nodded in sympathy. 'I might be off my head,' he said, 'but I have reasons to believe that one of my home-beat constables is moonlighting as that comedian.' He waited for the insinuation sink in. Ivor's nose wrinkled and his moustache twitched. Ivor dealt sternly with police officers who committed offences against the Met's disciplinary code. 'I sighted the constable today and I confirmed my suspicions tonight, well, as far as I could.

Gloria and the girls sent Daphne a poster of the comedian. The face on the poster matches that of a constable attached to my sub-division, a P.C. William Beckham. I might know for sure tomorrow when I make a telephone call to Blackpool.'

'I loathe piss-takers… You are quite sure, Jack?' Ivor asked, whistling through his teeth, his face showing a mixture of disgust and surprise.

'It will require investigation, of course. If it's he, then he is the one who performed his blue act in front of Gloria and the girls, the one who's causing you…'

'You don't have to remind me, Jack,' Ivor snapped. Then his face contorted a little, his nose wrinkling again, his moustache jerking like a hairy caterpillar on the move, just faster. That the whole episode was so much bad taste was registering quickly.

It seemed to Jack that Gloria had descended on Ivor like a nymphomaniac plague.

'I'll have to clear this up,' Jack said, 'sensitively if possible, keeping the reputation of the division clean. Frankly, I don't want to kick it upstairs. I never did like the SIB. They're never happy unless they reveal some dirt, no matter what station they descend on. I've given the situation some thought and conclude that "rubber heelers" investigating the situation would deal with it quietly, keep the problem on the division. Then I'd be able to sack Beckham, personally. A constable who is sacked without his full pension will do wonders for discipline, don't you think?'

Jack watched Ivor's face grow into a twisted smile. He thought it probably the one of sheer hatred for which he was notorious, the one he reserved for berating coppers who had discipline issues. Ivor might never have liked the sound of performing in the sack, but when it meant a copper quivered in front of him, waiting to hear that "the sack" was his fate, that was different.

It confirmed what Jack needed to know: Ivor was on his side. When angered, Ivor's mouth contorted and his tongue clicked against his top palate, sounding as if he sought to siphon out a saliva-filled hole, vacated by a deeply-rooted molar.

Ivor was also having difficulty controlling his face muscles and spluttered, 'Other Forces might have a lenient attitude to their men moonlighting in demeaning occupations. Here in the Met, we keep to the script. We will rid the Force of skulduggery and corruption, wherever it raises its ugly head. He produced two exceedingly loud 'Clicks,' with his tongue then said, 'Jack, count me in. Whatever it takes, we must get the piss-taking bastard.'

Jack wasn't about to mention what Daphne's conditions were for returning to the marital bed. Ivor didn't need to know these demands, for him to find a couple of likely lads for the investigation he had in mind. 'I'll need two officers who you consider expendable if anything goes wrong,' he told Ivor, 'ones with the relative experience for an investigation of this sensitive nature. Officers of whatever rank will do. They must have some blot on their copybooks. Under threat, they must be manageable. They must also be the types who will do the rubber heeling, "duties elsewhere", quietly and without fuss.'

Ivor looked into the distance as he thought ahead to a successful outcome in which he would play his full part.

Jack forced a smile, thought of the saying he had heard somewhere, probably at a bloke's celebration in the nineteenth hole of a golf course: Ivor did have a faraway look in his eyes like a pig pissing.

'I have two jokers in mind already, Jack. They are two piss-takers of the highest calibre. Jocks, who, I am sure, are only a day or two away from dropping themselves into the inextricable mire. With the usual threats of the sack and the loss of pensionable rights ringing in their ears, their boots will smoke on their accelerated transit to your door. After I've been through them with the verbals, their minds will focus very quickly on the task you have in mind for them.'

Jack smiled and relaxed a little. He was happy to have Ivor on board and keen to root out misconduct in the ranks. With his reputation as a strict disciplinarian, Ivor would have a notebook full of potential officers who were walking a fine disciplinary line, not only the two Jocks he mentioned. 'Don't be too hard on them. I wouldn't want them to resign the force before you deliver them to me. I need them. I may even have to offer up some carrot.' Whoever the jokers were, he planned to send them incognito into the "I.Q" to find out if Billy Bagman was gigging there.

'I'll have my half-hour with them and enjoy it,' Ivor said. 'What you do with them after is your affair. I'd sack them and it would be bloody good riddance, too.'

******

Rowley was standing on the steps of the Lodge building, shaking hands with Lodge members and visitors as they arrived for the degree meeting. He put on a happy-to-see-you face. Inwardly, he was uneasy. During lulls in arrivals, he stepped out into the street, looking in each direction for the arrival of a black cab with Jack aboard. In his anxiety, he continually patted the side pocket containing the small parcel that he hoped Jack would accept without question.

When Jack's cab did pull up, Rowley was pleased that he left Ivor to pay the driver and quickly mount the stairs.

Inside the building, he gripped Jack by an arm and tugged him into his changing room.

Behind the closed door, Rowley turned to face Jack, taking hold of his upper arms. Rowley saw the darkness ringing Jack's eyes, read unhappiness there and dejection in the way he hunched his shoulders. Rowley felt confident that Jack was malleable, that he'd be able sell him the idea of a blind date.

Myrna had already communicated the results of her conversation with Daphne, who had accepted the idea, eagerly.

'Look, Jack… I've arranged a blind date for you,' Rowley said brightly and beamed a smile directly at Jack. 'You must be interested in shedding your load, in a manner of speaking, and forcing yourself out of these sexual doldrums. I see the problem written on your face. It tells me of a lack of bed sports. A man recognises that on the face of another and it speaks of an ache, both mental and physical. It's there…crying out, deep…and if you don't do something about it now, I will forever see it there, permanent, etched, when you could remove it completely by agreeing to my suggestion. Seeing your unhappiness, makes me deeply concerned for you.

'I want to help. I think if you met up with one of the sexy but reserved women I'm acquainted with, the usual arrangements applying, relief from your pain will come quickly.'

Rowley knew his whole, woeful story, Jack was sure; that he had sussed out every detail, had interpreted his face, a billboard showing his problem in large capitals. Even so, the suggestion that Rowley provide him with one of his old girl friends, as he had previously done on the Costa del Sol, shocked Jack. Wasn't Rowley going over the top in thinking that a blind date would sort out a best friend's problems?

'Don't you think you're overstepping the mark, Rowley? At the very least… being a little presumptuous… that I'd mess about with one of your… your old flames in my own backyard… on my own manor?' Jack said, his voice rising, his attempt to sound manly failing. The anguish he was feeling so strangled his vocal chords, what he said came out squeaky, unconvincing.

'Oh, how I feel for your…your balls-ache… Brother,' Rowley said slowly, spelling it out for him. 'You have become embittered, sucked on the crab apple of life, the sour skin of which still sticks in your craw. If I am correct, your face tells me that Daphne hasn't restored your nookie ration. If it were I…I'd be desperate for nookie by now. Knowing your sexual appetite, you're desperate for it now, too. Believe me. I'm just trying to get your leg over a nice-looking woman who will appreciate your need and ease you through this tough time.'

Hanging on the walls of the changing room were photographs of Past Worshipful Grand Masters. All looked suitably sombre in their Masonic finery. Jack thought they were all staring at him, waiting for him to make the correct, manly decision, waiting for him to place his trust in a Brother Mason.

Rowley's photograph had been the latest addition. Shortly, his own photograph would be up there and remain for a hundred years, until they were stowed in some time capsule for posterity.

Jack calmed. Yes, Rowley had always been a true friend. Although there were times before their friendship blossomed when he had been rather envious of his accelerated promotions. Then, he had always shrugged his shoulders resignedly and thought, 'Well, without a degree in Zoology, what can I expect?'

It was true. Although failing to gain a commission as an Army officer at Sandhurst, Rowley had taken a degree in Zoology at a Polytechnic and, after resits, had gained a poor degree. He then attended Hendon and, after hardly any time spent on the streets, Bramshill Police Training College. After the Prospective Senior Officer course there, he and other officers with degrees, whether they'd ever make good police officers or not, had found their own personal slipway, on the fast track to the upper echelons of the force, well greased. None of them would have had done any real policing. Rowley's record confirmed his mounting of the promotional ladder to his present rank, faster than any other police officer had.

Jack was beginning to give a little, seeing Rowley as not being too presumptuous at all in assuming he'd dally with another woman so close to his home. Because Rowley saw there *were* too many pressures building up in his mind and body, knew that powering them *were* too many painful days when he was too scared to touch his balls. Rowley had observed him closely, could see the affect that *too* many sexless nights lying alone in a cold, lonely double bed was having on him.

Quickly, Rowley's idea began to tantalise, as had each holiday together after the first one they'd taken on the Costa del Sol. He puzzled where might Rowley find an old girl-friend for him and who might she be? That could be a problem. She must be acceptable, but hadn't Rowley's word had always been more than good on that score.

Probably, he'd line up one of his ex-conquests, most likely a trustworthy old flame sworn to secrecy, a gorgeous one, one of the many that he had seen hanging onto Rowley's arm at Masonic balls. Always, he had snake-like slim, gorgeous, sexy creatures with him. They must be like bloody boas and wrap themselves around him in bed, he had thought.

The twinge he felt in his Y-fronts was turning to hardness, confirmation indeed of his interest in Rowley's arrangements. If he didn't move soon, it would be difficult to hide.

Rowley was winning him over. Yet, many of his contemporaries thought Rowley took too many risks with his reputation. Of course, they were probably jealous. No young, attractive WPC escaped his attentions. Rowley was a handsome bastard, had charm, a wicked sense of humour, and the most outrageous of chat up lines.

WPCs, if the grapevine was correct, threw themselves under him with surprising regularity. There were rumours too: Rowley was well hung. Jack perked up. Well blessed in that department himself, he would not be embarrassed in the company of any woman Rowley had attracted and had no doubt given a good, substantial pleasuring. The twinge in his Y-fronts increased commensurate with the idea of fucking one of Rowley's women friends and doing a better job of it than he had.

Later, the Lodge's business over, Jack joined Rowley in his changing room. Sipping whisky and relaxing, Rowley thought Jack looked a lot perkier, definitely up for getting his leg over again. 'Choosing the correct location took a bit of thought on my part,' Rowley said. 'Rest assured, though, the location I've chosen will be secluded, dark and romantic. Your date will approach from one direction, you from another. There will be no embarrassment. Nothing should compel you to become acquainted with each other's identity until you're doing things...having a lot of fun and well into the date. Get the pun?'

Rowley was sure that when Jack and Daphne came together, realised that they'd been set up to meet, they would wrap their arms around one another and that would be the end of their nightmare, simple. Jack was almost sold on the idea of the blind date; he couldn't let him back out now.

Although he had relaxed a trifle, doubts still lingered in Jack's mind. Could he go along with it? Should he go along with it? If there were a disastrous outcome, and there could be many permutations of potentially ruinous incidents, what then? Shaking his head as a touch of panic overcame him, he said. 'I can't believe I'm considering going along with this. Christ, Rowley, what happens if Daphne finds out? That would be the end; no way back if it all turned to rat shit.'

Rowley saw Jack's face sag a little; he had to make his answer reassuring. 'It's as secure as a Masonic secret is. Believe me, as a Brother. You have my word on it.' Rowley took hold of Jack's arm as Freemasons do. 'Don't I always fix you up with a special woman, nice, sensible, one who knows the score, is sensuous and sensitive?

'You richly deserve to enjoy this woman's company. She'll attend to your every need. Believe me, it's the brotherliest thing I have ever done for a friend. I'll get satisfaction just knowing you'll feel better afterwards, you know.' Rowley winked. 'The secret someone will ease the pain, eh, Jack. You'll charge at her like a man possessed. She's woman enough to take all you have, if I've done my research correctly. It will keep you going until your prunes are drained regularly again... as they say on the street... until things change at home, as I'm sure they will, soon.'

Jack sighed and looked at the floor again. 'I don't have a lot of options at the moment, do I?' he mumbled.

'Be a sport,' Rowley said. Jack's eyes left the floor. Rowley tried to lock onto them. 'Go to the hairdressers tomorrow, have a trim, a facial massage, and relax. Get "something for the weekend", nudge, nudge, wink, wink,' he suggested. 'You know what I mean: "a packet of three".' All the time Rowley was moving his head from side to side trying to fix Jack with his stare.

Jack's eyes were dull and he cast them downwards, towards his feet again. 'If I know this woman, you'll need all of them.' With a hand in the crook of the opposite arm, Rowley gave Jack a sign: an upward-lifting arm, indicating the woman was sexy. Jack looked up and Rowley quickly took hold of his arm. Then, taking Jack's right hand, Rowley applied the Master Mason's grip.

In the other hand, Rowley held an envelope. 'In this you'll find the instructions for meeting your blind date,' he said, holding it beneath Jack's gaze. 'She has similar instructions. You won't miss each other.' He shoved the small squeezable package into Jack's hand and forced his fingers around it, 'This package contains your disguise. Your date will be wearing a Maggie Thatcher mask and wig, so you'll recognise her easily. It's easy, Jack,' Rowley said airily. 'It's Halloween on Sunday. You'll meet her then, that night. No one will take any notice of you. You'll be just another partygoer meeting up with a friend. It's easy-peasy, Jack… don't you think?'

Jack gave a muted grunt of agreement. There was no prospect of him returning home to find that Daphne had lifted the exclusion order on her body. Something just had to cheer him up. He weighed the package in his hand and looked at Rowley, squarely, for the first time. Ideas began to run amok in his head. He saw pert, firm breasts swaying temptingly in front of his searching lips, seductive perfumes toying with his nasal receptors. He warmed, imagining the closeness of a woman to him again, his fingers tracing the knicker line where they encircled her thighs. Suddenly he was hard, in more pain. His stomach muscles tightened. Pangs of anticipation attacked him. 'The blind date with this mystery woman, nothing can go wrong, can it?' he pleaded.

Rowley smiled his assurance. 'Nothing, Jack. Just relax. Give it a chance. It will work. If you do, your dreary, sex-starved days are over. On Monday morning you'll be singing my praises and be feeling like the old Jack we all know and love.'

Then they retired to the bar and mixed with other brethren.

Chapter 15

The BBC midday weather forecast, on Sunday, All Hallow's Day, warned of a deepening low-pressure area and gales lashing the south of the country for the next twenty-four hours. As predicted, that afternoon, the skies darkened, clouds rolled in from the west and wind-driven rain pelted relentlessly.

Lunch over, the Sunday Times read, Ivor stood looking gloomily from a window, watching the rain bouncing off his garden. He was in a sucker stance, crouched forward, nose to glass, his feet well apart.

Gloria, wearing slippers, sidled silently towards him. Standing behind him, unnoticed, she thrust her hand between his legs and tweaked his testicles from the rear, vigorously. Ivor shot up straight and let out a roar, followed by, 'for heaven's sake, woman, get your mind up above my navel, will you? It *is* Sunday after all!'

Gloria fluttered her eyelids and adopted a girlish tone. 'We ought to have a matinee, dear. Why don't we lay down doggy-fashion on the Chesterfield and watch the afternoon film? This is a day for getting your back into something other than the garden.'

Following the tweaking, Gloria couldn't resist pawing Ivor every time he came close to her. As the afternoon wore on, he became increasingly unhappy with her attention and opted for escape, rapid and immediate. Throwing a coat over his head and pushing his feet into his wellies, he made a dash for the garden shed.

Delving deep into mulch and compost, busily potting and transplanting, he found a degree of contentment. The rain drumming upon the tin roof had a soothing effect and it didn't talk back with stupid, sexy prattle.

There was no "trick or treat", no guisers singing at their door, no frivolity in the Bunce household early evening on All Hallow's Eve. It pleased Ivor that Gloria hummed a tune, most of the time to a CD she played. Knowing her position relevant to him was important, especially to his testicles, which were still paining him. The gardening programme repeat on TV kept his eyes glued, but he had tuned his ears to pick up any sound indicating Gloria's proximity. For the remainder of the evening he kept mum and stayed out of her reach.

******

The late-turn constables at West Clegham nick paraded for duty at 1:45 pm that afternoon. On the Superintendent's day off, the whole relief felt safe to sip a mug of tea in the canteen before hitting the streets.

Half an hour later, Hamish and Harry, feeling no warmer for the fortification their tea had brought, were standing in a High Street shop doorway, considering using a bus to get to their beat. Rain and the sleet blew in sheets. Dustbin lids, assorted rubbish and wheelie bins jetted crazily along the street. It was a dangerous and miserable place to be for users. Their interest in police work was slumping further into the negative.

'Any Sunday on late turn's a bloody pain. I can't remember a wetter day this year and the rain shows no signs of abating,' Hamish said.

'Aye, you're right,' Harry replied. 'Even being Halloween couldn't brighten it up.'

'I hate foot patrols in the rain. I'm soaking with sweat already beneath this cape,' Hamish said.

'Is the sweat blowing up and down the cheeks of your arse affecting them like the downpour is the streets?' Harry asked.

'Aye, my breeks will soon be sodden. Without a changeable wind pattern blowing in that area, I'll have no hope of drying them,' Hamish answered, pulling at the seat of his trousers.

'This pissing rain signals autumn's here and winter's icy grip isn't far off. Soon we'll be shivering in our boots, not swimming in them,' Harry reckoned, dancing the toe of a boot over the wet pavement.

'I'll be glad when we're all at old Tonks' retirement do later tonight, after we've booked off,' Hamish said, 'I'm looking forward to supping a few pints of Guinness.'

'Aye, but you'll have to keep your nether reaches dry for that,' Harry reminded him and winked in his direction. 'You don't want a damp performing area.'

Hamish and Harry's duties that late turn were to patrol retired Constable Tonks' community beat. Within the beat's boundaries were some of the finest properties on the division, and the sprawl of Clegham Municipal Park. In their present demeanour, they treated this beat no different than they would any other. That afternoon, the heavy rain was washing away any responsibility they felt for preserving life and protecting property anywhere, into the already overflowing gutters.

A bus ride later and a short walk from the stop they took shelter in a shop doorway. Hamish groaned, took his helmet off and dried the inner leather band. 'It's grim here too. I'd love to spend the rest of the shift tucked up with a cuppa in a nice warm kaff's kitchen. Pity there's neither kaffs nor shops open around here today.'

Harry nudged him with an elbow, taking his mind from a steaming brew. One of Constable Tonks' avid neighbourhood-watching old dears was trudging up the street, bent against the wind. Wearing wellie boots, a plastic headscarf, an open raincoat beneath which an apron billowed, she braved the weather. Joining them in the shop doorway, she brushed water from her brow, turned her face upwards and said, 'I know it's pissin' wet, officers, but some kids have been setting off fireworks in the street. Frightened my cat to death, they did. The old tom scurried right up a tree, it did. There for hours it was until, whisker-sodden, it scuttled down, branch-to-branch, to safety.'

'That's terrible, my dear,' Hamish said and 'tut-tutted' for effect.

'The cat's warmin' at my hearth now, but the kids were rascals and under age, officers. Shouldn't have fireworks on them at all, cheeky beggars. Belted off sharpish, they did, when I mentioned calling the police. Dropped these though,' she said. Digging into her apron pocket, she found and handed Harry two fireworks.

'Constable Tonks trained you well. It's terrible weather, and you've done the right thing bringing us these. What did you say your name was?' Hamish asked. 'It's for my report. The Superintendent might write and thank you for this.'

'I'm Mabel Bell from 6 Ditchburn Street.'

'Well, Mabel Bell from 6 Ditchburn Street, you've done a grand job, that you have. We'll take these fireworks and make them safe. That'll be an end to it,' Hamish told her, arm around her shoulders like a loving son.

After she had gone, Harry grinned. 'Bangadebang!' he said and held the fireworks up in front of him, inspecting them for rain damage.

'Those will go down well later,' Hamish said. His smile waxed cheesy as he leaned back, seeing if Harry had gotten his drift.

'I know what you're thinking, Constable MacNab?' Harry said, 'I was on to you quick. I know you know some shirttail lifters use the "cottage" as well as the park, but do you think they'll be seeking cover tonight?'

'Bloody right I do, Constable MacSporran, and I smell a great laugh here.'

At 7:30p.m., they took their meal break. By 8:30, they again waited to board a bus. If anything, the weather had worsened as darkness descended.

Although a restricted service operated on Sundays, buses were available that would drop them at their chosen destination: a small shopping arcade situated across the road from Clegham Municipal Park gates. Sheltered in an inner doorway, unseen, in the dark and well protected from the storm's ferocity, they waited and watched.

******

Preparations for blind dates were underway in the Dewsnap household. For four painful weeks, only screeched 'Fuck offs,' from Daphne had shattered the silence. Now she was watching him folding his Masonic apron, preparing the regalia case, her eyes blazing. He shrugged. What's she's going to have a go at me for this time, he asked himself.

'I see you have dressed smartly in shirt and tie, charcoal grey flannels and black blazer both newly dry-cleaned. You won't get far in those shoes tonight, either. You've another fucking woman, you bastard. That's what this is.' Daphne said, nastily.

The marital spat and worries concerning the night ahead had Daphne pent up, feeling bitchy. It was all getting to her and she was responding petulantly to the attire Jack had chosen to wear.

Jack had noticed Daphne going for a shower earlier, after which she reappeared in a clean change of shroud. He had shuddered, picturing her lathering her body beneath the spray. Excruciating balls ache, nervousness and taut muscles couldn't prevent him thinking what might have been.

Why the outburst now, he wondered? In her present sulk, she wouldn't have missed his assistance beneath the spray. Surely, she couldn't have any suspicions. Preparing his regalia box on a Sunday could only mean one thing: he was leaving for the Lodge and another practice session. He had attended many and without any fuss.

'I'm on my way to the Lodge. It's not necessary to dress formally for a practice, you know that,' Jack said, stroppily, whilst attempting eye contact. Daphne turned and walked away from him. Shaking her head and thumping her feet, she mounted the stairs to her room. 'Typical womanly reaction,' he mouthed, and stared at her back, glumly.

Jack was beginning to see the whole blind date escapade as a ridiculous exercise. He muttered to himself, 'I must be mad, absolutely mad to go along with Rowley's plan. Sexual needs, huh, at my age I should be able to live without them.'

When he was single, he had attended some crazy Halloween thrashes in Section Houses. Sometimes, coppers were pleasuring naked girls they knew not who, each with their masks still in place. He had thought nothing equalled the stupidity of this act. 'What a desperate character I've become,' he conceded with a sigh. Shrugging, he pulled on his black gabardine raincoat.

The weather he'd face walking between his parking place, which he had yet to suss out, and the meeting place, sounded horrendous. The rain pelting the windowpanes was unrelenting. He looked down at his polished shoes and harrumphed. He usually wore them to Lodge meetings. Tonight they were a part of his deception, though unsuitable for walking in a waterlogged park.

It was 8:30 p.m. exactly, when he passed through the door from the kitchen into the garage, clambered into his BMW 5 series and reversed out. The gusting wind shook the car and the rain drummed on the roof. Reversing down the drive, he started the windscreen wiper. Through the clearing glass, he saw the curtain in Daphne's bedroom move. For some reason, she was checking his departure. He thought that a change. The road was clear of traffic so he reversed out and drove off towards the park.

******

Daphne watched Jack leaving. She knew the Masonic apron-box lying open indicated his attendance at his lodge's practice session. It also answered the question of his casual attire. Being uptight, she found shouting at him made her feel better. Jack had no idea she was about to leave, too; but he had answered her prayers by leaving before her. Now he had gone, she quickly dressed, pulling on the black two-piece trouser suit, newly purchased and kept hidden from him.

Ever since Myrna had told her of the date over the telephone, she had been on edge. Soon after hearing of the arrangements at the Thursday night meeting, the worries had started to consume her. She hadn't eaten properly since. Now anguish surged through her breasts. Blood coursed jerkily through her veins, pounded against her forehead, panic gripping her.

The dalliance was outrageous, barking, but she desperately needed a man. She gripped tightly the Maggie Thatcher mask Myrna gave her. Looking at the rubberised face, she saw in it a symbol of strength, the red lips weapons ready to bark in defence of her actions. Then, quite oddly, the words of the Pina Colada song were fizzing around in her head, the number being a favourite during her girlhood. Were the words the same tonight? Were they asking her something? "Was she tired of her hubby, had they been together too long?"

She shook her head. Her recall of the words was murky, as murky as the night was.

At 8:45 p.m., Daphne set the household alarm system. She covered her shoulders with a full-length waterproof and read again her instructions. They said she ought to approach the park entrance from the east, on foot, at 9 p.m., exactly. Parked in the other half of the double garage was her Peugeot 106, a birthday present from Jack. She reversed out of the drive and motored towards Clegham Municipal Park.

******

Jack arrived close by the Municipal Park a few minutes early. There were no other vehicles parked in the vicinity; therefore, no courting couples lurching car suspensions and liable to upset him further. The spot he chose to the west of the toilets was discreet, giving him a clear view towards the park gates, but not of anyone approaching on the pavement from the east, the direction from which his blind date would appear.

Parked up, he needed to flick the wiper to clear the rain-lashed windscreen; the storm wasn't easing and extra large raindrops were falling from trees to thud onto the roof. Through the rain, he made out the footbridge, fifty yards away, traversing the street from the shopping mall to the public toilet.

Mists, kicked up by the deluge, shimmered beneath the street lighting, subduing outlines. Shadows danced frenetically, trees swayed erratically. The gusting, whooping wind clawed at the shrubbery overhanging the park railings, bending and straining the branches.

Jack ran his fingers around the steering wheel, flexing them, pounding his head on his knuckles. He deplored his situation and sounded off, 'Boom boom, what the bloody hell are you doing here, Jack Dewsnap? What kind of madness affects you? What devils are playing with your emotions… and manifesting themselves in your painful balls?' Daphne, Daphne, Daphne, why are you driving me to this…being an utter bitch…withholding your love… sex…for all this time?'

He mused: his covert loitering in a dimly lit street, close to Clegham Borough Municipal Park toilets, on a dirty, wet, Halloween, would shock people he knew in high places. That he toyed with the Elvis Presley facemask lying flexible and rubbery on his lap and was waiting to meet with a blind date arranged by his Masonic brother, Assistant District Commissioner Rowley Beaverton, would shock them more.

Jack didn't feel he was an untouchable within the force yet, though Rowley seemed to act as if *he* were. Only promotions to come would give him an extra coating of Teflon invulnerability. The discovery of this foolhardy venture could prove costly. He could see humiliation within the Job, a hounding out of it even. 'Blast Rowley,' he said then breathed in through his teeth. 'This had better be good!'

Two buses had passed by the park gates without stopping. The third one pulled up beneath the bridge. He wondered who'd want to get off outside the park gates in this weather. Could it be a night watchman? Was it his date? The bus pulled away.

Two coppers had dismounted. Holding onto their helmets, they hurried stooped towards the mall. Two piss-takers who can't be bothered to complete their patrol on foot was Jack's immediate reaction. There was still time for them to move on, but if they hung about, began doing their job properly, they might stop and question suspicious loiterers.

He recalled the mall had a central passageway with several doglegs. Meandering for a several hundred yards, it connected with an adjacent street. Buses on that route ran back to Clegham High Street. That was the answer. The piss-takers, intending to remain dry, had come to check this part of their beat before returning to the High Street by the other bus route.

This was Ivor's patch. A word with him about his coppers using buses to get around their beats was out of the question. Ivor would want to know the day, date, time and place of the occurrence. He couldn't give him that information.

******

Hamish and Harry had observed figures, their targets, arriving at the park's public toilet or "cottage", the off-hand name constables had for such a building, which stood bleak and rain swept on the pavement opposite.

Hamish appraised the situation. 'It was a copper in the importuning squad who gave me the gen about this area, by the way. In the dark and in good weather, pervs use the park. Small groups, mainly twosomes, form over there outside the park gates then disappear into those dense rhododendron bushes to do their own thing. They probably do someone else's thing, too. On dirty nights like this, the pervs were reportedly mud shy. That'll be why the eight we've seen so far have gathered in yonder "cottage".'

'You don't like shirttail lifters much, then?' Harry asked

'If they don't bother me, I'll not bother them. Tonight we'll be giving them laldy, but only for the laughs we'll get.'

'The lifters in the cottage might not think it's funny to have their moments of pleasure blasted,' Harry prompted.

'No, no, later, they'll feel enlivened. A couple of extra blasts will have added thrusts to their enjoyment, got them closer to buttocks. They will bless us,' Hamish disagreed. 'What time is it, by the way?'

Harry glanced at his watch. 'It's almost 9 o'clock. Why?'

'I think all the "cottagers" have booked in.'

******

Sitting waiting for the witching hour of 9 p.m., Jack was nervy. He fumed and did test fittings with the mask. His mind was becoming super-active by the second and skimmed over the problems that had begun away back. Problems that had brought him down, feeling bloody foolish, desperate for sex, to that drenched street.

He left his musings and cried aloud, 'Bugger it!' It was time to get across the road and watch for her arrival. He picked up the mask, stepped out of the car and pulled the coat collar around his neck. He locked the car with a flick of his key fob, looked right then left. He could see little through the driven rain.

Walking stooped, he crossed the road towards the park railings. In the restless shadows of the wind-whipped shrubbery, he saw some concealment. He eased the mask over his head, down over his forehead, and then twisted it into position, lining the holes up with his eyes. The reincarnation of Elvis Presley trembled. He felt very much alive, but still the pangs of guilt wrestled with his conscience.

******

'Look, there, Hamish, two late-comers, wrists all limp and dangly, are walking towards one other. One's coming from the west this time. They're both doing the Govan glide, though.'

'More likely the Leith walk they're doing, especially if they're rear gunners, eh, Harry?'

'Are we having a wee go at one another?' they said together, both chortling softly.

'Are you keeping count? How many is that now?' Hamish asked.

'I've counted ten all together, including these two,' Harry said.

'Half of them must be rear gunners unless they have swivel turrets, Hamish said. 'Look at old sneaky there. Whoever he is, he's creeping up in the shadows of the tall shrubbery near the park railings.'

'They're definitely two seedy types mincing along in the traditional shabby raincoats of their calling. The larger one, I think his signal to the one approaching is "RU12". They're well wrapped up and protected from this pissing weather, I'll give them that,' Harry said. 'They look odder than the others did. Funny heads those two have.'

'We couldn't tell who they were from here anyway,' Hamish said.

******

Jack breathed in, shuddered and uttered, 'My God, what am I doing here?' The figure approaching from the other direction with a purposeful stride held down a wig and looked so much like the Iron Lady herself, and this was his date.

He kept close to the railings, the dancing shadows falling on him, and walked head-down towards the park gate. The wind tugged at his mask. Rain blew through the eyeholes fuzzing his eyesight. Passing from the shelter of the shrubbery across the entrance to the park, a stronger gust briefly unbalanced him. The "getting to know you" few words in the park he once had in mind were definitely out… what could he do? Where could he take her? His mind raced.

Then they were face-to-face, heads a trifle bowed, embarrassed to be there in their silly masks, both thinking how ridiculous they must look. He reached out, took hold of her two hands and held them gently, the rain trickling between their fingers.

Daphne felt his skin, soft, slippery too, as his hands gripped hers, gently. He obviously was the Civil Servant, the gentleman Myrna had said he would be and she looked up.

'Where can we go?' Jack mumbled, his throat was tight and a lump was rising fast. The rainwater oozed through eyeholes of the rubberised faces of "Maggie" and "Elvis". It ran down over Jack's lips and he sucked it in to ease his dryness.

Daphne sighed, couldn't speak. The Pina Colada song was there again..."Do you like Pina Colada, getting caught in the rain? Like a worn-out recording of a favourite song..."

'Terrible weather,' Jack said and shrugged his shoulders. He wanted desperately to hear her voice, his sounded so anguished and distorted through the mouth of the mask dripping with rainwater.

Behind the eyeholes in the Maggie Thatcher mask, his blind date's eyes flashed back at him, reflecting the street lighting. He stood looking, indecisive, rooted to the spot by them. He realised he had to make a move quickly, before they were both drenched.

In desperation, he took hold of an arm, gently nudging her towards the toilet block and the shelter of the bridge. There, he could engage her in a quick chat and find out what she expected of him. He would suggest the mall and telephoning a taxi from there, going for a meal at a nice restaurant, a night in a country pub, or to her place, quickly.

The door to the Gents gaped open. A dull light flickered from inside. Floodwater poured down an incline into a drain.

Adjacent with the entrance, she grabbed him by an arm. Fiercely pulling at his coat, she dragged him through the door.

Inside the Gents, the smell of old urine, disinfectant and Harpic gripped Jack's nostrils. His head spun, disorientated by the gloom, the smell, and the mask… which Rowley said he hadn't to remove yet.

Daphne's metal heels slipped on the cement floor. She steadied herself and dragged him in further. She had a man in her grasp, her juices were running and she wasn't going to miss out by appearing timid. She had done worse in the boiler house of the Hospital when she was a nurse… with Jack. Cubicle doors seemed stubborn and unwilling to budge when she pushed. Suddenly one gave to her shoulder pressure. She stepped inside and pulled him in behind her.

******

By 9:05 p.m., ten individuals had entered the Gents.

'The job's a good one, Victor One,' Hamish said in a Captain Mainwaring accent. 'Has all the necessary equipment been prepared?'

Harry searched beneath his cape, found a tunic pocket. In a lisped, Sean Connery voice he confirmed, 'The two explosive devices are present and correct, Sunray.'

'Have you the detonating device, Victor One?' Hamish asked.

'Detonation device is ready. The lighter indicates a full charge of gas. The 69's still in progress, no one has come up for air, and the nozzle is turned up high,' intoned Harry. 'It will be effective, even in this weather.'

'Very good, Victor One.'

'What's the tactics, then, Hamish?' They had moved to the mall entrance, ready to face the conditions.

'The staircase on the Park side passes within a foot of the roof of the Gents,' Hamish explained. 'My informant told me of a gap in the protecting railings around the roof large enough for me to haul my bulk through onto the roof.'

'What about a skylight?' Harry asked.

'We're okay there. Some of the skylight's diamond-shaped glass panels are missing. They've probably been banged out to give voyeurs pleasure.'

The wooden steps of the bridge looked worn and as slippery as glass. Standing facing the upward stairs, Hamish scuffed a boot over the bottom step's surface and tested for adhesion. 'Careful,' Hamish said, detecting slipperiness, and ushered Harry in behind him for the passage across.

Crouched low, crossing steadily, one hand holding down their helmets, the other holding onto the handrail, they withstood the rain-laden gusts threatening to unbalance them. The rain hitting the wooden decking and the wind blasting and whistling through the metal gantries deadened the sound of their passage.

******

The light above the urinal flickered, went out then came back on again. Daphne didn't need light. Letting out a gasp, she threw her arms in his direction, wrapped them around him in the gloom. Jack's arms flew around her. Immediately he lifted her arms around his neck.

Wet facemasks squeaked together. Moans shuddered from bursting lungs, exploding through rubber lips. Arms squeezed, hands wandered, caressed, up and down backs. Passion, denied for so long, rose in the two mortals.

Daphne thought she was acting like a common hussy, but she had come too far to back out now. They separated and he closed the door behind him, reached behind her, and put the seat down onto the pan. He was a gentleman, after all, she mused. He had prepared a throne for her.

Daphne sat down, her legs flagging. Holding him close, her arms found their way beneath his raincoat to encircle his bum, which felt firm, clenched. She moved her hands, searched for and found the line of his belt and trouser top. She pressed her cheek to his stomach. She felt the tension in his muscles when she playfully squeezed his "six-pack", feeling the heat oozing from his body. He placed his hands on top of her head. He moved the wig around, gently. She began massaging his trouser front. They both moaned in unison. Feeling the power of his manhood, hard, straining, she searched for his zip, mad for it.

******

Across the bridge now and at the top of the downward steps, Hamish signalled his intention to descend and for Harry to stay put. He reached the Gents outer door and signalled back to Harry that he was going inside. The only light available shone in intermittent bursts from a solitary fluorescent tube; black at both ends and close to the end of its useful life, it faintly illuminated the urinals A wee bit of luck for the sitting tenants, Hamish mused, noting all of the cubicle lamps were out, too, personal privacy secured.

The wind was thudding into the building, but Hamish tiptoed anyway. In front of the urinal, he unzipped, aimed at the stainless steel and sprayed. Although he was excited, he breathed quietly, naturally, in a casual manner. In the act of zipping up his fly, he cast his head downwards, in a low reconnaissance, projecting his line of sight beneath the raised door bottoms and dividing partitions.

******

The magical, unique, soft metallic purr, made only by the male trouser-fly, sounded as Daphne lowered Jack's zip. Loosening the belt, she allowed his trousers to fall to the floor. Four weeks was a long time for her to remain celibate. She would take her time and enjoy the fruits of the blind date. Ripping off her mask and wig, she casually threw them behind her.

She found her head stuck beneath his raincoat, in a darker place. She felt for and found a pair of thin white legs, shaking uncontrollably. Her hand brushed his erect cock, poking out, pointed heavenwards through the opening of his Y-fronts, the touch making her quiver. Pulling the pants down to his knees, his cock sprang back, smacking her beneath the chin. She cupped his testicles in both hands. Strangely, they seemed suspended, almost vertically, springing up and down in her palms, as if fixed to pieces of piano wire… She had never seen Jack's like this.

Jack shuddered, groaned loudly, louder still when she gently squeezed his testicles.

Strange, Daphne thought, were the balls actually vibrating in her attentive hands? It was a wholly new experience for her and certainly, Jack's had never given her that sensation.

Daphne held his cock between her upright hands, as if she was at prayer. She rolled it and kneaded it, caressed it and blessed it, twisted it and kissed it. She ran her lips along the length of it, along the top of it, along the side of it, along the bottom of it and she blew on it hotly and heavily. She thought Jack would have liked it that way, too. She allowed it to touch the end of her nose gently, smelling the soap residues, detecting its recent cleansing. She allowed her tongue to play around the end of it, licked it, worshiping it.

. Then she took him full in the mouth, her lips ringing him tightly, sliding, her tongue moistening, giving him the full deep-throat treatment, gently and skilfully. Quickly, she drifted away into an erotic, dream-like trance.

******

It was as Hamish had thought. Four-legged men seemed to occupy each of the five cubicles. A double nap-hand, he mused. Within two of the cubicles, all the feet were facing one way. Within the other three, two feet faced one way and two the other. Even in the gloom, he could just make out trousers and underwear captive around ankles.

Tiptoeing quickly and quietly away, he retraced his steps and reached the outer door. A door-bolt, entered into a hole on the floor, kept the door open. He removed the door-bolt and very quietly, he drew the door closed behind him.

A supple twig, blown from a tree in the storm, he used to secure the hasp over the eye, preventing anyone opening the door from the inside.

Nimbly and excitedly, he mounted the stairs, stopping when level with Harry. He said breathlessly, 'Four-legged men in each of the five cubicles.'

'What are they doing?' Harry asked eagerly.

'In two of the cubicles, all the feet are facing one way. In the three others, they're not. Most have their kecks and skiddies lying on the floor around their ankles. What do you think they're doing? None of the users are potting and dropping their guts. The others aren't providing assistance at jobby time. Let's get to the hole, quick.'

Ducked low, they squeezed through the broken fencing onto the reinforced concrete roof. Hamish stopped and pointed towards a spear of light coming from a hole in the skylight.

It was the "bomb bay". Hunkering low and in procession, they reached it. Hamish felt for its edge and knelt on its raised surround. He pulled Harry down with him, shortening their shadows. Then he cast his eye over the hole, peered through, turned his head and placed his ear close. There was no sound. He reported quietly to Harry as he straightened, 'Definitely heard the gentle flip-flopping of a bobby's helmet.'

The rain gusted with ferocity, lashing the roof. Water sluiced everywhere. No pedestrians were out in the rain. Some vehicular traffic, stationary at the traffic lights of the junction about three hundred yards away, were just visible.

Harry produced the fireworks and the lighter set at high flame. Hamish pulled on gloves and took hold of the two Super-Strength Thunderclap Bangers. He said nothing, but knew the little beggars losing them had missed a bit of fun. Harry lit the blue touch-paper, which started to sparkle.

******

Daphne was lingering in that palace of ultimate ecstasy, her head blissful. Would it last forever? No. Indications were that a huge, perfectly formed globule of pressurised semen was about to arrive. Jack's body began to jerk, his knees to sag, and he roared as his orgasm neared.

The globule thundered from his cock on its ejaculatory trajectory, reaching escape velocity on its restricted flight path. A great sob of relief and satisfaction accompanied it together with long, drawn-out cries of, 'Yehhhsss… yehhhsss.' The semen thumped into the base of Daphne's epiglottis, split into two parts and smashed into her tonsils left and right.

She coughed and gasped.

The erotic trance that had transported Daphne to that heavenly place, high above the plateau of sexual tranquillity, suddenly reversed. In an instant, she was crazily plummeting back through the wormholes of her mind through distance and time. Words of an alien Pina Collada song broke through. They didn't mention "making love at midnight in the dunes of the cape". No…, where had she heard these words before?

"AND SHE SWALLOWED HIS PINA COLADA, Oh Blimey, O'Reilly, Olé!"

******

'Bombs away,' Hamish said. The bangers spat out stars as he dropped them through the holes.

Keeping their profiles low, they quickly crossed over the footbridge. Halfway across, two loud, booming bangs sounded. Inside the Gents, total darkness came instantly. The third explosion was the fluorescent lamp disintegrating, blown from its fitting by the resultant shock wave.

The silence following lasted until the first screeched, anonymous utterance of 'What the fuck was that?'

******

The words of the song died in Daphne's head as the first of the three explosions reverberated around the walls of the Gents. Just as suddenly, her teeth clamped together, spring-loaded, like a gin trap snapping around the leg of an unsuspecting animal. Jack was withdrawing slowly, but jerked back suddenly when the second firework exploded. Daphne was exiting her trance and her clenched teeth drew blood, biting unintentionally, deep into his withdrawing cock. Jack writhed in pain, trapped, his back tight against the toilet door. The third explosion coincided with a sound of breaking glass, the gloom turning to total darkness.

Unexpectedly, the sounds of men in a panic erupted all around them. Daphne sat stunned, on her throne, alone. She felt her companion turn, somehow open the door and hop out, underpants and trousers around his ankles. So much for him being a gentleman, she thought.

The others she had suddenly become aware of in the building were banging on the entrance door, crunching glass beneath their feet. One bereft inmate screamed, 'Some bastard will pay for this!'

Jack ripped off his mask and tossed it behind him. Unsteady, in a panic, he stumbled and hopped about in the dark, his trousers and Y-fronts still beneath his knees. Hands brushing over him indicated that several persons were using the toilet that night. A hand took hold of his pained cock and he immediately knew what type of man was closing his fingers gently around it. An affected voice said, 'My, you've shot your load already, ducky.'

'Over here, Claudie,' an anguished voice cried. The hand left him before he could hit out. Jack bent over, grabbed for his pants and butted someone in the back. As he searched for his Y-fronts, hands lifted the tail of his raincoat, found and parted his buttocks. He felt something warm and hard, bobby's helmet shaped, starting to probe. Jack pulled away, clenching his buttocks tighter than he could ever remember.

He could see no one. He threw an elbow back, connecting with a nose, crunching it back onto an invisible face that let out a groan. No way was he going to speak. No way was he going to let anyone recognise *him*. Then something smelling of shit hit him on the side of his face. He raised his hand and pulled away the used condom. Feeling like throwing up, he said beneath his breath, 'Rowley's going to pay for this. Fucking right he is.'

******

An eternity seemed to pass, though it was only a couple of minutes. A loud rattling and banging of a door opening preceded the cold gust of night air that blew into the building. Feeling the draught, Daphne tidied her attire and left the cubicle in a hurry. Pushing past a hobbling figure in a working overall, she kept her head down, a hand over her face. Getting back home before Jack returned from the Lodge was all she could think of. She had to shower away the smells, all the memories of the Gents. After the practice-session at the Lodge, Jack would remain with the boys for the harmony. It often kept him late.

Chapter 16

At 11 p.m., that Sunday night, while Gloria fussed in the kitchen, Ivor took the opportunity to slink away and shower. Tenderly he bathed wedding tackle, which recently, in his loudly voiced opinion, Gloria had cruelly wrenched from the realms of the unemployed. In clean pyjamas, he prepared for an early night. He felt knackered these days and knew the reason why.

In the bedroom, he uttered a prolonged groan. Gloria was already there selecting from the mountain of vitamin-pill and potion pots collecting on his bedside cabinet. He felt his dander rising, felt that he had to rail at her. Stuttering and spitting, he became stiff with rage. 'I'm too old for these stupid concoctions and bloody foolish sexual antics!' he said in a high-pitched voice. 'I think you ought to go and have your hormone levels tested…. bloody vitamins… whatever next?'

Gloria was determined that someday soon he'd really enjoy sex. Unperturbed by his outburst, she grouped pills into two separate lines, pointing out his evening's and the morning's doses.

In a light mood, she began skipping around the bedroom, tidying and hanging clothes in the wardrobe, telling him as she tended to the chores: 'I don't care if your more commendable asset is your adherence to the Met Police General Orders. I don't care if you are punctilious, always punctual…well not nowadays, or that you have a reputation as a strict disciplinarian. Neither do I care that those traits stood you in good stead in the promotion stakes.'

Gloria stopped at the wardrobe door, nodded her head, turned and looked around the bedroom, run her fingers lightly over the wardrobe's mahogany sheen. 'Your promotions may have raised our standard of living, too,' she continued, 'however, since my return from Blackpool, I've looked for the sexual satisfaction missing from our marriage since our honeymoon. Since resuming fucking, you haven't ever brought me close to a multiple orgasm. However, we will make it yet, you and I, darling, you wait and see.

'When we were first married, our fucks were pathetic. Now your short, stubby little cock cannot even retain a hard-on for two fucks of an evening. I know you are older now and your libido is low. However, do not fret. The vitamins and other fortifying agents will enhance your performances. I will have you fucking the way big boys do. Fortunately, for *you*, I have the hots for you all over again… otherwise I'd be looking elsewhere for a well-hung, satisfying stud to do the business.

'Remember that night not long after we first met, when I pinned you down in that shop doorway? Then your cock was springy and came to life readily. When I played with you, I had you ejaculating, splashing your load over the doorknob and the letterbox. Your breath came in short gasps and you dared not make another sound until that sergeant had passed. Well, you might not like it, but I feel like that again. I require your participation. I need you to give me sexual satisfaction. I've missed too many good fucking sessions over the years. Sex is making me happier than I ever thought it could. I intend to keep my sexual goody basket topped up… *vitamin pills and fortifying agents or not.*'

'I don't like your choice of words,' Ivor bleated. 'They demean you. I'm not happy to take any part in your sexual games.' He sat on the edge of the bed, prodding the pills around with a finger.

'If I tell you to play sexual games with me, you will,' Gloria answered him curtly. 'There will be no permissible excuses. The vitamins and other remedies will boost your libido, when they kick in. When you begin to enjoy fucking again and wake up every morning feeling dead randy, I will take extra snacks from the goody basket… so be prepared for it.'

'I'll be bloody dead, anything but bloody randy,' Ivor croaked, his voice trailing off.

'Come, come, soon you won't know your own strength. Starting tomorrow, I'll feed you like a fighting cock. Venison T-bones, Aberdeen Angus fillets of beef sautéed in unsalted Danish butter and Extra Virgin olive oil, and a selection of Sainsbury's imported organically grown exotic vegetables will grace your plate. I need a meaty man… oysters will be not be included on the menu. Of course, there will be bedtime snifters of the best vintage ports and brandies. I've read in women's magazines that when the two drinks are combined they guarantee to raise the blood pressure through erectile gristle and prolong erections.'

Ivor blanched. The thought of a prolonged erection pained him. He would rather suffer Jack Dewsnap's prolonged case of sore balls than that. It seemed he had become Gloria's puppet. Though he had wriggled in an effort to extricate himself from his ordeals he felt Gloria would misuse him until she had put these crazy sexual ideas out of her head. 'I'm aghast,' he said, 'that I now have to engage in sessions of grunting, straining, slobbering, kissing, sweating, heaving, and if you were to start this carry-on before we sleep, having to sleep on the bloody wet spots. When is it ever going to end?'

Chapter 17

At a safe distance from the park toilets, Hamish and Harry took a breather. 'I feel settled now,' Hamish got out, still somewhat short of puff. Blotches of mould streaked their waterproofs, evidence of the fences and walls they'd bounced off as bouts of laughter overcame them.

Handkerchiefs in hands, they dried tears from their eyes and raindrops from their helmet peaks. 'That was the most outrageous firework display I've ever attended. Guy Fawkes himself would have approved.'

'Guy Fawkes… eat your heart out.' Harry said, laughed, spluttered, reeled into Hamish and wound an arm around him. He had used Hamish as a prop each time the need occurred and it had happened often since crossing back over the bridge. Mostly while making shocking guesses at the havoc they had caused amongst the users.

'My sides are splitting,' Harry screeched, hardly able to speak. 'I hope none of the cottagers were near sharp objects when the bangers went in,' he said, spluttering and in a rush to get the words out.

'Their flip-flopping days might be over,' Hamish said between hanky dabs.

'With damaged helmets, they won't be seeking blow-jobs for a while,' Harry said. He felt raindrops running down his back and pushed his collar up and under his helmet.

'It'll be a great laugh in the canteen, by the way.'

'Ken, as long as nothing's gone tits up, like we were seen.'

'There's nothing for us to worry about, I'm sure. Only daft bastards the likes of pervs and us brave weather like this. Now we need to move fast. I need time to settle down before my performance on stage later tonight. I also thought we might mump a curry on the way. We missed out the other night,' Hamish said and looked towards Harry for encouragement to mump a nosh.

'That's a great idea… You know, Hamish, when I was a kid in Leith, we never had Indians.'

'Aye, Harry, Govan was the same, by the way. The only Indians I saw wore baggy trousers, had silly looking beards, and were off the Clan Line ships that tied up down at the docks. They bought all the shite of the day from the local junk shops.'

They set out towards the "Spice of India", an Indian restaurant on the manor. Whilst mumping a nosh there the previous week, they'd found the kitchen a bit unsavoury, though not enough to put them off calling there again.

Turning into the dark alley leading to the kitchen's back door, wiping rain from his helmet, Hamish said, 'I think all coppers are addicted to cups of tea whether it's brewed in the canteen or out on the manor. Some go a bundle on Chinese food, especially the chow mein, even when they know the cooks get credit for assisting the bean shoots to germinate by pissing into the bins they use. As for me it's curries, especially the ring-burning vindaloo.'

'Fuck, the door's bolted,' Harry said, lifting the latch. His torch beam illuminated the smelly dustbin standing outside the door, brimming with curried leftovers. Chicken bones and remnants of red tandoori specialities stuck out from a morass of yellow rice, bits of naan bread and chapattis. A wet cat squealed, streaked from behind the dustbin and raced away.

'You're out of luck, Harry, there's no number twenty-nine on the menu tonight,' Hamish teased. 'And if the cat's been feasting on that crap, it'll have a scorched ringpiece by morning, like us, with any luck.'

'That's some rammy going on inside. It sounds a busy night for the kitchen staff,' Harry said, hearing the loud, staccato Asian chatter.

'Good reason for the bolted door. More likely, it's to keep out mumping coppers,' Hamish opined, and smiled cheesily.

The reason the door might be bolted was forgotten as he banged on it loudly, shaking it on its hinges. Hurried footsteps sounded inside, then the anguished cry of, 'Waat you waant?'

'It's the police, open the fucking door,' Hamish shouted back.

The bolt was drawn and the latch lifted. The door opened and Hamish shouldered his way in. A small Asian washer-up cowered, his face upturned towards the two wet figures. Hamish's hand appeared from beneath his cape and patted the washer-up on a shoulder, matey-like, but wetting it. 'Don't go out there, Lofty, you'll drown,' he warned.

They passed along a pathway formed by stacked bags of rice and onions, large jars of mango chutney, tins of spices, trays of onion bajis and tiers of papadums ready for serving, towards the cooking area.

The warm, inviting miasma of oriental smells pervaded everywhere. In the distance, they could see the chef speedily lifting his feet and dancing backwards to avoid the flames leaping from a frying pan.

The pathway was narrow and under a low ceiling. Hamish was leading the way. Ducking to dodge cobwebs laden with the shrivelled corpses of flies and bluebottles, he threw an arm back over his shoulder. A web-load of dust and dead things cascaded over Harry.

'Big shite,' Harry chided, brushing the mess from his waterproofs.

'The sanctuary beloved of all hungry, curry-mumping coppers and brave Jocks,' Hamish voiced to no one in particular and smacked his lips noisily.

Curry colours streaked the wall above the range. The smell of hot fat, scorched spices and garlic tinged the air. The stockpot gurgling on a stand above a gas flame held broiler-chicken bits, onions, garlic and spices, all adding to the tantalising, spicy aroma.

Hamish spotted a stool and lurched towards it. Moving it with a boot, he placed it next to the stockpot and sat down.

The owner, Mr. Kava Naqvi, Hamish buttonholed in conversation. Kava was engaged in a triple function: he dried plates, other crockery and his runny nose with the same manky, used tablecloth.

'Business is good, eh, Kava?' Hamish asked, winking at Harry.

'Business is never good. Rates are high, chickens, garlic, ghee and spices expensive. I pay my staff too much and I have three wives and twenty-one children to keep back in Pakistan. The wife I have here, she takes the rest of my money and spends it down the bladdy bingo hall. I cannot make money in present circumstances,' he replied. He glanced at Hamish, surveying him low. Knowing police appetites, he didn't make eye contact, just wondered what cheap offering he could get away with next.

'You waant coffee, tea, sugar and milk?' Kava didn't like the look of Hamish; he was big and his appetite might be the same!

'I'd rather have a curry,' Hamish said, eyeing up the cups Kava was drying. 'It's a cold and dirty night out there.'

'Wat you waant, Vindaloo, samthing warm?'

'A King Prawn Vindaloo will go down nicely,' Hamish said. 'What about you, Harry, do you fancy the same?'

'Get it on a plate,' Harry said. 'I'm starved.'

Kava winced.

The chef began his preparations. Plunging a ladle into the chip pan, he transferred some multipurpose oil into a blackened frying pan and rattled it onto the range over a roaring gas flame. Using the same ladle, he scooped some spices from boxes and mixed them into the sizzling oil, along with the same amount of chilli powder. A devilish grin cracked his face. The potion seethed and Harry reeled. Hamish licked his lips; there was torture to come. The chef tossed in some soused onions, blending them in with the spices and flames leapt from the pan, the hot oil spitting out and igniting. A paltry portion of smallish shrimps he tossed into the fiery mix. Two scoops of stock from the pot completed the recipe. When the stock had boiled off and thickened, the chef served the fiery dish on beds of congealed rice.

Hamish immediately attacked his meal and began wolfing it down. Harry nibbling gingerly at the edges of his, waiting for it to cool, took time to look about the kitchen where activities were disturbing.

Waiters were buzzing about, chatting away to each other in their own language, scraping leftovers into another curry-encrusted dustbin, before dropping the plates into a sink of murky water. In the adjoining sink, an assistant chef busily assassinated chickens, slitting their throats with a curved knife. Bleeding them to death was a religious requirement. The birds had already suffered cooped up in battery cages, where they'd spent most of their lives and where frustrated neighbours had plucked their rear ends bare.

A canopy of steam rose from the sink of boiling water along with a flurry of feathers and billowed around the assistant chef. Blood spurted from the necks of birds fluttering and flapping in their death throes. The assistant tore at the sodden carcasses. It seemed before the birds were dead; they were still jerking as he removed skin and feathers together: plucking made simple. He gutted them with the same knife and threw the innards into the dustbin. In quarters, the chickens disappeared into the kitchen staff's own curry pot.

Hamish was completely unperturbed at the ceremonial and shouted across to Harry. 'Are you ready for a top-up?'

'I've had enough… bagged up,' Harry said, shunning the offer and wafting a hand over his tongue, poking out through overheated lips. 'You've to perform your act later, remember, and I'm already worried if I'll feel okay in the morning.'

Kava ignored their empty plates, showed complete disinterest in providing further curries free of charge. 'Thank you for not taking more food from a poor man,' he said, sniffed and re-wiped his nose on the cloth.

Kava chose two cups, newly dried, dropped a teabag into each and splashed in some milk. While he poured in hot water, Hamish lurched to his feet and looked towards Harry for guidance, his eyes asking the question: 'Did you see what wiped those cups dry?'

'Hamish would like another free prawn Vindaloo?' Kava asked stressing the free. Then he felt safe. Hamish was up on his feet and looked ready to leave.

'No, you can relax,' Hamish said, sucking at the tea, his lips lying lightly on the rim of the cup Kava handed him. 'The chef can have the rest of the night off. Young Harry and I have business to attend to.'

Kava left them and went out front, into the restaurant. Harry said, 'I appreciate Asian businessmen, whatever their race. They work hard and their principles are good. Keep on taking money until our arms drop off describes it. Consider this, though. Knowing, as we do, how many coppers take advantage of their generosity, those first principles must take a severe backward step for Indian restaurant owners.'

'With the lurch towards unprofitability first noticed at about the same time as coppers discovered the hospitality available once inside the back door,' Hamish said, getting his mate's drift.

The weather hadn't improved as they left the restaurant. Booking off time was close and the station was only a shortcut away. More nonsense beckoned. Once off duty, they were meeting up with most of the strength of West Clegham nick to raise funds for Constable Tonks' farewell gift.

Chapter 18

'There's little doubt; coppers working out in the sticks understand policing priorities better than those "uptown", and that's why we're all here tonight.' In the function room of the King's Arms pub, the manor pub known locally as the "Rozzers' Arms", Harry was addressing those of the milling throng stood with him. Midnight, the witching hour, neared and laughing coppers, most of them hot and sweaty, some supposed to be on beat duty, some not, were standing in groups quaffing beer. All had bought tickets to raise funds for Constable Tonks' retirement gift. Some of them would return to their beats in the early hours of the following day in no fit state. Others, like Hamish and Harry, would parade again for duty at the tortuous hour of 05:45 the following morning.

The entertainment had been continuous since 10 p.m. Any copper with a singing voice, a joke to tell or something to say had got up on stage and done his bit. Hamish's act, though a secret, coppers thought could be nothing other than hilarious. Hamish's sense of humour and indifference to his duties had aroused curiosity in some coppers on the same relief, and others who also plodded beats on the relatively tranquil, "out in the sticks" manor.

Some throaty chuckles erupted. Harry had begun explaining how he perceived the ensuing mayhem within the Gents following the bombing raid with squibs. 'Headlines in the Clegham Weekend Advertiser might read like this. Police suggest explosions in bog were fairies banging away at magic rings. Or this: fairies using bog are hospitalised. Bruised rings among the injuries. Clegham Council explain. Explosions linked to escaping methane gas from a busted ring.'

While working early turn the previous week, Hamish had spent his afternoons liaising with the pub licensee. Known affectionately as Fat Bob, he was a balding, retired, marine electrician with a penchant for, and ability in, the art of sound control and the production of special effects. Together they'd set up the show's format using magnetic solenoids, gas cylinders, small explosive charges and a Moog synthesizer.

At ten minutes to midnight, Hamish dragged Harry towards the dressing room, to begin preparations for his performance. Pieces of theatrical equipment made Harry curious. Nothing took his interest more than the stout, six-foot-tall wooden post covered with a stocking of blue velvet, standing on a plinth of roughly hewn, heavier wood. 'What the fuck's that?' he enquired, quizzically.

Hamish was undressing, but turned and said, 'It's the farting-post. I suppose it's a sort of vertical straining bar,' Hamish said. With one leg still in his uniform trousers, he demonstrated with a firm grip on the post.

Hamish's wardrobe was a huge pair of ex-American Marine's trousers purchased from an Army & Navy store. A trapdoor, tailored into the rear, opened to show a joke-shop-purchased, skin-tone-coloured, plastic buttocks set thrusting out of the serge.

'My performance tonight I've taken seriously, Harry. I've a lapel microphone to clip to the side of the trap door. It will give my performance authenticity. A Moog synthesizer produced the sounds requiring tonal quality at the top end of my high-pitched deliveries. The Sub-Base woofer, a Frequency-Resonator and an echo chamber produced the thunderous bass required at the bottom end of the scale.'

Fat Bob stood at the control desk, tweaking sliders and turning knobs. The speakers squealed at the stage front and he moved the sliders back to predetermined marks. Suddenly a thought struck him and he rocked back on his heels then wiped a tear from an eye. 'This must be the funniest act I've ever promoted. It'll bring the house down. Your mates are going to end themselves when you play the whole of "The Londonderry Air". I'm just glad I don't have to introduce you, I'd be laid flat out, pissing myself.'

Hamish was about to imitate one of the heroes of the Victorian era, Joseph Pujol, an elegant Frenchman, blessed with a sphincter of extraordinary elasticity, whose stage name was Le Petomaine, famous as the "first fiddle of flatulence". He could inhale air through a hole in the seat of his trousers, then control its expulsion in a most melodic fashion. He convulsed audiences on the French cabaret circuit with his birdcall imitations and tunes on his flatus flute, including "La Marseillaise", complete with cannon shots. Twenty years back, Leonard Rossiter had portrayed him in a film. Hamish was attempting nothing so elaborate. He would fart "The Londonderry Air", though in reality, he would act out a recording of sounds generated by the Moog.

Harry's first contribution to Hamish's act was to place the farting post on the chalk mark on the stage.

Out front, coppers gathered around, watching him place the post, their faces turned up, showing interest in the proceedings.

Suddenly, the curtains billowed outwards. Hamish pushed through and lumbered towards the farting-post. His face was wreathed in his cheesiest smile and shone redder than the skin of an Edam cheese. Reaching the post, he gripped it double-handed and stood, legs-akimbo.

That action cued Harry to perform a spot check. To one side of the stage, he found two extra-long back scratchers and moved behind Hamish. He pulled down sharply on the trousers' trapdoor and stepped back in mock horror. To chortles from the audience, he threw his hands over his eyes. Using the small hands at the ends of the poles, he made to inspect Hamish's buttocks, peering into the chasm with one eye, then the other. His tap on the lapel microphone boomed through the speakers.

'Thorough investigation of the performing area reveals no mechanical devices, penny whistles, clarinet reeds, sousaphone mouthpieces or evidence of small explosive packages. What you hear will be Hamish's educated sphincter performing this wonderful, old Irish favourite,' he announced on his return to the stage front.

Hamish straightened up, grimacing. For the benefit of the audience, he placed a hand in the small of his back, feigning pain. Then he gripped the farting post and appeared to be concentrating.

The lights went down, the audience hushing to coughs and half-smothered giggles. To total silence, the strains of "O Danny Boy, the pipes, the pipes are calling", played with perfect tonal quality, mimicking faithfully the strains of Uillean Pipes, filtered through the speakers. Every note came over clear, played in tune and with precise timing. Fat Bob pressed a button, released some compressed air and the stage curtains directly behind Hamish ballooned, as if a tent ripped from the ground in a hurricane. A roar of approval rose from the audience. "From glen to glen and down the mountainside", had sweet resonance and timbre.

The difficult part of the air arrived. Hamish had to go up scale: "If sung it would be And I'll be *heeeeeeere* in sunshine or in shadow", he reached the top-most note with perfect strength, accent, timing and astonishing piquancy. The top note held, cued Fat Bob into further action. Dust eddied from gaps between floorboards, and an empty pint pot, sitting on the edge of the bar, shattered into several pieces. The devastation, caused by a small explosive charge, gave the impression that a high-pitched, anally generated, sonic wave had disintegrated the glass.

Mature individuals fell about, rocked and reeled, were overcome and speechless. It raised serious doubts whether the night-shift attendees were capable of completing their duties.

Hamish showered and dressed. Back in the function suite, he found the many pints of Guinness, bought by appreciative colleagues, building up on table. In the course of the next hour, he laughed uproariously and supped them all. As the witching hour passed, his belly was heaving, under strain and suffering the prawn curry fighting Guinness for dedicated passage through his bowels.

Chapter 19

Jack raced from the Gents to the car, opened the door and slumped inside. A trail of persons unknown to him were splashing through the rain and racing the other way. No one moved towards him. He moved the car and parked up in another secluded spot. He had to kill time. Hanging around, too, was the smell of the human shit, displaced from the condom as it struck his face. Injured, dishevelled and smelly, he couldn't return home to shower until he was sure Daphne was upstairs and asleep.

He reclined his seat and eased his cock from his Y-fronts. Even in the subdued interior light, the laceration streaking red down the length of it looked bad. His spirits soared, briefly, on thinking the injury only looked jagged and sore because he was flaccid. The deepest laceration was to the head, which had his spirits plummeting. In the end, it *was* bad. While his cock healed, it would be tender. When healed, anyone feeling around it would easily detect the ridges of the wound and an inquisitive eye couldn't fail to miss it.

He hung a handkerchief out the window to dampen, then gently dabbed at his cock and removed the blood, the remnants of his ejaculation and saliva.

He glanced at the interior mirror. His reflected features were spelling out a message, particularly for him: 'someone you know has had you over, you sad bastard.' Excrement was sticking to his face. He dabbed at where he could see. The smell was still hanging about, as was the affected voice hammering away in his brain, saying, 'Over here, Claudie.'

The house was in darkness when he pulled into the drive. Indoors, he acted casual, taking the stairs slowly, his normal way for that time of the morning. He entered the bathroom and locked the door. In the mirror, he saw a brown trail of shit spilling from an ear, spattered chunks of it sticking to the lobe. He puked into the pan. Ripping up his soiled Y-fronts to pieces, as Hulk Hogan does a T-shirt, he flushed them and the puke away.

Using some diluted Dettol, he sponged his cock clean and then wrapped antiseptic gauze around it. In the bedroom, he tucked his cock and its medicated swathe gently into a clean pair of Y-fronts. Then he crawled into bed. He spent some time lying on his back, silently cursing Rowley, before finally falling into fitful sleep.

Chapter 20

The drinking session in The King's Arms carried on until 2 a.m. The night shift attendees staggered back to their beats, some showing regret at having to leave. Others telephoned taxis and went home. Hamish and Harry were the last to leave, drinking malt whisky with Fat Bob, until he slid down the bar and flaked out on the floor.

Harry lived in the single coppers' section house, close by the nick. A corkscrew run and a few bounces off walls as wet as the ones he had encountered earlier and he was home. As his ear descended towards the pillow, the ceiling circled before his eyes. He closed them tight and sleep came quickly, soothed by the rain pattering on the windowpane and the threnody of the wind finding gaps in the loose-fitting frame. Lying heavily in the pit of his stomach was the at-odds mixture of Guinness and curry, which rumbled noisily, assuring a restless, dream-laden night.

*****

Hamish staggered into the station yard trying to recall where he had parked up his moped. In his path to where he thought it should be, he found the duty inspector's car. Lurching and giggling, he urinated over the driver's door handle.

Hamish's transfer to West Clegham nick meant he rode his moped west along Bow Road to get home from work. Nothing had improved regarding the moped. He still had to pedal it like hell to encourage it to fire into life. Wanting to get home quickly, he could do without its idiosyncrasies.

He recovered his moped and straddled it. Rocking perilously, he leaned to one side, feeling for the petrol valve and the carburettor tickler.

The road home had an initial, downhill slope for at least one hundred yards. Pushing off with his feet, the clutch disengaged, the moped gained speed down the slope. When Hamish engaged the clutch, the machine shuddered into life, its exhaust banging and smoking. Vibrating under its load, the throttle wide open, it reached the speed of 15 mph, bulldozing his bulk through the wind-driven rain. Hamish always rode flat-out, looking awesome in the saddle. Fortunately, not many persons were abroad for him to put the shits up at that hour of a wet morning.

An area car had parked up in the shadows of an alley, its crew steadily munching at curry carryouts and uninterested, for the moment, in miscreants that might pass by their gaze. Hamish flashed past and saw them there. The radio operator, looking up to lick sauce from his fingers, spotted his mock salute.

Speeding at 15.3 mph, his head down low, Hamish heard the engine of the police car burst into life, then the ding of its bells. The car pulled alongside, a hand and a head sticking out of the front-passenger-door window. Another hand, flailing a length of naan bread from the rear window, signalled him to pull over and stop. Hamish looked up. Both radio operator and observer recognized him. Leering and laughing they shouted, 'Fuck off, fat Jock bastard.' The area car accelerated, the crew dumping carryout containers, hoping to hit him with them, before turning down a side street up ahead.

The complex of flats and maisonettes in which Hamish lived housed, in nearly every case, a police recruit and his family desperately saving the deposit to purchase a private residence. Escaping the morbid depression of living in barrack-type housing, too close to many others doing the same job, was usually only achievable thus.

Hamish and Jenny had lived in the complex for nigh on ten years. Alas, Hamish was the exception to the saving rule, spending a small mortgage each month on booze. For that reason, and his other shortcomings, Jenny was ever ready with a tongue-lashing for him.

Hamish cut the engine and freewheeled silently towards his front door. Usually, Jenny was in bed by midnight. On the rare occasions that she was still up when he arrived home in the early hours, pissed, he had received a barrage of verbal abuse.

Through the open kitchen window, he heard the Hoover purring away. Normally, it sounded like a well-contented barber's cat. Now, like the barber's cat, it was proving to be just as unproductive. Bangs and loudly exclaimed obscenities floated out as he looked in. Blearily, he made out Jenny's moist and heavily freckled face, unhappy that the machine wouldn't pick up the crumbs he had dropped on the floor at lunchtime.

She was practicing on the Hoover before getting to him.

Jenny was a small, rotund woman with remarkable physical strength, character and a Scottish accent that hadn't faded during her years in London. Hamish always stoked the blazing moods she had. With calf muscles like Himalayan Sherpas, she had walked all over him many times.

'Where have you been raking to at this time of the morning, stink bomb?' she yelled at him. Staggering through the front door, Hamish had a blurred view of the muscles of her tongue, her tonsils, her stance, arms folded across her chest, looking cross. Hamish's eyes were incapable of fixing onto any object for more than a second. He just wanted to feel an ear hit the pillow, not use it for listening to her.

Unsure of his attention, she berated him anyway, while dispensing what she considered was sound advice. 'Isn't it time you mumped some Warfarin suppositories, stuff them up your arse and rid yourself of the rats you keep up there?' she enquired.

Jenny's complaints about his habits were old hat to Hamish. As he had to be up again at 5a.m. he wasn't about to waste time arguing. He hung his waterproof behind the door and bustled past her, eyes focusing poorly, charily towards the stairs. Jenny stood behind him and watched his progress, ready to rebuke swiftly any stumble or trip.

He reached the top safely and entered the bathroom, pausing there to urinate. In the bedroom, he sat swaying on the edge of the bed, undressed and threw his clothes carelessly onto a nearby chair. Toppling over, his ear an inch from the pillow, he heard Jenny bawl at him, 'You've pissed all over the floor again, you fat, useless pig!' Five minutes later, Jenny had set the alarm for 5 a.m. and tumbled into bed, keeping a safe distance from his back.

******

The electronically generated numbers on the radio alarm said 5 a.m. and sleep in the MacNab household was about to end. Hamish was snoring compulsively with stentorian resonant clamour. His mouth was agape and he slobbered a colourful, oriental variety of mucus onto his pillow. His body was jerking convulsively and strange, guttural utterances interrupted his bouts of snoring. Beneath the sheets, short, fruity, reverberant animal noises purred from an orifice elsewhere on his anatomy.

Behind him, her back to his, but space aplenty in between, long-suffering Jenny lay. The loose cardigan she wore on top of her nightie protected her shoulders against the removal of bedclothes in the night by the pig sharing the bed with her.

Hamish is dreaming as he surfaces towards wakefulness; then, he freewheels into a full, technicoloured nightmare. He cannot prevent his transportation to a strange, forbidding place. His face creases, he blows bubbles from pursed lips and he frowns. His wet-eyed mother looks at him from beneath straggly, unkempt hair. She mouths and he lip-reads, "My rebel son."

For fuck's sake, has he committed a heinous crime or something? Rain is falling heavily upon his father who, damply, from beneath a flat cap, is offering him advice. 'Keep your wallet in your back pocket and your breeks well-fastened and you'll come to no harm.'

He gathers his father believes that if an Act of Parliament made him a copper, then only an Act of God will make him a gentleman. Why this shit now he questions, his mouth working silently, words not forming?

Now he's on an express train. The carriages are rattling and twisting, the wheels singing along the track. The diesel engine is roaring. He's mystified as to where it's heading. He notes that he's naked and sharing the carriage with two women wearing army khaki. One looks nice and inviting. She is standing pawing him, her fingers smelling of curry, vinegar and-chips; slowly, her nails are moving down his chest and over his belly towards...

The larger of the two women is lying on the facing seat, making animal sounds. An empty whisky bottle, screwed-up newspapers, curry carryout packages and some cold chips are sitting on the window shelf. He smiles. A party they've had and he wishes he could have joined in. The chip he reaches for floats away, out of his reach.

He hears the squeal of brakes and the train stops almost instantly. The reclining woman begins to levitate from the seat, moves sideways and then slowly sinks to the carriage floor.

He falls onto the other seat together with the pussy with the paws. He puckers his lips towards hers, seeking a kiss. His lips never reach her sweet-and-sour smelling pair. Silently, she is mouthing a name, He reads, 'Big Jessie.' Is that her or *me*, he wonders. He plunges his puckered lips in the direction of her tantalising mouth and again they fail to connect. Breasts, big and inviting, are bulging from the top of her blouse. He stretches both hands out towards them, to fondle them quickly or the erection paining him will be of little use.

The woman levitates from the floor, does a magic carpet trick out of the door and becomes vertical in the passageway. He assumes she is going for a pee. His pained bladder is telling him he is desperate for one, too.

Big Jessie isn't into kissing. Always, always, she moves her pouting lips beyond his reach. Beckoning, she encourages him to touch the breasts she is jiggling in her hands. Smiling stupidly, he reaches for them.

There's a jolt as the train starts up. The carriage door opens with a bang. A khaki object in level flight passes down the corridor. Peeing Woman appears at the doorway, grinning hideously. She has a toothless hole in the centre of her face. It's where her mouth should be and it reminds him of the Govan entrance to the Clyde Tunnel. Feeling bilious, he sees her eyes cross and one of them go walkabout, wildly rotating in her head, spinning psychedelically, like a top.

Big Jessie points a finger with a lengthy and ragged nail at him. She crooks her finger, summoning him into the passageway in the direction from where pee woman has just returned.

Big Jessie beckons and leads him towards the toilet. A door swings back and forth, banging hard against the jamb.

He sings:

'There are pricks and bollocks on the wall.
Some are large and some are small.'

A coating of technicoloured vomit reaches up the walls to some humorous drawings appended there by an unknown artist. He chuckles. His body shakes. There is pleasure in toilet humour.

On a morass of spurious stomach contents staining the back of the pedestal, the lost dentures, open wide, grin back at him and circle a spewed-up green pea, like a dog chasing its own tail.

He sings:

'This is a bridge too far.
Who left the door ajar?
She insists he picks them up.
But he's not a mucky pup.'

He carries the teeth wrapped in newspaper, along the corridor and presents them to Cakehole Kate (his new name for her). In the void of her mouth, lubricated by spew in turmoil, they slip easily into place. The lips closing around them become a blemish in the side of a turnip, which turns into a sheep's mouth holding the turnip in a vice-like grip. Suddenly he hears a welcoming interruption, for he desperately needs a piss, 'Ron Davis, The Under Secretary of State for Wales, who was…' The radio alarm has gone off. It's 5 a.m. and the dream ends. The thump he gets in the buttocks from a heel attached to Jenny's muscular leg, is the practical alternative to the snooze alarm, and power-kicks him further away from her.

'Get up and wipe up your spew, you filthy pig,' she rages at him.

Eyes wide, sticky and not fully awake, Hamish slid his feet out the side of the bed and into the wet, slippy and sloppy mess. The view between his knees points to his feet having spread a film of regurgitated curry and stuff across the bedside carpet. From the undigested bits of shrimps mixed with Guinness and goo oozing from between his toes, he guesses the spew is his.

Ten minutes later, quickly showered, dressed for the elements and still feeling a tad unwell, he straddles the moped and heads towards West Clegham nick.

******

In the section house, it is 05:29, one minute before his alarm rattles out its unwelcome message. Harry is dreaming. He's suffering from sudden bladder loosening. Nightmarishly, it seems he's contracted a previously unknown prurient disease. It's pissing him off and his feet lift sharply, as if he's doing drill while floating over rough terrain.

It seems he's trekking through the Kyles O' Bute, searching deep gorges, apparently bent on profitably spiriting away a pretty sheep before the winter mating season begins. The rabid condition known as "Sporran Rash" appears from behind a gorse bush, attaches itself to his sporran, and begins assaulting the fur. Large holes are appearing.

He thinks the sporran useless and throws it away. The rash, making a dash for a tilt at his kilt, begins to streak across the mazy network of his filibeg. At the hem, displaying mountaineering skills of high quality, it transfers to his knees.

A crude man appears. It is Hamish. Hamish is making rude noises and applauding a pincer movement that will direct the rash towards his testicles, which he is caressing protectively in both of his hands. If not the rash, then the stream of hot water he detects running close by will scald them.

Discomfort is multiplying by the second, spreading rapidly and creating pressure around tender parts. Hot liquid is splashing onto his toes. His knees are jerking and his feet stamping.

Pain is wracking his feet. He feels weightless setting off with rocket-like velocity across heath and heather, remnants of his filibeg flapping behind him, for Edinburgh. At midnight, he is sweeping up Princes Street, where he meets seven sailors on shore leave from a gigantic floating toilet block docked at Leith Harbour.

Pulling remnants of his apparel tightly about him, limiting the drag, he accelerates towards cooler climes. Red, raw and rabid, he is hurtling through the night like an Earth-locked comet, arriving in Wales under a steaming cloud of his own creation. Suspicions there are he's a piss-artist arriving late for an Eisteddfod. Assurances are on hand: while playing in the nude he will be popular and big out front.

Zit-infested fans, each with small, black moustaches positioned directly beneath their noses, and of Germanic naturist pursuits, are taking a poke at him, pelting him with bananas, half-strangled jellied eels, and dangerously out of sell-by date, rock-hard, Welsh cakes. He can smell pickled onions.

The cry of "Pissports…pissports" is dragging him closer to wakefulness. Rude questions are blasting from the lips of Dai, the local excise and immigration Johnny, ever alert for the arrival of midnight intruders using old sheep-drover's trails and transporting parasites without a permit.

The cries of 'Ma Sporran,' 'Ma Sporran,' are prising his eyes open. He is standing at his sink, cock in hand. Sergeant Dai Morgan, the block caretaker, is watching him as he directs a stream of piss into the plughole. The hot tap, running full-bore, is spraying his testicles and splashing onto his toes.

The sergeant is standing framed in his doorway, bathed in the backlight of the passageway. He switches Harry's room light on and says loudly, 'You fucking drunken prick, MacSporran, why don't you invest in a piss pot?'

'I've had a troublesome night's sleep,' Harry says aloud.

At 5:30 a.m., Monday morning, the single constables' section house had become a hive of activity. Peaceful sleeps were ending. Alarm clocks with differing tones were ringing out. Doors were banging and loud voices on every landing were waking early-turn constables from their slumbers.

******

At 5:45 a.m., Harry wobbled into the parade room at West Clegham nick, glanced quickly around, then joined some friendly faces, which he recognised as fund-raising-night attendees, gathered at the rear of the parade room. They all look hung-over and in no fit state to take up a beat. Shuffling their feat, they were all manoeuvring for a place behind another copper, in attempts to hide their inability from the sergeant.

The strained put-put-putting of Hamish's moped filled the yard. He, too, looked the worse for wear as he shouldered the door, lurched into the parade room and stumbled towards the rear wall. Close to Harry, he wheezed 'You don't look good.'

'Kettle calling pot, eh?' Harry replied.

Sergeant Shrapnel entered. At risk of him noticing them, the feat shuffling continued.

'Your eyes are like, er, two cherries in a snowman's face,' Harry said.

'Aye. Right. My head's thumping. It was worth it, though. A great night, wasn't it?' Hamish said, jamming an elbow into Harry's ribs and waxing into a naff smile.

'Watch it. Don't draw attention. Your breaths smell like the Taj's dustbin with added cat's piss. It'll crease Shrapnel if he gets a whiff.'

Sergeant Shrapnel, his diligence slipping, shagged-out and baggy eyed from Maggie-lust, yawned repeatedly and allocated beats automatically, detected nothing amiss.

The sergeant appointed Hamish and Harry to the same home beat.

Wanting to forego the usual pre-beat brew up in the station canteen, Hamish cajoled Harry away from the canteen steps. 'Forget the canteen, it's fresh morning air we need. We'll get all and more on the walk to Ted's Diner. Other coppers tell me it's a friendly, early morning eatery. We can take our time there over bacon butties.'

'That sounds good,' Harry said, 'the curry festering in my guts overnight is restless and I'm needful of something to calm it.'

'I'll suffer full-blown indigestion if I don't get my hands on some Rennies,' Hamish predicted.

The weather remained wet and blustery, the sky overcast, pointing to another shift wearing waterproofs. When Hamish's thoughts turned to grub, though, he would waddle his encased bulk through worse to get to it.

Ten minutes into the shift, dripping water and looking even more pallid, Hamish began to wobble, his breathing becoming patchy. Visions of Ted's Diner, just around the corner, kept him going.

Harry was trying to match Hamish's pace. He was unable to draw level with him. They both slowed visibly, the diner in sight. Harry said, 'It might only be an illusion, Hamish, but your belly always appears to be two feet in front of me. No matter how fast I walk, I never seem able to get past it.'

'Och, don't worry, you're doing well by the way, we're almost there.' Hamish stopped abruptly a pace from the door and allowed Harry past. 'There you are. You're in front now. I'll let you through the door first. It's your turn for the teas and the butties.'

Chapter 21

Jack awoke at 7:30 a.m. on the Monday following Halloween. He was alone again and on this occasion, glad of it. He hadn't slept well and the gauze bandaging his cock had worked off during a twitchy night. Now, an erection, if he couldn't control the blood surge quickly with a negative thought, was about to stretch ripped flesh. He got out of bed, opened the curtains and stood by his bedroom window. In the dreary, morning light he watched and listening to the rain pelting the glass. Blanking his mind, he stood until he felt the surge ebbing.

He chilled when he viewed his damaged cock, shuddered and breathed in deeply through clenched teeth; the lesion furrowed jaggedly and deeply into his flesh. Carefully, he lifted his cock, laid it in the palm of a hand and turned it gently this way and that, examining it. Pulling his foreskin slowly back, he viewed the gash on the head. He feared it would heal leaving a noticeable ridge. 'Suffering fuck!' he erupted. Anyone seeing it would suspect only one thing: contact with a tooth had caused it, 'suffering fuck!'

******

Ivor didn't think his situation desirable either when he awakened at 7:30 a.m. that morning. Gloria had risen earlier and already a mug of ginseng tea was sitting steaming on his bedside cabinet. Then he heard her climbing the stairs again. 'Crikey,' he cried and leapt out of bed. She could return, sex in mind, and made a grab for him!

'Why can't I have the Earl Grey tea that I like?' he asked her, bitterly, as she entered the bedroom.

'Because the ginseng will fortify you for this morning's fuck,' Gloria replied.

'OOOooooOOOh, not that again.'

'Yes that again; this time, with some assistance from a new friend.' Gloria held out her hand, a Dr Blakoe's famous energiser ring in the palm, for Ivor to get a good view.

'What in heaven's name is that?' Ivor bellowed, his face twisting. She moved the ring back and forth beneath his nose, making sure he had a close up of it. His fears heightened. Only one part of his flagging anatomy fitted the hole in the rubberised, doughnut-shaped object.

'I saw it advertised in a magazine and ordered one,' Gloria explained. 'The device will fit around the base of your cock and stop it from drooping. The device will help keep your cock nice and hard until the vitamins kick in. Bring it to the kitchen with you. This morning, we will try it out whilst performing in a new position. In doing so, we will attempt to prove Billy's idea of shagging to time an egg. If you don't perform to the standard I require of you, your eggs will be runny and you will not like that one bit, my dear.'

Ivor shaved slowly. This morning an unexplored "Vale of Sexual Hell" awaited him in the kitchen, of all places. The look on the bleak face peering back at him from the mirror horrified him and suddenly, a sharp spasm indicated the proximity of a bowel movement. Seated in the WC, he spun that out. In the shower, he washed all over twice, dragging that out. Gloria's demands could wait. 'Time a bloody egg? Whatever bloody next?' he blurted, and spat out shower water in a display of disgust. 'The silly woman does not know what she is saying or doing.' He dried and dressed in boxer shorts, trousers, braces and shirt.

On the stairs and in the hallway, his slippered feet scuffed miserably and clicks sounded from the corner of his twisted lips. On the walls of his route of inestimable despair, reminders of a happier past life hung. Framed photographs showed him smartly attired in the uniform of each rank in which he had served. Some showed Gloria wearing the uniform of the Salvation Army.

Gloria's preparations for the morning's session included the provision of appropriate music. The lounge Hi-Fi unit thudded out the smooth round sounds of Mike and the Mechanics' "Looking Back over My Shoulder". 'She's playing that number too bloody often and too bloody loud,' Ivor whinged, feeling doubly accursed as he entered the kitchen.

Usually, he breakfasted on two three-minute boiled eggs and a side order of toasted, buttered soldiers. From the evidence presenting itself so far this morning, that wouldn't be the case now. There were no expectations whatsoever that he'd enjoy the alternative: the surprise sexual position. He cursed his luck, 'Time a bloody egg. How ridiculous! I'd still be leading a contented life had she not seen that blue comedian, bloody Billy Bagman.'

Gloria was leaning over the kitchen sink, her nightdress depicting Jurassic park characters hitched up over her shoulders. Girding her backside were black, crotchless knickers, fitted back to front and thrusting towards him. The view didn't turn Ivor on. Expressing his disgust, he sounded 'Aaaaaaagh.'

'No, it's not the pirate position this morning,' Gloria said, then wiggled her bottom and encouraged her knickers to slide slowly to her ankles. Her hands appeared behind her, the fingers of each taking a grip on her spotty, cellulite-furrowed buttocks, which she then swung about whilst holding them apart.

'I suppose I'm to feel enticed,' Ivor whined.

'Forget your whingeing,' Gloria railed. Then she quietly cooed, 'Will you shawft me in the kitchen this morning?'

Ivor had heard Gloria repeat the joke when he wasn't supposed to hear and guessed that if he repeated those words, the entire distressing affair would be over expeditiously. 'Aaaaaaagh,' he grimaced, groaned and asked sullenly. 'Why do you wish me to shawft you in the kitchen?'

'Because I want to time your eggs.'

'Are you preparing hard ones or runny ones?'

'Hard ones.'

'You'll be bloody lucky,' he gasped, mournfully.

'You've spoiled it. You should have said I gave her a runny one and left,' Gloria scolded.

With a 'Humph,' he let his trousers fall to the floor. The boxer shorts followed. Flaccid and in no mood to engage in any of Gloria's games, he nevertheless attempted to raise the necessary erectile gristle… Ginseng's promise was still many doses away. Hammering his cock onto Gloria's reddening buttocks had little effect either.

Beleaguered and desperate, he slipped the Dr Blakoe's ring into place at the base of his cock. 'Bloody instrument of phallic torture,' he wailed.

His cock turned red and hardened. Taking a firm grip on Gloria's ample love handles, he swayed, grunted, thrust blindly and missed, hit the wrong spot and cursed before finally entering her.

Coupling initiated, Gloria's hand shot out. Two tactically placed Sainsbury's brown, free-range farm eggs she dropped into a saucepan of salted, boiling water. Previously prepared, it was bubbling away on the gas range.

With his boxer shorts lodged around his knees, Ivor's arse began working like the proverbial "fiddler's elbow". Despairing that the fiddler hadn't chosen a shortened number and desperate to complete his role quickly, he dragged into his mind the filthiest pictures from the dirtiest books he had ever seen seized by police. The Diplodocus on Gloria's nightdress, a much-treasured birthday present to her from a favourite niece, stared back balefully and jerked in sympathy with her oscillating shoulders. Underdone eggs or not, he wasn't about to break the three-minute shagging record.

Words leaping into his mind kept time with his laboured thrusts. Jack......Dewsnap……you……lucky……bastard.

The rhythm accelerated and the words kept coming.

Whap……whap…..click….whap…click..whap..whap..click until the sound of his loins crashing against Gloria's buttocks obliterated his thought processes.

Ivor's knees had weakened and, as he ejaculated, he slumped away from Gloria to sit on a chair. Gloomily, he viewed his blood-gorged cock. Mortified at what he saw, he uttered two rapid 'Click, clicks,' clawed at the energiser ring, tore it off and threw it away from him as if a piece of rank ordure.

Gloria lolled over the sink, breathing heavily, sucking on the collar of her nightdress. Ivor saw this as an act of fanciful, multi-orgasmic satisfaction. Immediately his displeasure turned to anger. How many more times might he have to participate in this madness? Suddenly he had a burgeoning hatred of anyone who might have insalubrious thoughts. At the nick, he'd be particularly scathing and nasty towards constables. He had earmarked two Jocks who had given him woe for special attention. They would get some comeuppance for that and for making disparaging remarks about Freemasons!

Chapter 22

A second, much cooler and prolonged shower had done nothing to calm Superintendent Bunce's ire. He drove from his home to the station incensed, the sink-ender the prime mover behind his mood. A disappointing breakfast of runny eggs and burnt toast had added to his fury. 'Bloody late again, damn the woman,' he muttered, turning into the station yard. 9:27 a.m. had flashed up on the car clock.

Bursting through the front office door, he found Sergeant Shrapnel at his desk, checking the expenses payment book. The sergeant thought the Superintendent looked of a mean disposition, demanding tactful handling. He was gaunter, watery-eyed, haunted looking, his jowls sagging and red. 'All correct, sir,' the sergeant said crisply then remained quiet, keeping his distance.

Finding nothing worthy of rebuke during his initial inspection, the Superintendent did the books. He had calmed somewhat by the time he opened the Occurrence Book. No incidents of any consequence reported, he closed the book with a 'Humph.'

The front door opening caused him to lift his eyes towards it. An unhealthily thin, sallow-faced man, wearing an overall marked "Clegham Council Sanitation Department", had entered, holding at a distance a supermarket bag.

The prospect of meeting the man didn't sit well with the Superintendent.

Fully stretched the man might have stood six-foot-five, but there seemed little prospect of that happening. He hobbled grotesquely and negotiated the door with difficulty. The Superintendent quickly noticed the man's unusual problem. He seemed to walk two paces forward, then one back. His left hip wilted outwards with each forward step, then waxed inwards each time he flung the right leg forward past the left one. The right leg's movement required extraordinary fleetness to miss the inward rush of the left leg, as had one's eyes to witness it.

He seemed to take ages reaching the office counter. The Superintendent stood up from the desk and eyed him quizzically, puzzling where he had seen him before. He walked to the front counter, arriving at the same moment as Sergeant Shrapnel. 'You're Harpic Harry, if my guess is right?' the Superintendent ventured.

The man reached the counter and grabbed it for support, gasping for breath. 'Naw, naw, guv, you've the wrong fackin' bloke, guv,' he said, coughed, wheezed, removed a yellowing handkerchief from a trouser pocket and blew a nasal rasp into it. 'Arpic fackin' Arry is my second in command. 'E's the wan wot's got his right thigh facked, shot to fackin' pieces in the war, wasn't it. Easy to make a mistake wiv us fackin' pair, he hirples completely fackin' opposite to me, loiks, but we're both fackin' brilliant at the fackin' hokey fackin' cokey,' he volunteered in his strong cockney accent.

The Superintendent wished he hadn't asked, pulled a face at the sergeant and said, 'I remember now, you're both attendants at the conveniences outside the Municipal Park gates.'

'Yeah, you've got us now, guv, but my name's Dan, not fackin' 'Arry, and I's the fackin' Superintendent up there, guv; I's the same rank as you, see.'

The Superintendent's nose wrinkled in distaste. Clicks were imminent.

Dan placed the bag on the counter, opened his coat, and proceeded to entertain the Superintendent and the sergeant to an impromptu song and dance routine. Spinning like a dervish on one insecure leg, he began singing:

'I'm Dan fackin' Dan the fackin' lavatory man
Superinfackin'tendent of the shithouse fackin' clan
Picking up fackin' papers, hangin' up fackin' towels
Dancin' to the fackin' rhythm of rumblin' fackin' bowels
Flip fackin' flop…. hear them fackin' drop
Honky fackin' tonky that's the facki..........n' shite hou..........se bl...........ues.'

Surprisingly, the Superintendent saw some amusement in this new irritation, Dan's gyrations cracking his sombre face into a smile. His eyes flooded and he even stifled his habitual clicks of annoyance. The sergeant curled up at Dan's dancing routine and smacked the counter, speechless.

Taking charge, the Superintendent let out a loud 'Ahem,' and asked, 'What can we do for you, then, Danny boy?'

'Well its fackin' loik this, guv, last noight I's was locking up the conveniences loiks what I's fackin' do every fackin' noight, but last fackin' noight I's decided to locks them up early cos ov the wevver loik. It was fackin' pissin' dahn. You'll remember that, guv. I's drove me fackin' Lada dahn to the conveniences. You've probably seen it parked up there, guv, its a fackin' brown wan an' goes like a fackin' bomb it dahs but I's never exceeded the speed limit, guv,' he said, looking intently from the Superintendent's face, then back to the sergeant's, looking for them believing his claim.

'Well, when I's pulled up outside them at abaht quarters to ten there's a fackin' hellish row kammin from the Gents. It was pissin' dahn with fackin' rain roight, oi've fackin' told youse that already, and I's was wonderin', wot the fack's going on here. Just then, I's fackin' thought I's seen a fackin' black camel going over the fackin' footbridge in the pissin' rain. Well I's fackin' thought at the time, if that's not a fackin' camel, then it certainly fackin' looks loiks two fackin' coppers' helmets, bobbing up and fackin' dahn, making their way to the other sides of the fackin' road. I's dismisses this from me fackin' moind roight as I's approach the fackin' bog door with all the fackin' screamin' kammin' from it. There I found sam kant had closed the fackin' door and secured it wiv this piece of a fackin' tree.'

Dan delved into the supermarket bag and produced a twisted twig. Sergeant Shrapnel, quickly and without much thought, interjected: 'This Sam Kant, can you identify him?'

Dan and the Superintendent turned, looked at the sergeant, each not quite comprehending how a serving sergeant could be so naive and so stupid.

'Remind me to have a word with you later,' said the Superintendent and gave him one of those "stupid boy" looks so favoured by Captain Mainwairing types.

'Well I's had to go back to me fackin' Lada, wots got a fackin' M.O.T, guv,' Dan continued, 'legit loiks, to get a fackin' pair of fackin' pliors what I pulled the fackin' tree out wiv. Then I's opened the fackin' door, and abaht ten screamin' fackin' fellers run past me, smellin' fackin' 'oribble. Reckons they all must ave fackin' shit in their pants over samfin'. Bad fackin' Ruby, I's thought. I's shone my torch in when they's gone loik, no other fackin' kant there but the place looks loiks a fackin' bomb had hit it. Anyway, I's locks up for the noight, officially this toime and leaves it till mornin'. Well this fackin' mornin' me and moy fackin' mate, 'Arpic 'Arry, we opens ap at fackin' noine. Wot a fackin' mess. Fackin' shit, blood, glass and spew everywhere. We looks rahnd, and this is wots we've fackin' fahnd.'

The twisted twig dispensed with, Dan reached into his coat pocket for a pair of rubber gloves, pulled them on with practiced ease, before reaching into the Aldi bag for the next piece of evidence.

'These here are fackin' shit-flavoured condoms, if's you'll pardon the fackin' expression, guv, wivout any fackin' lav juices, but wiv identifoible traces from the upper reaches of some geezer's chocolate speedway.'

The Superintendent's jaw dropped. Sounding prudish he said, 'Oh, how bloody awful, what creatures use such places.' Directing the sergeant with a wave of his hand, he said, 'Get a sample tray, will you, to put this lot in?'

'And this here is a fackin' Oirish Jig, a fackin' toop, loiks wot we fahnd dahn wan of the fackin' bogs.'

The sodden, sparse, gingery hairpiece, he dropped it onto the sample tray. Delving deeper into the bag, he dragged out two facemasks. One was of Elvis Presley, which had a high rubbery forehead and attached black locks. The other of the steely-featured Maggie Thatcher, that went with the gingery hairpiece.

'Must have been 'avin' a fackin' gover… eh… mental, fackin' gangbang,' said Dan, his face lighting up.

'And these two fackin' fings here, I's finks they's fackin' been bangers for fackin' Guy Fawkes fackin' noight if youse was to ask me.' Another rummage produced the remnants of the two squibs, sodden, and blown asunder.

'Is that everything?' the Superintendent asked. The clicks were back; irritation was setting in. Only the sight of ranting Dan's unfortunately twisted body leaving the station rapidly had any chance of preventing them.

Dan finished his descriptions by delivering a wholesome message for all at the station. 'Fackin' yeah, that's it; we've cleaned ap an' are open for fackin' business as usual. If I's moight say so guv, its good to see your fackin' coppers dahn there samtimes, wot wiv all those perverts and fackin' shirttail-lifters, wot's offrin' their deaf and fackin' dumbs to wan an' Tex Ritters to the other and sucking' each others fackin' dicks. 'Onestly, guv, when your fackin' coppers appear to have a good, serious crap its loik a fackin' breff ov fackin' fresh air in the place. Fackin' roight…innit?'

'Right, sergeant,' prompted the Superintendent, turning away from Dan and pointing thumb over his shoulder in his direction, 'get a constable down here from the canteen, pronto. Get Dan out of here, into the interview room, and get a statement from him. In the English language would help. While you're at it, get two constables down to the Taj Industry workshop. See if anyone living close by saw anything, if anything identifiable was left behind.' He breathed in deeply. 'Tell them to take care. I don't want to hear of any of my constables being gang-raped on cloth-cutting tables by a bunch of cock-crazy Asian women.'

His hand stroked his forehead as he thought. He reasoned someone had thrown fireworks into the toilet, whilst perverts were using the place for their disgusting practices. He shuddered imagining what had transpired the instant the fireworks exploded. Though it answered the question of the artefacts, Dan had found there: some disguised, panic-stricken poofs-in-a-hurry had discarded them.

Met lore told of similar happenings occurring, on all divisions, too. Mischief-making policeman had extracted some sort of delight from pulling such pranks. This incident had occurred on the home beat policed by MacSporran and MacNab. Dan had witnessed two helmeted figures leaving the scene. He pulled the hand away from his head and uttered, 'Humph, I need seek no further, "The Jock Connection". It would *surprise* me if they've nothing to do with this. I think *I* might just be able to tie them in with this and the sweatshop incident,' he told the sergeant, standing nodding his agreement.

Dan was in the interview room when the sergeant, in an instant of unusual flippancy he immediately regretted, said to the Superintendent, 'Will we record both these occurrences under the Tadgergate Mysteries, sir?'

The Superintendent looked at him witheringly, as he did at stupid constables. Emitting an extra deeply draining, 'Click click,' he stormed out in the direction of his own office, up on the next level.

*****

Sergeant Taffy Moriarty, a capable, highly rated and trustworthy officer, ran the Superintendent's office. He opened all mail not marked personal, read it, assigned importance to it, and sorted it in the order of attention the Superintendent ought to give to it. An ex-Welsh Guards drill sergeant, Moriarty had lost none of his devotion to all things bullshit. His mania for discipline was such that coppers thought him a silly old fusspot. He kept his uniform immaculately pressed and his boots, which were always highly "spit and polished", were lore among probationers at the station. They believed mini castors replaced studs on the soles of them, answering the question of how he could perform the precise and speedy boot manoeuvres for which he was famous.

The Superintendent hung his hat behind the door, walked quickly across to his desk where he slumped into the chair behind it. A pleasing cup of steaming Earl Grey together with a chocolate-coated digestive biscuit waited him. It was a duty Sergeant Moriarty took on, knowing Superintendent Bunce favoured that tea and digestive.

He pulled the mail tray towards him. Monday's mail was always heavier than usual, a full tray of bumf from The Yard, usually. It was a dull chore, but he had to do it.

Before he had picked up the topmost letter, the one chosen to be positioned such by Sergeant Moriarty, because of its importance; he heard a strange, muffled sound coming through the open door of the sergeant's sub-office. Rather like stifled mirth, he thought.

The letter displayed the crest of office of the Mayor of the Borough of Clegham. The Mayor had addressed the letter to Superintendent Bunce, and not to the Officer in Charge, it was, therefore, for his eyes only.

He read:

Paddleville Towers,
69 Park Avenue,
West Clegham.
26th Oct.

Dear Superintendent Bunce,

We are very good friends through our Masonic interests, as our wives are, through their ladies circle and their occasional outings. The weekend they spent in the seaside resort of Blackpool, is an example of this.

However, even with these friendships in place, I feel I must write complaining of the behaviour of two of your constables stationed at West Clegham Police Station, even if it puts me in a wretched light.

The Mayoress and I knew of the good work accomplished by Constable Tonks, while he served as community police officer for the beats that include our residence at 69 Park Avenue. Indeed, his effectiveness in cutting down all criminal activities and implementing an innovative "police watch" system in the area is a legacy, which will live long after he has gone.

I became aware of Constable Tonks' imminent retirement when, last Wednesday, The Lady Mayoress telephoned me in my office. Breathlessly, she told me Constables MacNab and MacSporran were at Paddleville Towers collecting for his retirement gift, and she sought my advice in deciding the size of a donation for him. These two constables are the subjects of my complaint.

The Lady Mayoress and I discussed the contribution we should make towards Constable Tonks farewell gift. However, we failed to agree a figure. The Lady Mayoress suggested, because of our eminent and dignified position in life, we ought to donate ten pounds. I was not so agreeable.

I'm sure you remember the very embarrassing situation in which I found myself recently. During the last local council elections, Constable Tonks had the temerity to charge me with urinating through the letterbox at the home of my pathetic Liberal Democratic Party opponent. In addition, and what made matters worse, Tonks charged me with being drunk and incapable of taking care of myself. This charge, if proven, would have done me severe political damage. It was a great relief to me when you stepped in, as a Masonic brother does, and had the charges dropped. 'Fuck them and give them a pound was, therefore, the instruction that I gave The Lady Mayoress.

I have noticed my wife's behaviour has become rather unusual, and her sexual demands on me (yet unfulfilled I should add) rather strange. All, it seems, in an effort to time my breakfast eggs in a bizarre manner that I had not previously heard of. This abnormal behaviour is a recent manifestation, appearing quite suddenly after our wives returned from the weekend in Blackpool.

I have also intercepted a letter written by The Lady Mayoress, addressed to the Central pier in Blackpool, requesting literature and a membership form for the fan club of one called Billy Bagman.

Even so, I didn't expect the greeting or the "after the party was over" scenes, which I encountered on my return home from the Mayoral office, late that Wednesday afternoon. On opening the front door, I found The Lady Mayoress skipping around our home, almost naked, wearing only a pair of black crotchless panties, back to front, and a sublime smile that I found inexplicable at that moment.

However, I soon found a trail of her clothing and undergarments, scattered up the stairs and across the landing leading to our bedroom door. On entering the bedroom, I found both of the single beds completely trashed. Three stumpy, solid-oak legs had broken off each bed, the stuffing and springs limply hanging from the mattresses.

Footprints from boots dotted the wall behind the headboards, drawing out the numbers six and nine, which is the number of our residence. At the foot of the beds, I found pieces of toenails, (small packet of samples enclosed) both male and female. One can only assume they were painfully detached during throes of passion.

The chandelier had fallen from the ceiling; obviously swinging from it took place before its draping over my destroyed bed. My Victorian commode was less a chamber pot. After use, someone had placed it upside down to drip its contents onto of my Mayoral hat, sitting above my robes hanging from the coat stand.

Following this bacchanalia, in which The Lady Mayoress fulfilled some foolish sexual fantasy, she took this pair of adventurers to our kitchen. There she prepared for them lobster thermidor, fillet steak Diane, and completed their stuffing with my favourite chocolate profiteroles.

She then provided Irish coffee, using my twenty-five-year-old Jamieson's Irish whiskey, and finished off their meal by offering my very best Havana cigars. Being non-smokers, they refused.

The Lady Mayoress has since explained that it was her idea to provide this level of largesse. The other happenings mentioned, she said, were at my suggestion. Of course, I do not agree with her version: that I had told her to fuck the two constables, then give them a pound.

I will have to watch my choice of words. The Lady Mayoress obviously used the liberal translation of my response to the donation towards Constable Tonks' retirement fund that suited her best.

However, before rumour that The Lady Mayoress might be a raving nympho engulfs your station, I beseech you, as a good brother, on the square with me, to discipline Constables MacNab and MacSporran in such a way that it secures their silence.

Yours sincerely
Algie
Algernon Rideout
MAYOR of Clegham

'"The Jock Connection"! The bloody Jocks have been performing there too; fornicating with Myrna, ruining beds, using Algie's po, whatever next?'

The words were leaving his lips when crazy giggling and a profusion of thuds boomed from Sergeant Moriarty's office. 'Sounds as if he's in the throes of an apoplectic fit,' he said, furrowing his brow. The sergeant's boots were thumping onto the floor. 'He'll be through it if he doesn't stop,' he said, panicky now. Then he heard louder hoots and guffaws punctuating the thumps.

Slapping the letter down on the desk, he rose from his chair and crossed to the sub-office door. Sergeant Moriarty was standing stiffly to attention, his eyes wild, froth flecking his lips, his whole body quaking, repeating the words that had motivated his condition: 'Fuck them, give them a pound.' His helmet was sitting crookedly on his head and back to front. It rocked when, with startling pedal dexterity, he completed a left turn and bellowed, 'Fuck them, give them a pound.' He then marched two paces forward. Reaching the end of his desk, he came to a dynamic halt, his boot studs leaving deep inundations in the floor covering. A left turn, his body ramrod stiff, two paces forward, then one left and an about turn, took him behind his desk to his chair, into which he collapsed. He threw the Superintendent a parade ground salute and shouted, 'All correct, saaaar. Fuck them, give them a pound.'

The Superintendent was not amused, the risibility of the situation passing clean over his head. He was in complete control of the situation, even if his sergeant's sanity had disappeared behind a distant planet. MacNab and MacSporran were blameworthy in the two odd cases angering him that morning. Especially the latest case where, it seemed, his right-hand man had "thrown a wobbler" on reading the letter of complaint against them.

It confirmed his opinion: the Jocks were two of the worst type of piss-taker. They had created stirrings of indiscipline amongst his constables. They had found uncommon ways to cause unrest for some inhabitants of his manor. They had succeeded in infuriating him, thrice. This time, they'd left behind incontrovertible evidence of their guilt; he had sussed them out, now he would have them. They would pay for their waywardness, insolence and their lack of interest in the Job. *They would not like his verbals.*

He picked up the telephone and dialled the front office. Sergeant Shrapnel answered. 'Telephone an ambulance and ask the medics to bring a straightjacket with them. I have a problem with Sergeant Moriarty's sanity,' the Superintendent said, his tone restrained.

Chapter 23

The town hall clock was striking 11 a.m. as Hamish was pushing Harry onto a bus. Its route would take them from Fred's Diner to a stop near the nick. The chimes signalled that their mealtime was nearing, though they didn't need any more grub. Their recovery from the previous night's excesses was slow and neither of them felt well.

On the High Street, the bus tyres sluiced rainwater over pedestrians already sodden. The windscreen wiper lashed at the continuing downpour, scuffing it away with wide swipes, the driver leaning forward to obtain a better view.

'I'm beginning to feel queasy,' Hamish complained, standing close to the door and swinging in sympathy with the bus' motion.

'I'd have thought the six bacon and egg butties, the several cups of tea, the handful of Rennies and the three aspirins you threw over your neck in Ted's, would have settled your guts and cooled your head,' Harry said. 'It has mine.'

'Och, I've never felt good on buses. There's always the whang of cigarette smoke, exhaust fumes and spew in the background. I'll feel better when I'm settled in the canteen and have a hand at cards.'

Hamish was sweating and had turned facially ashen. Harry thought him about to throw-up and stood away a pace.

The bus driver had diagnosed Hamish's condition and dropped them off outside the nick.

Arriving in the yard, an incident worthy of a second look was presenting itself. An ambulance parked close to a staircase exit had its back doors wide open. To Superintendent Bunce's instructions, paramedics were struggling to negotiate into it a jolting stretcher upon which a straitjacketed figure lay restrained.

They both nosed forward to get a better picture of the events, certainly not to assist. Sticking out of one end of the restraint was the puce, organ-stop-eyed and ranting face of Sergeant Taffy Moriarty. Out of the other end, a set of boots, once immaculately polished, were keeping time to an unheard, jitterbug beat.

Shocked, they both mouthed, 'All correct, sergeant.' It was no malevolent deprecation; they'd not had time to consider any.

'Fuck them, give them a pound,' Sergeant Moriarty spluttered back at them.

'Strange one that,' said Harry as they ambled on towards the canteen. 'Sergeant Moriarty's gone a little potty by the looks of it. Pressure of working under Bunce's beady gaze, I bet.'

The Superintendent's eyes followed them; the rest of him vibrated down into his shoes. His hands made clutching gestures at his side and his moustache was twitching madly. Hair stood out on the back of his neck. Beside-himself anger was contorting his mouth. Dredging deeply, he uttered 'Click, click, click,' followed by 'aaaaaagh.' Never had the progress of two constables ambling towards the canteen steps had such an effect on him.

The ambulance left for the local mental hospital with Sergeant Moriarty screaming from the back, 'Fuck them, Buncie Boy, give them a pound.'

The Superintendent leapt up the stairs to his office, completely forgetting how knackered he felt and why; the kick from what he was about to achieve had revitalised him. Behind his desk, he settled for a moment, got his breath, gained some composure and quelled his excitement. He picked up the telephone and rang the front office. Sergeant Shrapnel answered. 'Arrange for MacNab and MacSporran to parade in front of me at noon,' the Superintendent snapped. 'And bring to my office all the forms I'll require for a constable about to resign the Force… in duplicate. I don't have to tell you this is confidential, sergeant, not a word of this to anyone. You have that?'

'All correct on that one, sir,' Shrapnel replied, ever mindful of their brotherly affiliations.

The Superintendent sat back and thought of the invective he would use: two barrel-loads, one of vitriol, the other of venom, which he'd let fly at his victims, extracting great pleasure whilst doing so. 'Huh, "The Jock Connection",' he said aloud, threw his head back and stared at the ceiling. 'I'll have them squirming, floundering and blubbering.'

The tension on his face eased briefly. Coppers of their ilk would not appreciate for one moment the duties of rubber heelers. Most coppers coerced into investigating colleagues suspected of some indiscretion or other, saw it as a shit task. However, if Jack Dewsnap needed two malcontents to perform "duties elsewhere", as he knew the business of rubber heeling, then that was fine by him.

He moved from side to side in his chair, his eyes rolling at the thought of rattling their cages, having them crap their pants, shocking them to the core, ensuring their compliance before dispatching them to receive Jack's orders, knocked groggy. Even the flimsiest of chances of remaining in the Job would look good to them, when he had finished his verbals.

******

Both Hamish and Harry played their hands in the card game somewhat mechanically, showing little interest in their cups of tea. Hamish's stomach turned often at the sight of beans and stodgy gravy sloshing around islands of chips on the plates coppers inexpertly carried back to tables from the servery. He stuck it out and his luck was in; winning several hands, small change rattled across the table towards him, along with the bad losers' grudging comments. About to deal a hand, he heard the rustle of waterproofs and a copper's voice close to his ear. 'Remember what you told me last week,' the voice said, 'the bit of daftness at the sweatshop, the little cocks, big cocks thing? And last night, what Harry said happened at the bog.'

From the beery whang of the copper's breath, Hamish knew he, too, fought off a hangover. 'What are you trying to tell me?' Hamish asked and turning his nose away from the voice.

'Two coppers are on their way to take statements at the sweatshop. Another copper is in the interview room debriefing Dan, the bog attendant from the park gate Gents. If the Super suspects you two of any involvement, prepare for a broadside. He looked grim when he arrived late for duty this morning, and any complaints he has received since won't have improved his mood. Pass my warning on to Harry.'

'No need,' Hamish shrugged, 'he's got fuck all on us,' he said, confidently, turning and facing the copper. Changing the subject, he asked, 'What's wrong with Taffy Moriarty?'

'He suffered severe mental trauma this morning, soon after the mail arrived,' the copper told him.

'Has someone sent him a ribald tale of naughty goings-on with sheep on the Brecon Beacons, the Welsh prick, isn't it,' Hamish said, mimicking the sergeant's accent. 'And that's fuck all to do with us either, by the way.'

The game ended as the meal break finished. Hamish flashed a handful of change at Harry who had lost a small amount. 'That's the way to do it,' Hamish poked at him.

'You've won enough for another round of teas, then,' Harry responded.

******

'Where are we off to now?' Harry asked. They were crossing the yard, making towards the street and on to their beat. He wished to confer with Hamish how they'd get through the remainder of the shift. Hamish hadn't time to answer or pass on the warning. Sergeant Shrapnel opened a back door and gestured them over. When they were close enough, he told them quietly and with a haughty look of contempt, 'Don't know what you two jokers have been up to, but the Super wants to see you in his office at noon. It's better you tidy up, he's not in great humour.'

They both stopped in their tracks; memories of their most recent indiscretions were leaping quickly into their minds. Two of their daft capers were now the subject of enquiries and most probably would be the topics of the Super's interview.

Sergeant Shrapnel looked on pleased. His message had furrowed their brows. He would remember with relish their reaction to it.

Downstairs in the copper's locker room, a futile and half-hearted smartening-up of appearances began. It proved difficult on unpolished, rain-bleached boots; an impossible task on shapeless uniform trousers, sodden and then dried out, on each day of the previous week of torrential rain.

Both were wringing water from the bottoms of their trousers. Hamish was thinking as they set about that task. 'Take this in,' he said. 'If Bunce just wants to know why these two occurrences happened on our beat, we'll tell him the Neighbourhood Watch Scheme is working well, but couldn't prevent them. We'll tell him we saw watchful faces peering avidly from rain-streaked windows on the lookout for criminals, but it was too wet for them to get out and be active as far as the park gates. That's in our favour. We'll tell him we walked our beats those shifts, braving the rain, and saw nothing suspicious because we weren't near those locations. We'll bullshit him, devotion to duty and all that, make it sound good.'

'He won't believe the devotion to duty bullshit. I'm sure no one saw us entering that dark alley, or loitering near the park gates. There should be no witnesses. We know what Bunce will be thinking, though. He'll have read the conduct reports that accompanied us here from our uptown nicks, by now. Although we've only been here a couple of weeks, he will want us to be guilty, responsible for the incidents, have a go at us, sack us maybe, for his own pleasure, make him look good in the eyes of his superiors,' Harry said, sounding downbeat.

'Any copper who bombed a busy "cottage", like we did, would have seen some humour in it. That copper having attained a senior rank, of course, would never admit to it. Bunce will never have done anything of the sort. He's not that type; he won't be interested that we are both pissed off with our lot since returning to beat duty. He definitely won't understand why we decorated one shithouse interior then blasted fuck out of another, just for amusement. He will expect us to have accepted the mind-numbing boredom of walking beats and checking door handles as part of the Job, until retirement,' Hamish said.

'Aye, you're right, no sense of humour there.'

'So that just leaves our shagging session with the Mayor's wife to worry about.'

'Do you think someone might have shopped us?'

'We've not bragged about it to anyone, kept it secret, like we said. I don't reckon Myrna would give evidence against us. She would have complained the same afternoon if she were. She squealed herself out on top of me, remember,' Hamish said boastfully.

'Who might, then?'

'The Mayor might have complained to Bunce, his Masonic brother. He might guess we both fucked his wife. The three legs I broke from his bed might just be the clue he needed. He wouldn't have bought that his piss-pot had wings for it to end up where we left it.'

'What do we do if he has complained to Bunce?'

'We left nothing behind us, except perhaps a wet spot or two on the bedding. Myrna will have washed the sheets. She won't want to bear witness.

We can describe her satisfied smile as she showed us out of her house and tell of her demand that we call around again, soon. If he believes that, we might not need to plead that Myrna took advantage of us, dragging us into the house, throwing us onto a bed and demanding three-in-a-bed sex with us. I'll look and act unperturbed beneath Bunce's gaze. I'll tell lies to explain away anything he accuses us of. I'll take great pleasure confounding him. We should be experts at bluffing. We listened to plenty of our collars practising that art.'

'Aye, I'll lie too. If it all goes tits up for us there's always the Police Federation who will give us representation.'

At noon, Sergeant Shrapnel led them up the stairs and paraded them outside the Superintendent's office door. Enjoying himself immensely, he barked, 'Bring yourselves to attention… and when I open the door… march in… come to a halt in front of the Superintendent's desk… make a brisk left turn… throw a salute. I will leave then… he will tell you to "stand easy". Understand?'

The sergeant knocked, opened the Superintendent's door, commanded them 'Left right, left right, quick march, parade halt, left turn,' and announced, 'Constables MacNab and MacSporran, sir.'

'Very good, sergeant,' the Superintendent said curtly, not looking up from the neat piles of Met Police forms on his desk. 'I'll take it from here.'

The sergeant closed the door behind him.

The Superintendent lifted his head. His eyes were watery as he scanned across both their faces. His top lip curled back a trifle. He gave a solitary sniff, wrinkled his moustache, widened his jaws and opened his lips slightly. Drawing them back into a snarl, he revealed teeth that whistled as he sucked air through them. 'Stand easy,' he barked and exhaled noisily. The slow, double, 'Click, click,' was his way of showing his complete and utter contempt for them.

The Superintendent enjoyed verbally slating coppers he had an issue with, using choice words, spat out to emphasise his disdain, in his controlled, grating voice. He would treat the Jocks similarly. 'You are two despicable, miserable, slimy, parasitic nematodes,' he began, squirming with pleasure in his chair, 'you are brazen, iniquitous, wanton, undisciplined and a contemptible pair of egregious yahoos. Masquerading as police officers, you leave nothing but havoc and heartache in your wake. You acted shamelessly at your last stations and nothing has changed since your hasty transfers here. At those other stations, overwhelming relief must have prevailed when they disgorged you like so much excreta from their strengths.

'It is also a well-known and verifiable fact that coppers of your reckless demeanour abuse "the cloth". Your uniform becomes some sort of gratis credit card to you. Wearing it, you obtain food and other forms of nourishment from the so-called mumping holes you visit, on duty. Off duty, you no doubt extract cheap deals from shops and pay nothing in the restaurants on my manor.

'Rab. C. Nesbit types, the Big Yin, the Tartan Army, filled with Buckie wine, the swally, might applaud contemptible behaviour in your Govan and Leith. You might gain plaudits from skulking bravehearts roaming in the gloaming, and in the heather and bracken of your glorious hills of home. However… rest… assured …your dissolute conduct here in the Met we take very seriously and... as you will discover... it breaks the Metropolitan Police Disciplinary Code.

'A complaint this morning and another last week, of lewd and base practices that have occurred,' his voice then rose suddenly, almost to a scream, '*on your beat, on my manor…* has offended my ears.'

He then settled back into his chair to take a breath, before looking at them squarely. 'Mr Abdul Rashid, from Taj Industries, has complained of an illegal entry made to his women workers' Ladies. On the walls of the small room, indecent drawings painted with black felt-tip pen appeared overnight, to the rancour of the owner and the mental disturbance of the Asian women.

'In addition, this morning, the attendant from the toilets outside the Clegham Municipal Park gates has told me of an odd sighting. He will swear he saw two helmeted police officers, *on your beat*, making their getaway across the footbridge following an incident that took place there last evening. I have various, disgusting pieces of evidence found at the scene. I have the firework remnants which were used in a most distasteful manner to discourage perverts from using those premises as a meeting place.'

The Superintendent looked from one to the other for signs of twitches, the tics of betrayal, that in his experience, the guilty showed.

Hamish stood impassive, gave nothing away. Harry shook his head, casting doubt on the Superintendent's words. The Superintendent didn't think their gall admirable, he just pulled his lips back and reassumed his contemptuous stare.

'Have you anything to say about these happenings on your beat?' he asked, his eyes darting, piercing and observing closely, first one and then the other. His experience told him that a rash remark from a copper, like anyone else under suspicion and knocked out of their stride, might betray them.

'No… no,' they mouthed casually, as one. Hamish added, 'It's been a rough two weeks weather-wise, sir. We've been soaked every day. We never got very far onto our beats. We certainly didn't get to those areas of our beat that you name.'

Harry cleared his throat. 'What Constable MacNab is telling you is correct, sir, we mainly patrolled this end of the beat because there are more places to shelter from the rain. We were still actively policing during the incessant downpour, sir.'

'What you tell me is utter pish MacSporran, but I can confirm this. Constables are taking witness statements from workers at both of these establishments. You have an opportunity to come clean...now.'

Confident the Superintendent could pin nothing on them regarding the two episodes in question; both shook their heads, feigning innocence of the charge. Again as one they replied, 'No sir, nothing to do with us, sir.'

'I have this Polaroid photograph taken by Mr Rashid. It clearly shows why the Asian woman found these drawings monstrous and obscene.'

Harry's handiwork was clear. The photographic reproduction was good. Harry thought it a shame to deny the artistry, but he did. 'It's obviously a child's prank sir and nothing to do with us.'

'Yes, a kid, sir. That's the culprit,' Hamish said, nodding, 'and I'm surprised that you are accusing two adult policemen of such childish behaviour.'

The Superintendent snorted and said nothing, but he thought plenty. MacNab's remark was typical of a piss-taker. An adult policeman, who did he think he was kidding? They should be showing some discomfort by now, though, but there was none visible and he hadn't yet proved anything. No shaming confession appeared obtainable from this pair of prurient-headed and misguided incompetents. He saw they were looking over his head now, completely ignoring him, their eyes probably on the manor map, on the wall behind his head, dotted with a number of coloured pins identifying different crime scenes. They were probably looking for the coloured pin shaped like a bog brush.

Of course, he had expected their denials. They knew, as he did, it would be hard for him to prove indubitably their involvement. However, the undeniable evidence he had on another matter he was just about to deliver.

'Utter pish… complete and utter pish,' he erupted sharply and positioned better his chair cushion. Telling words were only moments away from utterance and his voice changed in tone. 'You enjoy working Constable Tonks' old beat, click, click?' he asked curtly, his face looking a crumb happier.

A mumbled 'Yes' answered his question and their eyes were now on him.

'You called at certain homes there collecting for his retirement gift?' With his shoulders drawn back, he looked from one to the other, stern again, while reshuffling the Met Police forms. Then he slumped back into his chair, awaiting their reaction.

The Superintendent easily spotted their unease and their quick intakes of breath, thinking it an indication of guilt.

Had Myrna squealed on them? The Superintendent's drift changing suddenly towards their collecting for Constable Tonks had them both reliving their afternoon with the nymphomaniac at 69 Park Avenue. Her standard of entertainment, her great charm and her even greater sexual gusto had impressed them. She had also fed them extra well for their efforts. Surely, Bunce could know nothing about that. She didn't seem the type of person to give the game away. She had enjoyed shagging them too much for that and had extended an invitation to return for more.

The Superintendent removed the accusatory letter from beneath his blotter.

'A letter of complaint arrived this morning, the author, Algernon Rideout, Mayor of the Borough of Clegham. His grievance relates to your visit to 69 Park Lane, last Wednesday, when you requested donations there. It goes on, and I'm sure you know the details. You seduced Mrs. Rideout…'

'No!… No!' they butted in with shouts.

'…there,' he said loudly, cutting off their protestations. 'There… you treated her no better than a silly countryside hump; a hussy, took sexual advantage of her while she was highly emotional and fragile.

'In addition, I'm none too happy about the havoc it has wreaked on the mind of my clerk, Sergeant Moriarty, a deeply religious God-fearing man, who read the letter of complaint this morning. He is from the Welsh valleys, a member of the Chapel, the Chapel choir too, and had, until the arrival of the Mayor's letter, an existence sheltered from life's crudities.

'Reading the letter's contents has turned his mind. At this moment, I have serious doubts about his future in the Force.'

'Nothing to do with us, sir, and we're both sorry about Taffy, aren't we, Harry?'

'Yes we are, but come off it, sir, that's a terrible accusation to make. We would never do any such thing,' Harry said, face more hangdog than usual, his hands up and opened out in front of him.

'We were there looking for a donation, okay,' Hamish conceded, 'but nothing like that happened. I have Constable MacSporran to back me up on that, sir.'

'MacSporran has nothing with which to back you up,' the Superintendent told Hamish sharply. 'What you both are telling me is utter pish. A packet of toenail remnants, collected from the floor at the foot of his bed, the Mayor enclosed with the letter. Every fool knows that DNA testing will prove, conclusively, the presence of you two in the mayor's bedroom, conducting yourselves in a most disgraceful manner.'

The Superintendent eyed them, one then the other. He thought he had them on the run and warmed inwardly. The two clicks he then emitted were ones of pleasure.

The jagged toenail shards looked miniscule rattling about in the bottom of the clear plastic bag he waved at them. The Superintendent followed their eyes and saw Hamish peering at the pieces of plain toenail lying together with some painted bits. He wanted to progress this quickly; otherwise, he might find hiding his delight a difficult exercise.

'Yes, yes, yes,' he said airily, 'I could ask you both to bare your feet so I can inspect your toes for bits missing. However, I don't need to do that. DNA sampling will prove categorically one of the toenails found with those of the mayoress belongs to one of you. The Commissioner will not approve of your deeds that day. Especially when you were *on duty* at the time of the alleged occurrence, click, click.'

The Superintendent sat back, top lip drawn tight, waiting to rejoice when their discomfort showed. He would have liked to see MacNab and MacSporran turn exceedingly glum. Instead, they just looked squarely back at him, Bloody recalcitrants, he thought. He left his chair, went to the office door and picked up a brown-paper mat. They hadn't noticed it on entering. Now they did; clearly visible on the paper were the wet sole prints of both their boots. 'Now,' he said, 'there's the issue of the sixty-nine pattern drawn on the wall, behind a bed, in the bedroom of the Mayor, with the sole of a boot. This is another clue to you being in the mayor's bedroom; another prank to talk your way out of, adult policemen.'

He didn't give them any time to consider this new allegation. Quickly he was back behind his desk and telling them their options. 'As I see it, you have two choices,' he said, while messing with the forms on his desk. Levelling the edges, he purposefully reformed the files into two neat piles. It made them take notice. 'Your first option is to resign *now*.... I have the relevant forms here. We can complete them *now*, and then you can go your merry way. Resigning the force means, you will leave with the good conduct report, which neither of you deserve. Your shortened length of service will horrendously decimate your pension, too. I believe the full pension is your Holy Grail. Yes?'

The words excited him, made him fidgety. He moved his chair back to view better any discomfort they might show and dredged up a click, click of well-emptying strength. He expected they'd be thinking their days in the Job were numbered and they'd begin to sway unsteadily, bump shoulder to shoulder.

There were no pallid complexions to see, no dripping sweat or trembling movements for him to view, no squeaks from tightened vocal chords to hear, no indications that their arseholes were oscillating half-crown to sixpence in size and about to cave in, as he thought they should.

My second option should rock them, he thought. 'If you are unwilling to resign now, the other option involves the Commissioner. He will assess the offences against discipline and decide your fate. If you were to take that route, it is my duty to inform you that dismissal, if such were the result of his findings, and dismissal is how I would rate the outcome, would be without the good report, and without any pension. Employment opportunities in Civvy Street would, I think, be considerably less enhanced by the lack of good references.'

They just stood stationary and unblinking in front of him, pictures of innocence. One stood like a totem pole hewed from the wide-girthed trunk of a Californian redwood, the other one from a branch of a trim spruce. They still were not acting like guilty parties, which he was sure they were.

It had him thinking: he hadn't caught them red-handed and without excuse, as they had been when they worked "up town". Now it occurred to him that they were aware of the complaints procedure and that they could take advice from Police Federation Lawyers.

Every force in the country would have had, at one time or another, a police officer resorting to that device. Many of them would have erred by straying from their beats and been caught doing similar, sordid mischief. Many would still be serving officers today; he was sure, with some of them reaching the higher ranks. Indeed, with Gloria in that doorway….

Quickly, he left the recollection, realising that an enquiry would drag *this* entire sordid affair out into the open. Algie's allegations couldn't become common knowledge; he had requested secrecy to preserve Myrna's good name. As a fellow Mason, he saw that was important. As was Jack Dewsnap's urgency to acquire a duo the likes of these for "duties elsewhere", even if *he* had his doubts that this pair of rascals could assist anyone.

He got in quick, in case they began quoting him the Police Federation line. 'Interestingly, there is a third option which I have not yet proposed. It might well be your salvation.' The merest shadow of a smile played around his lips.

'A third option you say?' Hamish asked. He was about to ask for legal representation, but thought he'd listen to the offer.

'Yes… Commander Dewsnap requires two constables to undertake special inquiries of a covert and confidential nature. Should you acquiesce, the Commander has told me he will remove the finality of resignation and loss of pensionable rights. He may also have something of interest to offer you both, up his sleeve'

It took a moment to realise the nature of the slippery lifeline on offer to them. They stood face to face now, aghast, reading each other's mind and not liking what they read: they were in the mire. On duty at the time, leaving behind toenail scraps and the footprints featuring the number sixty-nine on the bedroom wall meant they were deep in trouble and unable wriggle out of being in the Mayors' bedroom. Police Federation lawyers might plead a good case, perhaps get them off, no guarantee, though…more than likely they'd just have a fucking good laugh. It seemed that they didn't have any options: it was duties as "Rubber Heelers" or the sack.

'I don't like this at all,' Hamish said, looking blankly at Harry.

Chapter 24

Hamish took the telephone call at his home, late on Tuesday morning. With his ear an inch from the earpiece, he glowered; he pictured the smug look on Sergeant Shrapnel's face as he gave him instructions to present himself to Commander Dewsnap, in his office, at divisional headquarters, East Clegham, at 2 p.m. that afternoon. 'Bastard likes to see us in bother and him a Jock, too,' Hamish said, his hand covering the mouthpiece.

'You're to present yourself along with MacSporran to the Commander,' Shrapnel told him. 'And you've not to discuss the subject of the meeting with anyone…get that?'

'Aye… aye… get on with it,' Hamish replied, not feeling like exchanging pleasantries with the sergeant.

'Pack a bag. Apparently, you'll be gone for a week or so. Old jeans and T-shirts are the preferable dress code. It sounds as if brothel-creepers wouldn't be out of place either.'

'Aye… aye… that's enough. You've your tuppence worth in. What else?'

'A cover story has been devised, suggesting you're taking some accumulated annual leave.'

'Is that it?'

'MacSporran asks you to meet him in his section house room at 1 o'clock.'

'I'll be there. By the way, sergeant, I hope nothing curable ails you while we're away.'

Jenny bawled 'Food' in his direction as he put the handset down. He trundled his weight into the kitchen, sat down and gave her the news: 'I'm off for a week or so. It's a special job for the Commander. Don't expect to hear from me until it's finished.'

'Good riddance. Don't bring your dirty washing home and expect me to perform miracles removing a ploughed field of your disgusting skidmarks,' she berated him as she surrounded his plate with a selection of sauce bottles. 'Learn to wipe your arse properly,' she said, before turning quickly and throwing her shoulders back.

Hamish wrinkled his nose and glowered at the plate of corned beef, baked beans and chips. 'I hope there's a decent curry house where we're going,' he shouted towards her retreating figure, 'this type of grub gives me the shits.'

******

Harry was standing staring into the mirror at the two "piss-holes in the snow" returning the look, when Hamish rapped on the door, walked in and dropped his holdall with a thump. 'This room reeks. There's a whang of overnight occupancy by a man worried he's about to become a rubber heeler. Your window needs opening,' he said, summing up the atmosphere.

A rumpled duvet kicked from the bed onto the floor suggested a traumatic night's sleep.

Harry's baggy eyes had Hamish straight in with a jibe and a diagnosis. 'Those bags are the first signs of being sent on a shit job, they are,' he said.

'Okay, Doctor MacNab,' snapped Harry, peering closely at Hamish for signs of sleeplessness, 'I suppose you're going to tell me you've had a wonderful, restful, full night's kip.' Hamish looked bright. Harry turned away and returned the duvet to the bed. Getting in his own jibe, he sniffed, and said, 'And I suppose you've filed down the rough edges on your shattered toenails. I've checked mine. They're all intact.'

Hamish looked in Harry's mirror, grinned at his own reflection, turned and said, 'Aye, okay. I know what you're saying. Guilty as charged. I've used a bastard file to smooth mine over. I can't remember losing any and didn't know bits were missing until Bunce waggled that bag at us.'

'They never snagged when pulling your socks on?'

'No. All that shagging had tightly curled my toes. Mind you, the thought of dragging a sock over a rough toenail makes me go all quivery and funny. You're right about one thing, though. I did lay awake for some time last night giving thought to our situation. I was trying to reason out the third option,' Hamish said. 'It was obviously made at the Commander's behest.'

'Aye, Bunce had such a go at us, you could tell he wanted rid,' Harry said.

'Aye, you're right. Nasty piece of work, that. I think the Commander must be desperate. Why else would he put the hard word on Bunce to find a pair of coppers to do some dirty work for him?' Hamish asked.

'If my police experience tells me anything, he's on the trail of a copper with a worse record of piss-taking than ours, if that's possible. Or maybe a wee personal vendetta is going on somewhere,' Harry said.

'It could be anything. Maybe he and another member of the Force are vying for the same "bit of stuff on the side" and he wants some dirt on him. His missus might be playing away from home. It could be anything like that. Old coppers have told me that, in the past, gov'nors have used their strength for anything from digging their gardens, putting on their bets with illegal bookies, and taking their girlfriends to the abortionist,' Hamish said.

Harry's face became set. 'There's a big gripper influence in the Job. It could be Dewsnap is doing someone in the funny handshake mob a favour.'

'What's a gripper?' Hamish asked.

'Come off it…I know you ken fine,' Harry erupted. 'There's no need to tell you it's one of those blokes that goes about crunching knuckles. I know you've come across them in the Job. They're everywhere, the Job's blighted with them.'

Hamish laughed. 'You're right. It's just the gripper handle. That's a new name for an old problem to me. Remember when you saw Bunce greeting

Dewsnap in the station yard, the handshake between them, and the incautious remark you made at the time. They wouldn't have liked that, wouldn't have liked that at all. Something about removing snot from each other's knuckles, wasn't it?'

'Ken what you're on about,' Harry said, 'but there's no point in us speculating about what the Commander wants us for. I'll pack some gear and then we can go.'

Harry opened drawers, chose a selection of necessities, placed them into a toilet bag and stuffed the lot into his holdall.

'Don't forget to pack your latest VIZ. That might be the only humour we get for a while,' Hamish said.

They left the section house and hitched a lift in an "area car" to the DHQ.

******

Walking a little easier at 9 a.m., Tuesday morning, with his cock still bandaged, Commander Dewsnap entered his office. On his desk he found Superintendent Bunce's report on the two constables he was expecting later that day, and their records of service. He looked at their records of service first. Those would allow him an insight into all of their police experience. Using the comments on their abilities from their former gov'nors, he might just be able to rate his prospects of getting Daphne back into bed with him.

Initial reading of the reports surprised the Commander. The two experienced and once well-regarded detective constables seemed to have jeopardised their careers in moments of madness.

A moment of whimsy had him smiling. He thought a mind pollutant, a virulent, distressing contamination, a pernicious plague, had struck them down. He pondered that, at Halloween, something similar must have struck him down. Perhaps the blame lay at the door of some maddening tomfoolery plant, its mind-pollutant borne on the cyclonic winds blowing from the depths of mirth gulch, in the region of comicality, during the silly season.

Then his face soured. Had he not suffered the pain apparent when politicians tampered with the workings of the Force? The promotion of graduates with degrees in zoology, with no streetwise experience to talk about, galled him, as did Rowley's roller-coaster rise to the top… and his madcap ways.

The Commander remained deep in thought; Sunday night hadn't been his only moment of rashness. He recalled his on-duty meetings with Daphne in the bowels of St Mary's hospital and his sooty and dishevelled reappearances from the boiler room. Political correctness within the Job hadn't raised its ugly head then. Many constables had their nookie on duty. He suspected there were some intrepid ones who still did. The thought of his gov'nors catching him in the act had always turned him cold. They'd never caught him, of course. As far as he knew, none of his colleagues had suspected his recklessness.

He was the young constable who witnessed Gloria's assault on Ivor in the shop doorway, heard his squealing, his moaning, saw the whisking of his short, stiff cock and watched the sergeant's unsighted walk past. His account had reached every canteen in the inner divisions. For a brief moment, he felt a pang of compassion for MacNab and MacSporran. Perhaps, unlike him, the wayside had upped to meet them.

The Commander broke from his thoughts, shuddered, and picked up his Superintendent's report. Several pages long, it began with his knowledge of the two coppers. From page 1, he was able to ascertain what he had always suspected anyway. Ivor relished his part in flushing out and providing the two coppers for "duties elsewhere". In his report, he crucified their integrity.

On page two, he penned their nicknames. Individually they were "Extreme Drollery in a Bannock", and "Fun in a Bun", collectively, the "Jock Connection". Jack would, Ivor also stated, be able to ascertain instantly which copper was which, from the first moment they entered his office. The first and most serious indiscretion listed he said was indubitably provable, which he could dangle in front of them, if they proved bolshie-minded enough.

Among other things, it involved the destruction of beds at Paddleworth Towers. He smiled at the thought of Algie remonstrating with Myrna about the shagging of two coppers. Coppers *were* still getting their nookie on duty, okay. The thought of it all tickled him. "Fuck them and give them a pound," sounded like another joke he had heard at the nineteenth hole. He had never thought the words of that joke would prove enough to unhinge the straight-backed pillar of rectitude, Taffy Moriarty.

The header on Page 3 read: "FIREWORK ATTACK ON THE CLEGHAM MUNICIPAL PARK GATE CONVENIENCES." The Commander gulped and his eyes immediately jumped to the first paragraph. He read hastily the listing of articles-found-at-the-scene, recognising some.

In detail, Ivor wrote of a provable sighting putting P.C. MacNab and P.C. MacSporran at the scene. It brought back the searing pain of teeth indenting his cock, its slow, flesh-ripping withdrawal, the three frightening explosions, the abrupt darkness, and his mingling with persons he couldn't see, screaming their fucking heads off… groping him…one trying to shaft him! He had no recall of the sudden, electric joy of ejaculation or the curing of his lover's nuts, the moments vacating his mind before the outer door of the Gents had opened.

Letting out a yelp, the Commander grimaced, clenched his teeth together and forced his chair back. Suddenly he was shaking with rage, kicking out at the desk, his thoughts suddenly a long way from mirth gulch.

The coppers' names seemed to leap from the page at him. He seethed. There, in print, were the names of the causes of his pain and embarrassment and he was about to entrust them with "duties elsewhere"! He had seen them previously too! The two insolent bastards he had seen in the yard at West Clegham. The ones with the poor view of Masonry; the ones who'd conned a lift on a bus whilst on duty; the ones he had seen entering the mall opposite the park gates!

Ivor highlighted the two coppers' previous experiences in various departments, thinking it was useful. It didn't mollify him, even though a moment ago he had thought that himself. Shit for shooting from cannon into no man's land was his reaction now; muck for spreading thickly on fields and ploughing in. 'Pimples on a pig's arse!' he shouted, repeating the words hollered by a habitual criminal he had once arrested, 'I shall have the pair of them!'

At 9.15 a.m., Ivor telephoned. The call dragged him away from thoughts of vengeance.

'You have read my report, Jack, on the two Herberts I found for you?'

'Yes, and thank you very much,' the Commander said, though he still wasn't completely convinced there'd be a successful outcome to his plan. He calmed, clamped the phone between his ear and shoulder and began looking through the morning mail at the same time.

'They're a pair of wayward Jock oddballs, Jack. However, I saw through them. They would admit to nothing, click, click. Tried to have me believe some complete and utter pish. I presented them with incontrovertible evidence. Eventually they wilted under the burden of guilt. Birling in their boots, they were, as my old granny used to say. It was a nice feeling, Jack, like being back in the CID, turning the screw, you know what I mean?'

'Yes, you have done a good job, and speedily, Ivor,' Jack said calmly. 'I owe you one for that. I will instruct "The Jock Connection", as you term them, and send them into the "I.Q." today. I've done some preparatory work. Results could come earlier than expected.'

'Oh I do hope so,' Ivor emphasised. 'We cannot employ coppers who will not give their full time to police service. There is no room in the Job for piss-taking bastards the likes of Beckham… or Bagman, whatever his name is. His telling of god-awful jokes has transformed Gloria into someone I do not recognise. This is just not on. Before I go, Jack, here is some mental pabulum for you to consider. If the opportunity arises at the culmination of their duties elsewhere, sack the Jocks.'

'Food for thought indeed, Ivor,' Jack said, 'and I know if I need your assistance in any other delicate matters, I can count on you. See you at the next Lodge meeting, drinks on me of course, 'bye.'

His lunch consisted of coffee and a sandwich taken at his desk, then an hour poring over the Daily Telegraph crossword. The mild relaxation over, he freshened up, and at 2 p.m., was sitting rather calmer, awaiting the arrival of the two Jock oddballs.

His telephone rang. It was Rowley on the secure line.

'How did it go, Jack?' Rowley asked cheerily. Jack placed a hand over the mouthpiece, straightened his body and groaned. Rowley had said he richly deserved the company of the blind date. Didn't he know she had cannibalistic tendencies? After what happened, he needed time to think up the correct reply. He didn't want to offend Rowley. Perhaps he didn't know the woman. Perhaps she was just some randy bitch. Perhaps the odour of stale male piss, Harpic and disinfectant drove her nuts! He was wary. 'W-w-w-well,' he stuttered, 'eh, eh, not quite as good as I had hoped, Rowley. I don't think we quite hit it off.'

'I'm shocked, Jack,' Rowley replied. He sat in his office at the Yard, his face screwed up in puzzlement. Was Jack kidding him? What could have gone wrong? 'I honestly thought you and she were compatible. I thought she would get your head sorted out. I thought you'd be telling me this morning your life was back on the tracks.'

'No such luck,' Jack said brusquely.

'You found out who she was then?' Rowley asked. Instantly, he regretted asking.

'No!' Jack thundered.

Hearing from Jack that they hadn't hit it off, and he not having received a report back from Myrna as to how the blind date went, it relieved Rowley to hear 'No' from Jack, even if it was loud enough for him to finger his ear. What could he possibly have said if Jack had said 'Yes' and the date had turned out disastrously?

'We didn't even get our masks off.' Jack continued bitterly. 'And I don't want to know who she was either. Right from the beginning, I thought she wasn't my type. Your efforts were all heart, I'm sure. However, I think I'll organise my own love life from now on.'

A rapping on the door, he thought convenient and said, abruptly, 'That's my next appointment at the door, Rowley. I'll see you at the next Lodge meeting, okay. 'bye.'

'Drinks on me, Jack, 'bye.'

'You bet, Rowley.'

******

On opening the office door, following the gruffly uttered shout of 'Enter,' from the Commander, a similar thought crossed both Hamish's and Harry's minds: the day they saw him shake Superintendent Bunce's hand in the station yard, he looked different to what he does now. He was sitting behind his desk, in an upright, high-backed chair, his tunic draped over the back of it, looking facially shell-shocked. He wasn't stooped. Quite the contrary; his hands were flat on his desk, pressing downwards and, as he looked them over, he raised his buttocks from his chair. He was relieving some lower-body discomfort, they guessed.

His healthy facial bloom was missing, now it was grey. Dark bags were hanging beneath his darting eyes, dandruff covered his shoulders and his hair was unkempt.

Sitting looking at them, piercingly, it was as if he had never seen two such pieces of excrement; like a cautious, infirm pedestrian suspiciously eyeing a twice stood-in dog shite smeared over the frosty pavement they were about to negotiate.

The Commander quickly worked out the significance of the personal nicknames. P.C. MacNab's stomach protruded over the belt holding up his overstretched jeans. His old mother would have said she'd rather keep him for a week than a fortnight. He saw in him the child who took delight in turning sunflowers away from the sun a little each day in the same direction. They'd end up twisted like him… and tied in knot. He should be on a diet or ousted from the Job for unfitness alone and were those eyes of his sparkling or just laughing at him?

In MacSporran, he saw a slim individual with an angular, saturnine face who, at Myrna's, must have done most of the shagging.

The Commander sat thinking of the information he had and to which they were not privy. He knew, but they didn't know that he knew, that they were responsible for the stinging lacerations to his cock. The secret of his tattered bobby's helmet was his… his alone, and he would prefer it remained so. He still felt like firing them from some sort of cannon along with a ton of shit for causing it. However, their compliance was important for his scheme to work. He needed Daphne back, desperately.

'At ease, boys, and pull up a chair,' he said, with a sniff, whilst smiling thinly. Sweeping an arm towards two wooden, straight-backed chairs, he indicated they move them to the side of his desk.

'Things don't look too good for your future,' he said, using his best commanding voice, after they'd settled and he had their attention. 'Superintendent Bunce's report sets out a horrendous portfolio of indiscretions.' He picked up the report, flicked through the sheets crammed with typing. To ensure that both Hamish and Harry would see the red typing, he then casually tossing it onto the desk in front of him.

'However, things can change. With your co-operation, and I mean full co-operation,' he looked at them meaningfully, looked to see if they were taking in his words, 'your careers can take off again. I have personal inquiries requiring a certain diligence and secrecy. For if it were known that I tackled the problem this way, my career would look as flimsy as yours does right now.'

'How do you mean take off again?' Hamish interjected.

'I'm against the policy of ousting clued-up coppers to make places for inexperienced graduates. On this division, I consider the experienced detective constables working my patch to be irreplaceable. With your arrest records, you could fit permanently into the department here. Do you get what I'm saying?'

'You're saying you're short of two capable thief takers in CID?'

'You have a cheek, MacNab, but yes, though not immediately. I've looked at your record of arrests. I consider officers with the experience you pair can provide are hard to come by. I'm also sure the mental aberrations placing you in front of me today wouldn't have happened had you remained in plain clothes. I understand your frustrations, though I cannot agree with your reaction to your demotions. However, there's a catch.'

'A catch?' Hamish asked.

'You've heard of "duties elsewhere"?'

'We've both heard of "rubber heelers",' Harry piped up.

'"Duties elsewhere", is slightly different…ahum. It is usual that only the keenest and most diligent of officers will carry out this type of investigation. Such officers realise that the Force will never sanction this method of collaring chummy, even if it's the only foolproof way of doing so. The officers also understand that such investigations are highly controversial and probably illegal. The investigation I have in mind for you is of a highly personal nature and…and probably illegal, too. Nevertheless, the same rules will apply to you. The investigating officers resign from the Force first…'

'What!' Hamish bawled.

'…so that any fall-out cannot damage the Force… MacNab… don't get uppity with me. I think you've little choice in the matter.'

'Superintendent Bunce never mentioned that aspect of the deal,' Hamish complained loudly.

The Commander picked up the report again, waved it at them, chucked it down, and said, 'There's no deal. Realise this… there's enough dirt here for me to ask for your resignations now. You have the Federation lawyers to fall back on, okay. You could win, keep you jobs, okay, but you'll be stuck in uniform until you reach pensionable age. Do this successfully, and you're back working in plain-clothes… all right.'

He looked at them looking at each other, watched them shrug shoulders, heard the 'Aye, he's right,' from MacNab and the 'Ken,' from MacSporran.

'What's it all about then, Commander?' Hamish enquired.

'It's about a copper working the Irish Quarter home beat. It's an unusual place, it's likely you'll never have heard of it. It's on my manor and over the years, we've come to know the place as the "I.Q.". It has remained tolerably policed since Constable Beckham took over home beat duties there some twenty-five years ago. He has proved a very efficient, diligent officer with an admirable work ethic. Arrests are a rarity, but a phenomenal amount of traffic process, mainly offences committed by company reps and visitors, comes out of the area. Seldom, if ever, do we have the delight of seeing a local inhabitant in court.'

'If we decided yes to your terms, is there any current Irish problem we'd need to worry about?' Harry asked.

'A good question, MacSporran, but no, it's an interdenominational community. Records show they were mostly interested in pub lock-ins years ago. Probably still are, though there's been no report of any licensing offences in Beckham's time. You may assume Constable Beckham has his finger on that pulse.'

'So what's your problem with him?' Hamish asked.

'I have confirmed reports that he is moonlighting as a comedian as far north as Blackpool, using the name Billy Bagman. I suspect he might be gigging within the "I.Q." in pubs and clubs,' he said, hoping to hell he was.

'You're having us on,' Harry said, muffling a guffaw.

Hamish looked equally surprised.

'I've the info on him,' the Commander confided.

'Do you want to run him out of the Job, sir; is that what this is all about?' Harry blurted.

'I'm not in the business of ruining careers,' the Commander snapped. 'What *I* require of you is this. Firstly, confirm my suspicions. Once confirmed, find out if Constable Beckham is gigging anywhere on the manor, and if he is, get me into a gig. It's as simple as that. I have a personal reason to see his show.' He gave them a cold smile only, giving nothing away. 'Can we leave it at that?'

He lifted the desk blotter and produced a copy of an A4 size poster. Pushing it across the desk, he said, 'This shows the caricature of "Billy Bagman", the comedian. You will note one important and instantly recognisable feature. He has a mole type appendage to the fore and left of his nose as you look at it, and protruding respectively from it at 3, 6, 9 and 12 o'clock, is a prominent single hair.'

He then produced a photograph of William Beckham, taken at the time of his recruitment.

Constable William Beckham

'You're right, . Constable Beckham's photo does have similarities to the caricature. The mole-like appendage, with the four hairs radiating at the correct hourly intervals, makes him a dead-ringer,' Hamish said.

'Billy Bagman really does look the alter-ego of Constable Beckham.' Harry said and nodded his head in agreement.

The Commander smiled, happy with the interview's progress. 'I have made certain arrangements to expedite your early, incognito arrival and acceptance into the "I.Q." It's better to have a cover than to go in cold.'

He arose from his chair, walked stiffly and stilt-like towards the south-facing window, beckoning them to follow. 'That Ford Transit down there is a hired rental van. Your names are on the agreement and it's insured. I've paid. You look after it. It's not a rough old nondescript. I've had adhesive lettering stuck to the sides, advertising the double-glazing company, Practical Integrated Glazing Systems. Inside you'll find two pairs of overalls and some relevant leaflets. The leaflets you can shove through letterboxes in the "I.Q." as part of your cover. In them, there's a strong hint. The glazing company is looking to fit a show house free with their product. Such a carrot should at least get the locals interested and talking to you.'

The Commander threw the transit keys towards Hamish, then ushered them back to their chairs. 'Finally, men,' he said, looking slightly apprehensive, expecting an outburst, 'I presupposed your decision, took the liberty and tentatively booked your lodgings and food at The Norfolk and Suffolk Hotel. You will find it at the end of Termonfechin Street, around the corner from Ringaskiddy Square. I believe this is a genteel establishment, dedicated to temperance and run by an elderly, well-regarded Irish woman. You will receive bed, breakfast and evening meal there. Other meals are down to expenses, which will only be paid on the successful completion of the task.'

'Reckoned we were a soft touch, sir?' Harry asked.

Hamish squeaked his chair back along the floor, and said, 'Aye, got us nicely, sir, got us nicely.'

'I needed someone. It just happened you were available. You put yourselves in this position, not me. You need the job. The Job doesn't need piss-takers, quality ones even less.'

The Commander lifted his gaze from them and moved behind his desk. He found and handed them two identification cards showing they were consultants for Practical Integrated Glazing Systems. Warrant card photographs were already in them, suitably doctored. Two sets of resignation forms, already filled in, he produced from a drawer, and motioned them forward to sign.

'These will remain in my safe until your return. Nothing will give me greater pleasure than to see them shredded after your "duties elsewhere". Now, your warrant cards, please.'

He placed the cards together with their signed resignation forms into his safe. Then he handed them a map of the manor, the "I.Q." circled.

*****

They were stunned. Signing the forms and leaving the Commander's office without their warrant cards was a bummer. To have them returned, they'd to embark on a bizarre pantomime in an "Irish Quarter". Unhappy, they shook their heads. Hamish mumbled, 'Our bad luck, by the way.'

They loaded their bags into the van and set off for the IQ.

A mile or so into their journey, Hamish loosened off, 'Fuck, it's just registered,' and pulled the van into a lay-by and stopped. 'I want to check something.' He left the van and walked to its side. 'Suffering fuck, Harry,' he bawled, and scratched his head, 'I was right.'

Harry got out, sensing a problem. 'Look at this,' Hamish said, pointing at the lettering on the van.

'It's what he said it was,' Harry said.'

'Aye, but look at the capitals. What do they say?'

The first letter in each of the four words had been capitalised and emboldened. While the wording certainly advertised Practical Integrated Glazing Systems, the capitals boldly spelled out "PIGS"

'You're right, Hamish, Suffering fuck! The job's gone tits up already!'

******

The Commander watched the van leave the station yard. For the first time, "PIGS" registered with him. He smiled; it was a bit of a blunder. The inhabitants of the "I.Q." might extract a degree of humour from it. If they did, he was sure that MacNab and MacSporran had the pedigree to handle it.

Now, he was convinced, it was just a matter of time until he returned Daphne to the marital bed. He could hug, hold and make up for lost time…but not before his injury healed.

He hadn't told anyone of the telephone conversation he'd had earlier in the day with the manager of the Central Pier theatre, Blackpool. Nor had he told anyone he'd discovered Constable Beckham used his home address as the comedian's forwarding address. He had already proved PC William Beckham was Billy Bagman. If the Jocks were good detectives, as their service records suggested, they ought to find that out for themselves, easily. Catching PC Beckham gigging anywhere as Billy Bagman, might be more difficult.

The manager of the Central Pier theatre told him that Billy Bagman had only performed on one night during the past season, standing in for a sick comic. Hearing he would perform there for the whole of the following summer season had caused him to raise an incredulous eyebrow. Encouraging was the news that Billy Bagman would be "keeping his hand in" by performing in his locality, and at this time of year. 'Stop worrying, Jack,' he told himself, 'things will turn out just fine.'

******

One hand on the steering wheel, Hamish began rummaging with the other in his bag. He pulled out a urine sample bottle; it seemed he'd had an idea in mind for some time. Turning south onto the A406 north circular road, the direct route towards the river and the Irish enclave, he pulled into a roadside café.

'What are you up to now?' Harry asked.

'I'm going to give Mr Sanctimonious, Bastard-faced Bunce something to remember us by. I didn't appreciate the denigrating way he spoke of our Scottish sense of humour or our heroes, by the way,' Hamish said, laughing. 'Anyone who's as irritating and as pedantic as that poser is deserving of some comeuppance. Let's have a cup of tea in this kaff.'

Inside the café, he ordered three cups of tea; one each for himself and Harry, from the other, without milk, he filled the sample bottle.

'What's your game? Are you letting me in on it, or what?' Harry asked, still not up with his mate's thinking.

'I'm going to stop off at a notorious Pub where drug dealers hang out. There, I intend to buy a packet of speed to mix with this tea. Then I'm sending the bottle to Ricky Croker, the famous investigative journalist at Thameside Television. The note I include will tell him that Bunce has, and for some time too, doctored the tea in the nick canteen with amphetamines to make us more alert and to get more work out of us. He's too astute to believe that, but it will cause a stir when Bunce gets to hear of it, as I'm sure he will. I'm going to cite Sergeant Taffy Moriarty as an example of an over-zealous hyperactive, tea-drinking workaholic, now languishing in Clegham Mental Hospital, suffering from a serious amphetamine-induced mental disorder. They'll undoubtedly check that out and find this letter to be at least half-true.

'I'm just going to sign the note... "Mr. Policeman".'

PART TWO

OPERATION "IQ"

THE INVESTIGATION

Tuesday

There wasn't any sign on the faces of Hamish and Harry that they saw amusement or fun on offer, as they peered from the transit van's cab towards the Norfolk and Suffolk Temperance Hotel.

Seeing Hamish's furrowed forehead and screwed up eyes, Harry piped up, 'Don't look so glum, Hamish, It could be a hoot. The colour scheme choice is sure funny. Walls all emerald-green, window surrounds sills and door stiles lilac, where else would you get that but in an Irish Quarter or a Disney film.'

Hamish said, 'Disnae work for me.' From the driver's side of the van, he'd seen a sign, a shamrock-shaped board fixed above the entrance. Gold coloured lettering, trumpeted the hotel's abstemious purity. It said no alcohol, inebriates or itinerants allowed on the premises. He said, seeing some risibility in the words, 'It looks as if the good lady in charge of this colourful hotel is a first-class mickey-taker.'

The hotel looked well maintained; the spotless windowpanes reflected the last rays of orangey sunlight. An alleyway parallel with the side of the building, just not wide enough for a transit to squeeze through, was the entrance to the hotel car park.

'There's the wrinkled face of an elderly woman looking out that downstairs window,' Harry said. The face backed off and a scrawny hand replaced it, pushing a scrawled notice to one side that said, Ring Bell And Enter. The woman began waving it about to catch their attention.

'Entering a booze-free zone's hardly an attraction, but it's four o'clock already. Booking in now seems sensible.' Thrusting a thumb towards the window, Hamish said, 'I was going to say let's meet the licensee, but that's a no-no.'

Parked up outside the front door, the van locked, they entered a small, reception area reeking of polish. A shiny-topped desk filling one corner had a residents' registration book with a brass call bell sitting on top. A board with a row of hooks attached and fixed to the back wall dangled room keys. The lopsided Alcoholics Anonymous calendar, two months out of date, showed September had thirty days. Outmoded drab millinery, thick with blue-tinged hairs, yellowy scurf, and stuck with highly ornate hairpins, festooned a corner-standing hat stand.

A variegated mongrel, looking the full fifty-seven-variety make, lay stretched out on a tattered leather settee. Friendly, but disinterested in their arrival, it wagged its tail once. Lifting its head, it cast dark eyes in their direction and then flopped back. Hamish positioned his fist above the bell, only to think better of making the "ding" when he saw a hand wafting a curtain hiding an inner doorway to one side.

The elderly woman on the end of the hand had a pronounced stoop. Her blue-rinsed hair, mundanely styled with tight curls, had an old-fashioned metal hairgrip hanging precariously from strands at the back. It bounced as she walked and she moved fast for one so frail. Her faded housecoat flew open and her wrinkled face waxed into grumpiness as she cast her eyes over them. Every short step she took her Stephenson's Rocket steam-engine-shaped slippers sounded a chuff. Her false teeth, slack on her gums, clacked as she walked. Chuff, clack, chuff, clack, she sounded.

'I'm Miss Gillhooly. What is it you want?' she asked stiffly. Her voice, which retained traces of an Irish accent, had an edge, sounded as if she didn't like the look of them. She cast her eyes away from them towards the dog and tossed it a raw Brussels sprout. Reaching the reception desk, she raised the wooden flap and went behind.

'Our boss has booked us in,' Hamish said, leaning on the desktop, eyeing her.

'Don't lean on the counter, stand up straight so I can have a good look at you,' she said, fussily, her voice rising. 'You'll ruin the varnish,' she said, polishing the counter with her housecoat cuff. 'I'm careful who I book in here. Who did you say you were?' she asked, moving the bell to one side and opening the guest book.

'We're from Practical Integrated Glazing Systems,' Hamish said.

'Holy mother of God, Holy Jesus, the Holy Father, Mary the blessed virgin, mother of Christ, Joseph, Mother Teresa and Father Murphy, double-glazing salesmen is it?' she shrieked. Using a thumb, she thrust her top denture back onto her gum, sucked on it, then snorted, tossed her head back and let out a cackling, derisive laugh. 'I'd have thought your boss would've had more sense than to send double-glazing salesmen here. Father Ted, eat your heart out, there's dafter about than you after all. Is your boss as silly as that drunken old lag, Father Jack?'

'You must know him?' Hamish asked, sounding surprised.

'No, no, but the last lot of know-all, gullible and stupid salesmen were really ripped off here, weren't they?' she replied, cackling louder. 'Show houses were all the rage, whole streets wanted one and whole streets were into devious shenanigans.'

'Aye, that's as maybe, but we're more experienced and have a better product than the easily-duped lot,' Hamish said. It was the first piece of sales patter to come into his head. 'We won't make the same mistakes.'

Miss Gillhooly gave a scornful sniff. 'This isn't Craggy Island, you know. We'll see if you can triumph over the crafty Irish folk living in this neighbourhood,' she screeched. 'Potty training is no longer a part of higher education here, you know. Now then, let me see. Your boss has booked a room with two single beds and a sink. B and B with an evening meal is what he asked for. There's a shower at one end of the corridor and a toilet at the other end on that floor. You're my only residents and I've nothing in to prepare a meal for you tonight. There's fast food outlets round about so you won't go hungry I'm sure. Will that do?'It's also the best I can offer.'

They both nodded their agreement. Hamish returned to the transit van to collect their bags. While Harry was hanging about, teasing the dog with the sprout, Miss Gillhooly issued further instructions, 'And when you use the toilet, you make sure the extractor fan is switched on.' She gave out a loud, phlegmy cackle. What she said obviously seemed funny to her.

Hamish returned with their bags. Miss Gillhooly was standing hunched-up in a corner, behind the desk, on the telephone, placing an order with her butcher. 'Send me two pork chops, a pound of your cheapest pork sausages, small ones, and a pound of streaky bacon,' she said loudly.

The dog looked forlornly in their direction and wagged its tail slowly, as if knowing there'd be little to get his teeth into from any leftovers of the order. With its front teeth, it continued to juggle and nibble disinterestedly at the unappealing raw sprout.

'Leaning on the desk, Miss Gillhooly said, sounding less strident, motherly even with advice. 'I should have mentioned it before, but before you go upstairs, park up your van safely… before Bebe comes along and nabs you.'

'And who might Bebe be?' Hamish asked, dropping the bags and groping in his jeans pocket for the transit keys.

'Billy Beckham is our community police officer. A very good one, too,' she cackled. 'He doesn't suffer fools gladly. Interlopers and strangers entering this neighbourhood have to beware. He'll do you as soon as look at you. Take my word and park your van up properly. Drive around the corner into Kilkenny Avenue. You'll find a parking-place under a streetlight there. It'll be easily seen from your bedroom window.'

'Morpheee,' she piped, and instantly a small, weasel-featured head poked from behind the curtains covering the door through which she had earlier bustled.

'Take the gentlemen up to the big room, will you? Show them how to use the conveniences, especially how to lift the toilet seat. Keep them free of those horrible yellow stains you men are guilty of leaving behind you… *and*,' she said loudly, casting her eyes over them, 'show them the hotel rules. In particular, point out the ones about *no drink or women* to be brought back to these premises.' She ran an eye over them as she spoke, taking special note of Hamish. Giving him swift weight appraisal, she said. 'And make sure Fatso here uses the reinforced bed, the one with the eight empty Guinness crates supporting the springs… I don't want him falling through my ceiling of a night.'

'Eh,' Hamish uttered, hearing the one name that his recent "up town" detractors had omitted to call him.

Hamish left to move the transit.

The full-length Morphy appeared. He was an ancient gent who stood a good five feet tall in his wellies. Soaking wet, he'd weigh seven stone. He wore a pair of soiled, ragged trousers held up with a length of hemp rope. His collarless shirt, as grubby as the trousers, was done up at the top with a collar stud.

He looked sheepish beneath Miss Gillhooly's gaze and attempted to lift the two holdalls at once. He, too, spoke with an Irish lilt. Unable to lift the holdalls, he let out a wheezed 'Bayjasus.'

Hamish returned from parking the transit, blinked when he saw the full Morphy. They picked their bags up and followed him up a flight of stairs.

Daft he wasn't. Morphy had an eye for a bargain, or in this case, a gift. Instantly, on settling Hamish and Harry into their room, he declared his interest in new double-glazing for his home.

'I missed out last time on the offer of turning my home into a show-house,' he said with a begging-bowl face, and sulking-dog's eyes. 'I offered my house, it's not very big and I said I didn't mind showing folks around, but I wasn't chosen. Quite despairing I was, to be sure.'

'Aw that's a shame… I'm sure you were,' Hamish said and pulled out two advertising leaflets from one of the bundles. 'If you're interested in us using your home this time, put your name and address on these. Leave them at the desk for us and we'll put it in the draw we have to see who will win the honour. We'll do our best for you and put it in at the top.' Hamish gave Morphy a knowing wink.

'If I could afford double-glazing, I'd take my month's holiday back home in Dublin. The extra week I'd spend in Donegal,' he said, a sly smile creasing his face. He went on to explain. 'My name's Morphy O'Richards, not Murphy. It was me Mammy what named me. She never told me if she called me after the electric toaster or somebody with an atrocious Irish accent.

'I'm only the handyman here, you know, and I don't get paid. In fact, I'm handy at most things for which I don't get paid. I even help Constable Beckham and he doesn't pay me either, but he says I'm very handy, he does. He says I'm as useful as a thumb on a wanking hand. Comedian, he is.' Laughing at his own story, he coughed himself into a prolonged, rasping, asthmatic wheeze.

Allowing Morphy to ingratiate himself upon them was an old detective's device for courting sources of information. Inquiries began immediately. 'Does Constable Beckham take a drink in any of the pubs around here, then?' Hamish casually asked. Morphy's answer to his a question could be worth knowing.

'To be sure, depending what night of the week it is, you could find him in any three of the two of them,' Morphy rasped. 'He likes a pint of Guinness with the boys, that he does, and he plays in the pub league at darts, dominoes and pool. Tonight he's playing pool for the Navigator's Den against the Shankless Music Bar. Get yourselves over.

'There's a great pint of Dublin-brewed Guinness on tap there It's much better than the London-brewed stuff they put out in other pubs I've been into.'

Morphy coughed and wheezed some more then left them. On his way down the corridor, he cleared his throat and stopped at the toilet for a spit.

Laid on his bed, Hamish produced a copy of the Clegham Advertiser newspaper, bought from a passing paperboy whilst moving the transit to the safer parking spot. A section advertised the entertainment available to pub and club goers within the Clegham area. 'If proper detective work is required on the Commander's "wild comedian chase", then this is where we ought to start,' he said.

Throughout their service together in the CID, Hamish and Harry had tossed ideas around whenever clues to the identity of a chummy were hard to find. Often their joint minds had conjured up a different line of enquiry that they should make; often, they beat senior detectives to the door of the perpetrator the Met sought.

On cue, Harry sat up; he had caught Hamish's drift, his detective's mind triggered. 'Ken fine, have a look, see if he's gigging. Think about this, though: If we were to look at back copies of that paper, for the last twelve months, we might find advertisements for Billy Bagman performing locally. If he performed in this area, around this time last year, say, he might just be doing so again now. It's not the festive season yet, but he might be tuning up for a Christmas spectacular by performing a charity gig in a church hall or some other institution. Tickets might be available for a performance at one of them. Our job is over when we get a couple for the Commander.'

'For our sakes and the Commander's,' Hamish said, 'I just hope he is gigging. What will we do if we don't find Billy Bagman among the advertised performers?'

'Asking the local entertainment agency if he's gigging in the area will cause suspicion,' Harry said, 'could warn him that rubber heelers are on the ground. We can check every advertised comedian act working in the area, surprise guest artists too, especially in the pubs in this locality. He could easily be using another stage name, but we must be on the right track. Hasn't Morphy just confirmed he's a comedian? That was a cracker about his wanking hand. He couldn't have made it up; he's not that bright.'

'The Commander will be pleased when I tell him you sussed that out,' Hamish faint-praised him. 'I'll also be giving your sheets a stiffness test in the morning. Your thinking is good, though, and we can hope that Morphy's comedian thing is our first real clue.'

'What are we going to do if we get concrete evidence that this Billy Bagman is about to perform?' Harry asked.

Hamish was all the while thinking. 'If we value the opportunity of getting back into plain clothes, there's no contest. Mind you, grassing up another copper will be hard to stomach. However, the Commander seems to have given us a get-out clause. He hasn't said he wants to have him resign. He just wants to attend one of the moonlighting copper's gigs.

'There's more behind the Commander's need than meets the eye. I couldn't even begin to guess what it is. I'll sleep on it tonight. By morning, I might have a solution. One thing, though, we must remember not to use the name Billy Bagman in any conversations. We don't want to give the game away.'

Their eyelids lowered as the last strains of the B.B.C's. six o'clock news faded. Refreshing and recharging forty winks loomed compellingly. Hamish had a final thought before sleep overcame him. 'If Miss Gillhooly loads your plate with Brussels sprouts tomorrow night, are you going to down them all?'

'I'll ask for seconds. You'll eat up yours, too. Didn't you notice the size of that dog's bollocks?'

******

It was 9 p.m. when they left the Norfolk and Suffolk Hotel. Being undercover, as it were, they'd both put on black leather jackets and jeans. The attire fooled Miss Gillhooly, fussily dusting the reception. She gave them the once-over and sniffed derisively. 'You won't pull any birds in the pubs around here dressed like that,' she cackled.

They thought their destination, Ringaskiddy Square, was unusual in that it was circular. Its central area was a car park; fringed with tall trees it was large enough to hold a hundred vehicles. Parked shrewdly, surveillance of most of the buildings on the square's periphery, housing commerce, colourful and quaint shops, pubs and entertainment venues, was possible. People with familiar Irish surnames owned many of the businesses.

A one-way road system circled the square and served the car park's several entrances and exits. Streets radiated off the square's outer circumference at regular intervals. Spurring off the streets were narrow, cobbled, "olde worlde" alleys, giving access to loading bays servicing the shops and the back doors of other businesses with on-square frontage. Street and store window lighting illuminated the square.

The weather wasn't helping them see much detail as they made their way. Scudding clouds obscuring the moon prevented prolonged bursts of the moonlight adding any brightness. A wintry wind from the direction of the river, funnelled through the pedestrian-free streets.

The general lay of the immediate area noted, they decided to seek refreshment. The Navigator's Den, the subject of Morphy's good report, was the only pub in the square doing good business, cheering and laughter coming from within.

Hamish pushed through the swing doors. In front of him was a wall of sturdy, Guinness quaffing men, all with ruddy, windblown faces, wearing black donkey jackets decorated with well-known, construction company names and logos. Their interest was the illuminated pool table on which the Navigator's Den was playing the Shankless Music Bar in a "pool-league" match.

Suddenly groans erupted from all around. The opposition had just pulled back into contention.

Hamish pushed his way through to the bar, ordered two pints of Guinness and placed a ten-pound note in front of him. He thought it a minor event in any pub in the land even on a Tuesday night. Some customers standing close by saw it otherwise. Some whispering took place. Quickly, it became evident why.

'Are you the boys staying down at the, er, eh, the "Two Focks" and looking for a show house for your double-glazing?' the barman asked, as he handed Hamish his change. He tipped a wink to his cronies standing by the bar, and feverishly dried some glasses while he waited for their part-poured Guinness to settle. 'I can always spot clever people looking to show off their great wares,' he confessed.

A glance passed between Hamish and Harry. It hadn't taken long for the barman to hear of their presence. The barman was fiftyish and spoke with a Dublin brogue. His sideburns were turning grey and he had a small bald patch towards the back of an otherwise good head of blonde hair, shoulder length and tied back in a ponytail. From his casual clothes, facial wrinkles and happy outlook, he looked like a rocker now rocking towards superannuated years. His body shape would do nothing for bulimic woman. A T-shirt, with the logo, "Call Down The Moon", the title of an album made by the famous and still-going-strong Welsh rock band, MAN, stretched around his considerable paunch.

'What do you mean by the "Two Focks"?' Hamish asked. 'It sounds a bit Irish to me.'

'You're almost right there, but you're wrong. The "Two Focks" is what old Granny Gillhooly's Hotel is known to us as around here,' he said, grinning slyly. 'It's short for Norfolk and Suffolk. It's been standing since before the Irish influence in the area. If it hadn't stood that long, today, it'd be known as the "Two Fecks".'

'I see,' Hamish said, nodding his head. At the same time, he spotted Morphy sitting by the door; now he understood where the barman had gained his knowledge. 'We haven't started our sales campaign yet, but if you're interested in the show house draw, I'll drop off a couple of leaflets, see if we can fix you up.'

Grinning broadly, the barman tipped his cronies another wink. Returning to the pumps, he topped up their pints, leaving space at the brim for the compulsory, Guinness head of froth. Handing them over, he said, 'If you're into heavy rock, I can get you a couple of complimentary tickets for tomorrow night's gig at the Shankless Music Bar.' He pointed a finger to the front of his T-shirt so they'd notice it. 'They're Welsh. One of the great rock bands of the seventies, they were. The best band ever to pound hearing in this area,' he said knowingly, poking a finger into an ear.

Hamish nudged Harry and pointed out Morphy. He was nursing a part-consumed pint of Guinness and looking towards the pool table. 'Let's take a seat with our first interested customer,' Hamish said. The barman and his cronies laughed loudly, seeing some humour in the statement.

Seated, with their backs to the wall, Harry was quickly aware that the variegated mongrel they'd seen at the hotel was beneath the table; it's inquisitive, wet nose was sniffing between his legs, perhaps looking for another game with a sprout.

'Ah, take no notice. It's only Timmy. He likes yer. He's a grand, intelligent little fella. He can walk backwards and wag his head. He's just pleased to see yer,' Morphy cackled. They could hear him well over the hubbub of the pub.

The excited sniffing continued, the dog's tail thwacking against a table leg, rocking some empty glasses. Suddenly, it leapt forward, his tongue lolling out of his head, its front paws landing in Harry's lap.

'Watch your knee, I think he fancies it,' chuckled Hamish. Slapping Harry's thigh, he encouraged the dog with tongue clicks. 'Come on boy, up here, do your stuff.'

'Fuck off,' Harry said to Hamish, then repeated the instruction to the dog.

'I've just lost his brother. He died. Timmy's very lonely now.' Morphy cast a sad eye at them and pushed back his chair.

'Aw. How long has his brother been dead?' Hamish asked.

'Well, if he had lived until tomorrow, he'd be dead a fortnight,' he told them. 'Lay down you daft bogger and be quiet!' he raged beneath the table at Timmy, who settled down to lie quietly alongside their feet on the floor.

Festooning the nicotine-discoloured, wallpaper-flaking walls of the bar, were artefacts of historical interest from the locality, depicting fifty or more years of local navvies at work and at play. Displayed examples of spades, some worn down to the wooden shaft, had write-ups explaining their different usages. Tales told of some operators, blessed with a long working life, who had worn out two or more spades.

An old sepia photograph showed a gang of navvies on a building site, thronging around a large, circular, newly dug hole. The write-up beneath said: "The Cutting of the Sod Ceremony. Construction commences on the Circle Line."

Hanging next to it, a more recent photograph showed a gang of older, mud-splattered navvies, circling the same hole. The write-up said: "The Topping Out Ceremony. Construction of the Circle Line is completed."

A photograph of a peculiar-looking family didn't look out of place among the others.

The write-up beneath said: “The blighted O’Hooligan family suffered from a rare genetic disorder, known in the locality as Guinness Ear.” Each had a cigarette sticking downwards from an earflap, a symptom of the complaint.

‘I’ve an idea what causes that disorder, by the way,’ Hamish said, spotting the photograph.

‘What do you ken?’ Harry asked.

‘Well, take this scenario. For maybe twenty years, you drink twelve pints of Guinness nightly, that’s twelve times twenty, times three hundred and sixty-five. When you multiply all that lot up, what result do you have?’

Harry’s eyes began to move about in his head as he did the mental arithmetic.

‘That equates to a lot of drunken sleeping time, and Harry, I know you’re well aware of this fact: Guinness is one of the best soporifics known to man. Once your head hits that pillow it will never move until morning. That’s a lot of time sleeping on one ear now isn’t it?’

‘That’s eighty-seven-thousand and six-hundred pints,’ Harry said. ‘Aye you’re right.’

‘After twenty years of pissing it up, one ear starts lying closer to the head, Hamish continued. ‘Eventually, in extreme cases, it’s usual for the outer ear to fuse itself to the side of the head…’

Harry interjected. ‘Adding another sixty for the leap years, that’s…’

‘ …that’s enough, Einstein. It leaves a narrow pocket between ear and head. Most of the O’Hooligans I’ve met worked as carpenters. They all kept their pencils stuck in that flap.’

‘Daft bastard,’ chuckled Harry, throwing his head back.

A dead-fly encrusted, framed photograph of an elderly man was hanging beneath a dim, nicotine-stained light fitting. Harry asked. ‘Who’s the old geezer dressed in what looks like the very best of navvy gear? The spotless donkey jacket, black, string bow tie, white silk shirt and white wellies look class.’

‘Boys, those photos you’ve looked at are a part of the navvy joke section. It’s the greatest spade handlers in the world doing a bit of self-deprecation. They all drank here in the Navigator’s Den. That photo there, that’s the world-famous Grampy O’Sullivan, the greatest liar ever heard in open contest, dressed in the bib and tucker of his profession.’

The write-up beneath the photograph said: “The Legendary Grampy O’Sullivan, deceased, local luminary, with-drink orator, and the winner of the Navigator’s Den’s Liar of the Year contest for fifty-seven consecutive years.”

Morphy slurped at his pint and removed the froth from his chin with the back of his hand. ‘He could lie the breeks off you Scotties, I can tell yer,’ he said. ‘The last time he sat on the “lying down pouffe”, that thing stuffed with duck fluff laid there in that glass case, he brought the house down with the most wondrous of lies.'

In the display cabinet, standing close to the pub entrance, a silver trophy, tarnished with age, sat upon a green-velvet plinth. The inscription around its rim said: "The Tom O'Pepper Trophy."

'Aye, that's very apt and Irish considering the devil threw the legendary Tom Pepper out of Hell for telling lies,' reminded Hamish.

The write-up beneath said: "The Tom O'Pepper Trophy has remained uncontested, since Grampy O'Sullivan won it fifty-seven times on the belt end."

A coloured photograph of a stiffened diving suit, described as "The Wimmen's Monument", lay on the case bottom.

'Morphy, what's that coloured photograph and the other paraphernalia all about?' Harry asked.

'You're asking me something now, boys. I've told you, Grampy O'Sullivan was the arch-fabricator of untruths. Well, this pub was, and still is, to a lesser extent, the ancient cradle of fibbing. Bayjasus, it was, but didn't it all go a bit funny for Grampy that last time.'

'Why's that?' Harry asked. He was keeping Morphy wound up, storytelling.

Morphy dried his chin on the cuff of his donkey jacket, preparing for a lengthy tale. 'Well, he had an old biddy of a wife, didn't he, and she didn't like the prize he was set to win again. She might have been right. After all, he had won it for fifty-six years up until then. The first prize was always a fortnight's holiday in a horse-drawn caravan in County Donegal, with enough free Guinness and Old Paddy whiskey to blur the memory of all those miles travelled over bumpy roads.

'The Granny aired her objections about the prize to Grampy in what I believe was an interesting, one-sided conversation that they had to be sure. "There's no way you're getting me into a rickety old caravan at my time of life. You're a feckin' silly old eajit. You getting all silly, sexy and passionate, thinking you can still perform. The last time you tried to throw that twisted old stump of a leg over my body, you almost broke my back."

'Well, she had been into the pub for a quart of Guinness to carry out, and had seen the prize list for the contest. She told Grampy to take the second prize on the list that she had seen hung up on the notice board, and told him not to come back home with any other one.

'She was a formidable old biddy and I can still see her in my mind's eye. Sitting by her newly Zebo-blackened hearth, she'd warm herself at the peat fire. She always wore a shawl of handmade Irish linen, crocheted with shamrocks that you'd hardly recognise amongst the other 39 shades of green. A broken clay pipe, throwing out more sparks than the fire, she'd hold between her one and only pickle-stabber of a snaggled tooth and the bottom lip of a pair irreparably stained from drinking stewed tea. Poor old Grampy, I felt sorry for him, quite often he couldn't get a word in sideways.

'On the night of the final contest here at the Navigator's Den, Grampy's home became rather bare. All the furniture normally used for comfortable seating, Granny had removed from the house and built it into a bonfire in the backyard. There she waited, expectant; the time was approaching for her to hear the thunderous uproar and the raptures Grampy received every annual Liar of the Year event, for as far back as she could remember.

'When finally the uproar rumbled the night air, she rubbed her hands together and sighed. Grampy'd be arriving home shortly with his entourage of inebriated followers pushing and shoving the wheelbarrow. Lashed on board would be the brand-new *divan suite* that he had won, and which she had set her heart on.

'Liberally, she doused the old furniture with paraffin. Taking a wax taper, she lit it with her pipe, by sucking on its stem strongly until it roared like a blacksmith's forge. Then she set the bonfire alight and the flames soared into the heavens. Bayjasus, wasn't it just her strong, womanly convictions that told her that she was doing the correct thing?

'The entourage arrived home with a diving suit, Grampy all the time wondering, "What the divil am I going to do with this eajit thing?"

'The following morning, Grampy mixed cement in the wheelbarrow and filled the diving suit up to the brass collar. He left it to set, fitted the helmet and visor, and erected it in his front garden with that plaque you see over there.'

The write-up on the plaque said: "THIS MONUMENT IS DEDICATED TO WOMEN EVERYWHERE WHO THINK THEY KNOW EVERYTHING."

'We've a right one here, Harry,' Hamish said, chortling.

'Aye ah ken, his story was almost as good as yours.'

'Ear, ear,' Hamish responded.

An ancient map of the Kingdom of Ireland, hanging skew-whiff on a wall, gave the locations and origins of Irish surnames. A display of photographs showed John Millington Synge, Flam O'Brien and George Bernard Shaw, describing them as wild, Irish writers.

A corner stage had a collection of rubbish dumped on it, gathering dust; interest in the old entertainment had waned with the passing of years and the changing tastes of customers.

On the opposite side of the bar to where they sat, stood the pool table, and on the wall, two dart boards and a notice board. A sudden stirring amongst the supporters standing and sitting near them suggested the pool match was becoming interesting. 'The opposition have pulled a couple of frames back,' Morphy explained, having followed the games played before they came in. 'Their pub we knew as the Hamshank Redemption, back in the good old days. Then they played jigging music on fiddle and flute. Nowadays their customers are a bloody load of hairy rockers, if you were to ask me.'

Constable Beckham was easily recognisable as one of the players approaching the pool table for the next game. Grizzly, with a hirsute, wart-blighted nose, care-worn faced, potbellied, he was out of place amongst the younger set of men making up both teams. His opponent broke the balls, scattering them around the table, leaving none easily pottable.

Taking his time, perusing, working out his first shot, acting much in the manner of Steve Davis as mimicked by John Virgo, he peered at the lie of the balls. Chalking his cue, he calculated angles and working out where the white ball would end up after each shot. Walking around the table, stealthily, lifting each foot high in turn, his cue held out in front of him, he prowled like a hillbilly in the film Deliverance.

Hamish nudged Harry and said from behind a hand. 'He certainly looks like his photo and I'd put money on him being Billy Bagman.'

'I'm so sure I wouldn't take the bet. Just look at his nose, there can only be one like that in the Job.

'The score is seven all, boys. Bebe has to win this game for the pub to win the match,' Morphy commentated.

Bebe chalked his cue again and blew the excess from the tip, like a professional does. Settled on his game plan, the bar hushed. Leaning over the table in an ungainly stance, his belly hung low, almost resting on his knees. Lining up his cue for the first shot, he wobbled, steadied then potted a difficult double into a corner pocket. Then with magical, deft and accurate flicks, his cue-arm a blur, the next six balls and the black thudded into pockets without allowing his opponent another visit to the table.

The Navigator's Den won the match. Fists rose into the air accompanied by shouts of 'Yes' from the other home players and supporters.

'That's our Bebe, that is,' Morphy said, gleefully, turning towards them and showing his toothless smile. 'We can always count on that man in a crisis. What a feckin' game that was to be sure. What a feckin' finish.'

Timmy, awakened by the noise, let out a muted yelp. Suddenly, a tear jerked into Hamish's eye. Nudging Harry with his elbow he asked, 'Is that smell attributable to human kind?' The stench wafting from beneath the table assaulted the nasal cavities of everyone close by. Morphy sniffed, narrowed his nostrils. The facial expressions of his table companions, the sight of some cronies moving quickly away, had him kicking out at Timmy who squealed in protest.

'It's those bloody sprouts, the turnips carved like bones, the bloody carrots made to look like Chinese spare ribs, and the parsnips whittled to look like Bonio that Miss Gillhooly gives him. I keep on telling her he isn't a feckin' vegetarian dog. It's not natural I keep on telling her. She keeps on telling me, "He looks so thin and hungry that he would eat the decorations from a hearse, scoff a tramp's chin rag.".'

'He smells as if he's already eaten a box of sprouts,' Hamish said.

'You tell a canny story, Morphy,' Harry told him, before escaping the stench. Slipping from behind the table, he headed towards the bar for refills.

The result secured, the home and away supporters and members of the visiting team drifted away, thinning the numbers left in the pub. The home team mobbed popular hero Bebe, a smile splitting his face. Declining no offer, six congratulatory pints of Guinness were soon stacked up at his bar stance. Listening to words of congratulation, he downed them in turn, quaffing easily.

Twenty minutes later, the last one sunk, he burped mightily and wiped his lips with the back of his hand. His belly began rocking, causing him problems as he prepared to leave. Try as he may, he couldn't budge the zip on his three-quarter-length, black leather coat. He gave that up and collected his cue case. Shouts of 'Good old Bebe,' rang out and he beamed his supporters a drunken grin.

Hamish nudged Harry. Bebe was nearing their table on his way to the door. He stopped, rocked, the small of his back bending inwards, his belly lurching forward, almost continuing without the rest of him. Playfully, he ruffled what was left of Morphy's hair, tipped him a wink and said mysteriously, 'I hope the old horsebox is ready for next week. The mists are coming.'

The presence of double-glazing salesmen in the neighbourhood having not gone unnoticed by him either, he cast his eyes over Hamish's girth then to Harry and said, 'Constable Beckham at your service. You'd better bring your credentials to my office in Kilkenny Street during my office hours tomorrow. I like to know who's touting on my patch.'

The bar closed on time. Returning to the "Two Focks" early had no appeal; the idea of trying out the Bally Balti, a Tandoori Pak/Irish restaurant they'd seen while driving into the "I.Q.", did. Their stomachs had rumbled all evening for a filling meal.

The restaurant's kitchen area, futuristic in concept, was open to public view. Behind a circular counter, the kitchen was shiny, immaculate. A ventilation system effectively dragged the cloying, oily residues away from the frying and chip pans. Asian chefs glided around each other adding ingredients to meals they were preparing, looking ill at ease wearing tall hats. With quick steps backwards from the range, they dodged flames soaring from spitting frying pans. Others skewered marinated meat, placing it along with potato scones into tandoori ovens.

Harry lifted his head from the menu and viewed the kitchen. 'An Environmental Health official calling here couldn't have any complaints. It's not like some we've dined in.'

Hamish's tastes in curry didn't change much and he settled on a king prawn vindaloo. 'Aye, they're ensuring that the preparation of Indo/Irish cuisine conforms to high environmental standards.'

Vindaloo-strength curries, with colcannon, potato scones and soda bread as alternatives to naan bread, chapattis and rice, were some of the specialities customers ordered. Able to see their meal's preparation and the ingredients used, customers would have confidence that it was both wholesome and tasty.

There was plenty of spicy sauce with the meal, which Hamish wasn't going to leave behind. He was using a portion of naan bread as a sauce scoop when he saw the restaurant door open. He kicked Harry lightly on the shin, making him take note. Constable Beckham had sauntered in and was making his way towards the counter. A several item take-away quickly appeared, the handles of the bags thrust into the constable's hand. He picked it up, thanked the manager with a brief handshake, and made his way out.

'I'm beginning to like this copper already,' Hamish said. 'Obviously, he's a lover of Guinness and curry. Straight through the front door he comes, picks up some nosh. No messing, no sign of payment offered: he's a grade-A mumper, just like us.'

'Ah ken, but it's the only way to get around an eatery with no rear entrance to the kitchen.'

Wednesday

Ricky Croker often arrived early at his office in the Thameside Television Studios. On clear mornings, he took inspiration from the sun cresting the Thames at daybreak, as it headed inexorably higher, to brighten even the dullest parts of the capital. He had congratulated himself often that the ships he saw heading out to sea, to faraway places with strange-sounding names, wouldn't sail as far as the boundaries of his enquiries.

Other TV journalists, he considered laggards. None of them found as many hideouts of wanted gangsters and paedophiles, and worse, than he did. He gloried in the content of his shows and the underhand methods he often used to gain information. Viewers loved him, thought him a paragon, a hero, and all manner of perverts and crooks on the run feared his arrival with his camera team at their doors.

Usually, his shows were shown once weekly in runs of six. Each Wednesday morning, during the run, he would dutifully check each detail of the video before transmission in its primetime slot. In the past, disclosing the whereabouts of some criminals had left him open to the threat of personal injury; consequently, he employed protection. The revelations broadcast in that evening's show were about a bank clerk who'd run off with a cool sum of money and the bank manager's wife. Ricky had found them living it up in Kyrenia, Northern Cyprus and saw no threat in exposing them.

After viewing the video, he sat back, sipped a mug of black coffee, content that he'd masterminded another major expose.

It was normal for him to hand over his dossiers of irrefutable facts to The Met or other, relevant criminal investigation branch. He expected them to act on his findings; they always did, but he suspected that some cops resented his successes. His methods of investigation got him up close to many of the faces on wanted posters, whose whereabouts police forces didn't have a clue.

On a daily basis, he received letters from a cross-section of the population, asking him to investigate alleged malpractices. Letters containing dubious or hard-to-substantiate facts, he passed to a team member for initial investigation. Bona fide cases, the team passed back to him for final consideration. Letters deemed from cranks, he binned. In the business of investigative journalism, he had to remain forever alert for the arrival of hoaxes.

That Wednesday's mail tray contained a bulky Jiffy bag. His assistant handed it to him unopened saying: 'When shaken, it sounds like a bottle filled with a liquid. It hasn't exploded so it's not nitro-glycerine'

Ricky opened it to reveal a urine sample bottle with a Met Police crest, filled three-quarters full with a yellowy liquid. A crumpled sheet of notepaper accompanied it; this he opened, smoothed out and read.

Dear Ricky Croker,

I filled this sample bottle from the tea urn in the canteen at West Clegham Police Station this week. When you've had it analysed you'll know that I'm telling the truth. Every time coppers go on duty at this police station, have a cup of tea in the canteen before proceeding to their beats, they all get uptight, cantankerous, and start racing about like headless chickens. It is a common occurrence that a whole shift of beat officers will start out walking to their beats and end up miles away. It has happened that coppers have walked beats on the next division, not knowing how they got there.

Recently, (and you will be able to confirm this), Sergeant Moriarty, an over-zealous workaholic, stickler for the book, and a good man, was admitted to Clegham Mental Hospital. He had suffered a mental breakdown while working in his office at West Clegham Police Station. Coppers believe this happened because of the extreme pressures he had to work under and his addiction to canteen tea.

Coppers are convinced that heir Superintendent, Ivor Bunce, is surreptitiously adding uncut Amphetamine Sulphate to the canteen tea. This is an effort, on his part, to have the few coppers left on his depleted strength cover all existing beats and foot patrols.

Once you have confirmed this fact, please assist the coppers of this station to overthrow this megalomaniacal tyrant.

I am a serving copper attached to West Clegham Police Station.

Mr Policeman.

Ricky Croker laughed aloud. How did police officers, of all people, expect him to believe rubbish like this? If a crackpot hadn't sent it, then it was a wind-up inspired by senior police officers peeved with his successes. About to bin the letter, it dawned that, some time ago, he had encountered a Sergeant Bunce. That the same sergeant was the Superintendent Bunce mentioned by the anonymous copper, had him thinking: did the letter contain just a morsel to get him interested in investigating Bunce for a different iniquity; one that the Mr Policeman didn't want to put into writing.

He had good reason to recall the name Bunce. Twenty years previously, as a young, highflying court reporter nicknamed Scoop, working for the Clegham Advertiser, he was driving his E Type to work one weekday morning. On his usual route, a police sergeant had annoyed him as he directed traffic through a junction, where a motor vehicle had destroyed the traffic lights.

Bugged that he had to stand stationary for some unreasonable length of time, he became explosive and his agitation festered. The sergeant, going about his traffic directions in a fussy but professional manner, allowed elderly women and schoolchildren to cross the junction safely to the detriment of the traffic flow. His temper soared as he approached the sergeant at the junction, seeing him grinning stupidly, as if enjoying hindering Jag drivers in a hurry. Facing the sergeant and from the safety of the car, his lips twisted and close to the closed side window, he had mouthed in his direction, sillily and petulantly: 'Fucking bastard.'

To the then Sergeant Bunce, his lip action must have been very readable. It happened that the sergeant had noted the words.

Next morning, daydreaming and preoccupied, he hadn't realised the crossing lights were still inoperative. Any opportunity of changing his route had gone and the traffic flow swept him towards the junction. To his consternation, Sergeant Bunce was there again, directing traffic in his usual, no-nonsense manner.

It became obvious to him that the sergeant had spotted the E-Type from afar. Blatantly, and with visible delight, he had hindered its progress, allowing only two vehicles at a time from his direction to pass through. When he expected passage through the junction, the sergeant had walked in front of the E-Type and stopped it level with him. Then he had smirked, turned his back on him and kept him stationary for fully five minutes.

Traces of a smile continued to flicker around the sergeant's tight-lipped face when he saw him shifting uncomfortably in his seat.

Eventually he waved the E-Type through, looking closely at him for further silent mouthings. None came; he had stared directly ahead, looking chastened. He eyed and noted the sergeant's number, which was visible on his shoulders. Through local Magistrate's Court contacts, he had discovered the sergeant's name. The surname was so unusual that he suspected the Met had only one Ivor Bunce on the strength.

If he hadn't recognised the name, he'd have disposed of the package. Many other cases more realistic and worthy of his investigation existed. The thought of discovering any of *this* senior police officer's follies and indiscretions was too mouth-watering to overlook and got the better of him.

His recollections over, he instructed his assistant to telephone the reception at Clegham Mental Hospital. Later, the assistant confirmed the admittance of a Mr. Moriarty on Monday morning, the Hospital declining to give reasons for the admission.

The authenticity of the sample bottle still perplexed him. Picking it up, he twirled it and watched the bubbles forming in the contents only to disappear again as the agitation settled. 'In for a penny, in for a pound,' he said aloud after minutes of reflection. 'Take this up to Rodney's in Harley Street. He owes me a favour and we might get a result,' he instructed his assistant, 'it might be interesting.'

******

At 9 a.m. on Wednesday, Hamish sat down opposite Harry for breakfast. Miss Gillhooly was fussing around the table, apparently looking for the sight of a crumb to dust away. She revealed her real intention when she snatched the cornflakes packet away with the cackled explanation, 'You've had enough of them!'

The second course consisted of one watery egg, sunny side up, one crisp rasher of bacon, further hardened in a microwave oven, one half-slice of fried bread oozing fat, and one small, wrinkled sausage. The round of thin, cold toast each and a wan, margarine spread didn't greatly enhance the rations.

Hamish, deep in thought, cleaned his plate, said little. Seeing this, Harry slipped upstairs to use the toilet, left him to his contemplations.

Back in the bedroom, he heard the results of Hamish's thinking. 'Harry, I'm going to pay a visit to the offices of the Clegham Advertiser and have a look through some back issues. I've an interesting proposition that I've thought about overnight and this morning. It will definitely be of interest to a Leith ram such as you.'

Hamish finished brushing his teeth. Harry wondered what was coming next. 'Yeah, what's that?' he asked.

'We'd be a lot happier if we had some idea what's going on within the Commander's head, wouldn't we?'

'I suppose.'

'The only person who might be privy to that info and who might impart it easily is Myrna, correct? Remember she told us that she wanted more nookie than her girlie friends in her daft club were getting. She's in with the elite, must know all their wives and will know or can find out what's going on, right?'

'Right.'

'And wouldn't it be to our advantage if we learnt something that we can use later if the shit hits the fan, spreads nastily, covers us, and the Commander won't give us our warrant cards back?'

'Great thinking.'

'Well, Harry, my rampant Leith ram with the elastic back, I think you ought to sidle over there and see Myrna this morning, slip her one, and pump her for that sort of information.'

Harry spluttered into the sink, clearing his mouth of toothbrush and paste. 'Now just hold on a minute… why me? Being there once before put us in this position… remember?'

'You're single, handsome and she liked the way you swayed your kipper-thin hips, as I recall. You don't have the weight to fuck up beds the same as I have, and you, she said, “Shagged like a rattlesnake”. I couldn’t possibly follow that.’

Hamish told it as he saw it, his hands open, outstretched, smiling benignly. ‘She’ll drag you in, have you away a few times, rid herself of another itch, and you’ll come back here looking shagged-out, hoping for the rest of the day off to recuperate. I’ll not be there to fuck up beds, so there won’t be any more complaints. Will there?’

‘You’re right.’ Harry had made his decision. Like any healthy man, he wasn’t about to turn down the opportunity of a shag. ‘If you think this is the best way to begin our investigations and gain some protection, then okay, you’re on. I’ll give her a ring first and see if she’s at home and receptive. I’d rather do that than risk a wasted journey. Then I’ll have a shower, rub on some fragrance designed to have women gagging for me, and change my skiddies.’

Hamish found the Mayor’s residential telephone number in the hotel’s telephone directory. Harry hung about until 10 a.m. before he rang. He reckoned by then, the mayor should have left for his office.

They found a phone box close to the parked transit. Harry picked up the receiver and dialled. Myrna answered. Harry unloaded his charm. ‘Hi Myrna, it’s adorable, thin-hipped, elastic-backed Harry here.’ Hamish grimaced at his patter. ‘Can I come over to see you this morning?’

Harry didn’t need the chat-up line. Myrna was desperate and tried to get him there quickly, but with restrictions. ‘Yes, hurry over, dahlin’, but don’t bring that big fat geezer with you. You know, the mate that facked two beds last time. Algie is kicking up fack about them getting destroyed, get it?’

‘Okay, Roger on that, no problem, see you in an hour, okay?’ He hung up and turned to Hamish. ‘That’s the arrangements made, I’m in, sorted, as simple as that. I could tell she’s gagging for me to fettle her again. She’s glad you’ll not be about, though. The Mayor’s going off his head about the two beds that fell apart when you had your two shags.’

‘That’s uncalled-for cheek, it was three. You know how easily I hurt. Now, if you’ve finished bulling your ego and poofing yourself up, I’ll drop you at the Underground on my way to spend a boring hour or two at the newspaper offices. When you’ve emptied your prunes several times, as I’m sure you’ll brag, you’ll find me around three o’clock in “The Paddy” café in the square. I’ll be there sitting thinking about the Job and our jobs.’

Harry took a direct train from Clegham South Tube station to Clegham Parkway, the nearest station to Park Avenue. Hamish set off for the newspaper’s offices in East Clegham High Street.

In the depository, Hamish found a bundle of newspapers covering October and November of the previous year. Dragging them to a window table, he viewed them in good light. Working through those issues, he came to the weeks that interested him. Carefully and methodically, he scanned the entertainment pages for advertisers with noteworthy entries.

In one Friday issue, he found that two pubs and one club in Ringaskiddy Square had advertised performances by a remarkably similar entertainer. Interestingly, the first anniversary of those gigs would occur the following week. In each case, the advertisement's only reference to the artist appearing was the underlined letters B B. Blodger's drag bar, while offering entertainment for cross dressers and transsexuals, also reminded their members that they could only get real B B there, that the show was strictly private and to look out their tickets now.

'It could be what we're looking for. I'm sure the underlined B B here can't mean bum and baccy...surely not... must be Billy Bagman, Bebe,' Hamish said aloud.

The Navigator's Den advertised a show couched in similar terms: "Plod along for the funniest private show of the winter season". "B B is back in time for the winter fog". "Look out your tickets now".

The Shankless Music Bar was also in on the act, advertising a show they described as, "Bringing Home the Bacon, Private Party, entry only by prepaid ticket".

Hamish thought Harry wouldn't have the stamina for an all-afternoon session with Myrna and that he'd arrive soon, albeit feigning he was shagged out. Close to 3 p.m., he took a table in the Café Paddy, next to a window. From there, he got good views of the only bus stop in Ringaskiddy Square. Slowly, he sipped at a mug of coffee.

Constable Beckham appeared in the square. He walked with a nonchalant, loose-limbed gait along the pavement, his helmet perched on his head at a jauntier than regulation angle. He laughed merrily with some dog owners out walkies when they displayed their poop-scoops and plastic bags to him. It suggested he didn't enjoy playing the game of pavement chess: dodging knight-like around dog turds. He nodded to all passersby, they responding with their own greeting. Schoolchildren were on their way home from school; they were very respectful towards him, saying their helloes without giggling.

He stopped to scrutinize various vehicles parked up, his eyes peering closely at windscreens, checking Road Fund Licence validity. Stooping, he checked tyre wear. Looking up at the parking regulations, he checked the restrictions in the time-limited parking zone. He took his pocket book from his whistle-pocket, licked a pencil, and noted the registration numbers of some vehicles. Then he moved on, his belly swinging.

Passing Oliver's Butchers Shop, his gaze strayed in the direction of the window and the hanging strings of sausages, only pausing on hearing his name called by the butcher, who had appeared at the door.

The upshot of a short confab and the pointing at the butcher's delivery van was permission for it to remain parked on double yellow lines while loading. Together, constable and butcher disappeared into the back of the shop, a bloody arm lying on the constable's shoulder.

Reappearing twenty minutes later, a little redder in the cheeks, the constable placed a wobbly, plastic bag in his side pocket. An experienced police watcher could only conclude that, after downing the steaming cup of tea laced with a tot of whisky in the meat preparation room, the butcher had gifted him a rag end from a beef fillet for his dinner.

He then completed a circuit of Ringaskiddy Square. Back where he started, he gave his attention to the illegal parking that had previously interested him. Flourishing his pocket book, he penned all the information necessary for a successful prosecution of that offence. Smiling, he placed a note behind a wiper blade of each offending vehicle, letting the drivers know he had reported them and that they should report with their "relevant details" to a police station. Ambling leisurely away from the scene of the offences, he seemed content with his afternoon's work.

Five minutes later, Hamish spotted him slouched and helmetless behind the steering wheel of a vintage, light-blue Morris Minor. Manoeuvring the car out of a tight parking place, he circled Ringaskiddy Square, before exiting down Kilkenny Street.

A red bus pulled into the square at 3:30 p.m. and stopped. Harry alighted and waited for the bus to move off. He crossed the square through the car park, a smile splitting his face, legs wobbling like a multi-jointed puppet. It was a message to Hamish, whom he had spotted looking out the café window: just look at me; shagging all morning and some of the afternoon has knackered me, but I'm happy and so is Myrna.

Hamish ordered two coffees and waited his boastful arrival at the table.

'How did it go then, O' great Leith Lothario?' Hamish asked scornfully as Harry sat down, looking washed out, his lips red and bruised from a session of heavy petting.

'Give me a minute to organise my thoughts, will you? I've a cracking story to tell that I know you'll like better than treacle bannocks.'

Hamish sniffed derisively. 'It cannae be that good.'

Harry slurped at his coffee and adjusted the sugar content 'I need to regain my strength, fast,' he said, benefiting Hamish with a wink 'Going to see Myrna was good, the right decision and I don't mean just for nookie. Myrna told me a right story of lust, nymphomania and sexual deprivation.'

'Och away, you're taking the piss now.'

'No, listen. I'll be as brief as I can, but it's serious. Myrna, along with Bunce's wife, Gloria, and that odious creep Shrapnel's wife, went to Blackpool for a long weekend at the beginning of October. There they saw a blue comedian. His show sent one normally staid women, she previously not knowing the bodily positions assumed when performing a 69, off the rails. It seems they all reeled home to their husbands, suffering degrees of rampant nymphomania. Believe me, that reference does include Myrna. There's a difference with her husband: he's a piss-artist and can't get it up,' he said smugly.

'You mean the blue comedian that might be our Constable Beckham. Billy Bagman; the one we think might be Bebe? That one?' Hamish asked.

'That one and that's not everything. The Commander wouldn't let his missus go to Blackpool. She cut off his nookie ration. I mean *totally*. She's told Myrna that there's definitely no nookie or cuddles for him until she sees the same comedian as they did. She's also told Myrna he sleeps alone. From him saying no to the Blackpool jaunt, and up to last Sunday..., think about this Hamish, he's been walking around each day with a hard-on trying to find a manly way of getting rid of it. Understand? The sort of deprivation a man doesn't need. His wife dresses in shrouds bought from the Co-op undertakers and wears them around the house, so she can ram home the message, sex, over my dead body.'

'It sounds if the Commander's been getting it a bit rough. It's a bit like my current standing with Jenny.'

'You've heard nothing yet. Myrna and ADC Beaverton attempted to get the Commander and Mrs Dewsnap back together on a Halloween blind date. They met wearing facemasks as disguises. It all went tits up.'

'What happened?' Hamish asked, 'we could do with some dirt on the Commander.'

'Now when I tell you this, I don't want you to collapse in the café and start weeping with laughter, drawing attention to us. Listen carefully. I will say this only once. Due to circumstances away beyond *our* control, the Commander, in an Elvis mask, his wife Daphne, in a Maggie Thatcher mask, neither knowing the identity of the other person, met outside Clegham Park gates, in a raging storm, for the Halloween blind date. You know when Halloween was. Does last Sunday night ring a bell? Got it now? And they met at 9 p.m.'

'Shit... we were there! We must have seen them!'

'That's not all. They were in the bog together when the bangers went in.'

'Suffering shit!'

'The way I read it, Daphne, Mrs Dewsnap that is, thinks she has severely damaged a man's cock, nearly parting it from his body. We now know that it was the Commander's cock. It happened during a sex act with which, I'm sure, you're familiar and, when teeth are not painfully nibbling, like a lot. Talking about cocks, when I left Myrna earlier today, mine looked like a meaty marrowbone newly savaged by a mad dog.'

'Bragging Leith bastard,' Hamish erupted, sounding resentful, 'I don't believe you, be serious. They didn't know one another, you say. Explain?'

'According to Myrna, they're still unaware. The masks and the darkness, remember? She spoke to the Commander's wife on the phone, after the blind date, casually enquiring how it went. Well, Daphne Dewsnap was in a dreadful state. She complained bitterly, as some women do, even when they get hold of a decent man, that the date had tried filthy things with her. "My teeth are sharp and I had to bite him savagely to get him to remove his thing from me, and I was clenching them tight when the bangs happened," she told Myrna. I suspect she couldn't admit to enjoying it.

'That's my story. The one you sent me to get. There's more, though. Daphne was tearful while admitting it to Myrna. As you can guess, she appeared none too pleased with Myrna for organising such a blind date. Myrna doesn't know how she's going to look her in the eye, when the women meet again this Thursday night.'

'Suffering shit!' Hamish repeated, following a sudden realisation. 'Thanks to Bunce's suspicions, the Commander guessed all along it was us that chucked the fireworks in.'

'Yes, Hamish, I think you could tell by the way he looked at us yesterday… he hadn't just missed an episode of "The Bill". He was all the way out of his pram, though, a rattle in each hand. He knew we were the ones who had caused him an ache in his helmet. Though, I reckon he'll send our warrant cards back express delivery when he knows that we know where he was at 9 p.m. on Halloween.'

'Aye, that's what I was thinking. It could be great insurance, keep us safe. We'll have him confirm us in the rank of DC when he knows we know. What else have we got here, though?' Hamish asked.

Sitting back in his chair, he closed his eyes and tried to pull the threads together. 'Now tell me if I'm going wrong, Harry. By your account, the Commander has an aching cock. That means he must be sore with us and whoever caused him the pain. He's also desperate to get his wife to share his bed again and that's why we're on this jaunt to achieve that end. His missus has given him the message, which is no nookie until she sees Billy Bagman perform. His wife doesn't yet know the damage she's done to her husband's cock. The husband doesn't know that his wife caused him the pain by damaging the said cock. The blue comedian who could get them back into bed together might be none other than Constable Beckham. I think we'll have to take the bull by the antlers to get any success with this.'

'Is, er… that not a bit of a contradiction, a misnomer?' Harry asked, pulling Hamish up.

'No.' Listening to Harry puff up the account of his morning and afternoon of lust had peeved Hamish. 'You Leith folks wouldn't know that expression. This is a queer beast we're up against here. There are many points to consider. I was worried that we could do this thing without dropping Bebe in the mire. The story you've returned with suggests that the Commander just wants us to confirm Constable Beckham is Billy Bagman. Then he needs us to get him into a gig, along with his missus, as you've found out, then he can put things straight… in a manner of speaking. I don't know how we'll achieve it, but in this community, if last night in the Navigator's Den is anything to go by, I think we're going to have some laughs and fun doing it.'

'Did your Govan-blue eyes scan anything interesting at the newspaper offices?'

'Aye, they did. It's not nearly as interesting as your story, though. What I found seems to show a link with the one known as Bebe. The use of the underlined letters B B in adverts I found for gigs taking place exactly fifty-one weeks ago were interesting. I think the underlined letters used might just be a code reminding the locals of his presence at the venues. It's probably their method of keeping secret the identity of Billy Bagman. We'll know for definite when we see this Friday's issue of the Clegham Advertiser.

'There's another thing we've to do, and I know you'll like it, you being a Leith piss-artist. We've learned a little about the Navigator's Den, but we must also visit the other licensed premises mentioned in the adverts, paying particular attention to notice boards, whilst on the lookout for tickets.

Blodger's nightclub is a cross-dressers' bar, but it doesn't open for business until Thursday night. Although it does seem it was open last year on the Wednesday for the B B show. Another is the Shankless Music Bar. We've had an offer of two tickets to attend a gig there tonight. So, if you agree, a further visit to the Navigator's Den tonight is on the cards to see our ingratiating barman and get the gig tickets he offered.'

'You're spot on. Killing two birds with one stone seems a bright idea. The locals might see us as entertainment-seeking double-glazing salesmen if we go to the gig, and the search for tickets to any show might not look so suspicious. It's reasonable to suggest, if Bebe's our man, we'll need tickets from whatever source for one of his gigs.'

*****

The police office was pokey, room for one copper comfortably, with a public counter, office space and a cell at the back. A standard blue lamp hung outside. Manned from 10 a.m. to 12 p.m. and 3:30 p.m. to 4:30 p.m. Monday to Friday, said a plaque alongside the door.

Bebe was on duty at the station when they called there at 4:15 p.m., laid back in his chair, dozing, his feet on his desk alongside two school jotters. He looked comfortable with his head laid back, rocking on the chair's back legs. The jotters' titles were interesting: one was Old Jokes, the other New Jokes. Hamish nudged Harry, pointed at them, and winked.

The index finger of Bebe's left hand was working dexterously, without apparent conscious instruction, deep within a nostril. His lips moved silently as if he was subconsciously rehearsing his act. His nose's wart-like appendage was gently oscillating, the hairs sticking out of it stiffly.

Hamish banged on the desk with a fist. Bebe jumped, the chair squealed onto four legs. His feet hit the floor, but he continued with the difficult nasal extraction, unperturbed.

'You haven't recovered yet from your session down the Navigator's Den last night,' Hamish ventured with a smile.

Bebe's educated finger withdrew. He looked at the extraction on his fingernail, then struggled to flick it into a waste paper basket, stuffed to the gunnels with food wrappings and crumpled paperwork.

Ignoring Hamish's question, he gathered the jotters and quickly put them into a desk drawer. Then he said snappily, 'I've been working flat out on some important cases and was resting my eyes.' He tapped his fingers continuously on the desktop, more than a little irritated at being caught snoozing and by strangers.

'We're here to show you our identification,' Hamish said, sliding their identity holders across the desk towards him. Bebe looked at them, gave a short whistle and, passing them back with a wry smile, said. 'I wish you luck on my patch, I really do.'

Back out on the street, Hamish said, 'I think it's about time we acted out our cover and shoved a few leaflets through some letterboxes, before darkness falls.'

Spurring off Kilkenny Street, they found residential Naas Drive. Doing a side each, their rattling of letterboxes disturbed the late afternoon silence. On reaching the end of the drive, residents were proving the popularity of double-glazed show houses. The sound of cackered clogs rattling the pavement drew their attention. At a distance, an old codger was pursuing them. A young woman, with a babe in her arms, joined him. Both were waving leaflets at them.

'Let's be off, we're doing too well here,' Hamish said, encouraging Harry to walk faster and get away from the area.

*****

As 9p.m. was striking on the town hall clock that evening, Hamish was pushing open the swing doors of the Navigator's Den, skilfully allowing Harry to enter first and buy the first round. The barman was working industriously. Many of his customers were already well oiled. He glanced up and looked over the top of the popular Guinness tap, to eye them pushing their way through swaying clientele. By the time they reached the bar servery, he had already half-poured two pints of their favoured tipple.

Noticeably, the barman had changed his T-shirt for another portraying a classic MAN album: "The Twang Dynasty". Making signs that he was anxious to speak with them, he came out from behind the servery. Ushering them furtively to a quiet, corner table, he took two tickets from a trouser pocket and pressed them into Harry's hand.

'My name's Barney, by the way.' He spoke in a hushed brogue, tipped them a wink, grabbed a hand of each and shook them vigorously. 'These tickets are for you boys to enjoy an evening of peerless seventies rock at the Shankless Music Bar. The band kicks off at ten. I'll be there, down at the front, doing a spot of head banging. The tickets are free. Keep it quiet. I wouldn't want my customers to think I'd a better chance than them in your double-glazing draw.'

'We'll have to be seen fair to others. You'll have to go into the draw with the rest, but your ticket will be close to the top.' Harry said, but returned him a huge, knowing wink. 'It's great getting free tickets for what must be a sell-out gig, though. I'm sure we'd have been disappointed, otherwise.'

'This show house thing has captured their interest,' Harry said as Barney left them. 'Obviously, it's a good wheeze. Barney and his customers are hooked on the idea of being warmer indoors this winter, without it costing them a bean.'

Taking a slurp from their glasses, they both looked for a notice board. On the wall opposite was a piece of pin board with a clutter of newspaper cuttings and other bedraggled announcements stuck to it. Among the personal adverts, they read requests for dart and domino team players and the private sale of household goods. They also spotted a dog-eared poster. It mirrored the advertisement that Hamish had seen in the previous year's newspaper.

'Bingo,' Hamish said, on seeing the poster that referred to B B being back in time for the winter fog. The show was being held the following Tuesday.

A voice directly behind them and one they'd heard before said, 'To be sure there's no feckin' bingo in here, boys, you'll have to go into town for that malarkey and wimmens' nonsense.'

'Hello, Morphy,' Hamish said, without looking around, 'you out on the town again tonight?'

'Come on over here.' Harry took Morphy by the arm and led him and Timmy to one of the long, wooden side tables. Feeling kindly, Hamish returned to the bar for a pint of Guinness and presented it to Morphy.

At the table, he took a pace back and peered beneath it, saw Timmy laid there quietly. Then he sat down, much to Harry's surprise, close to the dog's eruptive end.

'What type of glazing would you want fitted to your home, Morphy, if it were chosen as the show house? Gold plated panes with ten-millimetre gaps that reduce heat loss are the best.'

Harry was taking the piss.

'Anything Pigs can fit me up with,' he said, 'I worked out your van sign writing. Great idea, the whole rigmarole makes folks think about it twice, it does.'

'Tell all your old cronies that we'll put them in the draw. If they don't win, we'll swing them a good deal with an interest-free clause built into their agreements,' Harry said, tipping a wink to Hamish in the process.

Morphy's attention remained rapt during their chat; he didn't notice Hamish taking the tea-light from his pocket. Harry hadn't seen him purloin it from the Bally Balti food warmer the previous evening, either.

Hamish placed it on the seat close to him. Using a cigarette lighter, he quietly lit it. Nobody noticed. With the flame on the tea-light going well, he leaned back, casually, gaining a better view of the floor. He was interested in a position close to Timmy's fundamental, gas-emitting orifice. The space between Timmy's upwardly curling tail and his bollocks, laid spread out like a bunch of black grapes, he thought the perfect spot. The tea-light required precise positioning to avoid Timmy detecting any heat and to maximise effect.

Hamish placed the device. He then joined in the conversation.

Timmy was an unwilling convert to vegetarianism. Having fallen asleep, he was a picture of contentment, his black jowls slobbering. Occasionally, he let out short, muted yowls and tremors jerked his legs. Perhaps he was dreaming of chasing a rabbit through the foliage of his mind; a hare in its winter coat across the frozen tundra of his imagination, a slinking cat into the high branches of the tallest tree he could recall.

If those were Timmy's doggy fantasies, they were about to end. The methane building within his intestines from a diet of turnips, carrots and parsnips whittled into bone-shaped structures, had reached sufficient pressure to vent through an age-slackened sphincter muscle into the atmosphere.

Claws scraping along the floor were the first sounds of changes to doggie sleeping patterns taking place beneath the table.

Shriller yowlings and woofs followed, revealing canine concern and shock. Paws scuffled, then with a thud the table moved violently, spilling Guinness. In a rush, the canine equivalent of Halley's Comet shot from its refuge, a tail of flames streaming from its rear. Timmy's contorted face looked back at them whilst he chased his tail. Unfolding from the spin, he took flight towards the exit and darted between an entering customer's legs as if they were a croquet hoop, then through the door still ajar.

'Bayjasus, what's the feckin' matter with Timmy?' a mortified and bemused Morphy exclaimed, before taking off after his mutt, his short, wellie-clad legs slamming together in his haste.

'What the fuck was that?' Harry asked, chuckling. He was unaware of the cause, but saw the funny side of Timmy's horror.

'Heh, heh-ing,' and looking a little smug, Hamish showed Harry the extinguished tea-light, before slipping it back into his coat pocket.

'You're a cruel bastard, but I must admit it's as funny as fuck. For a time, you've had me thinking you were a dog lover. Maybe it's only the two-legged variety after all,' Harry reproached Hamish.

Ten minutes later, Morphy returned with a reluctant Timmy on the end of a lead. Aghast, he showed his drinking cronies the singed area on Timmy's coat. Pushing Timmy's tail to one side, he said, 'Look at his arse. It looks like the end of a sausage roll.' The incident was still a mystery to him and he asked, 'how the feck did that happen to my Timmy?'

'That's the first recorded case of spontaneous canine combustion, to be sure.' A knowledgeable bystander assured him, a smile creasing his face. Turning, he gave a nod and a wink to some of *his* cronies, past sufferers of reeking doggy methane and sponsors of Timmy's previous ejections from the premises.

'I never thought dog farts were so inflammable,' Harry said.

'Like yours, Timmy's farts are pure gas,' Hamish said, pointedly. 'The dog will think twice about dropping one in our company again.'

Just before ten p.m., they crossed the square to the Shankless Music Bar. It was difficult to miss, stood on a prime, corner site, illuminated by an array of flashing neon signs. Its windows were now billboards behind which acoustic insulation prevented noise escaping from super-loud rock band performances.

Sixty motorcycles had already parked up. Some seemed deliberately scorched, similar to those seen in the Mad Max movies. Harley Davidsons stood out radiant: the biker's pride. Most bikers dig heavy rock. This bunch, although looking wild and hairy, queued orderly and without menace to file through the venue door. A burly bouncer, who looked to be no respecter of such reputations, made sure they all had tickets.

Hamish and Harry joined the queue.

A thick fog of tobacco smoke enveloped them in the concert area. Surprisingly for a rock venue, with or without the presence of bikers, the smoke didn't contain the rich and heady aroma of burning marijuana.

The PA system was using twenty-one-inch bass speakers that created the low-frequency reverberations noticeable in the Z Z Tops number playing through the system, "Sharp Dressed Man". Eardrums pounded, air moved thudding into punter's bodies. Between the speakers, two guitar-amplifiers, a bass guitar-amplifier and keyboards were set up. Within the battered bass drum of the drum-kit rested a small, iron ingot. The kit would remain well rooted to the stage during the hour-and-a-half of frenetic pounding it was about to receive.

The stage backdrop was a painting of a three-legged pig with a teardrop falling from one eye. A zip of stitches in the pattern of a ladder where its nearside back leg should have been, joined up skin. Lettering above the painting said: "The Hamshank Redemption". The lettering beneath had one word: "Porky".

'If Porky was a dog with a back leg gone, he'd have great difficulty pissing up against a tree,' observed Hamish.

'If he was a dog, he'd have fallen on his arse, wouldn't be able to piss at all,' was Harry's take.

A framed cutting from an old Irish newspaper, fixed to one of the giant shillelaghs forming part of the bar, answered the mystery of the pub's name. They had time to read the cutting before the gig began.

It said:

CERTIFICATE OF BRAVERY AWARDED TO GILLICUDDY PIG.

*

Farmer Seamus Gilligan, aged ninety-seven, of Gillicuddy Farm, today received the posthumous award Porky, his trusty pig, so richly deserved.

The award, made by L.A.P.H.S. the LEGION of ACHERMORE PORCINE HERO'S SOCIETY, is *the* most prestigious accolade for heroism given to a member of the animal kingdom.

At the award ceremony, Gilligan proudly said, "Porky was a hero of the potato famine and I'm thrilled to receive this medal on his behalf. Without him, the family would have starved to death, to be sure."

Only when Gilligan told of how the leg came to be missing at Porky's slaughter, did the true story enfold…

Porky's sire, Perky, a four hundred and fifty pound boar, Gilligan killed and cured the same day. His mother, Matilda, a prodigious sow, had pigged many times. Porky was pigged in a litter of seventeen piglets of which he was the runt. Gilligan, fearing Porky's survival chances, took him indoors and reared him by hand in front of a well-stoked, peat fire.

Too small for stud duties, he had an early appointment with the local Veterinarian and Gelder, Mr. Flip O'Gooligon. While still young, and before ejaculatory urges appeared, the Gelder visited Porky, bringing with him his specialised castration tools. With a deft swipe from his sharp blade, a practised bite with his remaining, blackened incisors, and amid a crescendo of high-pitched squealing, he rendered Porky neutered. Thereafter, Porky became the family pet, as tame as a dog and twice as intelligent.

Porky had just turned two-years old when he saved Mrs Gilligan from a gang of notorious, murdering kidnappers. About to drag her away, the pig attacked their horse around the fetlocks before they were able to remount and decamp with her. This uncommon act of porcine heroism spared her life.

Then, in the summer of the same year, he saved Gilligan's youngest son from drowning. The son had fallen into a dirty, stinking, farm midden. Porky dived in after the child, pulling him to safety.

When he was three-year-old, he appeared from nowhere when sensing the farmhouse had caught fire. Unconcerned for his own safety, he rushed into the farmhouse thirteen times saving Gilligan, his wife, ten children and the family cat in another act of porcine heroism. So fast did he streak, not one member of the family received a scorch mark or a spot of soot on their person.

During the potato famine, the family came close to starvation and they greedily eyed Porky as a food source. Reason partly prevailed. Gilligan chose a sunny Sunday afternoon to render Porky unconscious by repeatedly striking him on the head with a shillelagh. While he was under this crude, latter-day anaesthetic, Gilligan removed Porky's nearside back leg and neatly stitched the skin back into place in a ladder pattern.

Gilligan, when asked why he didn't slaughter Porky when he had him almost dead, replied, 'How could you kill a wonderful, heroic pig the likes of that?'

During his lifetime, Porky survived swine fever, foot and mouth disease and many misguided attempts by a local prosthetic manufacturer to fit him with a wooden shank and wheel.

Gilligan eventually slaughtered Porky. He learned that Porky, in the pig's own opinion, had become too sophisticated and important to be associated with the Gilligans.

Gilligan said: "It was quite normal, and sometimes preferable, for Porky to lay himself down in our bed at night, with his head on his own pillow, placed between me and the wife. One night, she and I had gone to bed after a session on the Guinness, onion and kale soup, and plates of Munster peas. During the night, Porky, shaking his head and extremely disenchanted with us, got up from our bed, complained about our animalistic noises and behaviour and slowly walked away."

Killed and cured, Porky weighed a leg less than four hundred and fifty pounds.

Anon

*****

Pinned next to the newspaper cutting, a notice said the following Monday would be the Bringing home the Bacon night, Private Party.

A multi-cored electric cable linked the PA system to a mixing desk, which sat precariously on a forty-gallon beer barrel, positioned outside one end of the bar. Talking to the soundman, and partly obscured by the huge shillelagh-shaped bar upright, Constable Beckham raised his nose and sniffed the atmosphere. Patrons were showing respect for the constable by not smoking drugs in his presence.

At 10 p.m., a longhaired compere, sporting a Ché Guevara style moustache, skipped onto the stage from the rear, dodging the instruments and cables as he came. He grabbed the centre microphone and yelled into it, 'Please welcome onto our stage, these wonderful, if ancient, disciples of heavy rock, The MAN band,'

The band's poster was dated and showed the members when they were youthful. Now, to rapturous applause, a gaggle of facially haggard men filtered onto the stage and re-acquainted themselves with their instruments. Careworn and dishevelled they may have looked, but it had taken a thousand such gigs and hard living to create their current public image.

Mickey Jones and Deke Leonard plucked their guitars and fine-tuned them. Martin Ace played a couple of chords on his bass guitar to supple up his fingers. John Waters shuffled his stool and rat-tat-tatted each drum and cymbal of his kit with his sticks. Mickey, Deke and Martin, the singers with the band, approached the microphones, testing them with a few vocal clicks and a 'One-two, one-two.'

The band lurched into their first number, "Romaine". The audience members closest to the stage, swinging their heads about, madly whipping hair loosened from ponytails, head-banged to the detriment of their neck muscles. The crescendo of noise guaranteed each rocker auricular whistling by the gig's end; it would still be intrusive and troublesome on arising in the morning and for most of that day.

Hamish made signs that said, 'Let's scarper to the other end of the bar, as far away from the music as we can get.'

Barney the barman rocked in front of the stage, close to the sound, swinging his locks around his head in a frantic manner, his eyes closed, the music sending him.

The MAN band sounded top-notch, professional and musically tight. Their voices were rich, gravelly. All the numbers played, written by the band members, sounded superb.

At twenty to midnight, close to last orders at the Navigator's Den, Hamish and Harry had heard enough loud music and made to leave the rock bar. Outside, in the quietness of the square, their eardrums hissed. The hour and a half of auditory torment had caused white sound to dull their hearing, and the strains of "Bananas", the last number heard, wouldn't go away!

A large woman wearing a snugly fitting outfit was walking ahead of them as they made their way back to the Navigator's Den. Harry noticed that Hamish had quickly locked on to her. 'She has an ample rear end and love handles that *you'd* die for,' Harry kidded. 'I wouldn't like to see it in wide screen. She's extreme enough to interest you, though. I know you like women cuddly and that shape.'

'Aye, Harry, you're right. I bet her cheeks spread like Flora, eh?'

'Definitely some moving offences there, too, Hamish.'

'Her arse is as wide as the east end of that westbound bus you got off today.'

'Aye, ah ken. We must be looking at two tigers wrestling in a small marquee there.'

'She also reminds me of the Hammers this season.'

'Oh, why's that?'

'She's solid at the back.'

The woman turned and walked into the Navigator's Den. 'You're in luck,' Harry said. 'She's the lock-in shift coming on.'

The bar bustled with late-night drinkers, the duty barman failing to meet demands. 'You're right,' Hamish said, bustling through the crowd.

The woman, who looked about thirty years old, had gone directly behind the servery, hung her bag on a hook and started taking orders. She was wearing a tight-fitting outfit: a hunting-red coloured leotard over white tights. Her hair was peroxide blonde the ends dyed ginger and gelled upwards to spiky points.

'I like her crazy hairstyle. Cauliflower floret with blight I'd call it,' Hamish said, elbowing for some room at the bar.

Harry pushed in beside him and said, 'Ken, but I bet you're crazy about more than her hair.'

The barmaid flashed her false-eyelashes at Hamish and gave his torso the once-over. She probably noticed, approvingly, his rotundity matched hers.

Barney, his T-shirt and hair sodden with sweat when he returned from the gig, went straight behind the servery to man the beer pumps. The bar continued to fill with rockers coming from the gig, working fingers into their ears, jabbing at their own personal hiss.

Bebe swayed in and made his way towards the bar, his probing digit hard at work in an ear. He nodded, smiled, shoved a thumb high into the air and made gestures of recognition to customers.

At the bar, in the position he seemed to have made his own, a pint of Guinness awaited him. With one long quaff, he drained the glass, leaving beneath his nose a granddaddy of a frothy moustache. He had been in the pub no more than two minutes. Tipping Barney a knowing wink, he left the building.

Barney left the bar at pace, his untethered hair flying. The front door he slammed shut, turned the key in the lock, then fussed with window curtains. Sure that no light was escaping, he declared, 'It's a lock-in, folks, Bebe's benevolence.'

Hamish had watched Bebe's departure. 'You were right' he said to Harry, 'a lock-in it is. I must say I'm impressed with Bebe. He has great style and the right priorities. What a copper. Anyone taking the piss on his patch, he makes sure he knows about it.'

'It sure looks that way. He's taking the piss, too. That's plain to us professionals,' Harry said. 'He's had a great life here, you have to agree. Did you see him pay for that pint? I bet a lot of free Guinness went into that gut expansion.'

From customers' shouted orders, they learned that the barmaid answered to Rusty. Later, when she was out front, busily collecting empties at the rate of six pint pots per adept hand and placing them on the bar next to Hamish, she gave him blatant eye treatment. Harry whispered to Hamish, 'Admit it. You're crazy about fat birds with big, cuddly bums?'

'Aye, I have been known to lie down next to one. I'd have been safe behind most of them if I had been in the vicinity of an atomic blast,' Hamish replied with a smirk, 'she fits that scenario. A bizarre vision, and aw that.'

'Get a dekko at her. She looks as if she wants full oral sex with you,' Harry said.

'Piss off! What makes you think that?' Hamish asked, suddenly alarmed.

'She's got a face like a Kerr's Pink spud with sixty-nine eyes, and they're all looking at you,' Harry said.

'Piss off; I couldn't fancy that with her.'

Harry nodded knowingly. He could tell what Rusty's game was: each time she sashayed towards the bar, clutching empty glasses or without, she was sidling closer to Hamish. Turning to face Hamish he said, 'Look closely, Hamish, her fanny's slung in a hammock.'

Though Hamish recognised Harry's piss-take, he gave her a quick glance anyway, which was a mistake: she saw it. Hamish recoiled and turned towards Harry, trying to get a conversation going. For a moment, he was tongue-tied. More bad luck: his disinterest hadn't moderated Rusty's interest in him. Walking around him, she pushed in between them. Using her bulk, she separated him from Harry. Wanting Hamish to herself, she flicked her backside at Harry, nudging him out of the way, sending him skittling along the bar. Her eyes searched out Hamish's and locked on. Alluringly, hand on hip, her buttocks swinging, she asked, 'Buying me a drink... big, hunking, Jock boy?'

Hamish dragged his eyes away and cast them despairingly towards Harry, recovering ten feet away, down the bar, amongst some perturbed regulars.

Harry's actions weren't saying he was about to intervene and drag Hamish away; leaving him to Rusty's mercy and enjoying his discomfort from behind the safety of his pint pot was more like it. 'You're on there, Oh Extreme Rear-end Fancier,' Harry's lips said as he gave Hamish the short-arm sign.

'Well, er, eh, aye,' Hamish blustered. He had read Harry's lips, knew his game. 'What's your fancy?' he asked.

Hamish was leaning an elbow on the bar top when he felt Rusty grip the inside of his nearest leg in a pass of exquisite obviousness. Then, with Gascoignesque skills, her hand homed in on his balls and applied pressure. Parting her lips seductively, she purringly named her drink, 'You can get me a large Pernod with a Vimto chaser for starters... you big Jock bastard.'

Hamish felt a hand mess with his lunchbox, felt his bollocks lift a wee bit more slowly than the time he slipped down the canteen stairs. Rusty felt his legs parting and forced her knee in between them.

Hamish ordered. Barney was unable to contain himself and smirked continually. Setting up a double measure, he tipped Hamish a secret-sharing wink. Using her free hand, Rusty removed a squashed pack of Camel cigarettes from a pocket sewn into the back of her leotard and offered them around. 'Don't indulge,' Hamish said, but his eyes were alight.

Expertly, she used her free hand to light a cigarette. Inhaling deeply, she then let out a succession of perfect smoke rings, through large, rouged and puckered lips.

Hamish visualised an Indian boil sucker hovering over a ripe carbuncle with his hollowed-out bamboo tube. Skilled practitioners of the art supposedly achieved astonishing suction and removed puss with their lips pursed around such an extractor. Although Hamish loved a blowjob, there were limits to how far he would go for one. Surely, Rusty had nothing the likes of that planned for him. Smoke rings billowed about him; grinning broadly, he tried to stick his head through them.

Hamish felt arousal, then its quick dousing, albeit in an odd sort of way. Between his intermittent coughing bouts, he had given Rusty the once-over, up close. Gags from a comedian's routine suddenly came to mind: "She had a kind face, the kind that had sucked enough bell-ends to put a handrail around the Great Wall of China, swallowing more semen than the Bermuda Triangle in doing so." Instantly, he felt bus-ride squeamish. He definitely didn't fancy "giving her one" now, maybe at some other time, like when he was blind drunk.

Hamish's stiffy was fading fast. Rusty, feeling the rapidity of the wane, put her free arm around him, pulled him closer and gave him a playful squeeze that hurt. Thinking he was ignoring her and unresponsive, she stuck her tongue into his ear. There she left it, working it about, desperately attempting to instil life into that erogenous zone. Her body forced against Hamish, her breasts spilling upwards from her leotard like a pair of clootie dumplings.

Separating the items in his lunchbox with her dropped hand, she squeezed his cock, feverishly, roughly; any way she could so long as she could return him to hardness. Hamish felt dead from the helmet down.

Pushing herself closer, she skimmed her lips lightly and suggestively across his, letting them linger, before pressing them hard against his. Her tongue, long, warm, moist and gecko-like, forced into his mouth, darted, wandered around, probed deep. She was still after his body; Hamish had little doubt about it!

Hamish was finding her deep-throating tongue hellishly off-putting, almost making him gag. Thrusting an arm out as if he was stopping traffic, he pushed her away, letting her know he didn't fancy her, getting rid of her fast, before he spewed.

Rusty was expecting to hear lustful words from Hamish at this point in the arousal procedure. They weren't coming, even though she had made a sterling effort to enliven his tackle.

When Hamish did speak, his words definitely weren't what she was prepared for. No, they were words that she wouldn't admit to ever having heard before.

With a hint of seriousness showing on his face, Hamish said, 'How would you like me to ram my huge chopper up your fragrant, smoky little orifice?'

Rusty stood back, withdrew her dropped hand, her knee and looked at him, as if he was a steaming turd that she had just found in her handbag. With a flick of her wrist, the cigarette landed on floor in a shower of sparks, to disappear completely beneath her shoe. Then she retorted loudly and indignantly, making sure everyone close-by heard her reply to the obscenity directed at her. 'There's no way *you're* going to shag *my* hoop!'

Rusty was the butt of most of the jocularity that followed. She gave as good as she got, stating, when baited, that she had shagged many double-glazing salesmen before breakfast and wasn't going to let that fat bastard fertilise any of her eggs.

Hamish had succeeded in getting off the case.

The frivolities over, danger passed, Hamish and Harry chatted, enjoyed a laugh with some of the locals taking advantage of the lock-in and bought round-for-round with them. Some of them became quite relaxed and, from hushed, drunken, confidential statements, they were able to ascertain that there were no more tickets available for the strictly private "B B show, the following Tuesday, at the Navigator's Den.

The lock-in ended at 3 a.m.

Thursday

Ivor Bunce quietly tripped the alarm clock at half-past-seven, preventing it from ringing. He raised the duvet cautiously and slipped carefully out of the bed, leaving Gloria undisturbed, snoring, her double chins vibrating.

Before bedtime, she had left orderly lines of vitamin pills on his bedside cabinet. Tutting softly, Ivor cupped his hand, scooped up the pills and walked hurriedly to the bathroom. There he flushed them away, looking closely to see that none remained floating on the top. None did. His 'Click, click,' was a rare sound of pleasure. He had thwarted Gloria. Wearing a wry smile, he showered, dressed, and descended the stairs to the kitchen on tiptoe. This morning, the eggs would have their full three minutes and he'd enjoy them along with the toasted and buttered soldiers that he liked.

On the carpet inside the front door, he found Thursday's Clegham Advertiser. He carried it to the breakfast table, sat down and began flicking through the pages. While the egg pan boiled and his toast browned, he looked for anything that might interest gardeners, court reports and other such items of interest to a Superintendent of Police.

Nothing of interest found in the first pages, he reached the centre spread. Quickly, the sound of air sucked rapidly and noisily through his teeth disturbed the silence: his eyes had locked onto the intro of an article written by Jilly Trebilcock the sex-education therapist and agony aunt for the paper.....

A REAL CURE FOR ERECTILE DYSFUNCTIONAL IMPOTENCY IN YOUR MEN isn't just around the corner IT'S HERE NOW! It proclaimed...

In a trice, Ivor's jaw sagged. Open mouthed, he breathed shallowly....but read on.

Ladies, is seeking lasting sexual performances from your men your "Holy Grail"? Then your waiting is over.

From the sex and health-shop, there is Horny Goat Weed. It's only a puny enhancer of rampancy, promising plenty, but rarely would you have noticed the difference. Now you can dose your men with VIAGRA, which will get it up to stay up, guaranteed!

The significance of the article increased his breathing rate and it wasn't a sensual response. 'Bloody… crude… writing,' he spluttered. Looking towards the kitchen door, he wondered if Gloria had heard his rant from upstairs.

His eyes returned to the pages. Shaking with fury, opening and closing the paper in a temper, he nevertheless read Jilly's blow-by-blow descriptions to the end….

Many gullible sufferers of erectile dysfunction have fallen for the lure of "snake oil" panaceas. Amongst the array of "under-the-counter" quack remedies, horny goat weed is *the* most sought after product of its type.

This pungent, ornamental herb, harvested on Iranian hillsides, has had its devotees for eons. Perhaps believable is some advertising literature claiming that a herder noticed his goats becoming stimulated sexually after eating the plant. Unbelievable and overstated, the same blurb described the rampant antics of the males, and the submissive, tails-to-the-side ways of the females, thus: not only did the rockets fire, they entered the stockade through the gun-ports, broached the doors of the armoury and blew up the barracks as well.

Octogenarian men… can you believe this, competed with teenage rivals for the favours of available maidens. Doddering, groaning, priapic coffin-dodgers, an infusion of the weed supposedly giving their backbones renewed, band-saw springiness, flashing erections, magnificent, stiffer and enduring, doing the business? Come on!

It seemed that no animal or man was safe from an unwanted sexual coupling on those hillsides. Horses mated with cows and vice versa, producing jumarts; goats mated with sheep and vice versa, producing geeps and shoats. Biblical tales, though not ones I've read, confirm the presence of such nightmarish beasts. Obviously, man and beast were into anything that stood still long enough. And any hopping frog that stopped for a moment too long would surely learn quickly there were consequences to its inertia.

In my experience, that herb never lived up to its gloss. VIAGRA will: It works by relaxing smooth muscle around arteries supplying the male organ, increasing blood supply and constricting venous outflow.

Manufactured by Pfizer, it has the power not only to cure impotence, but also to give healthy, non-impotent, older men, the sexual performance of a twenty year old, some reported having sex six times nightly.

Initially developed for the treatment of angina, Viagra eventually became a disappointment. Doctors noticed their patients were reluctant to stop taking it even after surgery had dealt with their angina problems. One by one, users confessed that a wonderful thing had happened after taking the drug: their sex life had dramatically improved.

Ladies, get the pill and get it into your men. Two hours later, you'll find instead of holding putty in your hand, your man now has an amazing hard-on, sure-fire.

Ivor paled. The thought sickened him. If Gloria got her hands on this product, she would become an even worse middle-aged sex fiend. He imagined her rudely awakening him at five-thirty each morning, ram tablet over his throat, then reawakening him two hours later for him to find he had an erection he couldn't control.

Shifting his buttocks on his chair, he read the final sentence...

In a minority of cases, it has caused heart attacks and even death in the older male patients deemed sexually depressed.

'Crikey, that means me!' he grouched, stiffly clenching his buttocks, before skirting over the article on Impocreme, which said, If applied twice daily to the genital area, it would improve circulation.

'Is there no escape from these bothersome women and their unwholesome interest in all matters sexual?' he moaned softly. 'Sexy articles won't help to sell newspapers to this household.' In the grips of panic and rage, he ripped the page from the paper. Rolling it up into a small, tight ball between the palms of his hands, he threw it into the flip-top rubbish bin kept beneath the sink.

******

Ricky Croker arrived at his office at 9 a.m. that morning. Rodney, his Harley Street friend, had sent a fax, which he read. 'Ho, ho, ho!' he cried out as he saw the result.

His personal assistant appeared at his door with his coffee. 'You were correct? It's a positive outcome,' she buttered.

Ricky puffed up as he spoke. 'Yes. I was right to pry into this police thing. The tests found pure amphetamine sulphate and a cheap, supermarket-brand tea in the sample.'

He gathered his team members together: personal assistant, minder and cameraman. Then he briefed them on the sample results and recounted the incident occurring twenty years or so previously, which had rekindled his personal interest in Superintendent Bunce.

It surprised them. The sample was of questionable origin as was the scribbled note. To launch such an investigation, they, at the very least, expected him to offer a reason more germane and cogent than the flimsy one he had just presented. The team knew he never changed his mind, so they said nothing.

While on tenterhooks waiting the positive result, Ricky had sought out another court contact and obtained Superintendent Bunce's home address. The briefing over, he ushered them to his Volvo Estate, instructing the driver, 'Let's go to the Bunce household first. We'll think of a reason for visiting on the way.'

******

Gloria awoke an hour and twenty minutes after Ivor had left for his office. She checked his bedside table, verified his consummation of the morning dosages of vitamins and additives, rattled containers to confirm supplies for his evening dose and removed the empty Pro-Plus container.

Gloria hadn't yet introduced Ivor to the Stallion Pump. "Annie Slobbers" took several weeks to deliver, so she had journeyed to Walthamstow, found a seedy sex-shop and made an instant purchase. Desperate to have another look at it, she took it from beneath the bed and sat it on her lap. Maggie had said it was easy to use, and that it worked.

Her eyes skimmed quickly from the instructions for use to the expectations and prophecies. There they lingered. 'A rock-hard inch a fortnight,' she said aloud. Maggie was correct. The enlarger would increase the size and improve the longevity of Ivor's erections.

Ivor had rushed off to work and left the kitchen in a mess. 'Typical of him when he cooks his own breakfast,' Gloria complained, as she fussily tidied up, clearing his plate and eggcup from the table. Chores done, she sat down in her housecoat and slippers. She stirred a milky coffee and flicked the Clegham Advertiser open to the centre pages.

Gloria always made a beeline for Jilly Trebilcock's interesting and informative articles. Often they included simple remedies for many of the everyday problems besetting women. It initially miffed her to find Jilly's article missing.

In a trice, she progressed to extreme discombobulment. Ivor had to be the culprit, and she knew the reason why. The article had to contain something sexual. He wouldn't like that, so what had he done with it? He wouldn't have taken Jilly's article to work with him, her very name bode him ill. He hadn't burnt it… there was no smell and the kitchen was clean and tidy now, so…where? With a 'Humph,' she walked to the sink and checked the rubbish bin.

Moving eggshells, she found the ball of newspaper. Opened out, it was hardly readable and in need of ironing flat.

With one pass of the iron, steam suppressed, the bold print became clearer, confirming why Ivor had attempted to keep it secreted from her. Another couple of strokes of the iron would reveal all. With the electricity switched off, she turned the page to smooth the reverse side. The front door bell sounded as she was completing the task.

In the passageway, on the way to answer the door, she wafted the page, cooling it. The article ready for scrutiny, she opened the door.

A tall man wearing a trilby stood there, a full-length sheepskin coat covering the rest of his bulky frame. Although the face was familiar, she couldn't put a name to it right away. Behind the bulky figure, a man peered into the eyepiece of the large, professional, video camera. The winking light indicated it was filming her. To one side a bright, slender, leggy, young woman wearing a revealing mini-skirt, a short sheepskin jacket and a reassuring smile, held a clipboard. To the rear of the group, a stocky, sinister-looking minder hovered incognito behind Ray-Bans.

'Yaws, what can I do for you?' she asked of them politely, if a little imperiously. With a gasp, she clutched at her housecoat lapels, closing them and ensuring they covered her nightie.

'I'm Ricky Croker from Thameside Television,' the large man in the trilby replied, doffing his hat. In doing so, he noted, with eyes that had often taken interest in such details in print, the words on the torn piece of newspaper Mrs. Bunce was holding.

'Of course. I recognise you now,' Gloria replied loftily.

'My new series will highlight the lifestyles of important civil servants and their wives. It's kind of "through the keyhole" stuff. We pleasantly impose ourselves into your everyday life, interview you in your beautiful home and ask you a whole series of pertinent questions. We take you to quality stores and ask you to pick quality furniture, clothes, shoes, music and literature. Some of the products you may keep. We will also dine you in the most expensive restaurants with stars of stage and screen as your table guests, taping your conversations, that sort of thing.'

'Are you not supposed to make an appointment first?' she asked, looking at him squarely.

'Ah, ah,' he said. Caught off guard, he bowed obsequiously. He had been thinking of police reaction to the surreptitious addition of Viagra to their canteen tea. 'The element of surprise works in wondrous ways and makes for the best television.'

'I see,' she said, folding the page carefully, realising too late that she had been waving it about in front of their faces. 'You had better come in.' She couldn't turn Ricky Croker away; his visit would make a great story to recount when she next met the girls.

Ricky's personal assistant and the minder were experts in making discoveries whilst their targets were unaware. Unwittingly, Gloria ushered them into the kitchen, offered them a chair at the breakfast table and suggested coffee.

The cameraman panned around the kitchen and caught Gloria busily setting out her best china. She smiled readily, described the coffee-making process, named the coffee beans she preferred, and when asked to, found positions in light for better shots. Noting Gloria's co-operation, Ricky nodded discreetly towards the team to film elsewhere. 'We have permission to shoot some footage in an around your beautiful home?' Ricky asked. The cameraman reversed out of the kitchen door closely followed by the girl and the minder. Ricky stood up and removed his sheepskin coat from his huge frame, placing it over the back of his chair. Gloria turned from the stove with the coffee to find she was alone with Ricky.

Without delving into personal possessions, the team knew where to look for indications of drug abuse: discarded roaches in ashtrays, powder remnants in sachets, telltale residue lines on flat surfaces. The discovery of any of those could confirm a user in the house. Nothing incriminating revealed itself downstairs, they mounted the stairs towards the bedrooms.

Oblivious of what Ricky's team were up to, Gloria gabbled away merrily to Ricky, describing the more maidenly topics discussed at her Thursday evening "Masonic Widows' Society" girlie nights.

The toilet cistern top, a flat surface favoured by drug users and the bathroom were clean. The minder fitted a rubber glove, stooped on one knee and plunged his hand beneath the water line of the toilet bowl. From the floor behind the bowl, he retrieved a green and black capsule, which he placed in a sample bag.

In the bedroom, they spotted the array of vitamin containers and devices on what was obviously Superintendent Bunce's side of the bed. The stallion pump, still in its sealed box, and the Dr Blakoe's Energiser ring, ready for use, brought about sniggers. It wasn't the paraphernalia of the drug abuser, but they were interesting finds in the home of a top copper, especially at his side of the bed.

Ricky was glad to see his team reappear, although their disappointed looks told him they'd found nothing incriminating. Gloria had yackety-yacked, on and on. Told him about her wonderful friendships with the women who attended her blessed girlie nights and hadn't she given him the most boring account of her tambourine bashing days in the Sal Dal? He concluded that she was a bored and old female fart who kept the compulsory, yapping, blue-rinsed, coiffured and powdered poodle, which couldn't be far away.

Deciding to fish new waters, he threw out bait, attempting to reel in Superintendent Bunce's passions, likes and dislikes: 'Police Superintendents have extremely stressful jobs. At the end of each harrowing day in which he has ensured that the good policing of his manor continues, does your husband drink coffee, decaffeinated or otherwise, or a nice China tea? Or does he need something special, something fortified to recover from his mental toils?'

'Oh, it's usually tea. Only Earl Grey leaf will suffice for Ivor,' she confided, 'he says tea bags are for the masses, for the riffraff, his constables I think he means. He complains he only ever sees them when they are in the station, drinking tea in the canteen. Moreover, he tells me when they leave the station "thin air" envelops them. Apparently, they only re-emerge at booking-off time. He spits with fury at the thought of his constables hiding themselves away in some seedy mumping hole on his manor, drinking tea and feeding their faces when they should be fighting crime. Unapproachable he is when he tells me he suspects some of them are humping while they're on duty. Humping has only recently reappeared in my dictionary so I do have an inkling of its meaning. Yes, quite cross my Ivor becomes when he suspects his coppers are breaking the rules!'

Ready to leave, Ricky bowed low and made Gloria happy by promising her she would feature in the first show, once the project got off the ground.

The team found Clegham Mental hospital was an austere, weathered, red brick building, standing back from the road in floral gardens. To the girl staffing the reception desk the TV team members were famous visitors. She was immediately helpful and escorted them to the outside ward housing patients with stress-related problems, but deemed capable of handling visits from family and friends. There, a male nurse showed them to a private ward where Sergeant Moriarty lay comatose, propped up on pillows in a bed, an intravenous cannular in his arm.

'Mr. Moriarty is short of sensible thought processes at this moment in time,' pointed out the nurse. 'The drip contains a solution of drugs that will ease his stress.'

'No sign of drug abuse?' Ricky asked casually, his eyes skirting the ward.

'I shouldn't say this, but his symptoms are similar. We're waiting the results of a blood test. You know how slow the NHS is these days,'

Signs of life stirred beneath the sheets. The lower half of Sergeant Moriarty's body twitched and his feet began to move rhythmically. He lifted his head from the pillows and he blubbered with his eyes closed, 'Aht…enshun…eft… tarn… one… two… one two…halt… eft… tarn… halt…stand ate… ease, you blithering idiots, isn't it.'

The male nurse approached him, felt his pulse and placed a damp cloth on his forehead. 'Fuck them, give them a pound,' he got for his thoughtfulness.

Ricky looked baffled, slumped in a heap in the front passenger seat of the Volvo as the team travelled back towards the studios. 'What the fuck have we here that's worthy of our interest?' he quized. Without giving a team member time to answer, he began his own summation. 'We might have a police gov'nor doping his coppers' canteen tea with speed. Highly unlikely, I think. They then race off like headless chickens. Yes, I think we can all believe that of them. Then they might go walkabout, disappear off their beats where they might visit mumping holes, be on the piss, humping, or they might not.

Knowing coppers, we can believe they're all up to all of that; actively looking for a mump or a sly shag, in my book. We might have a police sergeant suffering the effects of drinking too many cups of the previously mentioned suspicious, police canteen tea or we might not. He's certainly nuts. At this time, boys and girls, we've nothing... absolutely fuck all… but we might as well have that capsule analysed. It has crossed my mind that whoever sent the original sample and note might be pointing us towards something bigger, more worthy of my investigation. It might not be immediately obvious to us, so we'll watch Bunce's house for a week, at the most, and wait and see if anything interesting or tasty turns up.'

******

Hamish and Harry were mobile, on foot, dressed in blue overalls, preparing to advertise PIGS double-glazing. It was 10 a.m. both feeling a trifle fragile and looking bleary-eyed, they busied themselves pushing leaflets through the letterboxes of houses in Skibbereen Street.

After an hour, they stopped. 'Two big lumps of lassies,' Hamish reported to Harry, 'are on our tail. They've been stalking us. I've watched them for some time, sussing out their movements. It started with them keeking around corners, keeping an eye on us, watching what we're up to. They look very fine examples of extremely fat pussy to me. They're after our bodies, I'd say. The last time you'd have seen pussy that big, it would have been roaring and rampaging around a cage in Edinburgh Zoo. Anyway, I'll tackle one and I know you'd give the other one, one.'

'No, Great Pussy Fancier, if I were you I'd be wanting to give both of them one.'

'Cheek, last night I turned down an offer of nookie from a ravishing bird with rust-tipped hair.'

Harry laughed. 'If you'd have tackled that, you might've fallen in and never been seen again.'

The stalkers revealed their intentions. While sheltering from a squally shower beneath a covered bus stop, the girls walked up to them, hand-in-hand, giggling. The heftier of the girls sported red hair, her mate, six inches shorter, had the same girth measurements and a shaved head. Overcome with girlish excitement, they both wobbled and threw an arm around each other for support. Hamish smiled cheesily. Seeing this as an indication of his interest, the girls moved close up to him and ran their hands over his chest.

The red head said, 'I'm Jemima. You could make me swank, smiler, if you glazed my pad.' Swaying their hips like grass-skirted Hawaiian dancers, they both eyed him lecherously.

They ignored Harry.

He was relieved.

Hamish sounded 'Huh,' bounced on the balls of his feet, a cheesier grin spreading.

‘Go on, ask him again,’ the smaller one said, encouraged by the beam on his face.

‘Darling, I’d rather masturbate than give you a pane for your sash,’ Hamish got in first, quoting glazier speak.

‘OOOO…ooooh, you *are* awful. Will you show us the special tool you use for easing the pane, then, you big darling?’ Jemima responded. Then she brushed her breasts across Hamish’s stomach, leaving him in little doubt that she was referring to pain.

‘We live in a one-bedroom flat at 71 Mayo Street,’ the shorter one said, ‘on the second floor, just around the corner, with great views over the river. You’ll find us easily. When you do, both of us will shag that massive arse off you.’ Hoisting both breasts on an arm and bouncing them beneath Hamish’s gaze, she said, ‘I know you’ll get to like my name. It’s Laura. Laura Dickie, that is.’

Jemima made an offer of substance she thought attractive to Hamish. ‘Drop what you’re doing. Visit us this lunchtime. We’ll have a big, fat sandwich… all three of us…if you’ve time. I know you’ll like my name, too, it’s Jemima Broadbent’.

‘You both have a bit of a bent broad about you,’ Hamish responded.

The squall blew over. They moved on, Laura and Jemima strutting in front of them, screeching hysterically and kissing each other.

Harry nodded towards their retreating figures. ‘If the sun was any lower, they’d blot it out.’

‘They’re a pair of fat, ugly, lesbian vultures,’ Hamish said knowingly, ‘otherwise I might have been there. They’re girls of the other path with a fetish for double-glazing salesmen and pain. That’s what I think of them. The Axminster rash scrapes on their chins are badges worn proudly by girls of that fraternity.’

‘Aye, ah ken, muffing by the fireside. Their attire of jeans, colourful lumberjack jackets and shirts, Jemima with hair cropped short, Laura shaved on top, makes them look very manly.’

‘The wellies they’re wearing are signs of their affiliation to and affinity with the Irish community, by the way.’

‘I notice both had their incisor teeth buffed flat.' Harry said.

‘Aye, it gives them a fearsome and demonic persona, and I doubt that a sensible man would touch them.’

‘Eh?’ A frown of disbelief creased Harry’s brow.

Harry’s disbelief at Hamish’s declaration, that he thought the women untouchable, proved sound later that morning when he detected Hamish’s surge of Interest in the stalking pussy.

They’d run out of leaflets and Harry had expected they’d eat a bar lunch, then spend the afternoon playing pool in the Navigator’s Den. As hunger pangs were consuming Harry, it seemed Hamish was developing a foolhardy and playful disposition. Then he got a dose of the giggles and the horn in equal proportions.

'I feel randy enough to take up their offer,' Hamish erupted. 'My hormones are causing havoc, surging through my prunes, and getting into my head.' Then he set out walking briskly, breathing heavily, torso swinging, towards Mayo Street.

Harry puffed along in his wake; still he couldn't get past him. The belly was in front again and it looked like staying there. 'They can keep the view across the river,' Hamish voiced over his shoulder. 'It's the size of Jemima's tits that attracts me. Sticking my napper between them and being the meat in that sandwich is…is…irresistible… I just cannae refuse.'

Turning the corner into Mayo Street, Harry still hadn't caught up. Hamish said, 'You've had your nookie this week… already shagged yourself silly… you said…remember? Now it's my turn… you can come along if you like and dip the shorter one… I've come down with a severe dose of the horn… in fact… I'm gagging for a shag.'

'You told me this morning that no sensible man would touch them,' Harry reminded him.

'When did you believe everything I said?' Hamish asked, his smile waxing strength-seven cheddar.

'You don't know what these two are like… they're strangers to us… they could pass all sorts of strange diseases on to you… where would you be then?' Harry thought it a mate's duty to point out the venereal hazards that could crop up.

Hamish let out a loud 'Ach! Jemima and Laura look all right to me. Jenny has been off shagging for several months… I must have nookie…desperate for it…that's it.'

'Go for it, Hamish, if you feel like that. My prunes are empty of juices and my bell-end is still raw, but I'll be look-out for you.'

'Bragging again… Harry, eh? I thought you'd be man enough to take the wee bird…Laura Dickie…she who likes it a lot… a laura times, off my hands.' Hamish turned into the block of flats, stopped and took several quick inhalations. Harry caught up, bumped into him and wheezed. Hamish took off again, found the stairs at the side of the building and took them two at a time to the second floor. He found apartment seventy-one and knocked heavily on the door.

'A sandwich it is then and if I have to nibble at it alone, then I'll nibble it alone,' he said as Harry joined him.

There seemed to be no way of deflating Hamish's raging horniness. 'So okay,' Harry said, 'you're hot for it and all that, ah ken. I'll have to come along as gooseberry. You've no idea what you're getting into.'

The door opened sharply. A hi-fi was playing loudly and vibrating the flat to the bluesy beat of Big Twist and the Mellow Fellow's, "300 Pounds of

Heavenly Joy". Inside, the two examples of extremely fat pussy were standing together, wearing bras and panties, their faces wreathed in wicked smiles. They reached for Hamish and four hands dragged him into the front room. There, jumbo mattresses that a herd of elephants might have slept on covered the floor. Viewing the foam spewing out like overfilled, milk jelly sandwiches, Harry mused: this must be an extreme example of damaged Feng Shui.

Wall decorations were of a contemporary nature; two were brown and rippled with a chocolate-flake texture. On the other two and facing each other, were unique, full-size, full-frontal photographs of the amazingly well-endowed Chesty Morgan. Past reports stated Chesty wielded the biggest tits a woman had ever shoehorned into a bra.

Harry sussed the girls' reasoning out. Chesty was the quintessential idol of the worshippers of the larger person. Hamish was a large person and he, being a candidate for such worship, fell into Laura and Jemima's worshipful bracket.

Over the fireplace, a cheap picture frame held a spoof diploma from the Goosey-Goosey College, Gander, Newfoundland. It accredited a Miss Laura Dickie with a First Class Honours degree in the ancient art of Head Humping. The First Principal, the Right Honourable Fellatio Hornblower, M.D., confirmed the award.

The kitchen stabled a clotheshorse. Straddling it was an outsize leather suit. A whip with skin-like shreds sticking to it hung from a pocket. A pair of spurred riding boots sat close by. The kitchen sink overflowed with unwashed dishes, articles of used underwear and a loofah. Sign-writing on the door the hosts had just dragged Hamish through, one arm already out of his overall, their hands on his arse, thrusting and guiding, said, "Head humpers of the world unite, for we alone know what is right".

Thinking he should quickly follow Hamish, Harry entered the room.

Evidence of Laura and Jemima's interests in sexual perversion existed wherever he looked. Decorated drapes, showing fat women whipping each other across the buttocks, hung around the four-poster bed.

Knee-high chamber pots stood at either side of the bed. While on the bed, naked and ululating like a Bantu tribeswoman, the hunkered figure of Jemima was active, her pendulous breasts hovering over Hamish's torso.

Laura, naked and equally pendulously breasted, displaying a hanging spare tyre of abdominal fat, had also joined in the fun. She had already removed Hamish's trainers, one of which she slung casually over her shoulder in Harry's direction. Whistling close past his ear, its cheesy slipstream made him turn his head away.

Hamish had no chance of lifting Jemima's jumble of hanging flesh when she turned and sat on him, her buttocks spreading across his chest, and began pushing his overalls and jeans down over his feet. Once they were free, she tossed them over her shoulder to land behind his head. Laura's lips were drooling, working up lather on Hamish's feet. With deft flicks of her tongue, she was removing winkles and portions of flaking athlete's foot from between his toes.

In the throes of panic, Hamish suddenly got vocal and began to struggle. The noises he made showed him less happy than had he been stuck in a barrel of week-old, unwashed baby's nappies. He moaned, groaned, he intoned, blustered and spluttered. In shouting, 'She's a fucking nutter!' his voice betrayed his rising fears of imperilment. Other sounds accompanying the outburst compared reasonably with the unrelenting boohooing of a teething child. Laura had pulled her lips wide and was biting Hamish's inside leg, leaving behind nipping teeth marks. Plainly, Hamish was about to experience a tooth in a tenderer place soon, if he didn't do something about it.

The position Jemima sought and had manoeuvred herself into was to do with a threat she had made some months previously. Unsuccessful at persuading a prior sales team to double-glaze her pad, at no cost, she threatened that one day a double-glazing salesman would crack like a nut between the cheeks of her arse. The nut now beneath her had become the subject of that threat.

Harry stood gawping at his mate's plight. His concern eased a touch when he saw that Hamish had seen a way to extricate himself. If successful, he wouldn't perish between Jemima's threatening buttocks or bleed to death from the molar lacerations Laura the head-humping leech was inflicting.

Hamish had retrieved his overalls. Rolled up in the screwdriver pocket were some leaflets he was keeping for Barney, allowing him to think he'd have several entries in the draw for the show house. He removed them, rolled and tightened them. In the right hands, it was a potent weapon. In his right hand, he used it to spear a spot deep between Jemima's buttocks.

The effect was instant. Jemima squealed, clenched her buttocks, gripped the weapon, fell forward and rolled from the bed, dragging Laura with her. Hamish slid his legs over the other side of the bed and lurched himself upright. 'I couldn't take much more of that,' he wheezed at Harry, 'meat in the sandwich, fuck that.'

Struggling for breath, he scrambled around the room searching for the rest of his clothing. 'Nookie seems a lot kinkier than I can remember it… thought she was going to invite me to visit a lower floor to give lip service. The thought of that and her talons skirting the periphery of my ring-piece put me right off, it did… fucking painful it would have been… I mightn't have come out from beneath that pair alive… you know what I mean?'

They hit the street running, leaving Laura and Jemima rolling together on the floor, slobbering over each other.

Hamish was still struggling to breathe, Harry still having difficulty keeping up. 'It's the Bally Balti,' Hamish said, sweating heavily. 'An Indian is just what I need to cool down.'

During lunch, Hamish's breathing regulated and his heartbeat steadied. Harry agreed. Hamish did need a spicy nosh to assist his recuperation. He had reservations, though, about the tale Hamish told as they ate.

'Do you know, I last saw an arse that was as big, as spotty and as wrinkled as the one that just straddled me? It was one night duty, during my first year in the Robbery Squad, on undercover duties down at the KG 5 docks. A strange ensemble approached me as I sat parked up in a nondescript. A little guy, a mahout I think you call them, appeared leading three elephants in a trunk-to-tail formation. I stopped him, as you do, just in case he had nicked them. "Where might you be going with these elephants?" I asked, sternly.

'"I'm taking them to a ship in the docks that is taking them home to India for mating," he told me in his broken English. I shouldn't have asked him where the mating was taking place. He let go of the leader's trunk, took me behind the last elephant, lifted up its tail, and pointed to the gash running for a full yard beneath its base, and said "There".'

Harry laughed loudly and said, 'Your stories are getting dafter, I don't know where you dig them up from.'

About 2 p.m., Hamish left a message on the Commander's answering service, updating him and requesting more leaflets: 'Interest in our brand of double-glazing is booming. To keep the natives calm, we require another five hundred leaflets. Suspicions are that Billy Bagman will perform here next week. Access to tickets for the performances is difficult, if not impossible to obtain. Our best efforts assured at all times, more info to follow.' The request was timely. Later, while checking out the transit van before knocking off, a crowd gathered, pestering them for more leaflets to enter into the show house draw.

******

The impending installation at the Lodge and the forthcoming "Ladies night", had thrown the "The Masonic Widows' Society" out of kilter. Myrna insistence that she host an extra meet at Paddleville intrigued the other girls.

As usual, Daphne was first to arrive. It was immediately noticeably that she was off colour, quite jaw-dropped, preoccupied, distant and sour. Her eyes never rested; they darted and never looked the other girls straight in the face. Her wine went untouched, her sandwiches un-nibbled and she remained silent during discussions. Having previously listened to Daphne describe the sexual acts the Halloween blind date wanted her to perform, Myrna didn't need to guess at the reasons.

Gloria collared Maggie, took her to one side and pumped her for information on how to use a stallion pump to obtain the best results. 'Get it out of its box,' she said. 'It's no good keeping it as an ornament. All you have to do is work Ivor up, get his cock right hard, slip it in through the seal into the chamber, then you pump like crazy. You'll find it's so magical watching his cock swelling. When you see it extending up the glass tube, you'll want to keep on evacuating it. When you take the enlarger off, I'm sure you'll be dead chuffed with the extra hard inches. Using them for enhanced your satisfaction.'

'Well, I might like the pleasuring given by a well-hung beast,' Gloria replied, a thoughtful look on her face, 'however; I'm not so sure about Ivor being eager to perform like one. He's much too attached to his little tiddler. I can't imagine him humping a super dong about. He'd need to wear reinforced undies, something like Linford's lunchbox. Somehow, I don't think he'd like that, but your details encourage me. The evening I try it out on Ivor might not be far off.'

Gloria waited until they'd settled before beginning her account of Ricky Croker's visit. She told them what Ricky said, repeated his questions about Ivor's choice of tea or coffee, and the prospect of selection for the first show of the series.

'You'll be on telly, then?' Myrna suggested. 'Lucky you. I couldn't have a film team here with Algie falling about.'

'Hope you smiled a lot,' Maggie said. 'You'll look photogenic on the box.

Daphne, still looking a bit detached, hadn't a question or a comment to offer.

Gloria took the newspaper article out of her handbag. 'Do any of you have your husbands on this new product, Viagra?' she asked.

Myrna had read the article too and, being a bit more adventurous than Gloria, had approached her doctor to obtain a Viagra tablet to show at the meeting. Seizing Gloria's lead, Myrna said. 'What do you think of this, then? It's Viagra!' She placed a plate on the coffee table with the small, blue, lozenge-shaped tablet in the centre. Gloria and Maggie were agog.

Daphne looked once then turned away. What was there of interest in the shape and colour of a pill?

'Can I touch it, Myrna?' Gloria asked excitedly. I thought Jilly Trebilcock's article on it was very good.' Leaning forward to view it better, she shuddered. ‘Perhaps a little will rub off on my fingers so I can stir Ivor’s ginseng tea with them. That might get him up a little more often.’

Gloria had noticed Daphne’s disinterest and thought to involve her. ‘Come on Daphne,’ she said cheerily, ‘you’ve done nursing. Give us some medical details about this erectile dysfunctional impotence that Viagra supposedly alleviates.’

Daphne ‘tut tutted,’ she didn’t know much more than they did, it being a new product for the problem, but she’d make something up to please them. Turning towards the girls, she said. ‘Remember that big, stiff dildo at the “Annie Slobbers” party? Well that’s the size of cock a healthy male ought to have.’ She looked around them all, grinning weakly. ‘That’s the size of the cock we expect to be holding when our man is roused.’ Myrna and Gloria looked shocked as women disappointed in their men do, Maggie a little less so now the stallion pump was working its wonders for Murdo, so she thought.

Daphne checked that Myrna was listening. ‘If a male isn’t healthy, is drinking too much, say, like Algie does, then Viagra will alleviate the dysfunction by allowing more blood to swell the bobby’s helmet, if you’ll excuse the pun. Jack has never needed anything like Viagra. If he needed it now, it wouldn’t do him any good anyway… you know the story… forget it,’ Daphne snapped. Her face had flushed, showing her upset, but she sniffed and continued: ‘A man needs invigorating blood surging through his gristle to gain a lasting erection.’ Daphne pumped her arm up and down. She was sure all the girls knew the meaning of the lewd gesture. ‘Viagra affects cock tissue allowing blood to circulate more easily through it. Thus, if we girls were to dope our men with Viagra, we may hope for several erections from them during a love fest. I believe erections will follow one another in quick succession, some might not disappear at all, whether our man is happy with them or not.’

Daphne had no more to say on the subject and sat back.

Myrna kept the chat going. ‘You can get your hands on Viagra on the Internet, but it’s bloody expensive,’ she explained. ‘Otherwise you’re going to have to drag your old geezer along to the quack and have his waterworks given the once-over for defects.’

‘Can’t this drug be obtained from a pharmacy without prescription?’ Gloria asked, rubbing an eye, attempting to hide her interest.

‘Definitely not. If your old man doesn’t have an erection problem, you won’t get any from the quack,’ Myrna told her.

‘What is this Internet thing?’ asked Gloria. ‘Is it easy to buy the drug from there?’

‘You’ll have to equip yourself with a computer to do the deal on, won’t you? Like Viagra, the equipment is bloody well expensive,’ Myrna answered.

'I don't know how Ivor would react if I ever managed to slip a Viagra tablet into his morning mug of ginseng tea,' Gloria said, 'perhaps he will get a stiff neck as he swallows it.'

The girls laughed.

Gloria had learned from the article that Impocreme applied twice daily to genitals, was an interesting alternative to Viagra, as was Libido, a pre-embryonic chicken egg extract from Scandinavia. Herbal V and the Ginger Stimulant were other aphrodisiacs that some women were using on their men. She had already decided that those products, along with the vitamins and other potions she forced upon Ivor, were tardy at getting him up. No quack remedy would work on him the way the article suggested or the way she wanted. From what she had read and heard, Viagra would. Ivor needed that extra something guaranteed to work quickly, and time after time. She eyed the tablet, her heart thumping. While the girls were engrossed in another topic, she moved the plate across the table towards her.

The evening ended with a demonstration. Myrna, using a portion of a cucumber carved to represent a cock, showed the girls an interesting way to fit a condom to their partners. Sucking the condom head into her mouth, she then placed it over the carving. Her expertise drew gasps from Gloria and Maggie.

The girls left abruptly at 10:30 p.m., when the Mayoral car pulled up outside and deposited Algie. Listening to him falling about in the hallway, Myrna cleared away the designer cucumber and condom. The Viagra tablet she couldn't find anywhere.

******

Hamish and Harry saw that the need to obtain tickets for one of the B B gigs was now top priority; suspicions were that Constable Beckham was definitely Billy Bagman. If any tickets for one of the gigs were available or entry by any other means obtainable, it seemed that stoking friendship with the barman Barney or Morphy afforded their best chances. At 10 p.m. that night, they entered the Navigator's Den, their minds set on that quest.

They found Barney working industriously, serving customers with gusto. He chatted freely over the bar and looked a great front man for the pub. His band allegiances had changed and now he wore a black T-shirt showing a pig's head, wearing dark glasses, a set of earphones and a joint hanging from its mouth. Above the pig were the words "A Head Rings Out" and beneath, the name of the band, Blodwyn Pig. Barney pointed a finger towards it and shouted towards them, 'They're on at the Shankless Music Bar, Sunday night.'

Rusty was serving other customers, whilst completely ignored them; only a contemptuous sniff did she throw in their direction. Barney poured two pints of their favourite tipple and served it up. Hamish struck right away.

'You'll want your leaflets in the draw, Barney?' Then he tipped him an easily translatable wink,

Barney turned without speaking, leaving them for a storeroom and his jacket. Returning, he handed Hamish fifty filled-in leaflets. Begging-bowl faced, he returned the wink.

Hamish thought Barney had read collusion in the wink. 'Good, good,' he said, looking at the leaflets. 'I see you've dotted all the Is and crossed all the Ts on these. We'll get them in the barrel, close to the top.' He returned the wink and smiled cheesily. 'Oh, by the way, Barney, this gig that's on here next Tuesday with this B B mystery artist, what's the chance of a couple of tickets for that? We'll pay,' he said, leaning forward, his and Barney's face close.

Hamish's winks were working. Barney looked around furtively. No one had heard the question; he thought it safe to reply. Desperation was driving him to acquire the free double-glazing and show house status. He saw that Rusty was coping with the punters' needs and ushered them further along the bar. He said quietly, 'There is no way you or any outsider will get a ticket for the mystery gig here or at the Shankless Music Bar. The tickets sold out twelve months ago. All of them went to solid and trustworthy folk from the Ringaskiddy Square area who can keep a secret. Believe me, to have free double-glazing and show house status I'd do it, if I could, but, and it's a big but, if you fancy chancing your arm to get them, I happen to know that eight tickets have been returned to Blodger's, the cross dressers' club across the square, for Wednesday night's show there.'

'People died or something?' asked Harry.

'No… not quite,' he said, his eyes everywhere, watching for anyone eavesdropping. 'Rumour has it that eight cross-dressers, regular punters at Blodger's, met in a "cottage" last Sunday night, on the other side of East Clegham. Apparently, an evil psychopath, deserving of having his knackers cut off and stuck up his arse followed by a hedgehog, arse first… their words, not mine… bombed the building. Tongue in cheek… I don't know for definite what they were discussing… I found out that all eight have been hospitalised suffering damage ranging from busted arseholes, lacerated helmets through to pedestal rash and damaged tonsils, and won't be doing the rounds for a while.'

'It sounds like it was a pretty shitty gang-bang, to me,' Harry said, shrugging with indifference.

'More like an old-time filthy fairy story with someone doing the dirty on a wicked queen,' said Barney smirking.

'I would say with a degree of certainty filth was involved there,' Hamish said, mirthlessly, whilst dying to let go a chuckle.

'The only way you can get your hands on these tickets is to visit Blodger's and make out you cross-dress. You'd better be quick. Buy them before someone else gets their hands on them. Go tonight.'

The glance they gave each other said the suggestion was preposterous. Both turned to look at Barney, whose amusement was twisting his face as he stood polishing a glass. 'Tonight at Blodger's is bikes and dykes night. Many of the boys go there for a laugh. Sometimes they come away with a fair piece of fluff. Other times they come away with a bit of fluff with a surprise hanging between their legs. It's up to you. If you can convince the sisters, or should I say, the brothers Malone, Molly and Dolly, that you're serious cross-dressers, they might just sell you the tickets. I'll phone them now. Putting a good word in for you is as much as I can do.'

'Not a Polly, then?' Hamish asked.

'Their parrot's called Polly,' Barney said, lifting his eyes.

Returning from the telephone, grinning and brimming with chat, Barney said, 'Success, I think I've cracked it for you. I've done them a few favours in the time I've been here. They owe me one. They tell me if they like the look of your coupons, the tickets are yours. They say you'll have to take all eight. No one will piss them about again, Molly Malone said. Remember this, though. No piss-taking while you're in there or you'll lose out and they'll heave you out. They're tough cookies. Both suffer from irritating piles. They won't endure another pain in the arse gladly. You'll know why when you see the ugly pair of vultures. They work the bar. The last time I saw pairs of lips the likes of theirs, was in a photo finish at Ascot. Mind you, it could have been at Aintree, because I'm sure they jump. I tell you this, though. If sheep had mouths the likes of theirs, they'd do a quick job on a field of turnips.

'A right tearaway went there one night. He sat at the bar and straight away got on the wrong side of them. Told them a medical joke, said their stools were shite. Then he asked who was responsible for their design. Dolly Malone bit bitchily and asked why he wanted to know. He told them that lumpy stools always hurt his arse. Mind you, you don't have to be a psychiatrist to work out where the ugly fuckers went wrong in their youth. They were obviously suckers for a big knob.'

The most worrying feature of the conversation appeared when they were leaving for Blodger's at 11 p.m. Barney had saved the news, perhaps savouring it for a time. He looked at them squarely when he delivered it, his eyes shining with a merry glint. 'Boys, attending the gig at Blodger's next Wednesday will require you to cross dress.'

The very idea caused Hamish to rock against Harry and both to exchange worried frowns.

On their way out of the Navigator's Den, they stopped beneath the doorway light. Both turned, looked directly at the other, but said nothing at first. Each had an image of what the other might look like transgendered.

'Did I hear right?' they both mouthed together once in the street.

Hamish would have had the greater difficulty getting into a frock and, therefore, more reason to think quicker. 'We'd have been laughing our bollocks off at those poor demented bastard's injuries had we not heard the cross-dressing bit. Not to worry, though, the Commander said nothing about us attending as well. We'll just have to tell him that all eight tickets are his,' he said.

'Nice one, nice one, that lets us out. Mind you, there have been times when I thought you'd suit a camouflaging frock.'

'There's no way you would've got me into a frock, job or no job,' Hamish blustered, 'though I'd love to see the Commander's face when he hears the good news.'

They walked across Ringaskiddy Square in silence until they reached Blodger's club. The club front door was painted a shade of peach, with a peephole at eye height, and a heavy, flying-phallus-shaped knocker for requesting entry.

Hamish picked up the knocker, banged it against the door and said, 'What makes you think this door looks like an arse? Wrong question, you'll have seen plenty and know how to effect entry into this type of club, coming from Leith.'

Before Harry could protest, the door opened. Hamish quickly pushed him forward, giving him the privilege of begging entry.

Two simpering, muscle-bound doorpersons towering over them took a fiver admission from each. The bruisers' comments and sniffs of disgust at their black leather jackets, T-shirts, jeans and trainers, followed them. Loud, reverberating music, from somewhere deeper within the premises, blasted along a passageway decorated cheaply with red-painted Anaglypta wallpaper. Full-length mirrors were spaced every few feet. Red lighting bathed the walls and the blood red, shag-pile carpet.

In the bar area, a disc jockey operated a disco from a pulpit to the side of the stage. Playing was the seventies classic, "Gangster of Love", by the band Talking Heads from their album, Sand in the Vaseline. On stage, a band's equipment was set up and ready to play. Lettering on the front of the base drum said they were Milk on the Turn. A poster in the passageway had said they were a Transvestite Cream Tribute Band.

The overdone, blood red, shag-pile carpet theme covered all the standing areas and up the front of the bar. Where punters mingled the most, the carpet was worn, dirty and sticky underfoot. Sprinkled with a deodorant powder, it smelled like Gold-Spot-treated dog's halitosis. The bar servery, finished off with a white Italian marble top, looked classy. Like the passageway, the walls of the venue were red, and had red, oyster-shaped wall-light fittings producing more blood-red glow. The servery area had a mirrored back panel basking in harsh, green fluorescent light; the ceiling above the public area shimmered in ultra-violet light. Above the dance floor, multi-coloured pin-spots spun, blitzers flashed, making it impossible to tell who was dancing with whom.

Close to the bar, Hamish bawled into Harry's ear. 'It's boys might be boys and, if you're lucky, girls might be girls. And Barney told us no fibs. Molly and Dolly do have Rottweiler-jawed facial attributes!'

'Ah ken, and close shaving has left no trace of a five o'clock shadow. They wear heavy makeup, pucker rouged lips, and have additional beauty spots that aren't doing their bit. They couldn't hide those Adam's apples behind cravats!' Harry bawled back.

Both Molly and Dolly were dressed in green frocks, fluffed out at the top to hide false breasts, and green wigs with long tresses that covered their buttocks. Flouncing behind the bar in sling-backed stilettos, they dispensed drinks and talked camply.

Above the serving-area, and in a dodgy position for those serving beneath, a full-grown macaw turned this way and that on its perch. During lulls in the disco music, it screeched optimistic words. 'Who's a pretty boy?' was just audible.

'The Malones have a bloody cheek putting frocks on!' Harry bawled into Hamish's ear.

'The pair of them must have found their genes in a lucky bag1' Hamish shouted back.

The bar didn't sell draught Guinness. The beers on offer were of low alcohol content. The gantry held the usual selection of spirits, all twice the price of a pub, as was Taboo, Peach Schnapps and other low-alcohol brands.

A Malone brother spotted them quickly and cast a wary eye over them from beneath heavy eyelashes.

'We're Barney's friends. He's just phoned about the tickets for us,' Hamish explained. The brother Malone flounced a step back, uttered a 'Huh,' and eyed them closely for signs of cross-dressing affectations. The unconscious act of placing an arm around each other and standing close together convinced the brother Malone. He fished into the space between the top of his frock and his shaven chest and handed over eight tickets.

'That will be forty quid, to you,' he lisped. 'And I hope you've nicer outfits for Bebe's show.'

Forty quid lighter, in possession of a pint of insipid bitter and a double Bacardi and Coke each, they claimed plush seats against a back wall. It was as far as they could get from the booming sound system. The seats, they found, gave a good outlook onto the bar, the dance floor and the standing area.

'This beer is piss,' judged Harry, looking through the weak brew. 'I've seen more hops in a dead frog.'

'Yeah,' agreed Hamish, holding his pint up to the light. 'It's so flat you could serve it in an envelope.'

The club filled up, most of the punters arriving in pairs. Hamish poked Harry in the side. Two women had entered holding hands, one of them looking quite odd. 'Look there,' Hamish said, nodding towards the newcomers approaching the bar. 'They're definitely lesbians, they are.'

'Do you reckon?' Harry said, allowing his gaze to follow their progress.

'See that ugly one. She has a vibrator sticking out of her hip pocket and I can hear its engine running from here. Looking for a bit of action, she is. She's an ugly fucker. I bet her name's something like Doris Doberman. What a dog. "Scooby Doo" looks better. I wouldn't shag her with a stolen dick, but take a look at her mate… what a doll.'

Harry, chortling away at Hamish's observations, agreed. The blonde girl had an attractive face, was braless, had a great set of tits sitting pert beneath a white tank top, looked five-foot-six inches tall and about twenty-years old. Her bum took many glances, fitted tightly into denims. Her blonde, bobbed head of hair, which she ran her fingers through continuously, showed her looks to good effect. He turned to Hamish and told him scathingly: 'I've seen what you'd shag with your own dick, remember,' 'But it does show, "Extreme Pussy Lover", that dogs still like to get their teeth into a nice piece of pussy.'

'Aye, and the older one must be twice the age of her partner if she's a day. The Johnny Ray hairstyle suits her and gives her a manly image.'

'Ken, her nose is as flat as a Pontefract cake and it looks filleted.'

'Aye, and her tits have been effectively compressed by the denim jacket, by the way. If that's supposed to make her manlier, then it works.'

'Ken, and I don't like that permanent snarl on her top lip either. It quivers noticeably when she eyes you eyeing up her mate.'

On the floor, Jemima and Laura, the two heavyweight and recent acquaintances of Hamish, gyrated and strutted their stuff. Being manly, there were no handbags around which to dance. Colourful nightclubbing wellies standing upright gave them a focal point and they danced in bare feet around them.

'Which one of them reminds you of Nijinsky?' Harry asked.

'They've both got horse-like arses so I'll take a rain check on that one. I just hope they don't feel like my company again tonight.'

'I thought a Govan hero like you might've been generous and given one of them a twirl. They're your mates now, you know. You were in love and could have been successful there, had a lasting relationship'

'After you,' Hamish offered. 'It took two showers and half an hour of scrubbing to remove the smell of Jemima's arse and fanny from my chest hairs.'

Half an hour later, the rush onto the dance floor heralded the arrival of band members onto the stage. They struck up and played “Strange Brew”, an old Cream classic. The guitar-playing Eric Clapton clone’s frock clung to his thin body. Jack Bruce’s clone played bass and wore a trouser suit. Ginger Baker’s clone wore a loose-fitting outfit that covered him and his stool; he thumped a steady beat from the drum kit.

In a bit of a Bacardi haze, Harry took to the floor for a solo gyration, remaining there for several numbers, smiling inanely and moving to the rhythm of the blues music. Shuffling his feet slowly and rhythmically, he weaved around dancing couples. The band played “Sunshine of your Love”, and the Clapton clone was singing, ‘I’ll soon be with you and give you my dawn surprise.’

Another solitary figure danced into view: Doris Doberman doing *her* solo thing. With her eyes half-shut, she swung her hips and smiled just as stupidly as Harry did. It perplexed him a bit that it wasn’t her blonde mate. He kept his rhythm going and slowly, their gyrating bodies shuffled closer, almost touching. Doris thrust her hips forward to the beat as if she sought a passionate rub against her mate. Harry noticed her flattened tits, and her firm stomach beneath her shirt. He pictured her six-pack rippling like the proverbial washboard; developed, he was sure, writhing in the arms of her doll-like mate.

Blitzers scattered a multitude of coloured lights, changing to the beat of the music. Pin-spots spun crazily across the dance floor and fell on the faces of dancers in an odd psychodelia of colour. Doris was smiling crookedly, controlling her thrusting hips and maintaining a discreet distance between them: she teased Harry and he teased her. It seemed no way was she going to allow him the pleasure of crotch contact, even fleetingly. The upward curl of her top lip showed the derision she felt for men, though the cockless, pretend fuck had continued for most of the number. The experience tickled Harry; he had even begun to enjoy the experience. Walking from the floor during a lull in the music the thought occurred to him: how could he have enjoyed it? Whenever he played a game of snooker, he never liked his balls close to a dike!

While Harry was doing his thing on the dance floor, Hamish had chanced his arm with Doris Doberman’s mate. He had spent some time leering at her and when she looked his way, he had tried to encourage her over to his table with winks and hand signals. When he visited the bar, her refusal of an offered drink while he stood close enough to get a whiff of her “gagging for it” perfume, pissed him off.

His lusting for her ended with a shattering jolt when he read ‘Fuck off, fat bastard,’ from her lips.

During the interval between band sets, she left the club, Doris’ hand firmly clutching her mate’s bottom and without a backward glance.

By closing time, both Hamish and Harry had the staggers, were reeling about pleasantly pissed and using the bar as a support. Hamish was holding up the remains of an insipid pint of bitter and owlishly viewing the dregs through the glass. Harry was holding a glass to his lips and edging the last of his Bacardi and Coke past the remaining ice.

As drinking up time ended, Hamish spluttered to a Malone brother raging as he sponged some parrot shit from his wig, 'You want to ring that parrot's neck.'

The DJ, seeing the Malone brother's reaction to the parrot's droppings, sensed the occasion and riled the recipient brother by playing a Hound Dog Taylor number, "Give Me Back My Wig."

The number over, the DJ wished everyone safe passage on their journey home and cued the final track of the evening.

Suddenly, the resounding crash of a door bursting open and it thundering back against a wall took everyone's attention. Molly and Dolly stopped dead in their tracks and stood, mouths agape, looking past some stragglers towards the sound. Both Hamish and Harry turned to see Doris bustling in, shoulders swinging, her waistcoat and shirt open all the way down the front, exposing breasts, which weren't as flat as they supposed.

She was making directly for the bar and her facial expression said she was about to get something off her chest, and soon.

Hamish didn't realise she was heading for him until she reached the bar. Pushing against him, she eyeballed him, down the flattened bridge of her nose, her hands on her hips, her face contorted, her breasts bouncing and her lips quivering with hostility.

Stamping her foot in fury she said, 'I noticed you fancied my mate…you big… fat…ugly…Jock bastard. I saw the salacious way you leered at her when my back was turned. Well, I have this for you. She's outside in the car park, laid out on the back seat of my car. I've stripped her naked… she's all wet and sticky… her nipples are standing out like organ stops. She's randy… as hot as hell… panting like a bitch in heat.' With a breast in each hand now, she jiggled them at Hamish and said, 'And she wants to know if you'd like to smell her fanny.'

'Oh I'd love that,' Hamish said, taken aback, a daft look on his face. Reeling half-pissed and excited, he slid backwards along the bar.

There was no escaping her attention. Acting on Hamish's words, she leapt forward, her face close to him. Throwing her arms about his neck, she placed her twisted, thin-lipped mouth over his nose, breathing out, deep and long, aaaaaaaaaahhhhhhhhh.

******

Hamish had little to say as they swayed and stumbled on their short walk towards the hotel; he just complained about the pink sound buzzing in his ears and the smell up his nostrils, which he thought should only ever be present on the side of a U-bend that's closest to the sewage farm.

And Harry was able to kid him that it was just another smelly old dog he had messed with and that he had no sympathy for him.

Friday

It was clear at breakfast that Hamish's head felt thicker than Harry's did. The food the denture-clacking Miss Gillhooly dished up was greasy, unappealing and the whites of Hamish's eyes glowed yellower than the egg yolks.

'Mixing Bacardi with beer has its after-effects,' Hamish said. He pushed his plate away, filled his coffee cup and yawned. The tepid coffee he downed in one gulp.

'Fermented sugar cane and hops are paining the Govan napper this morning, eh,' Harry said, sitting back quietly, at ease himself while viewing Hamish's discomfort.

'How come you don't have a thick head? Hamish asked, eyeing Harry.

'We Leith boys can handle our drink better. It's an east of Scotland thing that you wouldn't know about,' Harry jibed.

'I'm obviously not as bad as I look. At least I'd presence of mind to clock the Advertiser lying in the foyer when I came downstairs.'

'And.'

'The adverts are there, the same as last year's.'

'We're on the right track, then?'

'Aye, but we've another sore point to address this morning,' Hamish said, and began pouring another coffee.

'What's that?' Harry asked.

'Someone has to phone the Commander and tell him he has eight tickets to see a show in a glitzy drag bar, performed, we suspect, by the local home-beat copper.'

'Are you convinced we've got enough on Bebe?'

'Last night that Malone brother, oblique sister, be it Molly or Dolly, had a slip of the tongue. He warned us to dress better for the Bebe show, remember. Apart from that, it's all circumstantial. We've seen Bebe in the subdued light of a bar, in daylight and sleeping with his feet up on his desk. You must agree that in real life he looks more like his poster, facially wart-ridden that it is, than his photograph.

'He's an ugly fucker really, probably suited to a life on stage telling gags. Have you taken note of his gut, by the way? I thought I was bad, but man, the last time a saw a belly that size was on a long-dead donkey newly pulled from the Clyde.

'Then there's the small matter of his joke jotters. The covers had written on them "Old jokes" and "New jokes", respectively. I know they hardly constitute compulsive evidence, but he did have them on his desk and was rehearsing as he snoozed. I don't think he had just confiscated them from some snotty-nosed school kid, do you?'

'No, and I can detect the rancid smell of conspiracy among the I.Q. residents using Ringaskiddy Square pubs and clubs. I think the way they're keeping secret the name of mystery artist tells us something.'

At 9:45 a.m., Hamish tossed a coin and lost. He took on the daunting task of relaying their findings to the Commander, and he would take any rebuke.

The bright, fresh morning greeting them as they left the hotel had a chilly sting to it and Ringaskiddy Square glistened in the light of the low sun. Some stalls erected for the Friday morning mini-market had attracted some early morning shoppers. A brewery dray, parked outside the Navigator's Rest, dropped off bottled beer, barrels and kegs, leather-aproned draymen dispatching the lot noisily down chutes into the cellar.

The nearest public telephone box stood close by the transit's parking place. They were heading there when a small, green, vintage bullnosed Bedford horsebox jerked itself smokily out of Doonbeg Drive. It professed, rather optimistically, on first glance, to be a long vehicle, to have a Crane Fruehauf-manufactured chassis and Ifor Williams coachwork. Its springs looked stiffened. If it was donkey transportation, it had room for only three donkeys standing line abreast. Suffering from pre-ignition and its after-effects, it banged, rattled, and emitted black smoke on its way around the one-way system.

MORPHY O'RICHARDS, DONKEY TRANSPORTER, emblazoned in the colourful sign writing beloved of fairground wagon owners, decorated its sides and doors.

Dark shades covered Morphy's eyes and a black cap sat crooked on his head, the peak pulled down. An Eddie Stobbart driver's jacket, a few sizes too large, hung around his shoulders. Standing on the passenger seat, wide-awake and alert, Timmy swayed on four legs.

Hamish pulled Harry into a doorway. 'Remember what Bebe said about needing the old horsebox soon? It looks like Morphy and Timmy are out on a mission,' he said. 'Let's clock what he's getting up to from here.'

'All that smoking, jerking and backfiring it's doing suggests the horsebox is having its first run for some time,' Harry supposed.

Morphy drove slowly, tooting his horn at pedestrians hastening towards pavements out of his way. He turned out of the square and into Doonbeg Drive and then turned smartly right into Ballybunion Lane.

'If I'm correct, that lane gives access to the rear of the Navigator's Den,' Hamish said.

'It does,' Harry said. 'All the premises fronting the square back onto a lane or wynd. What's his interest down there, I wonder?'

Morphy took his time exiting from Ballybunion Lane. When he did reappear, he drove to a parking space at the junction of Skibbereen Street with Ringaskiddy Square. Parked up, he stopped the engine and studied what looked like a stopwatch.

'He's having time trials,' Hamish said observing Morphy's progress. 'Maybe it's a dummy run for something.'

Morphy fired up the engine, pulled away, drove the horsebox around the one-way system, turned into Nobber Avenue, then first-left into Ballyragget Wynd.

'That close gives access to the rear of the Shankless Music Bar,' Harry said. 'Could be he's timing different routes from his parking spot.'

Morphy seemed to take an age exiting the Wynd. When he did, he parked up in the spot he had just left and began studying the watch.

'If he's up to something with Bebe, then his next route will take him down Boggeragh Close and behind Blodger's,' Harry said.

'There are no signs of mist or fog yet. At this time of year, it's due. I think we should get into a position and see what he's doing down there, if that's where he's going?'

'There's a broken mirror on Timmy's side of the cab. Morphy can't see to the nearside rear of the vehicle. If we get into a position on his blind side we'll see what happens in Boggeragh Close.'

The horsebox had warmed up, the engine had ceased misfiring and its speed had increased. A fast ninety-degree turn and Morphy had exited the one-way system into Termonfechin Street. Another slick, ninety-degree turn into the narrow Boggeragh Close, and he was on the approach to Blodger's nightclub stage door. The horsebox's wooden structure lurched dangerously, almost smacking into the walls of the close.

In the warehouse entrance, their view was clear along Boggeragh Close. The horsebox slowed as it approached the nightclub's stage door, the creaking tailgate slowly lowering as it went. The tailgate touched the ground, remained there for twenty seconds, before the horsebox moved off, its tailgate rising and closing completely before exiting onto the one-way system.

They were out of the Close now and Hamish said, 'These events are too similar not to have something to do with Bebe. It's evidence, I'd say, of Morphy's practicing setting down and picking up at the stage doors of these premises. We'll need to do further observations. I know what my guess is, though. The Commander might also be interested in what we've seen just now.'

******

Sitting in his office that Friday morning at 9:30 a.m., reading his mail, the books done, the Commander felt edgy. He had expected MacNab and MacSporran to make contact before now. It was 10:15 a.m. before his phone rang. If it were they, he would be brusque.

'It's Constable MacNab,' the voice said.

'Forget the constable bit,' he snapped nastily. 'Unless you come up with the goods, you're plain mister. What do you have for me, MacNab?'

Hamish took the phone away from his ear and grimaced. 'Shite!' he said.

The Commander put down the letter he was reading. He had thought about asking what nonsense they'd been up to during their few days loose in the "I.Q.", then thought better of it.

'I've eight tickets for a show next Wednesday night. We believe the mystery artist performing is Constable Beckham.'

'You've what?' The Commander shouted, leaned forward, and placed both elbows onto his desk, eager to listen.

'Eight tickets costing you forty pounds, sir,' Hamish said.

The Commander calmed. It sounded good news. Eight tickets for a show, what show? Was that good news or bad? There might be a catch, he'd be cautious.

'You say Constable Beckham is appearing? Are you certain it's him?' he asked warily. He was nervous, but he didn't want to give it away in his voice.

'All evidence points to him. There are even adverts in today's local paper. Your tickets are for the gig at Blodger's, sir. It's a club in Ringaskiddy Square. It's down here in the Irish Quarter. We've obtained the very last tickets available. We thought we'd done well to get them, sir.'

The Commander couldn't tell whether Hamish was snivelling or taking the piss, probably the latter, he decided.

The Commander rubbed his forehead with his fingers, tried to weigh up logically what MacNab was telling him, and asked, 'What's the evidence that it's him?'

'Well, apart from a slip of the tongue by a local bar person, identifying Bebe as the artist appearing, he's the spit of his poster. We've seen his joke books on the desk in the police office and, we believe, we've witnessed his transportation being prepared for speedy entry and exit from three gigs he is doing here next week…'

'Interesting,' the Commander said, 'tell me, why Bebe?'

'P.C. Beckham is known as Bebe here in the "I.Q.". It's short for Billy Beckham, I suppose, and the artiste at the venues is cunningly advertised with two underlined capital B's. Bebe, sir, do you get it?'

'I think you're spinning me a great fanny, MacNab. However, I do appreciate you're working in a strange place. The residents are a clannish bunch. You're not going to get much help from them.' Remembering he already knew that Billy Bagman was Constable Beckham, he encouraged, 'The rest of the evidence is sound. You've done well. Keep your noses clean for the rest of your time there. You'd better send the tickets to the station. Send them today by courier, marked for my personal attention.'

'Will do, sir,' Hamish said. 'But there's one other very important thing you have to know.'

'What's that?' the Commander asked, suddenly worried.

'You, and whoever else you bring with you, or whoever you send in, will have to dress in women's clothes or they won't let you in. It's a drag bar, sir,' Hamish said, pulling a face and holding the earpiece away from his ear, fully expecting an explosion.

'It's a what?' The Commander did explode. 'I'll have to do what?' He thumped the desk. 'I don't much care for what I'm hearing!'

'It's not *our* fault if the only tickets available are for a drag bar, sir,' Hamish pleaded, talking quickly, to impart his information and get off the phone. 'Bebe is appearing for the local cross-dresser community. It's as I've told you. There were no other tickets available, and these only because of last minute cancellations that I cannot go into now. Billy Beckham is popular and protected by the locals. It seems no strangers ever get tickets for a Bebe gig here. We were fortunate. It's this or nothing, sir.'

The Commander sighed, wondering what he had gotten into. He responded, 'Send me the tickets immediately; I'm going to have to think this one out.'

The problem of finding the comedian and getting Daphne into a gig had consumed him. During this preoccupation, he hadn't thought a lot about Constable Beckham's offences against the Met Police disciplinary code. The code decreed "Whole time to police service" and Ivor Bunce, from his words, expected him to sack the constable from the Job. Now, Ivor wouldn't be pleased to hear the word scuppered used in relation to the disciplinary charges they hoped to lay against Constable Beckham.

That morning's mail had contained official confirmation that Constable Beckham retired officially at midnight that day, with a full pension, having served thirty years. Signed by Assistant District Commissioner Beaverton, it was inviolate. William Beckham, private person, would be performing the gigs in the "I.Q." The Commander had known nothing of the impending retirement. Constable Beckham had submitted his papers requesting permission to retire while he was testing beds and flattening heather with Daphne, when they were on holiday in Scotland, and had by-passed him. He thought the news ought to please MacNab and MacSporran; their reticence to grass up coppers was obvious.

He had no doubt; his knowledge of Constable Beckham's retirement compromised him. If he knew of the retirement, there was no good reason for him to gather evidence for disciplinary procedures against the constable. It was something that he didn't need to know. This was why he picked up the constable's papers, shredded them, and flushed them down the toilet.

That morning's mail had also brought an A4 envelope marked, "For Commander's Eyes Only". Though not noted for his sense of humour, Commander Dai Evans had passed on down the line the pile of offending pornography that MacNab had sent him. The covering note explained what trouble Jack could expect with this particular Jock added to his divisional strength.

Earlier, the Commander had flicked through the magazines. His ball pain was in remission, the curse of lover's-nuts gone. He still didn't need any stimulus that would activate and stretch his still-painful cock; that was a sure thing; a bit like the blind date that he'd dallied with.

He had found some lurid photographs of readers' wives with drooping tits and grotesque "love handles" and had thought that only the likes of MacNab and MacSporran could enthuse over them. Putting the magazines to one side, he thought of passing them along to Ivor at West Clegham; they'd really twist his face for him.

Some pages towards the back of one magazine had caught his eye and he returned to them now. An advert in an "Adult Relaxation" column filled him with intrigue: the mulatto transvestite Tattiana, she, he, or it, with the colourful and a nice body, was well hung, had big tits, and gave French without, active or passive, and would cum wherever the client wished. 'He, she, or it, is available for nights out anywhere,' the Commander mused. 'And he, she or it has a mobile telephone number.'

Suddenly, his thoughts were shocking him, exciting him. He was about to receive eight tickets for the show at Blodger's nightclub and one question began to intrigue him; he only needed six. Now, he pondered: did he have the balls to reciprocate Rowley's generosity and fix him up a blind date with the wonderful, exciting-sounding Tattiana? The abortive blind date Rowley had arranged for him, had surely earned his best friend the company of a person like Tattiana, and two tickets for the performance on Wednesday evening.

A little body-shake with mirth, a little more musing and a smothering of giggles, and the answer was there. Of course, he had the balls for it. Rowley richly deserved the embarrassing situation into which he would place *him*.

He left the magazine open, picked up the telephone and dialled. The earpiece burred away for a time before a sleepy, affected voice answered. 'Yeth, who is it calling?'

'Is that Tattiana?' the Commander enquired.

'Yeth, and who are you?'

'My name is Jack. What do you charge for a date and a night out in your company?'

'That depends on when, where and with whom, dear.'

'I want you for my best friend, Rowley, next Wednesday evening. He's a civil servant, too shy to ask himself. He wants someone nice and sexy to take to a party at a drag bar'

'My standard charge for a night out and an hour of extras later in the evening, his place or mine, is two hundred and fifty pounds. I travel by Mercedes… I pick up the trick… I don't come cheap.'

The Commander had his own account. Daphne, even if she cared, would never know about the payment. ‘Yes, that’s fine,’ he said. ‘Give me your address. Payment will be in the post this afternoon. I’ll phone you again with the instructions, which you must carry out to the letter. What you do after the party is entirely up to you. Rowley’s a great guy. Make sure he gets his rations, okay?’

Whilst replacing the phone, the Commander wondered whether his Assistant District Commissioner’s appetite for sexual dalliances in any way matched his taste for a fucking good laugh.

The Commander’s thoughts turned to Daphne. Since Halloween, he thought that she had been acting even odder and was unusually tight-lipped. The abuse had gone. There was something toying with her mind, he was sure of that.

He wondered if her feelings were thawing towards him. Certainly, her behaviour had changed; was he imagining that she was hovering closer to him now, sashaying about the house in one of her ridiculous shrouds and fragrant with an Estee Lauder perfume?

Perhaps it was a guilty woman thing. Perhaps, soon she’d throw herself into his arms. Could he count on that? He didn’t want to ask if she had a problem on discovering a bottle of antiseptic mouthwash in the bathroom. Instead, he presumed she had developed a sore throat or a mouth ulcer, a common symptom of stress.

The Commander then turned his attention to the business of the Blodger’s party. He didn’t yet know if he could coax Daphne to go with him. If she did agree, no way would he take her there by himself. The media had recently reported the gory details of a well-known Parliamentarian’s questionable dalliance on Clapham Common. The case convinced him that he must not be caught inside Blodger’s, armed with only the flimsiest of excuses for being there. He needed top-drawer support in the shape of a Superintendent, his Superintendent, to corroborate that he was investigating Bebe… well Bebe to him perhaps; to Ivor, he would be Constable Beckham. Yes, investigating the serious charge of moonlighting at a place like Blodger’s required an officer of that senior rank to back him up.

How could he manage that? Coercion came to mind. There was the promotion to Commander of Police Training at Hendon that Rowley had mentioned. Gaining that step-up, the prestige, the extra pay and added pension rights ought to interest Ivor. Yes, it really ought to, and in a big way. Ivor thought all hope of another promotion had gone. However, getting Ivor into a drag bar would be difficult. He would have to endure listening to Ivor pathetically squealing protestations and disgust at the idea.

Fuck! He remembered MacNab said they’d have to dress in drag. Ivor wouldn’t like that. No, he’d scream blue murder. However, catching

Constable Beckham in the act and sacking him on the spot ought to tickle his fancy. Would that be a big enough carrot?

Of course, he would have to invite Algie along for good measure. He couldn't see Daphne wanting to attend without Myrna and Gloria. They would be a necessary encumbrance. Sergeant Shrapnel's wife, Maggie, was one of the girls. It was hard luck on her. According to Ivor, Shrapnel was a crawler, told tales. There'd be no tickets for them even if he had two left over.

The Commander had few doubts regarding his abilities as a police officer and detective. He was well able to sow the seeds of misinformation among the unwary. Thus, he formed his plan. For it to work successfully, for a part of the time anyway, he'd have to keep all his guests in the dark. Daphne, unwittingly, would be the first link in the chain of events he'd instigate and that, he saw, had a chance of succeeding. He rubbed his hands together, smiled. 'Reconciliation, here I come,' he said aloud, and crossed his fingers.

Lifting his feet from the floor, he rocked back, forgetting about his injury. Rocking forward, he stretched for the telephone and dialled his home number. Daphne ought to have had her morning shower. The image of her standing naked by the phone, the wonderful fragrance of Estee Lauder shower gel filled his senses and he shuddered. The spasm from his cock was most unwelcome as he waited for Daphne to answer.

'Daphne, honey,' he said quickly as the burring stopped. He knew he was chancing his arm that she might still be interested or, at least, responsive to his suggestion. 'I've some wonderful news,' he said, feigning breathlessness. 'I've found Billy Bagman. We're going to see him next Wednesday night, in fancy dress. Isn't that marvellous?'

Daphne, in the nude just as he had pictured her, was posing in a way that had always made him reach out for her. She listened with muted interest; frostiness was her weapon, thawing slowly, her prerogative. It took a second or two before she responded. 'How do you know it's him?' she asked, growling throatily.

Should he ask Daphne about her throat problem and show his concern? He decided not to. 'Honey, are you well?'

'Of course I'm bloody well!' She retorted.

'Good… I've had two of my very best detectives working in plain-clothes. Ages they've been at it to uncover him,' he said, 'and at a great expense to the taxpayer. They've discovered he is working next week in a drag bar down in the Irish Quarter. Consequently, there's a need for fancy dress.'

'I'm still not sure I can trust you,' she said with detectable sullenness, but her hand moved up to her heart as it skipped a beat. Jack was going to such lengths to get around her. Without revealing her true feelings, she responded bitchily, 'If I go I'll be wearing a shroud just in case the comedian dies on stage.'

Jack had prepared for such a negative response. 'How sorry do I have to be for the Blackpool thing?' he asked. 'Haven't I paid the price, gone out of my way, out on a limb for you now with this? If you don't believe that I've found the comedian, or need convincing that he's the same one Myrna and Gloria saw, you can bring them along. They'll identify him for you. Ivor and Algie can also come. I haven't enough tickets to allow more than two couples to attend with us. Maggie will be disappointed, but that's the way it has to be. And we'll all bloody well wear shrouds, if you insist.'

There was a moment of silence.

Jack spoke again, encouragement in mind. 'Gloria and Myrna will definitely appreciate another evening of fun and laughter. The comedian seems to have had a great influence on them. I'm not sure about Ivor, but Algie will be up for it. Think it over, honey. Speak to your friends and I'll see you when I come home tonight.' He had tried to sound elated, tried to draw her onto his hook. Later, with a bit of luck, he'd try to get her onto the end of his cock, painful though that would be.

Daphne put the phone down on him without saying goodbye.

Jack expected that. He leant back in his chair convinced that he had sown the seed exceedingly well. Now he awaited its germination.

Daphne, during the early days of her pique, said that Gloria and Myrna had enjoyed themselves so much in Billy Bagman's presence that it had changed their lives. They would hardly turn down another opportunity to see him. Ivor would be the difficult one to persuade. The carrot of promotion dangling in front of him ought to lead him into the snare, though, guarantee his acquiescence.

Jack had to admit: whatever Ivor's disposition, he was eminently suitable for the position at Hendon. A bit long in the tooth for a promotion to Commander perhaps; however, he knew the Instruction Book and general Orders thoroughly. His experiences in command of his own sub-division were also invaluable attributes to take with him. Ivor couldn't have written a better CV for the job. He was sure of one thing in that regard: if Ivor wanted his backing, his word in the right ear, that he was the most suitable candidate, then he would need to show compliance and assist his Commander. His recommendation that Rowley need look no further than Ivor for a name to recommend would come at a price negotiated by him.

The results of his telephone call to Daphne came quickly. His dodge had worked. At 11 a.m., Ivor telephoned. Initially, he communicated the booking of a black cab to take them to and from the installation meeting.

'The cab will pick us up at 4 p.m. and return for us at 1 a.m. to take us home,' he said. 'Are these arrangements in accordance with your wishes…

click, click?' The Commander detected a little agitation in his Superintendent's voice.

'Sounds good to me,' he answered. Listening intently, he heard the flick of Ivor's paper knife. He pictured him sitting behind a small hillock of correspondence, coping inadequately and opening his mail without the assistance of a sergeant clerk.

'About this other thing, click, click, Jack, this Beckham...Bagman fellow, do you really think it wise?' he said, concern ringing in his voice.

'Is what wise, Ivor?'

'That six of us should be going to see this Bagman fellow's show. I believe it will be terribly unrefined, blue and probably takes place in some insalubrious joint that I'd not normally be caught in dead.'

'Ivor,' Jack hesitated for effect. 'Beckham, Bagman, rogue, piss-taking copper, whatever, he is one of my strength, remember. The moonlighting one... the one Gloria saw in Blackpool... the one that's caused all of your problems.' He waited for that to sink in then said, 'The back-up I need on this one must be of high rank, for corroboration purposes. You watching my back, verifying our intentions, will make being there safe for me. It's the only sure way of hounding him out of the Force. I'd have thought you'd be game to go to these lengths to punish severely the source of your problems...I'll see you at the installation tomorrow night and go over the details with you. I'll give you your two tickets then.'

'But...'

'Drinks on me, Ivor, 'bye.'

The plan was going well, though he imagined Ivor, doubts rising, twisting and turning in his chair.

Algie wouldn't renege on a night out with the boys, of that he was sure; he had the inimitably daft Myrna to ensure his presence, drunk or sober. He didn't feel it was protocol for him to tell Ivor of his conversation with Rowley. However, another telephone call now to Daphne, passing on some gossip, that Ivor was in line for the Commander's position at Hendon, ought to reach Gloria just as quickly, then Ivor!

SATURDAY

At 10 a.m., Hamish drove the transit into the Ringaskiddy Square car park. He sat chewing Rennies, while Harry sat by his side chortling at the antics of "Billy the Fish" in the latest edition of VIZ. He was lucky to get a copy. The manager of "Perry O'Dicals", the Dublin-based chain of newsagents, hadn't heard of the publication and had to order it especially for him.

Streams of early morning shoppers were working their way from shop to shop around Ringaskiddy Square, some diverting to the van to leave completed leaflets. Suffering obnoxious breath from Friday night's intake of

Guinness and prawn vindaloo, Hamish generously directed them towards Harry's side of the transit. Of the thousand delivered leaflets, the locals had returned fifteen hundred, many copied on computers or Photostatted. The locals looked on them as a lottery, the extra entries giving them more chances of winning the double-glazed show house.

At dusk, fog began rolling into the square from streets leading to the river. Thickening quickly, it settled low. Saturday night shoppers, looking eerie, walked stooped loaded-up with supermarket bags. Vehicles, fog-lights glaring, crept along, carefully negotiating the one-way system.

At 7p.m., they returned to the transit after a bite to eat. Harry complained of feeling tired and dozed off. Minutes later, when Hamish nudged him, the horsebox was exiting Doonbeg Drive onto the one-way system, its dimmed headlamps yellowing the swathe of fog. The horsebox engine purred sweetly and Morphy parked up in his usual spot at the junction of Ringaskiddy Square and Skibbereen Street. He switched off the engine and sat craning his neck, peering from each window in turn.

A minute later, Bebe's Morris Minor eased itself into Ringaskiddy Square from Cork Street and pulled up behind the horsebox. Bebe was sitting hunched up behind the wheel, wearing a civvy coat and pressing his nose to the windscreen. Morphy was peering into the fog, seemingly waiting for a pedestrian free moment. When the square had emptied, he flashed his brake lights twice. The Morris Minor's headlights flashed, answering the signal. The horsebox jerked away in a low gear and at high revs. A sharp left turn from the one-way system took the horsebox rocking into Doonbeg Drive. A sharp right took it into Ballybunion Lane, its tyres squealing on the cobbles, the route taking the horsebox past the rear entrance of the Navigator's Den. The Morris Minor, revving highly, followed closely, only a tailgate-length behind the horsebox.

The delay in the lane was as before; then, the horsebox sped out of Ballybunion Lane, well down on its springs. Morphy turned right into Termonfechin Street then raced it around the one-way system to its usual parking place at the junction with Skibbereen Street. The Morris Minor was nowhere in sight.

'Aha… Three guesses. Where's the car?' Hamish asked.

'Stop pissing about. It's in the horsebox. We both know that's the only explanation to this stupid procedure,' Harry replied.

A minute later, the horsebox engine revved up and jerked away from the kerb, leaving smoking rubber behind. It followed the same route and twenty seconds later reappeared with the Morris Minor a tailgate-length behind. The horsebox took up its usual parking spot, the Morris Minor stopping alongside it, Morphy and Bebe each holding up a thumb. Moving off in turn, they followed the one-way system until turning down different streets.

Hamish clapped his hands and said, 'Of course, you're right. We'd have been daft not to see it.'

'Using meticulous timing, Billy Bagman is using Morphy to expedite his arrival and departure from the gigs in secret. The horsebox is a Trojan horse,' Harry said.

'Working as a copper and moonlighting as a comedian contrary to the Met Police disciplinary code must have made him more than a bit neurotic,' Hamish said, 'and being found out probably worried him greatly. I'm sure there are easier ways of slipping into gigs incognito. This way must be working for him, crazy as it seems to us.'

******

The black cab picked up Ivor, called for Jack, then conveyed them to the Lodge. They travelled in silence although Ivor seemed quite agitated during the journey, fidgeting in his seat. On their arrival at the Lodge, he suggested that they have a quick chat in the Worshipful Grand Master's changing-room. Jack expected Ivor to have concerns and he had prepared himself to address them.

In the changing-room, Ivor quickly expressed his worries. 'Click, click, the women's grapevine seems a little ahead of me at present. Daphne has told Gloria an extraordinary and surprising tale that soon I ought to expect a much-desired promotion.' Ivor looked at Jack intently. He wanted answers. His moustache twitched excitedly as he rushed on quickly. 'What do you know about that, Jack?' Then he gripped Jack's hand firmly, as a Mason.

Jack smiled, felt an inner glow. These women just couldn't keep their mouths shut!

'Oh yes, I did mention something to Daphne during one of her more amenable moments. Quickest way I could think of getting wind of it to you. I couldn't officially tell you that Rowley was considering putting your name forward for the Commander's job at Hendon and had asked my opinion.'

Ivor pulled his cheeks up, widening his mouth, pleased with his superior's thoughtfulness.

'Between you and me, Ivor, my initial comment was that you were tailor-made for the position. Rowley agreed. However, do not jump the gun yet. The invitation to apply may be a day or two in arriving. A word from me in the right ear… on the square; then, who knows, Hendon could well be yours?' He gave a nod and a wink and awaited Ivor's reaction.

Ivor threw his chest out and rose onto the balls of his feet as he caught the drift. 'Honestly, Jack, I thought I'd be too old by now, all opportunities for further promotion gone. The Commander's number at Hendon coming my way is a wish come true.' Ivor's face beamed in anticipation of the pip above the crown on his epaulettes of rank. He had swallowed the bait, well and truly.

Jack felt it time to put stage two into effect. 'Has Gloria also told you that we will all have to wear a form of fancy dress on Wednesday night?'

'Fancy dress? What do you mean by fancy dress? Click, click, Halloween has passed. I thought it would be a straightforward observation before we "stuck on" the bastard piss-taking comedian, click, click,' Ivor said, with all the venom he could muster.

'It's a bit more complicated than that, Ivor. We'll have to see the show all the way through, and be wearing fancy dress. I thought that while we're there, we ought to enjoy ourselves. Make it a kind of belated Halloween get-together. We'll stick out like sore thumbs if we don't look like the rest of the patrons. Remember, we're going to gather evidence of a serious breach of discipline.'

Ivor didn't have an answer; he stood, thinking hard and furiously.

The installation ceremony lasted several hours. The following harmony began with a seven-course meal and a selection of fine wines, later in the proceedings, the serious drinking. By 10 p.m., solo singers were taking the stage. Some brethren, waxing emotional, sang along, their arms around other's shoulders.

Ivor was having a quick drink with Algie, already heading for oblivion, when Jack captured them at the bar and ushered them into his changing-room. The elevation to the throne of King Solomon had left Jack unfazed. Looking cheery and resplendent in his apron and other finery of office, he dispensed a large measure of Glenmorangie each from a private bottle and bid them cheers.

'Cheers to you, Jack.' Ivor's voice was squeaky and obsequious. 'You will make a stout Worshipful Grand Master and uphold all the fine tenets of the craft. I have always known you were born to be a Grand Master. It stands out in your dignity and bearing,'

'Bollocks, speak to Jack like a man,' Algie erupted. 'He likes his drink like the rest of us. One of the boys is our Jack. No bullshit with you, is there, Jack?' Algie reeled, his face red, eyes bloodshot, breath heavy with the smell of whisky, and placed his arms around Jack.

Jack saw Algie as a round-faced, popeyed alcoholic, a pseudo-listener like most councillors, and a master of the non-committal, walk-away answer. Myrna would have little difficulty persuading him into agreeing to attend this unusual night out.

'And it's a great idea, Jack, all of us going to see this Billy Bagman character,' Algie spluttered. 'I could do with a fucking good laugh. That wife of mine has been treating me awful. Been trying to get me up and performing bed sports for some time. The stupid bitch says she's going to get me off the sauce and onto this new stuff... Viagra or something, and then shag my brains out. Fuck that, Jack, I'd rather piddle down my leg and have a good laugh these days. Have you something in mind that we can go as?'

Algie was a pushover, and Ivor's eyes were looking up into his head, probably already swanking inwardly and imagining his denigration of slow-learning or sloppily dressed recruits at Hendon.

Suggesting the mode of fancy dress to his fraternal counterparts for the evening in Blodger's, Jack saw as the remaining hurdle. Algie would go dressed as a chicken if asked to do so. Ivor would be the difficult one. Seeing that he had become a little detached sorting out his Hendon head, Jack thought that now was the best time to broach the subject with him.

'Blodger's nightclub,' Jack addressed Ivor and Algie, 'has an unsavoury reputation as you know. It's also essential that we attend in fancy dress. I think it's better we all wear the same basic garment. Daphne has told me she wants to wear a shroud in case the comedian dies on stage. It's her idea, not mine. I would not like to thwart her on that one. A taxi will deliver a shroud and a wig to your addresses in brown paper wrapping. The only other accoutrement you'll require is one of your wife's brassieres, suitably padded. We all must look like women. Our wives must look like men who are dressed as women. We'll all look silly, I'm sure, so don't stress yourselves. It seems that is the charade we have to go through to achieve access to the place.'

'Sounds better all the time,' said Algie, now using Ivor as a prop. 'I think I know the place. There are two ugly fuckers behind the bar, poofters, back-passage heroes and all that.'

Ivor's thoughts on Jack's suitability for the exalted role into which had had just been installed quickly disappeared. 'Fancy dress, yes, click, click, is one thing!' he screeched. 'Wearing shrouds and brassieres, I just don't know about that! If I'm hearing correctly, it's more like a bent undertakers' convention we'll be attending.' Ivor's voice levelled out to a concerned whine. 'Are you sure this is not a highly questionable escapade, Jack?' He detached Algie from his arm, and stood with his hands clasped in front of Jack as if in prayer.

Jack had prepared for Ivor's squealing. 'Brothers, you are safe in my hands,' he said, evoking Masonic trust. 'Believe in me,' he said earnestly. Then he forced two tickets into each of their top pockets. Before they had a chance to make another utterance, Jack had dispensed double measures of Glenmorangie. Raising glasses, they all said, 'Cheers.' His fears about entering a drag bar without support were disappearing fast.

Jack found Rowley enjoying the evening with other members of the installing party. He seemed reticent to leave them and make himself available for a chat with him. No surprise there, Jack thought. After shaking all of their hands and accepting a whisky off each, Jack finally collared Rowley and guided him into his changing-room.

Rowley looked at him sheepishly, half expecting a personal and private rocket for the apparently abortive blind date he had organised.

Brimming with thoughts of his own revenge, Jack hadn't mentioned it. He was out for a bit of reciprocation on this one, a little payback if not the full vengeful package. Humiliation at the hands of a woman was one thing. A so-called best friend to embarrass him in such a beastly manner was another. In quieter moments, he still smelt shit and heard those words that made him feel like puking, "Over here, Claudie."

'Ah, Rowley, dear Brother,' Jack greeted, took Rowley's hand and gave him the Worshipful Grand Master's grip, which was reciprocated. Standing slightly stooped to convey the impression he pondered his words seriously, Jack placed his other hand on his forehead and gazed at the floor. 'Ivor, Algie and I are celebrating Halloween, belatedly, and will be partying at Blodger's nightclub, here on the manor, next Wednesday evening. There's a comedian performing and the girls are dying to see his show.

'Gloria and Myrna will be there. I've talked Daphne into coming along. We're both looking forward to attending. Our new beginning, don't you think? I'm sure you will wish me well with that.

'However, dear Brother, so that you don't feel left out of the arrangements, I'm inviting you and have organised a blind date to keep you company…I hope it's more successful than…well… er, enough said about that. Her name is Tattiana, a strapping, busty, mulatto girl with an extraordinary sexual appetite.

'She'll take a great deal of pleasuring, if I've done my job correctly. She'll pick you up in her Mercedes. After the show, she'll take you back to your apartment, where she'll sort out any of the pressing needs that are bound to have arisen during the evening. I know you are a sport. I'm sure you will be up to it… a man of your reputation with the girls.'

'Wednesday evening, you say? Sounds as if you have arranged a fun evening, but I'm sure I could have found a friend to bring along.' Rowley looked intently at Jack, trying to work out if his friend was screwing him, even though screwing a busty, mulatto girl had really caught his interest.

Algie staggered in, taking a corkscrew path, his Masonic apron hanging limply around his waist. He closed with them and they allowed him space. Swinging an arm around Jack, he spluttered, 'See you Wednesday for a fucking good laugh and a few drinks, eh, Jack? Coming too are you, Rowley?'

'Of course, Algie, I'm just making arrangements with Jack now.'

Got him, Jack thought, and proceeded quickly. 'Algie's in good spirits tonight. He's a bit like you, Rowley, always up for a bit of fun. He's pleased about his invite and his fancy dress. Now that you're joining us, I'll send along yours together with the instructions from Tattiana. I know she will pick you up from the front door of your flat, but the time I still have to confirm with her. We'll be arriving at Blodger's at a quarter-to-nine. What time pick up on Wednesday would suit you?'

******

Jack arrived home from the installation at 01:15 a.m. feeling uncommonly pissed. Many congratulatory drinks and toasts had passed his lips, but they were an allowable concession of the occasion.

The house, often in darkness when he had returned home late in recent weeks, had the master bedroom light on. He wondered was Daphne just being kind, expecting him home worse for wear, or was she in bed waiting for him.

At the front door, Jack fumbled for the keyhole and dropped the keys. The black-cab driver, recipient of a large tip, picked them up, opened the door for him, made sure he was inside with his regalia case and that the door had closed behind him. Jack mounted the stairs unsteadily, eyes crossed, seeing double and feeling ill. He pushed open the bedroom door, his heart pumping hard. Was it possible that Daphne was warming the bed for him?

With a groan, he flopped onto the empty bed without undressing. His eyes weren't focusing on anything. The ceiling when he looked at it started to turn, psychedelic lights flashed, spinning in his head. Vomit started to rise towards his gullet and he closed his eyes, fearing he might throw up. A black cloud descended and he was immediately asleep.

Jack had bottled up much of his emotion during the preceding days and he hadn't dreamt once during that time. Returning to consciousness as the late morning light turned the bedroom from dark to pale, he was about to delve into a mental backlog. Nonsensical, vivid, traumatic and haunting was the dream bursting through to the top of the pile…

Ringaskiddy Square was a circular wagon train of gaudily painted wagons, complete with canvas-covered accommodation, much like those he had seen in old cowboy films. Set in the nose-to-tail formation, it might repel intruders attacking from any point on the compass.

Outside and inside the circle were nightmarish, fathomless pits. A swirling mist hid the wagon wheels beneath axle-level. He had no idea in which area he was, really, but within a huge doughnut, he thought about right. The pit in the middle, stretching between the wagons, was signposted: Nookie Zone.

The outer pit was signposted: Nookie-Free Zone. He was sitting on a hard seat, behind a smelly, tail-swishing horse. Alongside him, but at some distance, he saw Daphne, looking ghostly and dressed in a shroud. It seemed she chose to sit as far away from him as she could possibly get, without falling off and disappearing altogether into the Nookie-Free Zone. Something odious lurking in the Nookie Zone had clearly gotten up her nose.

Sitting the opposite way around to him and Daphne, on the equally hard seat of the caravan behind, were Ivor, his wry-necked back watcher, and Gloria. Gloria hung from the seat and leered into the Nookie Zone, but the distance between her and Ivor matched that between him and Daphne, leaving the impression that Ivor didn't want anything to get up anywhere.

Across the circular pit, three wagons drew his eyes. Sitting on the appreciably more luxurious seat of the wagon inscribed: BLACKPOOL AND BEYOND. TRAVELLING PISS-TAKING EMPORIUM. ALL TYPES OF JOKES CATERED FOR AND THE PISS TAKEN WHILE I WORK AND WHILE U WAIT he spotted the piss-taker: the copper, Constable William Beckham, the one known as Billy Bagman the comedian, and at other times, Bebe, the one with the nasal appendage and its four easily-identifiable hairs. The piss-taker was wearing a small, "Kiss me quick" bedaubed helmet that sat awry and back to front, how any comic, piss-taking copper would wear it, and he was waving a stick of Blackpool rock at him.

The piss-taker had so many titles, Jack expected him to possess chameleon-like qualities. His well-founded suspicions became facts the moment the piss-taker spotted Jack's interest in him. In a trice, the piss-taker changed into a ragged little bagman sort of a fellow and lashed out at his horse, heading out for somewhere beyond reach of his investigation.

Boxed in, nowhere for him to go, the ragged little bagman sort became extremely agitated, turned red of face, coughed, spluttered and wheezed. The eruption was harsh and resonant, like the call attributed to egg-bound grouse, their nostrils bunged up with snot and pertinacious catarrh.

Then the ragged little bagman sort began trilling, making plaintive, mocking sounds, sounds never heard before the Blackpool bollix or anywhere else in the world. Jack knew immediately the ragged little bagman sort was mocking him by mimicking the mating call of nature's least-known paradox: the caponised toad.

Immediately in front of the piss-taking emporium, stood a Masonic Lodge-shaped wagon emblazoned: GREAT BEAVERTON, CHUCKLEHEAD AND PURVEYOR OF CODSWALLOP AND ROTTEN DATES GUARANTEED TO HAVE SNAPPING JAW QUALITIES.

Behind the piss-taking emporium, but away ahead by qualification, the Jock Connection sat on the rickety seat of a wagon with illustrations in tartan stencilling: MASTER BLASTERS. QUALITY SERVICE AT YOUR

CONVENIENCE. RECONCILIATION AND NOOKIE REPLENISHMENT SERVICES RECOMMENDED.

With a lurch, the wagon train moved off, rising then falling over invisible hillocks like a merry-go-round. Daphne began teetering dangerously on the edge of the seat, only to overbalance and fall then drift out into the space above the enormous pit, the Nookie-Free Zone!

Jack moved his bulk across the hard seat in a panic, fear gripping him. Might she disappear forever from his view into that most hated of places? No, no, no, he grabbed for her hand, holding it tightly and made to pull her in. Her arm was resisting him. She was pulling away, borne on the cyclonic winds blowing from mirth gulch in the region of comicality. He had to save her. Prevent her eternal confinement in that hellish place. His body jerked, his head thrashed on the pillow.

Suddenly, his eyes opened. They were sticky, blurring. Daphne was standing to one side of the bed, a cup of coffee in one hand, his hand in the other. The bedside radio was playing an Earth Wind And Fire number. Alongside the radio, on a plate, were a round of toast and two paracetamols. Looking down, he saw he had failed to undress.

'You've been dreaming, Jack, shouting out in your sleep about saving me from somewhere grim,' Daphne said softly.

Even her blurred image was beautiful. He wondered if his recent, nightmarish relationship with her had vanished as suddenly and as completely as the dream had.

The hand holding his, he squeezed gently, looking for a response, but she pulled it away.

'Not yet, Jack. Not yet,' she said quietly, patted him on the back of his hand and was gone.

Sunday

Ricky Croker's man had maintained an around-the-clock vigil at a discreet distance from the Bunce household since Thursday. Ricky Croker left nothing to chance, but nothing worthy of comment had happened, with the possible exception of Ivor's assisted passage home from his Lodge's installation meeting.

At 1:30 a.m. on Sunday morning, the driver of the black cab had supported him from the back seat to his front door. Gloria had watched the pantomime from the open bedroom window. 'You're nothing but a drunken old fool,' she had chortled gleefully at him. 'It's a good job some of your lowly constables cannot see you now. They would have a good laugh at your stumbling attempt at finding your own front door.'

Late that afternoon, it was a different story. Moments after a taxi had delivered a package, coaxing words from a woman preceded loud shouting from a bitter man. A mental flash had told Ivor what he might look like in the guise Jack had sent.

The package contained two silver shrouds, two cheap wigs bought earlier that day from a Sunday market and a joke-shop false moustache. One wig, bubbly and blonde, resembled Barbara Windsor's thatch, albeit only dark-night realistic. The other wig was black, sleeked back and attached to a light-rubber front-piece, emphasising a high forehead, the whole thing intending its wearer to look a bit like Elvis Presley.

Apoplexy visited Ivor minutes later when Gloria tried on her outfit and began to pirouette around the living room, shaking her hips.

'Come, darling,' she mocked. 'Come and dance with me the rumba of the dead.'

'The world has gone crazy. You *and* bloody Jack Dewsnap,' he shouted. He put his hands to his head and held it. It hadn't ceased throbbing all day from the excesses of the previous evening. 'First you fill me full of enough bloody vitamins to keep a thoroughbred stallion going through three consecutive mating seasons. Then you expect acts of fornication from me, with an *ever-increasing* frequency.

'My Commander, whom I have always respected, has gone completely bananas. Now he has come up with this vacuous idea to have me dress up in this ridiculous outfit. It's all to see a blue comedian whom I know I will hate as much as his blue performance, wearing this grotesque, hideous outfit, in a poofter's paradise… I have a good mind not to do it, it's…*it's just beyond a joke.*'

Gloria wasn't at all happy at Ivor's tack. She had visions of him backsliding out of the arrangement. To keep him on track so she could see Billy again she made him an offer he couldn't refuse.

'Ivor,' she said stiffly, 'do not *ever* consider reneging on your promise to Jack, and *I* promise to dispose of the vitamins you object to taking along with using the ring thing. Go through with this and you'll never have to take one again or fit the enhancing gadget. Of course, and I'm sure I don't have to remind you that, if you let Jack down, you'll not be considered for the dream promotion to Hendon.' The Met Police Training School position, she knew, was a thought-provoking subject.

Snookered and feeling extremely unhappy, Ivor ascended the stairs to their bedroom for a trial fit. In his sight, Gloria moved all the vitamins from his bedside cabinet. Along with the energiser ring, she locked them away in a bedside drawer. While the drawer was open, she took a sly look into her jewellery box, confirming the Viagra tablet hadn't disappeared.

Its appearance in the turn-up of her trouser suit after attending the last girls' meeting was a mystery which she might have difficulty explaining. Unnoticed, she pushed the stallion pump further beneath the bed.

Ricky Croker's man, observing the silhouettes on the bedroom curtains, reported that the Bunce's were preparing to go to a fancy dress party, one dressed as Elvis, the other as Barbara Windsor.

******

'Are you into blues?' Hamish asked Harry when, at 9:30 p.m., they were entering the noisy Navigator's Den. They had heard the music from afar and found the pub filled with members of the local "Blues Appreciation Society". The jukebox, switched off on each occasion they'd used the bar previously, blared out "Bad to the Bone," a number made famous by George Thorogood and his Destroyer's band.

'I don't mind it so long as it doesn't blast my ears like rock or a noisy woman does,' Harry replied, but his voice didn't get much above the jukebox's volume.

Barney saw them enter and asked Rusty to pour four pints of Guinness. He was having a night off and joined them at the bar. His talk was of the band, "Blodwyn Pig", playing at the Shankless Music Bar later that evening.

'They're the best blues band ever to have played that venue, and their leader, Mick Abrahams, the greatest exponent of the Blues guitar ever to grace its stage. Mick is famous, and an original member of the legendary Jethro Tull. You'll be glad of the chance to hear them.'

He pointed for them to sit down with Morphy, sitting by the door. Lifting two pints, he carried them over, handing one to Morphy, who chortled his thanks.

Barney slipped Hamish two tickets beneath the table as soon as he settled onto his stool. 'For the gig tonight,' he whispered behind a raised hand. Barney was in exceptional form and began entertaining them with some humour of his own. 'You missed out with Rusty. You would've got on well with her,' he nudged Hamish, smiled and gestured towards the bar, 'She likes a ballpark figure. She's computer-illiterate too, you know… never ever had a click on her mouse.'

'You could have fooled me there,' Hamish said.

'No kidding.' Barney said, 'Once she went for footballers… liked to play with two-footed wingers… though she never liked a foot up in the box, or the back pass, but she'd accept a ball floated in gently. Centre-backs were in for their great tackles and the slow or tardy she'd pull off after forty-five minutes.

'I met that Les Ferdinand once… he was getting onto the team bus at White Hart Lane, toting a wooden railway-sleeper over a shoulder…. I told him it was good to see him take some stick.

'Morphy could have been a rich man, you know. His missus phones him up one Saturday night he was working back shift. She says to him, "Morphy, I've got some bad news for you, some worse news, but some good news too." "What's the feckin' bad news you've got for me?" he asks. She says, "Remember those lottery numbers you asked me not to forget to put on for you today?" Morphy says, "Aye, to be sure, I do." "Well those six numbers you told me not to forget to put on for you, I've forgotten to put on for you." "Bayjasus what's the feckin' worse news?" "The numbers I've forgotten to put on for you have come out tonight." "Bayjasus," shouts Morphy down the phone, "What can the feckin' good news be?" "Ach nothing to worry about," says she, "there was no winners."'

'Have you nothing to say for yourself, Morphy?' Hamish asked between laughs.

Morphy was grinning away like a loony. He cackled and said, 'He's a lot of room to talk. He took his wife to see a male stripper…she told him she never wanted to see a small man again, so the focker goes out and buys her a magnifying glass. His wife's a strange woman that she is… especially about religious festival time. Good Friday past… to keep him at home, she tried to drive a nail through his foot. She can't focken cook either. When he married her, she thought cole slaw was a cold sore on her lip… and Brussels sprouts were cabbage balls. She told me once that she enjoyed a sandwich. Barney here says he's never seen anybody laying the other side of her in bed.'

'No kidding,' Hamish said. 'There seems no shortage of comedians around here tonight.'

'You'll know that for a fact soon,' Barney said quietly from behind a hand, then tipped them the wink to say nothing.

The Blodwyn Pig band was quieter than the Man band. The guitarist and vocalist, Mick Abrahams, had the audience drooling. His singing of some self-penned blues ballads, "Billy the Kid" more notably, was on par with his guitar work, which was what many in the audience had come to hear. He also let loose his guitar on some traditional classics. The band entertained for an hour-and-a-half until Clive Bunker gave a marvellous solo on drums. An Amen Corner number, "I Wonder Who," was the encore that finished off the set.

That Sunday night, The Navigator's Den didn't hold a lock-in. For a drink, the duo chose the Bally Balti, where they could sup a pint of Guinness whilst dining on a vindaloo of exquisite fieriness.

Monday

At 10 a.m. that morning, Ringaskiddy Square was a hive of activity. O'Rippers the Dry Cleaners was busily accepting best donkey jackets, denims and lumberjack shirts for cleaning. O'Hare the hairdresser, doing a fantastic business with short back and sides, jokingly advertised he'd do haircuts while you wait. Hairy bikers were queuing for straggly-hair-end repairs, beard shampoos and trims. Old Cobblers the cobblers was doing fantastic business soling, heeling, wellie polishing and patching. Only locals knew that a few days of humorous entertainment was about to kick off in some of the Square's venues, for which they would turn themselves out properly dressed.

A block up Kilkenny Street, smoke was rising from the ovens of Thaddeus Bunn and Son's bakery into the cold November sky. A pleasant, malty aroma, almost biscuity, tainted the air. Flour-white workers were carrying trays of steaming bread rolls, bread both brown and white and confectionery on their shoulders and loading the trays into waiting vans for distribution elsewhere.

Hamish and Harry, munching on rolls filled with crispy bacon, a breakfast supplement, sat aboard the transit in the car park, watching.

Bebe pulled up outside the baker's shop in the Morris Minor. Stepping out jauntily, in his civvies, smiling cheerfully at passers-by, he grasped and shook the many offered hands.

'Has he got the Lottery up or something?' Hamish asked. 'He's certainly more popular than ever today.'

Their greetings over, the bakery workers began loading a variety of bakery products onto the back seat of the Morris.

'It's at least his birthday,' Harry replied.

'I know a great copper when I see one. Has his freebies extremely well organised has our Bebe,' Hamish said, rejoicing in his voice.

Harry nodded his agreement, munched the last of his roll and licked the juices from his fingers. 'Just think what he's tucked away into that great scupper of a gut while he's policed this patch. Honest-to-goodness perks of the job though. We'd have done the same. Only we'd probably have been greedier.'

'Is that you having a go at me because I've got a bigger gut than Bebe, and you?' Hamish accused.

'You certainly look to be drooling over his perks,' Harry chided.

'Fucking cheek. I've seen you put away loads of mumped nosh.'

The four musicians from the Blodwyn Pig band shuffled out the front door of the Shankless Music Bar. 'Sleeping rough on the floor all night hasn't done their looks any favours,' Hamish said. 'They look dishevelled, unwashed and still tired.'

'The custom might have suited them better thirty years ago. I bet they slept on the floor because of the paltry wages the venue paid them to do the gig. Although digs must be cheap in this quarter,' Harry said.

'It must be very cheap at the "Two Focks".'

The roadies had already loaded the hire-van with amplifiers and other paraphernalia of a touring band. Packing themselves tightly in around the gear, the band set out towards their next venue.

Soon after they left, a specialist provider wheeled a PA system into the music bar. For a time that morning, it squealed acoustically as the soundman set up for the evening's gig.

It was dark by 6 p.m. Streetlights glowed with an orangey hue, permeating the first wisps of fog swirling into the square from the direction of the river. Shopkeepers had closed up for the night and the pubs were strangely empty. Locals, it seemed, preferred to stay at home, saving their hard-earned cash for one of the three B B gigs. By 7 p.m., Ringaskiddy Square was a desolate place, not even a pedestrian in sight.

Hamish had parked the transit in the car park, with a good view to the road and the expected crowd of bikers and rockers bound for the Shankless Music Bar. 'It's bang on half-past seven,' he said, 'and that's the front doors of the bar open.' As Hamish's voice died, they heard iconic popping sound of the first Harley entering the one-way system.

Harry had been counting. Ten minutes after hearing the first motorbike, he said, 'That's ninety bikes parked up. Bikers rev their machines inconsiderately. The smell of hot exhaust fumes getting into the cab is bloody awful.'

'Harleys have an irregular sound coming from their exhausts, a bit like my heart some mornings. I bet there's some stink beneath the leathers of the great unwashed,' Hamish replied.

The bikers were arriving dressed in winter leathers and safety helmets. Some had brought leather-clad "ladies" as pillion passengers, others their mates who, perhaps, had no wheels of their own. Carloads of unkempt, longhaired, leather-jacketed rockers arrived, adding to the throng.

By 8:30 p.m., three hundred patrons had packed into the venue. 'That's the Shankless Music Bar full, its door closed. Morphy won't be long now before he's on station,' Harry said.

And as he predicted, at 8:45 p.m. prompt, the horsebox moved into the Square, Morphy revving the engine, checking on its engine's readiness for the task ahead. Then he parked up in his normal spot in Skibbereen Street.

'He looks cool enough to be going out on a cross-border, donkey-smuggling mission,' Harry said.

Hamish, who didn't have a thought on the subject, just said, 'Aye.'

Five minutes later, the Morris Minor pulled up behind the horsebox, Bebe at the wheel.

At 8:55 p.m., Hamish said, 'Would you believe it? That's the fog billowing in thickly now.' The visibility in the square was reducing quickly, down to a few feet.

'With poor visibility, no pedestrians in sight, and vehicular activity nil, this is the right sort of night for a covert mission,' Harry said.

The horsebox engine turned over, fired, then purred into life. Bebe, hunched forward, peered over the steering column of the Morris Minor, waiting for the signal. Two red brake lights flashed on the rear of the horsebox. Morphy pulled away, Bebe following, close behind. Morphy drove around the square before angling towards Nobber Avenue. In the avenue, Morphy turned sharp right into Ballyragget Wynd, towards the venue's stage door, Bebe on his tail.

The taillights of the Morris Minor were just disappearing into the fog when the duo exited the transit and crossed the square. In the Wynd, thick fog obscured the lowering of the tailgate and Bebe driving the Morris into the horsebox.

Twenty seconds later, the horsebox had completed its task and chugged back through the fog, well down on its springs, to its usual parking spot.

On the stroke of 9p.m., a roar erupted within the Shankless Music Bar, announcing Bebe's presence on stage.

'In a few minutes, this patch has turned into a Paddy Brigadoon,' Hamish said as they reached the stage door. 'Hapless sorts might never find their way out of here,'

'I'd rather be in than out. This is a great patch. You could police it forever, easy. The locals swill Guinness, love curries, and they all seem to be humorous coves and game for a laugh.' were Harry's thoughts.

Listening at the stage door, they heard the eruption of acclaiming voices hush as Bebe begged silence.

'My wife's a lady…' Bebe began, 'she only farts in the car as I drive past a gas works. Mind you, she's a big woman… I'd have brought her with me this time, but they couldn't get her gob on the plane.

'I'm not saying she's got a big arse either… but whenever we're alone in a room together… it's always next to me.

'She went for a job on a gas pipeline that was going through the town. The foreman… Paddy… he says to her… what qualifications might you have for working on a pipeline, missus? I can work like a feckin' horse, she says. That's fine… says Paddy… but can you feckin' shite walking?

'Then she saw a job advertised in the local paper for an intellectual, sensitive lady of culture to work down one of those body shops. Now my wife thinks she has the sexiest hands that have ever hung on the ends of a woman's wrists. She wrote off… got the form… filled it in… sent it back… got an interview… got the feckin' job, but she never took to working with those feckin' undertakers.

'I was in Blackpool recently and thought I'd buy the missis a present. An amber brooch took my eye in a shop window so in I went… five-hundred pounds the girl said it was… why so expensive, I asked… there's a fly in it, the girl said… Yes… but can you get the zip in as well? I asked.'

As the gig ended, they returned to the transit. At 9:55 p.m., they were watching the fog lift and listening to the horsebox engine turn over then purr into life. A minute later, it moved off towards Nobber Avenue and Ballyragget Wynd. Twenty seconds later, it reappeared, chugging across Ringaskiddy Square into Skibbereen Street without stopping. A minute or so later, it returned. Seconds later the Morris Minor pulled alongside the horsebox. Bebe exchanged thumbs-up signs with Morphy. Then they drove off and exited the square, using different streets.

Tuesday

At 10 a.m. that morning, an audience of gawking pedestrians had gathered to watch the manhandling of the PA system from the Shankless Music Bar across Ringaskiddy Square to the Navigator's Den. Barney had closed the pub for the day while he prepared the stage and the soundman readied the PA system.

Rusty was helping Barney drag tables into a storeroom to make room for his regulars, the manual workers from the area. When a brewer's dray pulled up, he oversaw two draymen off-loading Guinness and lager kegs and a variety of bottled beers.

Bebe drove his Morris Minor into the Square, stopped, reversed up behind the dray and stepped out of the car. Again, he was in his civvies.

Watching from the car park, Hamish queried, 'What's he up to now?' The draymen had left their delivery task to greet him warmly.

'They're fetching him something from the cab, but I can't see what it is yet,' Harry said. The draymen were crouching low as they carried six crates of bottled Guinness and loaded them into the boot of the car. Some light, unheard banter took place, evident by the smiles stretching the faces of Bebe and the draymen. The draymen removed protecting gloves, their hands reaching out to shake Bebe by the hand. More easily heard from the transit were the sounds of hands slapping Bebe's back and the calls of 'Good luck!' and 'We wouldn't miss tonight!' Both draymen took from pockets and wafted, in Bebe's face, dog-eared tickets, bought a year earlier, cherished and kept safe since then. Raised thumbs indicated the pleasure of possessing one.

'I'll say it again, a great copper and well organised on a personal level,' Hamish said, grudgingly.

'We did okay, but never that well whilst working in civvies,' Harry said and nodded his agreement. 'If we had, you'd have not shared, drunk the lot yourself and got well-pissed without me.'

'Fucking cheek.'

******

That night, the doors of the Navigator's Den opened at 7:30 p.m. Soon after, and as if prompted by some cosmic calling, donkey-jacketed, wellie-wearing men and their better-dressed women drifted into the Square. The fog also began drifting in, seemingly on schedule. In an hour, it had thickened, cloaking the punters heading towards the venue. When the doors closed, three hundred ticket holders had crammed into the premises.

'Fog or not, their wee farce is working like clockwork,' Hamish said. 'It's elaborate, I don't see the sense of it, but they've organised it well and you can't take that away from them. Makes you believe Morphy's story about him being as handy as the thumb on his half-clenched fist.'

'I'm impressed with every aspect of their partnership,' Harry said. 'I'm sorry that we ever got involved in trying to end it. I'll eagerly listen to Bebe on stage again tonight. His jokes are bang on.'

The charade remained the same as the previous night. At 8:45 p.m., the horsebox entered the Square, Morphy parking up in his usual spot, Timmy sitting next to him. At 8:50 p.m., Bebe pulled the Morris Minor up at the rear of the horsebox. At 8:55 p.m., following the usual route, the horsebox travelled around the Square, this time making for Doonbeg Drive. Morphy corrected a swerve entering the Drive, slowed and steered to the left as he approached Ballybunion Lane, then did the ninety-degree turn needed to enter safely, Bebe close behind him. Twenty seconds later the horsebox re-entered the square, down on its springs, and parked up at its original spot.

At 9 p.m., roaring approval erupted as Barney the barman called Bebe to the Navigator's Den stage.

Hamish grabbed Harry by the arm, indicated he would lead across the square to Doonbeg Drive. There was no traffic to worry them, but the fog hung thicker in the Lane, where the uneven cobbles were also slippy. The going wasn't stumble-free for both men, making them glad to find The Navigator Den's stage door. The door had a low window. Pressing an ear to it, they were ready to hear a bit of Bebe's act.

'I had me first sexual experience down in a wood at the end of the village where I was raised. She was a lovely girl to be sure. We were both six years old at the time, but she said it was all right because she was sixteen days older than I was. I'd hung her knickers on the branch of a tree and I was just about ready to bury Fagin when the Mammy appears from behind a feckin' bush. What a feckin' clout she gave me along the feckin' ear hole… you could have heard the smack and my cries in Carrickfergus. That's a long feckin' way from Cork, I can tell you, to be sure.

Get up that feckin' road, you dirty little bogger she shouts at me and chases me through the length of the village. All the auld wifies were standing at their doors gawping. She threw me onto my bed with its corn-chaff filled mattress, making me wait there until Dad came home from work. I was feckin' petrified. At five o'clock... I hear the bike clattering against the railings and himself coming into the cottage. Then I hear this feckin' great commotion in the kitchen and their raised voices.

Dad comes into me bedroom… picks me up by the lapels of me pyjamas and carries me through to the kitchen. He drops me down on the floor and takes the biggest feckin' frying pan from its hook on the wall. The Mammy screamed loudly, fer feck's sake, you're not going to hit him with that are you, Dad. No… he says… if my lad has started feckin' at six… I'm going to cook him a steak. He'll need building up'.

Laughter drowned out the rest of the act and lasted until the raucous cheering indicated the end of Bebe's performance.

******

Sergeant Moriarty had languished safely comatose in the tranquilliser-enriched arms of Morphius for many days. He re-entered the painful world of the conscious about 3 a.m., five hours after the B B show in the Navigator's Den had ended. He lay comfortably in a bed. Several items of hospital equipment placed nearby interested him. A wedge-shaped, porcelain bedpan, inscribed with the words Clegham Mental Hospital, resting on a nearby chair, he thought noteworthy. It provided all the clues he needed to pinpoint his location. Subdued lighting from a small lamp on an adjacent table cast shapes onto the white walls. He found them soothing and he lay unblinking.

No reasons for his incarceration in a mental hospital were emerging; hindering his befuddled mind from thinking properly were the words, 'Fuck them, give them a pound,' which flashed repeatedly from a transmitter that wouldn't switch off, somewhere out there in the hinterland of his consciousness. Each time he heard the words his eyes filled with tears and he felt like giggling. Then, in a flash, he had the answer: in the yard behind the nick, a straitjacket had recently restrained him, binding him intolerably tight as he lay on a stretcher, surrounded by ambulance men and the leering faces of coppers.

An image fluttered before his eyes, like the flicker of an old movie, of Bunce's twitching moustache and him supervising his rapid removal and transportation to the mental hospital. He snorted down flared nostrils, shuddered and rubbed his heels up and down the bottom sheet in a cycling motion. He practiced stamping on Bunce, feeling a rising hate for him.

'Bastard,' he rasped and spat out a gob of saliva.

Sergeant Moriarty moved his arms and arched his body. The restraints had gone, but his ankles ached as if he had recently slogged out a lengthy route march. He moved his head from side to side without removing it from the pillow. He saw the sticking plaster on the back of his hand where a drip had once entered a vein, the plastic tag around his wrist with his name on it, and that he was wearing a pair of hospital pyjamas.

Sliding out of bed, he stood upright and walked unsteadily towards the ward door, the lino tiles cold on his feet. Peering through a door window, he saw an auxiliary nurse sitting alone behind a desk, along the corridor, engrossed in a crossword puzzle. At the window on the other side of the ward, he moved the curtain and saw the hospital car park. Beyond the car park, a perimeter hedge separated the hospital grounds from the illuminated yard of the hospital farm. There, long-term patients received therapy by tending to an assortment of farm animals.

'I'm in a ward on the third floor, and that farm is no more than one hundred yards distant as a screwy crow flies,' he muttered, scanning the scene. A twisted smile played around his lips, his thinking improving.

Groping through a locker beside the bed, he found his shirt, his uniform trousers and his socks, all freshly laundered. His boots were nearby, unpolished, smelly and still dampish after many days. He quickly dressed and stood again by the door, in stocking feet, holding the boots by the laces, his thinking racing now.

Brought up in a dour mining community deep in the Welsh valleys, life had been characteristically hard and restrictive for the young Moriarty. His parents were religious people who kept his nose in the catechism and the Bible. He hadn't encountered the word Freemason during his upbringing and, since becoming a police officer, no one had yet broached discussions on the mysteries of the "craft". His staid, uncompromising attitudes, lack of humour, abstemiousness and legendary parsimony had ensured no invitation came his way to become a member.

Freemasonry being a society with secrets, he had gleaned the little he knew of its inner workings while sitting listening to the malcontented spouting their bile in the canteens at the different nicks where he had served. That Masons were guilty of "riding the goat" troubled him. Some said it what he heard was jest, aired by the misinformed and the piqued when a promotion or an assignment they had fancied had gone to a Mason. Bunce had abused him, had trussed him like the proverbial stuffed chicken and had incarcerated him in a nut house. Standing at the ward window looking towards the farm, he thought "riding the goat" a bestial act.

An audible alarm sounded in the area of the desk. The auxiliary rose to her feet and reset it. She passed by the door that shielded him and entered another ward further down the corridor. Slipping out of the ward, he made for the stairs that led down to the ground floor. 'Retribution time,' he whispered, 'fuck them, give them a pound.'

At the stair bottom, he gave the automatic crossbar on the fire door a push. Another alarm immediately sounded within the hospital block. He rattled the door closed behind him and the crossbar fell back into position. The door had closed properly. The alarm stopped ringing a second or two later.

Standing and supporting his back against a wall, he put his boots on. The moon was high, giving limited shadow, but he found some and, unseen, he darted from the building towards a brick-constructed ducting, housing steam lines and other piping, running between the hospital boiler house and the farm. In the ducting, he edged along between insulated pipes and the wall.

Escaping steam, piped into water-filled pools, made farting sounds as he passed by. At the junction of the ducting with the farmyard, some rusty, small-mesh wire netting blocked his path. 'What a mesh you've got me into, Moriarty,' he said and raised a boot. He was directly behind a range of chicken coops from where he heard some clucks. 'Another big brown one laid for brekkie, my lovely chook,' he said and then sighed quietly.

The acrid odour of chicken droppings stopped him. He mused: the stench of dung clears bunged-up nostrils much the same as smelling salts do. It's funny, isn't it, when stench ought to do just the opposite.

He aimed a boot at the fencing. It gave easily. He made a hole large enough for him to pass through to the other side. He stood in the shadow offered by a tall hedge. Weaving his way through a range of coops he entering the farmyard proper.

In the still night, not a zephyr of wind blew from any direction. Then an owl twitted and flitted close to the barn, its highly sensitive ears detecting the frantic scurrying of a disturbed farm rat. In the distance, from the direction of the silhouetted farmhouse, he heard a raucous, cacophonic cackling. 'Aha, a half-strangled, dissenting nightjar shatters the silence,' he gurgled. 'The bird is unhappy that an incontinent inmate, not yet fully cured, has placed it beneath a bed.'

Across the farmyard, a small circular building stood out beneath the glare of the farmyard floodlights and the moon's fullness. It was the goat pound. A notice board fixed to the door had scrawled on it in chalk: "BINNY".

'A goat. I'm in heaven at last,' Sergeant Moriarty said quietly and breathed out slowly into the cold night air.

Wednesday

The Commander sat in his office looking at the wall-clock. It said 10a.m. He was pensive, felt twitchy and thrummed his fingertips on the desktop. For an hour, he had awaited a further call from his "duties elsewhere" duo. The call was overdue: the time for transporting his party to Blodger's drew near. When the phone rang, some minutes later, it was MacSporran on the line. It must be his turn for me to blast his ears, he mused.

'The PA system has arrived at Blodger's for tonight's performance. As far as we can tell, everything is on track,' Harry told him.

'My party will be arriving at a quarter-to-nine in a blue Peugeot people carrier,' the Commander explained. 'The vehicle has darkened windows. I'd prefer to park with some cover, away from the immediate vicinity, a short walk from the club. If I park the Peugeot up on the dark side of the transit, that should suffice. Is there anywhere suitable in the vicinity of Ringaskiddy Square?'

'The square's central car park is fine, sir. It's large enough and will have many empty spaces at night. I see no problems there. We'll be looking out for you.'

The Commander finished work early and walked from the nick to the hire-car company offices to collect the Peugeot. At home, he parked up in the drive and fussily checked that all the doors opened easily, the locks and alarms worked and that he had enough fuel for the journey.

While turning the handle to the back door to the house, it flew open. Daphne pulled him in, frisked around him, skimmed a kiss across his cheek, appearing in fine fettle. She had prepared dinner: fillet-of-beef, cooked rare, as he liked it, with a peppercorn sauce. It was the first time she had cooked anything decent for him since his decision on Blackpool.

They ate dinner together, but there was little conversation. It was close to reconciliation time and neither seemed willing to grab the nettles, admit to any wrongs.

Daphne told him his fancy dress was in the lounge, laid out, ready for him to put on. After dinner, Jack found it there. Immediately he began to breathe deeply feeling an urge to hold Daphne. Her bra, stuffed and lying on the sofa, ready for him to don, had that affect on his breathing and his legs, which began to quake so much he had to grab for the sofa back. Then he quickly braced himself. The pressed shroud into which he had to fit caught his eye.

By 7:45 p.m., they both had showered, dressed and were waiting to leave. Jack was looking at himself in the mirror, twirling a dark leather handbag and trying to ameliorate his excitement. Daphne shocked him by putting her arms around him, slowing him down, causing the handbag to fly off the end of his arm. She lay her head on his chest, listened to his heart pounding, then lifted her face and kissed him gently on his Maggie Thatcher rouged lips. Then she straightened the wig that had fallen over his eyes. He breathed in, shuddering, a painful stiffy quickly sprouting.

'You must love me dearly,' Daphne said, then breathed deeply, looking aliently monkish in her shroud and Elvis headgear. 'How could I ever have been so insufferable to you? How could I have driven you to these lengths? Risking your reputation, dressing up and looking so silly just for me, makes me want to take you to bed now and fuck you continually throughout the night and most of tomorrow.'

Jack, looking steely as Maggie Thatcher, was lost for words.

They looked each other over, realising the standoff had ended. Bed beckoned and they quivered in readiness. A sensual smile played around Daphne's lips. It told of her real feelings towards him, but she withdrew into herself and took a step back; there were places to go, people to see and she had a deal. 'Only after the comedian, remember, Jack?' she said, regaining her coolness. They stood holding hands. For a moment, déjà vu registered with them. Both thought that somewhere, sometime, in the recent past, a reverse mirror image of how they now looked to one another had crossed their paths.

******

In the lounge of the Bunce household, Gloria was having difficulties. 'Stand still, Ivor,' she reproached. He wasn't fitting properly into his shroud. It was much too tight and too stiff to pull over the stuffed brassiere. 'How can I push it back into place from the bottom of your shroud with your garden hoe if you don't stand still?' she scolded.

'You're pulling hairs out of my chest with that damned pole,' Ivor complained. The pole suddenly found a route between the brassiere and his chest and knocked him under the chin. He wasn't too happy with that either and jumped backwards.

Gloria held out a pair of her knickers towards him.

'If you think I'm wearing them you've got another think coming to you,' he shouted.

Gloria saw him as overwrought and tutted her annoyance.

'I'm keeping my Y-fronts on. Those bloomers need taking in anyway. They're much too big, they'd fall down, trip me up, and I'd break my bloody neck....which might not be the worst thing that could happen.'

'Have it your way,' Gloria said and handed him a black, patent-leather handbag.

'Do I really have to bother with that?' Ivor asked, imploringly, holding it away from him by the strap.

'You won't look the real Barbara Windsor if you don't. You must appear to have tried your best for Jack.'

In the kitchen and safely out of Ivor's view, Gloria prepared two cups of coffee. The Viagra tablet was now in finely powdered form, following its crunching in the mortar and pestle she used to grind spices. She brushed the powder into the coffee, briskly stirring it, looking closely to see that the powder had dissolved without leaving any traces, which she thought as important as the full dose slipping over his throat unnoticed.

Sitting disconsolately in the lounge when Gloria waltzed in with a tray, Ivor wasn't in the mood for noticing anything.

'Drink this coffee. It will calm your nerves,' she said, soothingly.

******

The Rideouts were having their own difficulties, which differed from the others. Algie was staggering about in the early stages of drunkenness and making a complete mess of his preparation, his arms caught up in the bra straps Myrna was trying to fit on him.

'I insist that this contraption of a brassiere is fitted onto my back, that's the nature of the venue we're attending, silly,' he said, reeling away from Myrna.

Myrna had suffered Algie's nonsense enough. Having sorted the bra straps, she pulled the shroud down over his head. He moved away, dragging her along until his head appeared. When he had steadied, she plopped the blonde Marilyn Monroe-type wig on his head, turning the thing around until he could see. Then she thrust a hand down his front and positioned his brassiere. Using chair backs for support, Algie staggered about the room. Myrna, hands on hips, looked at her mess of a husband and knew she was wasting her time. Exasperated, she pushed him down into a chair. A handbag of wildebeest hides and shaped like an elephant's foot she tossed onto his lap. 'Sit there, be quiet, nurse that, and wait for Jack, you drunken fool,' she ranted at him. She was getting very emotional and excited at the prospect of seeing Billy again. She would have preferred Rowley's company. After the gig, she would have ensured that his shroud became starchy, but something with more life about it stiff.

******

Time seemed to pass quickly for Sergeant Moriarty, sitting in his Mini-van watching Ricky Croker's man watching the Bunce household. During the day, he had seen the man lift his camera and scan the house with the zoom lens a number of times.

He deduced from his observations that an investigator of some sort also had an interest in Bunce. He couldn't work out why, and his presence there was spoiling the sense of occasion for him. He couldn't knock on Bunce's door and introduce him to Binny. In front of Mrs Bunce, he wanted to embarrass him by ask him if he fancied "riding the goat".

Binny's head was sticking through an opening in the boarding separating van from the cab. His tongue flicked in and out, licked and moistened Sergeant Moriarty's ears, making him quiver. 'Now, boyo, we'll have less of that,' he said and pushed Binny's head back through the opening.

******

Jack assisted Daphne into the people carrier, telling her to 'Clunk, click.' Close to 8 p.m., he pulled out of the drive and set out for Ivor's house. Driving carefully, he arrived there fifteen minutes later and tooted the horn.

The front door of the Bunce house opened and Ivor stepped out, Gloria pushing him from behind. They reached the car as Jack was opening a rear door. 'I must congratulate you on your choice of fancy dress,' he said as Ivor neared.

'It'll keep, Jack, I'm in no mood for pleasantries,' Ivor growled.

Jack was in the mood for teasing. 'Gloria has certainly kitted you out well, "Barbara".'

Ivor grunted, said nothing, lifted his shroud hem and slid through the back door.

'Belt up,' Jack advised.

'I've said nothing,' snapped Ivor.

'Securely, clunk, click, I meant,' Jack said. 'And watch you don't trip up in those high heels when you get out.'

'Click, click,' Ivor responded.

******

The horn tooting also aroused the interest of Ricky Croker's man. He watched the two oddly dressed figures leaving the house and totter towards the Peugeot. Through the camera's night-vision lens, he saw only shapes in greenish grey. The shapes didn't look like any of the two people he knew lived there. He was only certain that two people in fancy dress had left the house. He called Ricky Croker on his mobile, relaying his suspicions, and confirming he was following the Peugeot with the darkened windows as it headed deeper into East Clegham.

******

The horn tooting also alerted Sergeant Moriarty to the movement of persons outside the Bunce house. He watched closely and, like Ricky Croker's man, could only make out two shapes. Strange ones too and it confused him that they were wearing fancy dress. Knowing that the Bunces lived there alone, he immediately suspected they were accompanying someone of importance in the Peugeot. 'Aha… a fancy dress party they're off to, I'll be bound. Maybe it's even a ladies' night at the Lodge, isn't it, Binny,' he said quietly.

******

Ricky Croker called his minder. 'It's on,' he said into the mobile's mouthpiece. 'Get the team over to me quickly and pick me up. Wouldn't want to miss any of this. The Mayor and Mayoress of Clegham have just boarded the same vehicle as the Bunces, driven by a person unknown. Interestingly, the Mayor is swinging a hairy, elephant's foot around his head and has loudly told the driver of the Peugeot to get *his* knickers off.'

******

Hamish had found the darkest spot in the car park, where a streetlight had failed. He thought that at least, the Commander couldn't complain about the location. At 8 p.m., they were sitting watching Blodger's arrivals. Classy cars were parking up in the lit areas of the car park. Out of the cars, quaint, finely attired cross-dressers struggled. Some wore fluffed-out robes. Others paraded in tightly drawn-in Lurex two-piece trouser suits A few devil-may-care, screaming-queen types, making giggly noises, just pulled up under streetlights; it seemed, worries about anyone seeing them didn't perturb.

'Very wobbly on their pins, some of that lot,' Harry observed.

Hamish giggled. 'If the Commander is wearing stiletto-heeled shoes he'll find proceeding over the cobbles in a southerly direction quite difficult, he being a tall man.'

******

Commander Dewsnap turned the Peugeot out of Cork Street and began circling Ringaskiddy square. It was 8:45 p.m. Hamish spotted them coming and flashed the headlights of the transit. The commander pulled into the car park and then reversed into the space in the shadow of the transit.

Six persons stepped out of the Peugeot and milled around, fiddling with wigs and looking about the square. Hamish counted three Elvis Presleys with moustaches, one Maggie Thatcher, one Barbara Windsor and one Marilyn Monroe, shrouds covering them from shoulders to ankles.

The full moon shone briefly through wispy, wind-blown cloud. Trees bending in the wind cast strange, jerking shadows to merge with those of high chimney pots, lampposts, and the even stranger silhouettes of the Commander's party.

'Which one of you is the Commander?' Hamish asked quietly, unsure of who was who in the dark.

'Call me Jack,' hissed a Maggie Thatcher figure and belted him around the head with its handbag. 'Where do we go from here?'

'Over there, Jack, follow the rest of the ladies.'

'Watch it, MacNab,' Jack wheezed humourlessly through clenched teeth. He smacked him again with the bag and walked up close. Hamish heard the snap of the bag opening. Then he felt the envelope pushed into his hand. 'Your resignations and warrant cards,' Jack whispered. 'You've done a good job here. See me tomorrow in my office.'

'Nice one, Jack. Have a great time in there,' Hamish replied.

Humourless in front of the constables he might have been, but Jack was relaxed, felt off duty; he knew the real reasons behind their attending Blodger's and of the goodies he expected later from Daphne.

Ivor had set out that evening feeling he was definitely on duty (why else would he bloody well be there) and on the trail of a piss-taking, miscreant police officer. The evening couldn't end quickly enough for him. Perturbing him further and making him wish even more that the evening had never began, was the appearance, without recourse to sexual whim, of a weighty hard-on. He first blamed the vibrations of the vehicle, but his confidence in that diagnosis was ebbing as he felt no change in the condition stood on firm ground.

As he stood beside the Peugeot, his hard-on remained rigid, giving him no indication at all that it was about to decline in strength. Nothing had prepared him for the experience. Never had he felt such surging power. It worried him greatly that the condition might be due to some latent reaction to his close proximity to a drag bar and the company of others cross-dressed. While waiting for Jack to lead the party, he stamped his feet, which only caused the erection to bob, worsening considerably his disposition.

Jack held Daphne by the hand and set out walking towards the nightclub. Myrna held Algie steady and followed close behind. Ivor skulked sullenly behind Gloria, pushing down on the end of his erection, desperately trying to rearrange his problem, stop it from bobbing, but the shroud was tight and the handbag kept on getting in the way. 'Can't get the bloody thing lifted high enough,' he moaned.

Gloria glanced behind her. 'Come on, come on, keep up, you fiddle-faddling old fart,' she decried. Pleased when she saw that the Viagra dosage was kicking in, she gasped and said, 'Stick it out, Ivor, stick it out.'

'That's the bloody problem,' he said, his voice scratchy.

Jack and Daphne stepped up to Blodger's door first, their arms around each other, as if nothing silly had ever happened to upset their lives together. Gloria turned, dragged Ivor forward and held onto his hand. The doorman took the tickets, checked them carefully, but he had a look of doubt on his face as allowed the sextet to pass through.

A wall of hot, fetid air hit the party as they shuffled along the inner passage. It was no potpourri of pungent spices pleasurable to the nose, but a mixture of different perfumes, sweat, and the beer spillages of many years that had dried into the carpet. Jack's nose crinkled and Daphne raised a handkerchief. Ivor mouthed, 'Christ, what a bloody awful smell. It reminds me of my section house days, cheesy feet, sweaty bodies and beery farts.'

Gloria thumped him in the ribs and had another look down at his bobbing front.

Music pounded along the corridor, the PA system amplifying the bass beat of the Elton John number, "Don't let the sun go down on me", to which Jack pretended to twirl Daphne. 'Insane bloody noise,' screeched Ivor.

'We're in the body of the kirk now, I think,' Jack said on reaching the already crowded standing area. Pushing Ivor's wig to one side, he revealed an ear and asked, 'What do you and Gloria drink?'

'A glass of water from my filter tap at home, if you don't mind,' Ivor responded acidly. He had found a use for the handbag and was holding it over his embarrassment.

'Come now, Ivor. Don't spoil the show. We've a piss-taker to nail,' Jack reminded him.

'Oh, I suppose so. Make it G and Ts for both of us.'

Jack left the party standing, short-stepped it towards the bar, which was as quickly as the tight-fitting shroud would allow. He didn't look too closely at the real cross-dressers. A quick glance was enough to tell him that the fraternity had members of various shapes and sizes. Some were bodybuilder types. Some, apparently, had belts strapped tightly to the chests of their pipe-cleaner-thin bodies, forcing up pectoral muscles and creating small and sometimes hairy cleavages. Plenty had well-rouged faces, wore stunning, quality wigs, and swung an assortment of flamboyant ear adornments. He pushed his way through to the bar, opened his bag, ordered the drinks and, when they came, paid for them. One of the dissipated-faced Malone brothers served him. Suffering Christ, Jack thought, I hope he's classed as uglier than I am.

Jack returned to find Ivor trying to catch his eye. Scowling his displeasure, Ivor was showing him his full range of facial distortions and uttering his 'Click, clicks' most peevishly as he passed him the drinks.

With drinks safely distributed, Jack turned his back on Ivor to look around for spare seats. Claiming the wall seating were the elderly and the bizarre, faces thick with ash-white makeup, eyeliner and heavy lipstick. He noticed standing room in front of the stage and ushered the party there.

******

'Let's hope Jack's come up with the goods here,' Rowley's words were almost a sigh as Tattiana swung the Mercedes into the kerb outside his Docklands apartment block at 8:15 p.m., prompt, and extinguished the car headlights. Rowley was ready and dressed in the shroud, the fuzzy wig and the strap-on breasts that Jack had sent him. It was a crazy outfit but he liked it. Watching from the front balcony of his apartment, he saw Tattiana's legs stretch out of the open car door, slightly apart, a portion of inner thigh flashing in the street lighting.

'Wow,' Rowley said, shuddered a little and whistled. After catching the flash, he took note of the lithe movement that propelled the trim figure upright. Tattiana's hands brushed over her figure-hugging dress on the confident walk in high-heeled shoes towards the apartment block entrance. Rowley leant a little further over the railing to ogle some more. Drawing back, he lifted his hands as if in prayer and said. 'My word, on what catwalk did I last see a person so tall move so elegantly? In that outfit, poetry in motion describes her movements, and knockout describes Jack's choice.' He brushed down his own attire, made sure he was hanging okay within the boundaries of the shroud, that there were no embarrassing bulges, yet, and left the balcony.

In a stride, he was waiting in front of his security video-monitoring system for a vision to appear. When it did, Rowley liked what he saw in close-up. Tattiana had long black hair, light-brown skin, a large mouth with sensuous lips and looked a fun person. 'She's wearing a permanent smile and is that suntan or has Jack really chosen a beautiful and cheerful mulatto woman for me to pleasure by way of a change?' he mused.

Rowley answered the intercom with a welcoming, 'Coming,' entered the lift and was soon at the entrance door. Swinging it open, he gushed, 'You look so terrific, Tattiana. What a thrill and privilege it is for me to have your company for the evening.' That the hands he took hold of and the knuckles he pressed absentmindedly were unusually large for such an elegant person, completely escaped him. After all, he was looking into smiling eyes that had instantly locked on to his.

With considerable panache, Tattiana turned the Mercedes out into the traffic and pressed hard on the accelerator. Rowley rocked back, but a large, steadying hand grasped his thigh. 'Take it steady, old boy,' the husky voice soothed, 'let's leave the rocking for later.' The hand remained and began to massage the inside of his legs, tweaking and pulling at all the right places in between them. Rowley breathed hard; he could hump Tattiana forthwith. Turning slightly towards the teasing hand, he allowed his hand to wander and brush lightly over Tattiana's nearest breast. He caught a glimpse of brown flesh thrusting over the top of her dress. A light squeeze suggested the breasts were firm, fleshy and suckable.

Both Tattiana's hands were on the wheel as she turned the Mercedes into the car park opposite Blodger's club. Parked up, the engine at rest, Rowley left the car and strode, as fast as the shroud would allow him, to assist Tattiana's exit. Taking hold of an arm, he held onto her for the short walk to the club door.

Rowley was sure excitement shone from Tattiana's eyes as they reflected moonlight. 'You look so radiant, so well turned out for this jaunt,' he said, 'and we're only attending a function at one of the more seedier clubs in Clegham. When I take you "up town" clubbing, you'll look amazing.'

'I know this place well, Rowley. Enjoy it here first. Then we'll see,' Tattiana growled a seductive Eartha Kitt growl.

Taken in by Tattiana, Rowley didn't notice her familiarity with Blodger's club. He said, 'Oh, promise me you will.'

In Blodger's, Rowley looked for familiar faces. He desperately wanted to find Jack and his party and show-off Tattiana, but the crowd all seemed to have bouffant hairdos, were jostling for position and making it difficult for him to recognise anyone. Both Tattiana and he were tall and could easily see the stage from the rear of the venue. Taking a light grip on an arm, he ushered her there.

******

Ivor's enlargement was embarrassing him further; it had escaped through the slit in his Y-fronts. Now it poked out and was lifting up the front of his shroud, like a frontal corset stay fugitive from its restraint, and pulsated to an increasing beat. Occasionally, as it surged, Ivor's twisted lips uttered, 'Click, click,' the hubbub drowning his frustrations out.

Some cross-dressers noticed Ivor's erection. Thinking that it couldn't possibly be a corset stay poking out, they plumped for it being a display of flamboyant cockiness. The thought turning them on, some began squeezing past him to get a better look. Others, thinking a look wasn't good enough, rattled his throbbing helmet with quick finger-flicks, much to his consternation. When one lisped quietly into his ear, 'Nithe one, sailor,' his head turned sharply, his growling mouth taking up the position in space that his ear had just left a millisecond earlier.

Gloria, looking closely again, was startled further by Viagra's affects, and the audience's interest in it. Stepping back, she nudged Myrna then Daphne to look. Myrna stared at the throbbing prod, her face quizzical. Immediately, she guessed that the missing Viagra tablet was at the root of Ivor's problem.

Daphne was too preoccupied to look. Jack had entwined his arms around her. With her back to him, she squirmed and pushed, feeling his cock swollen against her.

Jack was still feeling some burning twinges, but he was beyond caring, feeling no pain.

Word of Ivor's problem spread through Blodger's as if conveyed by some lunar influence and set into motion a mincing faction of onlookers. With shoulders rhythmically swaying, heads turning from side to side, feet moving in small steps, they looked like a rookery of male emperor penguins, each with an egg held snug upon their feet. Shuffling in concentric circles, four abreast, the swirling vortex of deviant, jaw-dropped creatures, handbags held tight beneath arms, scrambled between Jack's party and the stage. Passing by, they bowed, uttered approving 'OOOOOooooOOOOhs' and nodded their heads in unison towards Ivor. Bestowing this unwanted honour on him, they ogled his discomfort, thinking him an ideal playmate. The returned evil glare and twitching moustache set above growling lips didn't deter them.

Ivor looked imploringly at Jack, but found no comfort. Jack was breathing deeply and quaking a little, had closed his eyes, his arms around Daphne, who was thrusting and jiggled her bum against his loins. Shuddering in his embrace, her eyes were dreamy; she wanted him again. No way was Jack going to leave his current heaven to take notice of any problem he had.

******

Morphy drove the horsebox into Ringaskiddy Square, swinging it around on reaching Skibbereen Street and executing a ninety-degree turn. Reversing back, he pulled up one foot from the kerb and parallel to it, in two movements. On cue, Bebe pulled the Morris Minor in behind him.

'There's no substitute for practice,' Hamish observed from the driver's seat of the transit. 'He's so good now he could have attended an advanced driver's course at Hendon.'

'You're right. Bebe's no mean car handler either. It takes great timing to negotiate a moving ramp,' Harry said.

Lights flashed on both vehicles; then they pulled away together, angling towards Termonfechin Street. In the street, Morphy slowed at the narrow entrance to Boggeragh Close, then turned sharply into it. Twenty seconds later, the horsebox reappeared to take up its usual parking spot, having taken the Morris Minor aboard and dropping Bebe off at the back door to the venue.

******

The lights of the horsebox were fading when the headlights of a Volvo estate flashed twice to high beam as it entered the square. Roger Crooke, complete with trademark trilby, his cameraman, his minder and his personal assistant were looking out from its darkened interior.

The headlights of the Volvo estate parked up in Nobber Avenue flashed. The arriving Volvo glided neatly alongside it.

******

Sergeant Moriarty followed the Volvo driven by the single observer that had followed the Peugeot into Ringaskiddy Square. He found a parking space a little away from both vehicles. He had watched the uptake of passengers at the Mayor's home; now he watched as the Peugeot emptied, without making out anyone with certainty.

'They're all bewigged and wearing Masonic shrouds, isn't it, Binny,' he said melodramatically, 'but if my guess is correct, the sextet will include Brother Dewsnap, Brother Bunce and Brother Rideout. They'll have their wives with them, of course. They're *all* very good friends. They're *no* friends of mine, but you'll meet them all soon enough, Binny. Fuck them give them a pound, isn't it? What do you say to that my honey-lipped, bearded friend?'

He left the van, used a tree for cover and watched Jack and his party walk across the square towards Blodger's nightclub. Portions of the neon sign advertising the venue had begun to flash and flicker. Both ends of the sign had developed problems. The B at one end, the R and the S at the other lit only infrequently. As Sergeant Moriarty neared the door, the parts of the sign that remained lit read: LODGE.

******

There was a surge of expectancy as 9 p.m. neared. Audience members, preparing themselves for the show, huddled in tight groups, holding their drinks in close to their bodies, a hand cupped to an elbow for support. With a swish, the stage curtain opened revealing a grinning Malone brother holding a microphone. 'Evening, sisters,' he simpered, lifting up his breasts and weighing them, one in each hand, Lily Savage-like. 'We have a wonderful show for you tonight, filled with unique gags and heard from the amusing lips of the one and only Mr Elusive himself, Billeeeee... Bagmaaaaan!'

Ivor tetched, the tip of his tongue moving rapidly between upper palate and tooth, utterly annoyed at the camp display.

Billy Bagman ambled onto the stage, much as Gloria and Myrna could remember he had done in Blackpool, and yet again to rapturous applause. On this occasion, though, swinging handbags circled the audience's heads and there were lisped cries of 'Nithe one, Billy'.

The soundman played a few bars of "River Dance" music. Billy gave a little skip and a jump, pushed his belly out, made it look bigger and wobbly. In the Blackpool theatre, the girls' seats were quite close to the stage. From where they stood now, Gloria and Myrna thought Billy's stomach looked a lot bigger than it had then. Certainly, the nasal appendage seemed more real, had four longer hairs sprouting from it. He looked more comical when he crossed his eyes and focused them on his nasal antennae.

Pacing the stage, he looked out at his audience. With a look of shock and horror, he crossed his eyes again. With a shake of his head, his eyes returned to normal. When the tittering at his antics subsided, he went directly into his act with a gag..

'I hear Bill Clinton's in trouble again tonight… they've just announced he's splashed out on another new dress for Monica…He doesn't need Viagra, does he?'

'There's a new pill out now called Pro-Viagra. It's a mixture of Viagra and Mogadon. If you don't get a fuck, you don't give a feck.'

Gloria gulped and rocked a little at Viagra's mention.

'I've just devised a new game that'll interest you ladies.' Billy looked around the audience over the end of his nose, peering closely. 'Well, I say ladies with a small L. It's called Viagra roulette. Thirty of you lot go to a swapping party. You place twenty-eight Mogadon pills in a bag along with one Viagra and one Aspirin. The lucky one gets to fuck someone who doesn't have a sore head while the rest of you get an untroubled night's sleep.

'My bird fitted me with a "knickerette" patch before I came here tonight. She said it would stop me fancying any of you women.' Billy gave the audience a deploring look.

'When I was young, the Mammy worked as a maid down on a farm. I'd to go there after school to wait on her finishing. There was a huge flock of feckin' turkeys running about, out of control, chasing me everywhere… making a terrible racket. I can tell you this…I was feckin' petrified. Dad comes up one night to take us home and I tells him I don't like the noise these feckin' turkeys are making. Never mind son, himself said. When you're older… you'll love the sound of a gobble. Still don't know what he means,' Billy said, grinning slyly.

'I've got a mate who wouldn't know he was having a sixty-nine if the bird was sitting on his face. He's so feckin lazy he married a pregnant woman.

'I once met a lovely young Chinese girl. She was as slippery as an eel in bed… shagged like a rattlesnake. Feckin' rattled like an MFI wardrobe. I tried my feckin' best but I couldn't get her interested in blowjobs or sixty-nines. She just didn't understand. Then I had this brilliant idea and I struck it lucky cos I went and learnt some of the Chinese lingo. Next time I took her to bed, I said to her...hay yoo...two can choo...yoo choo too.

'I met this lovely German bird... she was known as that country's Wurst undertaker. Loved to bury my sausage, she did.

'My bird's a noisy woman. She's on the short list to go around the deepest graveyards when they start awakening the dead.

'She thinks she has to give me a gobble just to get me interested in sex. I'd told her I needed a head start.

'I comes down the stairs this mornin' and she said to me... shag me in the kitchen will you? Why the kitchen I asked? Cos I want to time my feckin' eggs, she said. I asked, do you want a soft one or a hard one? She said I want it hard. So I gave her a runny one and fecked off quick.'

Jack had heard many poor jokes and obtuse one-liners, thought funny by the broad spectrum of well-read professional men he had the privilege of meeting during his career. He found Billy Bagman's routine new and very entertaining. The girls were all laughing, but Ivor looked haunted. Jack took a firmer hold on the forgiving Daphne, as she reeled, giggled and continued to press her bottom into him.

It was impolite to talk during the act, but following the runny egg gag, Gloria turned to Daphne and said, 'That's the gag that really got me going.'

'It looks as if Ivor's Y-fronts have something going on in them, too,' said Daphne, her eyes cast down and wide, looking towards Ivor's predicament.

'Bother, bother, bother,' Ivor fumed and stamped a foot. Sweat was running into his eyes and he drew a sleeve of the shroud across his forehead. His scalp itched and he scratched at it beneath the wig.

The tightness and the length of the shroud made it impossible for him to gain access and re-cage his cock within his Y-fronts. He looked about him for the loo, which he thought he ought to have done on arrival. Now, the very thought of him running the gauntlet of three hundred perverts to rearrange his person, skeletal fingers reaching to touch him as he hastened by, made him shudder. If he actually reached the loo, witnessed goings on similar to what the "The Jock Connection's" gross firework display had interrupted, he was sure he would vomit.

Worse was afoot. A heavy-breathing, bearded type, dressed in an outstandingly bright yellow, Lurex two-piece, had slipped in between Ivor and Gloria, elbowing Gloria unceremoniously out of the way. Fingering Ivor's handbag inquisitively, the bearded type moved it to one side, saw better Ivor's pulsating discomfort and looked as if he intended to apply for squatter's rights.

******

Hamish nudged Harry as the two Volvos pulled up alongside each other.

'A Cinderella late for the ball, I expect,' Harry said.

They watched for some time as the personnel of the Volvos conversed through open windows.

Neither Hamish nor Harry recognised any of the occupants, at first.

******

'What have we got?' Ricky Croker asked his observer across the gap between the cars as the engine died.

'They've all gone into Blodger's drag bar with about three hundred others. They're the queerest looking bunch of cross-dressers I've ever seen.'

'Are you sure? This could make a great exposure if it's true.'

'That's where they went, Blodger's. It's a well-known haunt of that fraternity,' answered the watcher.

'My hunch is proving correct. Let's get weaving,' Ricky Croker snapped. 'Cameraman, get a night lens on. We'll need good visual images. We don't want to miss any of this.'

******

The Volvos hadn't been parked together thirty minutes when Ricky Croker left his car, stretched his arms and looked around.

'Jesus H Christ!' exclaimed Hamish, recognising the large person wearing the sheepskin coat and trilby. 'We need to move fast.'

'You've forgotten all about that letter you sent him?' Harry supposed, also recognising the figure.

'I thought he'd have binned it. Obviously not! He's been on the case and followed the party here. '

'Suffering fuck… aye. They're on Bunce's track, okay, but now for a very different reason.'

'What a story for Ricky Croker if he videos them in Blodger's.'

'I can see the headlines now.'

'Aye, tell me about it. "I expose two very senior police officers, one suspected of doping his strength at West Clegham with amphetamine sulphate…'

'Don't forget the Mayor of Clegham.'

'…who were dressed up like tarts and cavorting with known perverts in a seedy, drag bar".'

'It'll make interesting telly.'

'None of Blodger's patronage will like their coupons flashed across the tube, nor will the Commander.'

'You're right. The situation requires urgent action.'

'But don't rush, we have our warrant cards back, remember?'

'Aye, the Commander has been as good as his word, which he should keep. If he hasn't guessed by now that we know about his Halloween capers, we'll put him in the picture.'

'Can't we leave Bunce to have the skin flayed from his back by cross-dresser tongues?'

'Aye, that would be a nice ending to this saga. I want to return permanently to plain-clothes duty, that's my end game.'

'Mine too.'

Hamish pointed towards the Ricky Croker party walking around the square. 'They look as if they're heading for Blodger's front door.' He thought out the situation quickly, touched Harry on the arm and nodded in the direction of the horsebox. 'There's the means of escape. That's all we can use. We daren't use this van or the Peugeot, the Commander's party might be seen boarding and the vehicles are traceable back to him.'

'Will Bebe not mind? Harry asked. 'After all, he'll probably guess that the Commander and the Superintendent are there to "stick him on" for moonlighting.'

'It will need a white lie, but if Morphy goes along with us using the horsebox to get them all out, it can't do Bebe's case any harm. The Commander isn't aware yet of this entirely different scenario. When the word reaches him that Ricky Croker and his camera team are about, he'll go ape shit and be thankful of escaping by any means.'

'You're right. Let's go.'

******

In his van, Sergeant Moriarty readied Binny for his introduction to Superintendent Bunce and his party. The shorty apron, purloined from his wife's kitchen, hung around Binny's neck and down over his front, which the sergeant thought the goat suited. Outside a Lodge, and in his imagination, Binny would look the complete Masonic goat.

Had the sergeant paid attention to the nether end of Binny, he might have chosen a more concealing garment and placed it at that end. Binny was hermaphroditic: AC/DC, a freakish, milking Billy goat possessing both male and female genitalia, and a full, milk-producing udder.

******

'We'll keep to the shadows and approach unnoticed, if we can, from the rear. Morphy might panic and piss off if he spots us,' Hamish said, setting out for the horsebox. At the horsebox, he pulled the driver's side door quickly open. Morphy stared at them, agog and dragged a hand up to his throat when Hamish thrust his warrant card under his nose. Timmy, wary in the presence of an arse arsonist, cowered down onto the passenger seat and whimpered, his rear tight up against the other door.

Harry pushed in alongside Hamish. Morphy scanned their faces. 'We need your help, Morphy,' Hamish blurted. 'Bebe's caught up in a plot by Ricky Croker, the TV journalist, to expose the people he's entertaining tonight in Blodger's. Bebe's Police Commander, a Police Superintendent, and the

Mayor of Clegham are in there with their wives. It's important we get them out unseen. Bebe's your friend. You wouldn't want him caught up with them in an exposé the likes of this, would you?'

Morphy lifted the peak of his cap from over his eyes, grinned impishly, looked from Hamish to Harry and replied. 'Boys, you're a bit late. Bebe's been a retired copper since last Friday, at midnight. He's no need to fear anything of the sort.'

'We didn't know that, did we Harry?' Hamish said, looking quizzically at Morphy.

'Well he is,' Morphy retorted, now looking squarely at both of them in turn. 'Using this horsebox is a farce. Bebe has never needed to get to these gigs secretly. It's all to do with the opening night of his summer season, next year, in Blackpool. It will cause a sensation, be on the telly and in the papers, when I draw up in my horsebox on the Golden Mile, Bebe reverses down the tailgate and drives down the pier a little way towards the theatre.

This is just a dummy run, to see if the springs hold up and give me practice. It's worked flawlessly, up to now. It's sad about your superiors, but if it's any interest to you, I happen to think that a palaver, like this, will get Bebe onto the telly and some press coverage now, and will be great for his new career.'

Morphy allowed his words to sink in for a moment, saw the looks of concern on their faces. 'But don't worry, boys,' he said, 'Bebe's a gentleman. He always was, always will be, and he was a great copper. He wouldn't want any grief to befall his old bosses. They never hassled him, he wouldn't want to hassle them. He'd want me to help them. It'll be a tight squeeze in the back, but to please Bebe, I'll play any part you want me to play in the rescue bid.'

Hamish, relaxing, said, 'Phew, we're pleased you're seeing it this way. Just do your usual thing at the usual time. We'll be there at the back door with Bebe and the other lot. We'll sort out the seating arrangements then. By the way, you *are* as handy as that thumb on a… what was it Bebe said about you again? Get on. Get away with yeh, Morphy. Be on time.' Hamish tousled Morphy's hat about on his head and left him giggling. Then they moved quickly across the square to Blodger's entrance.

******

Bebe had gigged for charity at Blodger's for nigh on twenty years, but only recently for the burgeoning cross-dresser fraternity. He varied his act in each venue, exercised the grey matter, kept his memory-bank fluid and honed the brogue he had picked up over his years policing the "Irish Quarter".

On cross-dressers night, he always finished with the bluer gags in his repertoire. The tasty ones: ones he had held back to the end: ones he knew ought to go down well with this audience. His act, as funny as ever, neared its end.

'The bird had me attend the hospital last week. I've been suffering premature ejaculation... She told the specialist it was getting on her tits. Straight up that is.

I bought her one of those pug dogs. Even with the wonky eyes, the flat nose and all the slavers, the dog still loves her.

The last time I heard a woman screaming cheese I wasn't getting my photo taken.

This morning I upset the postwoman. I stuck my cock through the letterbox. She was shocked that I knew where she lived.

I was out drinking with my pals last night. When I got home, I was more pissed than a nursing home chair.

It's said that championship contenders must have a presence in the ring. Yet I've never seen a cross-eyed boxer win Crufts.

I was at a women's boxing match the other night. A brute of a heavyweight was winning her fight, right up until the 12th round. Then...what a mess: her periods started and her second threw the towel in.

A woman weightlifter at the doctors said, 'I'm on steroids and have grown a cock.'

The Doctor asked, Anabolic?

Woman said, No, just a cock!

I was shagging away at a woman last night and got a bit tired, so I said to her, would you mind getting on top for a bit.

She replied, you haven't done a lot of raping, have you?

School suspended wee Jonny twice this week. The maths teacher asked him if he had 20 quid and then he gave Joanne, Claire and Katie £5 each, what would you have at the end. Apparently, 3 blowjobs and enough left for a kebab was the wrong answer.

The next day, the biology teacher draws a penis on the board. 'Does anyone know what this is?' he asks the class.

Jonny pipes up, 'Yes sir, my dad has two of them.

You sure, Jonny?' the teacher asks.

Yes sir. He has a wee one for peeing with and a big one for cleaning the babysitter's teeth.'

There was an audible intake of breath from both Jack and Daphne.

Billy rattled on: 'With all the sadness, killing and trauma abundant in our world presently, it is worth reflecting on the death of a very important person, whose passing went largely unnoticed. Larry Laprise, the writer of the song Hokey Kokey, died peacefully at the age of 93. The most traumatic event for his family came when the undertakers attempted to get Larry into the coffin. They put his left leg in: that's when the trouble started.

And before popping off home tonight, you skeletal attendees should think of this: in the early hours of this morning, police stopped a man carrying a shovel and a sack of wrists as he left the local cemetery. He's up in court tomorrow charged with being a necrophiliac wanker. Make sure none of you lot are lifted carrying a similar package tonight. Leave your spades in here if I were you.

And here's one for the road. It's the final one from me.

A mounted copper on a horse stops wee girl on her bike. Did Santa fetch you that bike?' he asks her. Yes,' she replied. Well, the cops said, better tell Santa to put a reflector on the back mudguard for you, and fined her £5.

Wee girl says to cop. Did Santa fetch you that horse?

He sure did, replied the cop, smiling.

Well you'd better send it back because the prick is supposed to be on its underside, not on the top!'

Moving to the centre of the stage while the laughter subsided, Bill Bagman prepared his finale. The soundman, on cue, eased up a slider on the mixing desk. Slowly he increased the volume. The audience heard the high-pitched scream, similar to that made by a Stuka dive-bomber, swelling through the PA system. The sound changed in an instant to a jet engine growl. The blare of a supersonic aircraft, exceeding Mach 1 in a dive, preceded the thunderous climax that ended the show. An ear-splitting explosion shook the loudspeakers, the reverberations crashing around Blodger's, some wig wearers clamping a hand to their heads, fearing a draughty dislodgement.

Absolute silence followed. Bebe gazed out across his cross-dressed audience. With the microphone to his lips he said, 'Did anyone see that bluebottle go through the sound barrier? I'm off!'

Only then did he notice. Ultra-violet light, shimmering from the ceiling, was reflecting off the cheap wigs of a party of six cross-dressers, standing directly in front of the stage. The three Elvis look-alikes were clapping, laughing, their faces pictures of pleasure, having enjoyed every moment of his show. When he took his bow, he looked closely at the other three persons standing alongside each of them.

The shock rocked him, nearly made him piss his pants.

Superintendent Bunce, stern of reddened face, his blood pressure raised and his moustache and top lip in jerking, gazed back at him from beneath the Barbara Windsor-style wig. The smile of sheer hatred, for which he was famous, creased his face as he hugged a handbag to his crotch, his arms straining, looking as if he was attempting to hold something down.

Bebe looked from him towards the tallest of the party. Beneath a Maggie Thatcher-type wig, he saw the steely face of Commander Jack Dewsnap. For all his facial severity, he looked relaxed, pleased with himself even, and he held an Elvis look-alike tightly in his arms. Bebe's mind, working differently than most, saw that performance as an "Adoration of the Maggie".

Along from the Commander, he detected the Mayor overheating beneath a Marilyn Monroe-type wig and giggling uncontrollably. His continual winking had irked audience members, already quite unhappy with his clowning. Bebe had seen the Mayor before in such a state, but he wondered why they all were here.

He had retired; surely, his ex-superiors, of all people, should know that. Didn't he have a letter from the Commissioner thanking him for his years of devotion to duty, and another confirming his pensionable rights? Any day now, he expected an invitation to East Clegham divisional headquarters, there to receive some token of his former colleagues esteem, affection and some words of thanks from his ex-Commander.

But this was not a farewell salute. In a place like this and with this type of audience, it would never happen. He thought it more likely to be some disciplinary enquiry. His ex-bosses were all barking up the wrong tree: he had retired. And even in today's liberal society, he couldn't see these particular prominent people being paid-up members of the transgendered union.

Bebe lifted his head on noticing the two double-glazing salesmen, whom he thought ill advised to be trading wares in the IQ, were in the club. In leather jackets and denim trousers, they stood out amongst the brightly attired patrons. Now, he guessed what they were: rubber heelers, also on a wild goose chase. They were acting oddly, though, as they pushed through the milling throng to get to the stage, disregarding the obviously ineffectual and homing in on patrons with the largest shoulders, lifting their wigs and speaking directly into their ears.

******

Hamish and Harry moved quickly between ears, passing the message: 'Ricky Croker and a camera team are waiting outside to "out" you on his show.' Several cross-dressers were mind-blown, even the several likely sorts capable of handling themselves. Agitated conversations ensued as the shocking message passed amongst them. Suddenly and dramatically the mood of the patrons changed, the hum of conversation abruptly rising and intensifying into a viperish hiss, the transvestite's rage stoked. Replacing it was the sound of swishing frocks, stamping stiletto-heeled shoes and the whooping of whirled handbags. Forming straggly lines abreast and strutting as one, the ungainly unit practiced handbag-swiping manoeuvres together. Then they began queuing for the exit.

******

'What the fuck's that?' Ricky Croker asked his cameraman. The team had gathered and stood huddled to one side of Blodger's entrance. Ricky was about to reach for the flying phallus and raise it to knock on the door, then to rush in en masse, taking the doormen by surprise, when he saw the helmeted figure of Sergeant Moriarty.

Smart in his ceremonial uniform, his boots bulled to a reflecting shine, the sergeant was marching Binny along the pavement towards them. Close by his side, the goat was charging fractiously and putting a strain on its lead. Coming to a halt directly in front of Blodger's door, the sergeant crashed his studded boots onto the paving and did a left turn, dragging the goat around with him.

'It's the arrival of the Galloping Sergeant Major,' observed Ricky Croker, sniggering. Waving his hand, he had the team spread out to obtain a better view of the uniformed apparition and his creature.

Binny turned along with the sergeant and Ricky saw the extra bits dangling beneath its abdomen. He pointed them out to the cameraman, who moved behind Binny. Dropping onto one knee, sensing interesting footage, he got close up, focusing in on the appendages, getting them all in for a shot.

'You've brought the goat to the right spot tonight, sergeant, but you'll both have to cross-dress to get it in there,' Ricky Croker said, his face splitting with amusement.

'Binny will be introduced to my Gov'nor and his friends when they leave the Lodge, sir,' the sergeant barked in parade-ground tones, whilst standing stiffly to attention.

Unused to crowds or to so much attention, Binny began to tremble. Both udder and scrotum pendulously swung, but in two different directions, their momentum critically splaying its back legs. Off balance and quivering in panic, it let go what seemed a never-ending, steaming arc of watery shit, which sprayed onto the pavement, some droplets landing around the cameraman, still focusing to shoot the best close-up shots.

******

Hamish found Jack's party at the stage front. Quickly, he placed his lips close to Jack's ear. 'Ricky Croker, his team and a cameraman are outside. It seems they've tailed you here. One of their cars followed you into the car park.' He took the piss a little: 'As you can see, Jack, I've prepared the cross-dressers for battle. I've let them know its Ricky Croker's intention to "out" them on his TV show. Some of them were chuffed when I mentioned TV, but anger quickly returned when the reality sunk in. They're in for a surprise out there, when this lot in here wage war, using those swinging handbags and the points of the shoes most are wearing. The talons I've seen will gouge deeply into faces, claw eyes out, even.'

Jack pointed to his ear, made out he wasn't hearing too well, and pushed Daphne towards the door to one side of the stage, beckoning the others to follow. Almost as soon as the door closed behind the party, pandemonium erupted in the venue.

The noise of the door slamming shut hadn't quite faded when Jack bellowed at Hamish, 'What the hell is this all about? You say Ricky Croker from Thameside Television is outside. He has a cameraman ready to film us? How do you know that?'

Hamish didn't have time to answer. Superintendent Bunce shouted, venting his spleen at his Commander, 'I knew this was a damned fool undertaking.'

'Let's get on telly,' chortled the Mayor.

'Be serious,' said an Elvis look-alike, knocking him in the side. Two other Elvis look-alikes stared on worriedly.

'We've discovered this tonight,' explained Hamish.

'He's been to our house asking what Ivor drank in his coffee or if he liked tea,' said another Elvis look-alike, smiling, looking pleased.

'I think Ivor is taking Viagra in his coffee. Just you look at the whopper he brought with him tonight,' said the Elvis look-alike who'd spoken first. Hamish quickly realised from the voice that Myrna spoke.

'Why are you all here anyway?' Bebe asked. He had watched and listened to the exchanges with growing interest.

'You're…nicked….you….piss...taking…moonlighting…comedian…con stable! Your pension has just gone up in smoke!' Ivor shouted, bouncing about. He looked ridiculous with his false bust and his invigorated problem jiggling stiffly.

'I'm sorry, Mr. Bunce,' Bebe said, not giving him the benefit of his rank, 'but I retired on Friday.' He watched apoplexy wax swiftly across Mr. Bunce's face, his mouth gaping.

Ivor's jaws had opened and locked. As if in spasm, his vocal chords paralysed. Ages seemed to pass before he screamed, 'You fucking what?' The revelation had taken his mind off his throbbing problem, but had turned his face beetroot.

'What's up, darling? You never use the F word,' said the other Elvis look-alike, clutching him tightly by the arm.

'Have you got me here dressed like this, when you must have known all along that Beckham was already retired?' Ivor screamed at his Commander, his voice returned, spittle streaming down his chin.

'Yes, Ivor, I'm afraid so,' Jack cut him off. 'I had to do this thing my way to save my marriage. You were brave to come along with me tonight and I won't forget it. You mustn't forget, though, that I'm recommending you for the position at Hendon.' Jack held on tightly to Daphne, her eyes still dreamy. He looked towards Hamish, then Harry. 'Yes, and I deceived you pair too. However, what arrangements have you made to get us out of here, MacNab?'

'Detective Constable MacNab, I might remind you,' prompted Hamish. 'We're not using the Transit or the Peugeot. Those vehicles, Croker can trace and he will if he sees any of you in one. The horsebox, he doesn't know about. Inside that, you can escape unseen. It will be at the back door in thirty seconds to pick up Billy. Somehow, we'll fit you into that. The driver will drop the Morris Minor off at the Mayor's place. Bebe can then run you home. Give me the Peugeot keys and I'll see it's delivered safely back to your address tomorrow. '

'Good thinking, Detective Constable MacNab, but what about this blasted cameraman?' Jack asked.

'That's all in hand, sir' Hamish said. 'Parliamentarians, Lords and Bishops are here tonight, posing as black market fruit jobs, closet queens, chocolate speedway travellers, whatever. Some of them are dressed in slinky, body-hugging garments that only last week paraded on the catwalks of Paris. None of them will want filming in garbs like that, when they leave a place like this, will they?'

Throwing a thumb back over his shoulder, he pointed in the direction of the club that was already seething. 'I've warned the doormen and a few of the bigger, fragranter apparitions about Ricky Croker and his team waiting to film them outside the door of the club. I wouldn't like to be in his or his team's shoes when these bandits rage into them. Puffballs they might seem, but pinched toes will be aimed at painful places tonight.'

******

The horsebox roared along the close and swayed to a halt. Morphy knocked twice on the back door of the club using a long stick. Hamish pushed forward, opened the door and checked the Wynd was clear. Taking the single step towards the horsebox, he opened the side door to the donkey accommodation. The Morris Minor blocked entry to the unused portion of the horsebox and there wasn't much space left there. No gaps remained around the car for even the thinnest of person to squeeze past. If all seven were to get away quickly, unseen, and unfilmed by Ricky Croker's team, they all had to fit through the driver's door into the Morris Minor.

******

Ricky Croker called 'Team!' and, flapping his hand, directed them to gather around him. He needed to check on their readiness since the foetid stench of goat shit had gripped each of their throats and jolted tears from their eyes. Sergeant Moriarty, oblivious to the bowel emptying session, stepped back into the mess, tightening the lead attached to Binny's collar. Binny fought the restriction, bucked, reared onto its back legs, and frenziedly head-butted at shadows. Binny was standing on its back legs and off-balance when Blodger's door flew open. The sergeant was spreading his feet apart as he tried to regain his balance.

Howling with rage, the first troop of aggrieved cross-dressers, the most mettlesome and demonstrative, emerged, handbags windmilling. Behind them, pushing and shoving, egging each other on with rallying calls of,

'Bitches to battle,' 'Fags to the fore' and 'Queens to the quest,' were several other lines of the first wave.

In the midst of the fracas, the sergeant's much-vaunted boots were sliding this way and that. He still looked official enough, but that didn't deter the first-wave troops pushing on past him, with no regard whatsoever for his authority. 'Out of the fucking way officer, it's him we want,' someone shouted gruffly.

A flailing handbag cuffed the sergeant on the side of his head. Over he went. The first line, six abreast, false breasts askew, were careering towards the tall figure wearing the sheepskin coat and trilby. Ricky was a bridge too far away. Drawing a line between him and the first troop was the deluge of slippery goat shit, spreading treacherously over the pavement. The first six cross-dressers pranced into the slurried area. Slipping and sliding, they grabbed at each other to regain balance, only to pull one another down into the mess.

Some shit-planed, dragging their clothing through it. Wigs jettisoned, risking recognition for the wearer. Stiletto heels crumpled, legs jerked apart at uncomfortable angles and skied into the air. Trousers split. Short and sudden ripping sounds told of seams parting. Snapping sounds told of stiletto heels wrenched from shoes.

The dull thump followed by 'Ohaaoooah,' were the sounds applicable to a goat's head splitting a set of bollocks hanging exposed through ripped trousers.

The sergeant managed to get to his feet. Fallen cross-dressers hauled him back, beat him down again, used him as a lever, their false nails raking down his uniform and snapping off. Using them, as they used him, he reclaimed his balance, but his boots were finding no adhesion in the mire and he fell backwards onto Binny, crumpling the goat's frail, splaying legs. Cross-dressers rising successfully from the mire, clambered over the sergeant, forcing his head and Binny's down, close together. The pressure upon them was great and the goat and he began to slide across the pavement. Close to the gutter, he threw his arms around Binny's neck.

Punctuating yells of 'Save my cherished buns,' and 'Get your dirty, smelly hands off me,' were Binny's miserable bleatings. 'Don't say things like that, Binny!' the sergeant roared.

The second wave formed a semi-circle, the flanks moving to the right and left, quickly around those remaining on the ground. The ones forced through the middle by pressure from the rear, tipped up and tumbled over comrades already plastered to the pavement. The sergeant and the twitching body of Binny lay beneath, covered in goat shit. Casualties from the second wave wielded their handbags in horizontal arcs, striking the groups pushing up the flanks, thumping into heads, bringing most of that group down.

It was turning into a complete goat fuck. An intact stiletto heel, launched in the horizontal plane and driven by a powerful, hairy leg, pierced and split asunder Binny's udder. A stream of high fat-content, health-endowing milk gushed from the yawning wound onto the pavement. The slipperiness increased tenfold as Binny slipped away to his own, goatish bisexual heaven. One last, dreadful bleat, forced from deflating lungs, trembled inexorably to a rasping croak. Binny was dead.

The flanks of the second and the third wave crashed on, reaching Ricky Croker and his team members. Handbags twirled, one striking Ricky a downward blow on the temple, sending his hat crashing over his eyes. His minder, seeing his boss in danger of falling beneath a horde of weird sexual adventurers, rushed to assist him. He, too, disappeared under a barrage of handbags and kicks. Pointed shoes, pinpoint accurate and directed at bollocks by the second and third waves and from reforming reinforcements of the soiled and limping wounded, found targets.

The fourth wave included those who had stood or sat at the back, the taller, the weedier, the stooped elderly, the lightweight and the ineffectual. Trapped in their midst and carried along involuntarily amidst the mincing stream, Rowley Beaverton and Tattiana struggled to stay on their feet.

Out on the pavement, they stood tall, above the throng in tumult, but less eager to join the assault. The cameraman was now recording the mayhem happening closest to them. A police officer's helmet had suddenly appeared, forced from a heap of writhing bodies. Feet in the heap were juggling with the helmet, keeping it aloft. It laid the clue for the ADC that one of "The Cloth" had somehow become involved. He saw it as his job to act swiftly: to save the officer and bring normality to the situation.

As he groped in his handbag, struggling to keep his wig on and his feet planted firmly on the paving, he found his warrant card and whistle, which good coppers never went anywhere without. He blew on the whistle and flashed his warrant card. The maddened mob ignored him, the disorder escalating.

Close to the heap and peering into it, the ADC caught the flash of a sergeant's stripes rising to the top like three fingers of a white hand. As he tried to identify a face among the mess of screaming people, the jumble of legs and circling handbags, his mouth widened in horror. The police officer, whoever he was, could just be fighting for his very life, suffocating, dying beneath that lot.

Then shock twisted the remainder the ADC's face. The churning mass had spewed to the top the carcass of an odd-looking goat. Turning bodies also brought into view several sets of bollocks, dangling through rips in trouser-suit bottoms and from the legs of knickers. Quickly, the penny dropped: Tattiana had large hands and firm breasts. 'Does she have bollocks too? He mouthed, 'Jack, you bastard. Bollocks.' The bollocks were those of patrons of the establishment, *which he had just left*!

Ricky Croker broke free. First wave cross-dressers had tired and were just milling about, gasping for breath, screaming abuse at each other and swearing. Others trooped towards parked cars. Some limped away uninjured, one high heel intact the other ripped off. Others, dishevelled and without wigs, their battle over, stumbling from the scene.

Ricky wasn't completely safe yet: the occasional swinging handbag still clipped him about the head. His cameraman had found safety behind a parked car and was shooting from the roof. Pointing towards the ADC, still whistling, warrant card in his hands, Ricky fought his way forward and shouted to the cameraman, 'For fuck's sake, get some footage of him!'

******

In the close, the loading of the horsebox with a human cargo was underway. Hamish said to Harry, 'Join hands like this, it's the fireman's lift method.' He turned to Daphne: 'Commander's Elvis, you're first, on here quick.' Together they lifted and Daphne scrambled into the car. Lifting her shroud to clamber into the back, Daphne gave them an eyeful of knickers and thigh. 'That's enough, you two,' Jack said, noticing how long they stared.

They both grunted while heaving Gloria, but she just seemed to roll over the seat backs like a sack of potatoes. Harry tweaked Myrna's bottom then run his hand over it. 'Naughty,' she coyly whispered. Algie was next up, flying in at speed, to crash into the back seat between Gloria and Myrna. Breathing heavily he managed to holler, 'Get stripped off… you're on next… never had my leg over in the back of a Morris Minor.'

Jack required no assistance. He stepped up and shuffled across to the front passenger seat.

Jack's rear end was disappearing into the car when Barney the barman staggered around a corner towards them, taking a shortcut home from the pub. Well-pissed, he sang incoherently. Recognising the two leather-jacketed figures, he staggered towards them and squeezed between the horsebox and the wall. Tapping both Hamish and Harry on a shoulders, he told them, with a great deal of drunken emotion, 'Thersh a great punk rock band called Scrotum Clamp, playing at the Shankless Music Bar, Thursday night. Shtickets are yours for the ashking as long as I getsh the doublsh-glazshed housh, okay, hic.'

'You're our winner,' Harry told him.

Ivor groaned. 'Surely not scrotum clamp,' he said loudly. With his back against a wall, he tugged impatiently at his shroud, eventually lifting it up to armpit level. Jerking down his Y-Fronts, he stepped out of them, made a rough check of his tackle, grunted as he saw his cock's enduring springiness, and then he put them on, back-to-front.

He stepped forward and up into the car. Hamish gave him a push and he lurched and lightly head-butted Jack. Ivor settled onto Jack's knees and then Bebe stepped up. Jamming himself in behind the wheel, he pulled the door shut behind him.

Harry closed the outer door, entombing them with the lingering fragrances of old mown hay and even older donkey droppings. Hamish thumped on the cab. Morphy revved up and roared off, the box hard down on its springs, into the night.

Bebe smiled. The smells reminded him of Blackpool. His new career would begin there next spring, the contract lasting for the entire summer season.

EPILOGUE

The journey to the first drop-off point took twenty minutes, by which time Algie had comprehensively spewed over Myrna. The horsebox smells and its swaying aiding the onset.

Morphy was taking great delight in his role as getaway driver. He drove the horsebox too fast around the roundabout at the top of the drive at Paddleworth Towers, the back wheels scattering stones onto the verges. Coming to a shuddering stop, he lowered the tailgate and Bebe reversed the Morris Minor down the ramp.

Without stopping for any expressions of gratitude, Morphy drove off. Bebe followed closely behind with the others when he had emptied the car of the Rideouts.

The jerky journey had caused Algie to turn facially a deathly white. In the lounge, he staggered towards the recliner where he sat down. A pull on a lever and his feet rose from the floor. His head rocked as the chair-back let him down. Instantly, he was asleep.

Myrna snatched the wig from his head. Then she set up a full-length mirror in front of the recliner, figuring it might shock him out of his alcoholism if he saw the shroud-clad figure rising in front of him when he surfaced.

Myrna picked up the telephone and rang Rowley's number. It wasn't very late and she guessed he would have a bedside extension anyway. She felt as randy as hell, lusting for him whilst listening to the telephone burring away. It was answered and the voice said, 'Yeth, who wanth Rowley?'

******

It didn't take the Bunces long to reach their bedroom. Once there, Gloria began impressing upon Ivor the need to fit the stallion pump when he was so terribly, terribly and uncommonly hard.

The device in place, he stood naked, in some pain and exceptionally unhappy, as Gloria drooled over the evacuated glass tube, 'Look, it's creeping up the tube now. You'll be hung like a donkey by morning.' Ivor heard those words as he fainted and crumpled onto the floor.

As Ivor wilted, he became immediately flaccid. The tube lost its vacuum with an audible sigh. Gloria, seeing the miserly millimetre of difference the penis enlarger had made, became quickly discombobulated. 'Next time, I must hang the suggested weight from the end of the tube, thus extending the range of the enlarger,' she said, but no one was listening.

******

At home, Jack and Daphne raced upstairs, tearing at each other's clothing. Naked and in the shower they gelled each other and rinsed, all the while their lips were glued together, locked, as if Siamese twins. Once dried, they walked, still joined, towards the bed.

Beneath the duvet, Daphne lay on top of Jack, felt his hardness, heard his moans, his passion, felt his hips lift, thrusting up to meet hers. Daphne left his lips to kiss her way down and over his body to the cock that awaited her lips, her ministry. From nipple to nipple, down his six-pack and into his belly button she nibbled and tantalised. Then she lifted and slid back, finding a comfortable, hunkered position from where to pay homage.

Suddenly, Jack's cock sprang up and rapped her beneath the chin. It took her back a few days to a time she wished she could forget. The same thing had happened then and her teeth had connected with the stranger's penis. Lifting her head to bring it down over him, she raised the duvet and allowed light to enter beneath it. It was enough for her to see the ragged outline of a healing lesion that was scarring the length of Jack's cock and deeply indenting his helmet.

'J......... A...... C......K?' she screamed and threw the duvet aside for a better look.

******

Detective Constables MacNab and MacSporran were sitting in the Bally Balti, their task finishing on a high note. Their jobs were secure, as were their warrant cards, tucked safely into pockets. For the first time during a long career together, they were unable to enjoy fully a late-night curry. Soon after the papadum course, they began to laugh and couldn't stop. At an adjacent table, a large, disgruntled man with a crumpled trilby raged angrily at his cameraman. Apparently, a splash of goat shit had smeared the video-camera lens, wasting the entire shoot, apart from a short piece of footage showing a goat's udder and bollocks swinging pendulously.

******

Finally, there would have been no yarn to tell, had the three women visiting Blackpool that particular Sunday not attended the blue comedian's show at the town's Central Pier theatre. However, because they did, many lives have changed and some futures are still not resolved.

In Billy Bagman's case, his performance that Sunday evening guaranteed his future as a top comedian.

A critical assessment, written by the Irish Times' entertainment critic, highly praised Billy Bagman's act. The article said: Billy Bagman, who appeared in his own show at the Central Pier theatre, Blackpool, on Sunday evening, has a unique act. Coming away with the blarney as he does, his lips are a blur and his soft, throaty, rich, round and resonant Donegal brogue sounds like two wet farts colliding on a dark night.

This gifted entertainer will become highly regarded, gaining notoriety as the master of the double follow through. Others will agree with what his poster so rightly claims: Roy Chubby Brown couldn't wipe his arse.

THE END

Printed in Poland
by Amazon Fulfillment
Poland Sp. z o.o., Wrocław

63320848R00159